Dedication. To those that matter, now and always. (You know who you are).

The Hurler

A Novel

Jack Talbot

Acknowledgements

Jean O' Sullivan of Red Pen Edits for her dedication, professionalism and guidance. My good friend Richard Comerford - a historian, a sage, a scholar, who combines wisdom and knowledge to offer clarity and understanding in an ever-changing world. Orla Kelly for her accessibility and knowledge. My wife and sons for their continued support.

Prologue

The demon resides in us all. It lurks in the shadows, patiently awaiting our moment of weakness, for it is then it will raise its head. And when it strikes, it strikes with a vengeance.

So it was for the man. An ordinary man. Decent. Until his world turned upside down and all that was good in him perished. Crushed; not alone by the sight he beheld, but by the letter.

It was with trembling fingers he extracted the document from where it was wedged between the bars of the gate and stifling a groan, he hesitantly unfolded the neatly creased sheets of paper. For he knew what they contained even before he studied them. His call to atonement. What else could it be?

Handwritten on foolscap pages, he recognised the slanted writing immediately. He had seen it so many times before, criticised it, corrected it, admired it. It was a neat hand, far neater than anything he himself ever inscribed on a page, and it was honest. Always honest. With a growing sense of dread, he slipped his glasses from his shirt pocket and set them on the bridge of his nose. A broad nose for a broad man. Solid. Now, shaking like a lamb.

Not realising, he held his breath. Released it. Held it again. His eyes, already haunted, scanned the pages, skimming over words that alone meant nothing but as a group would tell the entire tale, the weight of which could not possibly be lost on him. Not on him of all people.

Yet, still, he read, aware of nothing only the words, even as he staggered sideways. It was the gate that saved him. The very same gate that had abetted his despair. His grasping of its latch an automatic movement, not one borne out of any immediate desire for self-preservation. What he witnessed today had already taken that. And now more, as the offending pages slipped from his nerveless fingers.

As if from a distance, he watched them flutter away on the rising wind only to return and settle against the laces of his worn boots. Intended for him, and him alone. Suddenly, what remained of the emotional dam inside the man burst. First, his eyes welled. Then his limbs grew weak. Finally, he collapsed to his knees and sobbed. Deep, pain-ridden sobs, drawn from the very depths of him.

In desperation, he raised his head to the skies, pleading with the heavens, but in vain. It seemed the entire universe had turned its back on him then. And worse. Condemned him.

As he condemned himself.

Deep in the shadows, the demon heard his cries, and slowly raised its head.

For the waiting was over.

The time had come to strike.

Chapter 1

"My husband is missing," the woman said, her words given a sombre resonance by the quiver in her voice. It was early on the first Saturday of October when she dialled the direct line to Oldcastle Garda Station. The call was initially answered by Garda Fiona O'Malley who was a junior officer at the station. Quickly realising the significance of the call, Garda O' Malley took the woman's name and address, and some basic details before transferring the call to her superior, Sergeant Britney Kent.

"Coffee?" she mouthed as she set down the phone. In response, Sergeant Kent scrunched her button nose and gave a quick shake of her head.

"Late night?" she asked, her slender eyebrows raised, as she muffled the phone against the gentle swell of her chest. She could think of no other reason Fiona would even contemplate the station coffee which, at the best of times, tasted like it was brewed in an offal bucket.

"Early morning!" Fiona admitted, then added with a naughty smirk. "But, believe me, it was worth it." With that, she sashayed toward the coffee dock, her lithe figure demanding attention despite the square-cut profile of her uniform slacks.

Watching her go, Britney wasn't sure if she felt admiration or jealousy for her carefree colleague. Settling on a bit of both, she returned her mind to the job at hand and engaged with the caller. In her late twenties, the sergeant was approximately the same age as the woman she was about to speak to.

"Hello, I'm Sergeant Kent," said Britney, pulling her brown hair back from her heart-shaped face as she held the phone to her ear. "What can I do for you?" She spoke in the calm and controlled voice her training had instilled, and seven years of dealing with an erratic and demanding public had further honed. In response, she heard a deep sigh followed by an unsettling silence.

"My name is Stacey Rourke," the woman finally replied, her fragile voice barely audible as she introduced herself. "I live in Emmet's Hill." A sigh. "And I really need your help." The latter was added with such reticence that it was immediately clear to Sergeant Kent her younger colleague had read the situation correctly. This was more than just a run of the mill complaint about a noisy neighbour or an escalating property dispute. Picking a pen from amongst the paperwork scattered across her desk, Britney sat up in her chair.

It wasn't that things were slow at the station or that crime levels in Oldcastle were at an all-time low. On the contrary. Statistics showed that, year on year, petty crime was every bit as pervasive as it had been while drug-related offences were also on the rise. So too was violent crime. She was hearing unsettling reports of a new gang in town. An unknown group of violent thugs who were settling disputes with a hurley stick, baseball bat or steel bar – whatever implement tickled their fancy.

Yet here she was, stuck in the office filing paperwork and stamping dodgy tax certs for just as dodgy vehicle owners. The order confining her to desk duty had come directly from the station's top brass – Superintendent Harry Halley.

"And that's where you'll remain," the super had promised on issuing it, "At least until you bring your questionable paperwork skills up to scratch." However, Britney knew there was far more to it than sloppy admin. Even if neatness wasn't exactly her middle name.

"It's a rap on the knuckles," she told Fiona, the day she received it. "For my run-in with that pig of a nephew of his."

"Do you think?"

"Without a doubt, Fi. Flynn can't stand having his decisions questioned by a woman. Especially one that's just a low-ranking sergeant. If he gets his way, he'll have me looking for cats up in trees next."

In his mid-forties, Terry Flynn had been an experienced detective long before he arrived at the station.

"Is it true he was transferred out of Carlow because he was having an affair?" Fiona asked.

"With a young recruit, more than half his age." Britney acknowledged. "It was all hushed up and Halley got him quickly moved along. Pulled a few strings to bring him here so that he could keep an eye on him, I heard. Not that it made a blind bit of difference. From what I've seen, a leopard doesn't change its spots."

"But he's married with three kids, isn't he?" Fiona said, wrinkling her slender nose in disgust. "A good kick in the balls is what I'd give him if he was married to me. Super's nephew or not."

"Now that's something I'd like to see." Britney replied with a laugh. "Might knock that leer to the other side of his ugly face."

"What's his partner like?" Fiona asked. "Murray, isn't it?"

Britney nodded. "He seems ok. Been here only six months. Like Flynn, he watches everything but not in the same way, if you know what I mean. And he doesn't say much. But when he's stressed, he puffs his cheeks from side to side as if he's playing ping pong in his mouth. Did you notice that?"

"Yeah. I think it's kind of cute to be honest. He kind of reminds me of a film I liked as a kid." Fiona observed. "Uncle Buck!"

"Now that you mention it," Britney chuckled. Shorter in stature than Flynn, Murray was a heavyset man who liked to remind people that at fifty-four, he had an excuse. He had a chubby face, a soft voice, and apart from case work, he kept his business to himself for the most part. Consequently, Britney knew little else about him except that he was separated with no family, and currently lived alone.

Now, as she held the phone to her ear, Britney could see the pair through the glass pane of Flynn's private office. Lean with broad shoulders, dark, greased back hair and lines etched into his hard, angular face, Flynn did a damn good impression of an Italian gangster. Handmade suits and copious amounts of Sicilian cologne. At least, he claimed it was Sicilian. Yet, as far as Britney knew there wasn't an Italian bone in his body. At that moment he was in deep discussion with his partner, but at the same time watching her out of the corner of a bleary eye. Though their actions weren't animated, the atmosphere behind the glass certainly seemed tense.

To Britney, Flynn seemed to be laying down the law about something or other. It wasn't the first time she noticed that dynamic, or for that matter, wondered why Murray just sat there and took it. Perhaps, he didn't consider himself secure enough in his position. Not with the way Flynn masqueraded as the leader of the pack in this neck of the woods.

Let him think what he wants. For now, she was glad he was preoccupied. And to hell with Halley's instructions. She wasn't a clerk. She was a Garda. A sergeant. She needed to work.

"Hello Stacey," Sergeant Kent continued, keeping her tone even. "Why do you need our help?"

"Because…" The woman faltered as if second guessing what she was about to say. Britney heard an intake of breath. "Because like I told your colleague, he's missing."

"Who's missing?"

"My husband. He went to work last week and never came home."

For a moment there was silence on the line as Britney prepared to enquire after her husband's place of work but Stacey's timid voice drifted across the line once more. "I know everyone says I'm being melodramatic, but I'm really worried this time."

"This time?"

"He was never gone this long before. A night. Two at the most. But that was before the kids. Never this long."

Britney could hear her struggling with the emotion in her voice.

"He's gone, Sergeant. I know it. I can feel it."

"You mean, he's left you?" Britney asked. Though relief should have been the appropriate emotion she couldn't help but feel a little deflated. It appeared it was a counsellor this woman needed to deal with her predicament and not the police.

"No, Sergeant," Stacey replied before sighing heavily as if struggling with what she was about to give air to. "I mean he's dead."

"Dead?" Britney sat forward, perching on the edge of her chair.

"Yes, Sergeant. I think something terrible has happened to my husband."

"I see," Britney replied while subconsciously running her fingers over the identifying mark that facing the challenges of her own dysfunctional family had left her with — a faded scar so thin it could have been drawn by a pencil. Thin or not, it would remain a permanent blemish on the soft flesh of her left cheek.

The woman's statement was certainly of a serious nature, but all her previous experience suggested to Britney that Stacey Rourke was more than likely overreacting. Her husband had probably just gone off on a spur of the moment man-cation or had simply upped and left her altogether. And she simply couldn't come to terms with it.

It happened all the time. In fact, the majority of missing person cases that the Gardaí dealt with turned out to be runaways or people who needed a temporary break from it all. Still, the gravity with which this woman made her statement gave Britney pause for thought.

"If you could just give me some details, Stacey. To start with, what's your husband's name?"

"It's Jim. Jim Rourke."

"And you live in Emmet's Hill, you say?"

"Yes. In the houses near the front. Number 128."

Once she got talking, Stacey's voice steadied a little so Britney followed up with further relevant questions, all the while scribbling on a notepad as the woman dutifully provided her with the information she needed. Even if she had initial reservations about the true reason behind Mr Rourke's absence, she was duty-bound to check out any complaint, and even if that hadn't been the case, she wasn't about to turn her nose up at a shot at freedom. And a chance to catch up with Fiona out of the stuffy confines of the office.

Being of similar age, and perhaps desperate for a buffer against the overload of testosterone at the station, Britney had developed an instant rapport with the latest addition to the staff. Garda O'Malley had been transferred in three months earlier from Portlaoise as part of a government recruitment drive and her presence in Oldcastle, along with that of their resident IT marvel, Triona Maguire, brought the number of female Gardaí serving to approximately 30%. This was more or less in line with what the Minister for Justice outlined in his letter to the Commissioner at the beginning of the Minister's tenure. It was widely acknowledged that the force was supporting a big push on sexual equality which was all well and good, but a bit of a joke in Britney's opinion, considering the tolerance shown to Neanderthals like Terry Flynn.

Having garnered the details she needed, Britney reassured Mrs Rourke that she was on her way to speak with her in person. She hung up the phone and discreetly approached the desk of a young Garda named Ben Youngs to inform him that she needed to respond to a call. Ben was of slight build with dark hair cut tight at the back and sides, and a fringe cutting a line over intelligent eyes.

"Any excuse," he replied with a playful smile. Ben had come directly to the station from training college a little over a year earlier and in that time, Britney had found him to be a likeable character. A bit of eye candy too, which always helped.

"Damn right. Staring at these four walls day in, day out, is making me claustrophobic. To be honest, Ben, I'm convinced I'm experiencing the onset of cabin fever."

Ben's smile widened in understanding. "That treacle they call coffee doesn't help."

"Worse than Flynn's aftershave," Britney agreed with a glance toward the office. "If anyone is looking for me, I'll be back in an hour."

"And if Halley happens to pop in?"

"I'm on an early lunch…or better still, tell him I'm gone to get some new file holders. Colour coded ones. With directions for beginners. He'll like that."

Ben smirked in reply. "Fiona going with you?" he asked, a knowing look entering his amber-flecked eyes. "You two are thick as thieves since she started. Kind of cute how you've taken her under your wing." He paused and glanced toward Fiona who out of earshot was making a coffee at the far end of the room. "Or is it the other way around? No flies on our Fiona, I'd say."

"No more than on you, Ben. If you're so interested in her, why don't you ask her out? I see the way you look at her."

Ben shook his head. "I've only eyes for you, Brit," he replied smoothly. "You know that."

"Yeah, right. You've got eyes for all the single ladies. And some not so single, I bet."

The mild look of dismay that crossed Ben's features seemed genuine, but it failed to register with Britney as she returned to her desk to pick up her jacket and phone before heading for the exit. On her way out she caught Fiona's attention. Her colleague was more than happy to leave the treacle where it was.

****

For a man who'd always been admired for his physical prowess, chopping off a hand hadn't proved quite as easy as he had imagined. Though he had sharpened the small hatchet to a fine edge it took three solid blows to complete the job. Even then there were still a few tendrils of sinew and loose flaps of skin for his knife to deal with. However, with one clean cut, the blade's serrated edge duly obliged.

The efficiency of this final act was of scant relief to his victim. In fact, it went totally unnoticed. Because his victim had long before passed out.

For this temporary respite, the man was grateful. The screams of the pathetic thing had become grating. 'Some people found it so easy,' the man thought, 'to inflict pain, yet so difficult to endure it themselves.' The stench that now emanated from his victim's nether regions proved testament to this. As did the fear he had seen in his victim's eyes. Fear he took great pleasure in witnessing.

Reaching into his coat pocket he produced a small vial of smelling salts and held it beneath his victim's nose. The time for respite had passed. Though grating, the man wished to hear the screams once more. Needed to hear them. They chased the images from his head. Physical pain was such a transient thing. It was emotional pain that had the staying power. Its scars far deeper and invariably septic. Unhealing.

When the necessary slack was applied to the strangling cord, his victim coughed and choked on coming to. "Why?" he eventually croaked, his eyes lingering on the rectangular shape faintly outlined in the dark. A wooden box. Worryingly fashioned with a gentle taper from one end to the other. As if to fit the lines of a human body. A dead human body.

"You know why," the man replied before gripping the recently ruined left knee of his victim and squeezing hard. Instantly his victim began to writhe against the pallet to which he was bound, and tortured screams filled the space once more. The man smiled coldly. A scream for a scream. 'Poetic justice,' he thought to himself as he checked his watch. It was nearing ten a.m. Already he was behind schedule. He swore in annoyance, as much with himself as the pathetic thing that cowered before him. He had taken too long, indulged himself too much, and now if she came back early from her walk, his carefully set out timetable would be screwed. He might even have to kill her there and then. And that wouldn't do. It wouldn't do at all.

Because he had prepared. He had planned. And right was on his side.

With that thought a beacon in his mind, he set about finishing his work. Then, with the first leg of his mission complete he took the letter out of his trouser pocket. Unfolding it with care, he set it on the lid of the makeshift box that held his deepest secret. Having dipped the tip of his finger in the blood of his victim he now scrawled it across a name.

"Please forgive me," he whispered for only the darkness to hear.

****

It was a beautiful place, Britney always thought. The city of Oldcastle.

Fashioned in medieval times, the heart of the city was a reflection of its environment. Stone walls, slate roofs, timber framed windows, and doors. Soft over-plaster and pastel paints enlivened with intermittent splashes of colour. Tastefully created with time and care. Like the world around it. Overlooking it all was the majestic structure from which the city got its name. With four circular towers on the corners, joined by crenelated walls, the castle was constructed as a defence fortress by the Normans way back in the 1100s. Strategically positioned, it stood proudly on a rise above the river, its hand-cut limestone façade overlooking the city to the fore, and to the rear the expanse of land that once comprised its gardens. Today, those lands served as a public park, popular with joggers and families alike. Its ancient woods a natural and unblemished beauty.

By contrast, the outskirts of the town were a crime against nature – a modern blend of concrete, tile, and PVC. Factory delivered and hurriedly erected. It was to this type of architectural tragedy that Britney was driving. The concrete jungle that was Emmet's Hill.

On reaching the estate, they entered between two huge eyesores of buildings that Britney presumed were apartment blocks. She also surmised that a few brown envelopes must have been passed back and forth for the council to grant planning permission for such unsightly structures – russet brick, flat roofs, box steel balconies sticking out like hampered wings – to be erected in the vicinity of such a beautiful town.

As she passed by, Britney noted that life existed behind many of the large steel windows, but others were dark. Empty looking. Abandoned. The very way they'd make any observer feel.

Once past the tower blocks, they entered the estate and the buildings shrunk down to the more agreeable stature of two-story townhouses. Pebbledash, grey tile, PVC porches. Arranged in rows that ran back-to-back within spitting distance of each other.

The only relief from the concrete was a small green area boxed in on three sides by the unrelenting houses, and by the giant eyesores on the fourth. On this grassy respite, several children were playing a game of football which slowly came to a halt as, one by one, the children stood to study the squad car that drove past looking for house number 128. The children seemed more curious than wary, something which always suggested to Sergeant Kent that the estate was decent enough.

"Working-class but relatively crime-free," she explained to Fiona. "In the earlier days of its existence, this estate had a bit of a name for being a drug haven with lots of the houses rented cheaply to young lads with nothing but partying on their mind, but over the years, more and more families have moved in. Nowadays, we might get a call out to the estate once every six months, compared to at least once a week when I started five years ago."

"Do you think this call is a throwback to those early days?"

"Didn't sound like it. In fact, I'm not sure what it sounded like. What I do know is it feels good to get away from that damn desk." Britney cracked a gratified smile, revealing the slight gap in her teeth that even the endurance of two teenage years of train tracks couldn't quite eliminate. Her mother had wanted perfect, but, personally, she was happy with the result. The gap was an inheritance from her father.

"Speaking of freedom, feels like ages since we got out for a jog, Fi."

"How about Monday? The Castle Park? I haven't been yet, but I've heard the woods there are lovely."

"Nice coffee shop there too," Britney replied as she slowed the car, her eyes peeled for a particular house in the front row. "I could certainly do with a few days off. If I stick my head in that filing cabinet once more, it will morph into the shape of a drawer... And if I have to spend one more minute in the same building as Yabba Dabba Doo, I'll start calling myself Wilma."

Fiona looked at her blankly.

"The Flintstones?" Britney suggested.

"I know but...?"

"His name is Flynn and he's a stone," Britney patiently explained then waited for the penny to drop. It took a minute.

"Oh! Now I get it," Fiona said eventually, with a laugh that Britney found infectious. "Flynnstones."

"A match made in heaven or what?" Britney giggled but forced the mirth from her face as she pulled over to the kerb and parked behind an old but well-maintained Honda Civic with Northern Ireland plates. Undoing their safety belts offered a moment to compose themselves but still, they retained traces of smiles as they got out of the car.

They'd hardly taken a step toward the house when the door opened and a woman who appeared to be in her late twenties or early thirties stepped out. Wrapped in a pink bathrobe the woman sported white runners on her feet, the laces of which trailed loosely on the step. Framing an oval face, she had long and curly strawberry-blonde hair which would have been quite beautiful, Britney thought, under different circumstances. Now it was unkempt and lifeless, a stark complement to the dark bags hanging under her otherwise pretty, blue eyes. Britney didn't have to be a detective to know immediately she was looking at the haggard figure of Stacey Rourke. All traces of mirth disappeared.

"Thank God!" Stacey said with a tone of genuine relief as they approached the house. Her feet fidgeted on the step as if she was in two minds whether to go out and meet them or wait where she was. She chose to wait. A moment later, Britney noticed two more heads appear at the door, smaller profiles with dirty faces. They peered out either side of Stacey, their little hands clinging to her bathrobe as if to prevent her from leaving them too. Unlike the children Britney had seen happily playing on the green, these two had a shadow of fear in their eyes. Stacey's arms instinctively reached for them and drew them close.

"Hi," Britney said as she held out her hand, "I'm Sergeant Kent. I spoke with you on the phone. This is Garda O'Malley."

"Thank God," Stacey repeated. "Thank you for coming so quickly."

"Not a problem," Britney assured. "I could tell by your call that you are at your wit's end."

Stacey nodded. "I didn't know what else to do. It's not like him to disappear like this."

"I understand," Britney replied with a glance over her shoulder at the children on the green. Their collective eyes remained on her; the ball forgotten. Britney imagined there would be plenty of other eyes on them too, with the way the houses were situated. The valley of the squinting windows came to mind. The fact that Gardaí had visited number 128 would travel like wildfire. If there was anyone remaining in the estate that hadn't heard of Stacey's predicament, they would soon be brought up to speed.

"Can we go inside, Stacey? Perhaps we could make you a cup of tea?"

"Yes… yes, that would be nice," Stacey replied as she gently guided the young children by her side into a narrow hall. To the right of the hall, a doorway led to a small, neat sitting room which contained a battered couch, flatpack coffee table, and a dated looking TV. The TV was airing a cartoon Britney failed to recognise from her days as a kid but understood the objective wouldn't have changed – to keep the children distracted, especially now. On the walls were several family photos, and three or four of just the kids themselves, warmly hugging, their gap-toothed smiles taking centre stage. In one of the photos, the girl reminded Britney of herself at that age. Further along, a picture of Stacey and her husband on their wedding day hung in the corner above the TV. At the rear of the sitting room, a set of double doors led toward an equally spatially challenged kitchen.

As Britney followed Stacey deeper into the house, she detected a keen aroma of bleach and could hear the washing machine running in the background. Britney wondered if the distraught woman hoped that by busying herself cleaning, she could wash all her troubles away. And somehow in the process, bring her husband back.

The children, a girl, and a boy were no more than five or six and though morning was pushing on, they remained dressed in pyjamas. Britney assumed this attire had become the norm over the last few days. It could be like that with overwhelmingly stressful situations, she knew. Routine went out of the window as survival mode kicked in. Some people could barely manage the basics, such as drinking and eating. Even going to the toilet could become a chore. Getting properly dressed was always way down the list of priorities.

In the kitchen, Britney suggested Stacey sit down at the table while she switched on the kettle.

"Jim didn't take sugar," Stacey informed her after requesting the sweetener in hers, "but I can't drink tea without it." She turned to stare forlornly at a picture which hung on the wall behind her. Similarly posed to the wedding photo it depicted her and her missing husband as a smiling couple. "He was always onto me to give it up, but I could never seem to manage it. Imagine, he wouldn't use sugar but smoked like a trooper. Not when his father was around though. He'd promised Alan he'd given them up, you see, and didn't like letting his father down."

A lump stuck in Britney's throat. It wasn't lost on her that she spoke of her husband in past tense. Or that he might have considered himself a disappointment to his father. But then, what son didn't?

As she waited for the kettle to boil, Britney searched the nearest cupboard for a few mugs while at the same time discreetly instructing Fiona to gather some toys for the children to play with. She had spotted a small toy sword near the leg of the kitchen table and a doll lounging on the counter-top near the fridge.

"You've got two lovely kids, Stacey," Fiona said as she gathered up the toys. "They're the image of you." Almost instantly she regretted the remark.

"Thanks," Stacey mumbled, "but most people say they look like their father."

"Well, I bet they are full of mischief," Britney interceded, when she saw Stacey's eyes welling up, "like all kids their age."

"They are that," Stacey agreed, somehow managing to force her stubborn frown into a smile.

Glancing gratefully at Britney, Fiona bent down to be at eye level with the boy and girl who were now clinging to the chair on which Stacey was sitting. She smiled warmly and held out the toys. "I'm sure you'd both prefer to play than listen to us rabbiting on." When that didn't garner the desired reaction, she leaned in and whispered, "Your mammy has promised a special treat for whoever can play in the sitting room for the longest."

The boy and girl glanced at each other then looked to their mother for confirmation.

"Go on," Stacey insisted mildly. "But remember, no treat if you don't behave."

The pair hesitated a moment longer but then, as if some secret communication had passed between them, together let go of the chair and grabbed the toys, the girl grabbing the doll and the boy the sword.

"Arthur!" the boy declared menacingly – or as menacingly as his little voice allowed, as he set his feet like a warrior and brandished the weapon.

Britney smiled and held up her hands in mock submission. "I surrender, Arthur, and I bow to the king. Have mercy, sire."

"He's not Arthur, silly," his sister interceded in a giddy voice. "He's my big brother. Zac Rourke."

"And you are?" Britney asked playfully.

"I'm Cathy." Cathy had yet to learn how to fully pronounce her words, and her name came out like Cappy. So, so cute.

"Ok. Zac and Cathy, into the sitting room and see who can earn that special treat."

With that, off they toddled through the wide doorway. Britney threw them a reassuring smile as she closed the doors behind them, hoping they would settle there for a while. They didn't need to hear what was about to be discussed.

"You're very good with kids," Stacey observed when they were alone. "Have you some of your own?"

"No, Stacey." Britney replied with an involuntary purse of her lips. "Can't say I do."

If Stacey detected the regret in Britney's voice she didn't let on.

"Well, you should because I can see it in your face. You'd make a great mother."

Britney appreciated the compliment but at the same time wondered if the longing she felt to have kids of her own was that apparent. Sometimes the maternal craving was a physical pain and she often wondered if her heightened instincts to nurture were down to her mother leaving when she was a child. And, later, her father leaving her too. Only he couldn't help it. Still, she was only twenty-eight, she reminded herself, and had loads of time. But tell that to the irrational urges.

Just then an intermittent whistling came from the countertop. Welcoming the distraction of the kettle coming to a boil, she pushed her petty personal concerns aside and busied herself making the tea. Three cups of tea, one with sugar in it as Stacey had requested.

Once the tea was made, Britney set the cups down on some coasters that were scattered around the kitchen table. The table was almost wedged into one corner of the room, next to a pair of glass patio doors that led out onto a postal stamp of a back garden. There was just about enough room in the corner for the three of them to sit comfortably. Along with the coasters, the table displayed a set of placemats, some children's books and an open biscuit tin that contained half a dozen homemade buns and two empty bun-cases.

"The neighbours sent those over," Stacey explained with a grateful nod toward the biscuit tin. "They've all been so kind the last few days. Buns, biscuits, sandwiches. They just drop them at the door without a word." While relaying the generosity of the neighbours, she had pulled a Kleenex out of her pocket and was now dabbing her eyes, once again attempting to smile but failing miserably.

"People can be really supportive," Britney observed, noting that the neighbours already knew the score. She was about to add 'at times like these' but as yet wasn't sure what kind of time this was. Was Jim Rourke's disappearance voluntary or was there a sinister element to it? Was he even missing at all? With those questions foremost in her mind, she took a pen and notebook out of her pocket then sipped her tea while waiting for the distraught woman to relax.

"So, Jim is your husband?" Britney stated when Stacey had finally gathered herself. The simple questions were always the best to get the ball rolling.

"Yes."

"And his second name is Rourke?"

"Yes. Jim Rourke. He's from Ballyfeud originally. Used to hurl for them once. Actually, that's how I met him. After a match."

"I see," Britney smiled encouragingly. It wasn't unusual for a person under stress to offer up trivial information but better to have them talking than not. "Could you describe him for me, please?" On asking this question Britney licked the tip of her index finger then flicked open the notebook.

"Tall," Stacey replied. "Around six foot. With sandy hair and broad shoulders." She nodded toward the photo near them on the wall. "Handsome, I like to think."

"He is," Britney offered a brief smile in acknowledgment. "And you fear he is missing?"

Stacey's lips formed a thin line. Her tone was resigned when she finally spoke. "I don't fear. I know he is missing. As I told you on the phone, he went out to work last Friday week and just didn't come home."

Britney frowned. Hearing the statement in person added far more gravity. As did the dark circles highlighting Stacey's puffed out eyes.

"Is it like him to do something like that?"

"No. Not at all. He normally calls me every day to see how the children are or to let me know what time he'll be finished at. He hasn't called at all. Not once. Something terrible has happened to him. I just know it."

"And you've tried to call him, I presume?"

Stacey nodded. "A hundred times. His phone is off." She sniffed back a tear. "His phone is never off."

Britney scribbled a note of this. The fact that the phone was off, concerned her on two fronts. One, it was out of character and two, it would make tracing his phone extremely difficult, if not impossible.

"Is he on Facebook? Or email? Could you contact him that way?"

"No. He's not into that social media stuff. Can barely manage sending a text on his phone."

Not one for social media herself, Britney nodded in understanding. "You suggested when you called that your husband went missing before."

Stacey quickly shook her head. "Not missing. He'd just go to the pub sometimes and forget to come home. But that was a lifetime ago. Before the kids."

"And what does your husband work at?" Britney glanced at Fiona. The sober look on her colleague's unblemished face suggested she was every bit as concerned as Britney was.

"He's a carpenter. He has his own business."

"He'd have employees then? People who should have seen him at work?" Fiona asked.

"Yes. They should have. But they didn't. At least not since that Friday."

"You called them?"

"Yes. I called Brian Farrell who's his head carpenter. I called him that Friday evening after Jim didn't come home. Jim wasn't answering his phone so I thought they might be gone for a drink or something, but they weren't. Brian said Jim went off at lunchtime and never came back. I called a number of times since but nothing."

"Ok. Did Brian say where Jim was going?"

"He was going to the hardware. He does that fairly regular."

"So, he took his van?"

Stacey nodded. "Yes. A transit. It's still gone. But that's nothing unusual. Lately he'd been lending it to someone in work who needed it for nixers, so even if Jim was here, his van mightn't be."

"I see. And no one has heard anything from Jim since he went to the hardware. Did you contact the hardware?"

"Yes. But they say he was never there."

"I see." Now that did sound odd, Britney had to admit. "Can you remember what he was wearing?"

"The same work gear he always wore. You know those trousers and jackets with all the pockets. He called it his uniform."

"Along with work boots, I'm sure?"

Stacey nodded.

"Has he family close by?"

"Yes, his parents still live out in Ballyfeud, but they haven't heard from him either."

"And what about friends? Would he have gone to see any of them?"

Stacey shook her head. "Ever since the children came along, Jim has hardly gone out except to go to work. He was a great father."

There it was again – past tense.

She stared at Britney pleadingly and said, "He wouldn't just leave the kids."

It was a question as much as a statement. With that, Stacey's eyes welled up again. "He's hurt somewhere. I just know he is." Sniffling loudly, she dabbed her eyes with the handkerchief.

At least she didn't say dead this time, Britney thought, as she reached out and gripped the distraught woman's shoulder reassuringly. She could feel Stacey trembling beneath her fingers.

"You say he used to hurl. Did he like to go to games?"

"Sometimes, but not very often anymore. What with his business and the kids and all."

"If there was a match on Friday evening, would he have gone to that? Perhaps gone drinking afterward?"

"He hadn't planned to. At least he never mentioned it to me. Anyway, that was last Friday week, for God's sake!"

Britney wasn't perturbed by the needle that had entered Stacey's voice. She understood it was a mixture of frustration and fear that was upsetting the poor woman rather than real anger.

"Ok, Stacey. Now I'm going to apologise in advance because I have to ask you this. Is it possible that Jim is having an affair?"

Stacey stared blankly at her for so long that Britney wondered if she should repeat the question. Finally, she gave a sharp shake of her head as the momentary anger in her eyes turned to hurt. Or was it guilt? Britney couldn't tell but sensed something was off.

"He wouldn't do that," she replied with a note of finality. "Not to me and definitely not to the children." Her eyes momentarily drifted to some distant place and when they returned, she breathed out in frustration, "Jim is a good man. A kind and gentle man. He's not the type to go running around behind my back."

"Fair enough," Britney replied and made a show of scratching that idea off some imaginary list in her notebook. However, in her mind, it remained. Even though Stacey's convictions about her husband's inherent goodness seemed genuine, the possibility of an affair couldn't be ruled out. Jim wouldn't be the first 'loving' husband to have gone off to visit his mistress and not come home afterwards. Nor the first to be too cowardly to pick up the phone and tell his wife where he was. It was easier for some men to let it all drag out so that eventually the cheated-on wife would put two and two together herself. That way the dreaded confrontation could be avoided. Or at least kicked like a can down the road. Of course, the same theory could be applied to women, Britney reminded herself as she pondered the momentary expression she had registered. Hurt or guilt?

"Was he in any trouble? Money wise, maybe?" Sensing that Stacey was temporarily annoyed with Britney, Fiona took up the questioning. It was an age-old technique. What American crime shows sometimes called good cop, bad cop.

"I don't think so. No more than usual anyway." She shrugged as if to apologise for him in his absence. "Employing people is a tough business."

"What about in general? Does he go out drinking? Was he having trouble with anyone in the community?"

Stacey shook her head. "Jim keeps to himself these days. Doesn't even go to mass." She paused as if remembering something then almost instantly dismissed it with a shake of her head.

"What is it?" Britney encouraged sensing the hostility towards her had passed.

"We used to have a bit of a time of it when we went out. But that was a good while ago. Before the kids, like I said. Anyway, it was silly stuff, mostly. Just lads arguing about hurling. That kind of thing. Though he'd played, Jim wasn't a big fan of the organisation."

"Nothing recent?"

Stacey shook her head and once again wiped her eyes with the handkerchief.

"I see. Do you think this might have had an effect on him?"

Stacey shrugged. "Of course, it did, but he learned to keep away from those people. And he didn't hurt himself if that's what you're getting at."

"Not at all," Britney replied, struggling to keep the lie from her face. "Just trying to get a better feel on things. One last question, Stacey. Why did you wait until now to declare him missing? It's been well over a week."

"I don't know," Stacey replied quietly. Her eyes as wide as saucers, she was shaking her head as if bewildered by her own stupidity. "I just thought he'd come home. I really thought he'd come home. But now I know he won't." Suddenly her entire body started to tremble and within moments the tears that she had struggled to hold back up to now, flowed freely down her cheeks. There was nothing Britney could think to do only reach out to comfort her, but Fiona got there first. She wrapped her in a hug and whispered in her ear, encouraging her not to worry. That they would find Jim, and everything would be ok.

Even as she heard the words spoken, Britney was all too aware how hollow they sounded. If she was to take everything Stacey had told her as true, then the critical first forty-eight hours were already long passed. The investigation had moved from missing person into the realm of possible fatality even before it had begun.

It was clear Stacey recognised that too. She was inconsolable. Beyond afraid. She was already grieving. Fiona sat with her until her sobbing grew quiet, giving Britney the chance to have a look for a photo they could use of the missing man. There were a number of them to be seen but she settled on the one hanging beside the rear door that Stacey had earlier stared at as it offered the clearest image of Jim Rourke. In it, Stacey and her husband were holding hands but where Stacey was looking at her husband, Jim Rourke was focused on the camera. He was, indeed, a fine-looking man with brown eyes and sandy hair that was beginning to grey at the temples.

When Britney asked Stacey's permission to take it down, she got a mute nod in reply. The woman was clearly exhausted. It was obvious that over the last half hour she had been dipping into the bottom of the well just so she could answer whatever questions they might have, but now that she had made her statement the last of her strength seemed to drain out of her.

"Is there anyone we can call to sit with you?" Britney asked as she closed her notebook and prepared to leave. There was nothing more they could do there, at least for the time being.

Stacey shook her head, then took a deep breath as she tried to control her sobs, the handkerchief held up to her face. "I'll be fine." The words filtered out through the tissue as barely coherent mumbles.

Britney glanced at Fiona, suspecting it wasn't the first white lie the forlorn lady had told them.

"Are you sure, Stacey? We can call your parents if you want."

Stacey didn't look up as she crumpled the tissue in her hand. The way her body tensed immediately relayed to Britney that she had said the wrong thing.

"My parents died when I was a kid," Stacey informed them eventually. "I've been on my own since I was Zac's age."

"I'm so sorry," Britney replied, instantly recognising that this bombshell only compounded the worry Stacey must be feeling. The poor woman would understand all too well the effect her husband's absence must be having on the children.

"What about one of your neighbours?" Fiona suggested, a slight strain to her voice.

"It's ok, honestly. I have Jim's parents. They're always so good."

"I'm glad," Britney said, genuinely happy to hear Stacey had someone to lean on. She would need all the support she could get in the coming days and weeks. Perhaps longer. There was no telling how this would end. Or when.

With that heavy thought weighing on her, Britney set a card with the contact details for the station on the table and scribbled both her and Fiona's names on the back.

"If you need anything, just call. Ask for myself or Fiona." Once more, she laid a reassuring hand on Stacey's shoulder. "Anything at all. Day or night."

Stacey nodded, forcing a weary but grateful smile. "Promise you'll call me if there's any word of Jim?"

"I will," Britney acknowledged.

As she exited into the hall, Britney gave one final look back. The children, as if sensing their mother needed comforting, had already come back into the kitchen, the promise of a treat clearly forgotten. They ran to their mother and climbed up onto her lap then threw their arms around her – Zac on one side, Cathy on the other. A young family united in a grief that had yet to be validated. Stacey's tea remained untouched on the table, destined to turn cold. And later sour. The card now replaced the tissue in the despairing woman's hand, clutched to her breast like an amulet. Britney understood why. It was more than a piece of paper. It was a talisman. A shining light in the dark. It was hope.

Chapter 2

Approximately at the same time that Saturday, but more than one hundred kilometres from where Stacey Rourke desperately clasped the Sergeant's details to her chest, journalist Marie Cox climbed the steps of Swords Garda Station. She paused for a moment, to contemplate the box in her hands, and wondered, not for the first time, who would have sent her such a thing?

It had gangland written all over it, but she could think of no plausible reason why they would target her. Certainly not for her work as a sports correspondent. As for her her side-line business, she had been so careful to keep her involvement under the radar. As had her partner. They both had far too much to lose. What if they had made a mistake? What if she had made a mistake?

Feeling a concerned flush rise above high cheekbones, she dabbed her forehead with a handkerchief and pushed back several strands of blonde hair that had fallen over her celebrated face. To any onlooker, her unusually frazzled appearance could have been blamed on the heat of the day as it was an especially warm afternoon for October. Hot sun and blue skies, with not a cloud in sight, and the air as dead as the item she was carrying. An Indian Summer they called it. In recent years, Ireland's only summer.

"Great day for the match, Cox," a passer-by observed as she dallied, his voice sounding strangely muffled.

"Should be a cracker. In fact, I'm surprised you're not at it, getting in free and all."

Being chief sportswriter for the biggest newspaper in the country – Independent News – Marie had grown accustomed to being recognised around the capital, and to the little jibes regarding what people saw as her exalted position. Therefore, she wouldn't have spared a thought for the strangely attired man if not for the fact that she'd spotted him already that morning, not long after leaving her apartment with her newly acquired gift.

"While the rest of us have to pay an arm and a leg," the man added as he moved quickly along. "By the way, say hi to Hitler for me."

Though she didn't get a chance to see the man's face she could imagine the sneer that accompanied the words. Hitler was the nickname his many detractors used for Ade Fagan, the president of the Hurler's Association of Ireland. The HAI, as opposed to its counterpart, the GAA, was fast becoming the national game's main governing body. Having been founded in secret on November 1st, 1984, it was but a pup in comparison to its more established peer, yet it boasted over one million members, with dozens of teams in every county across the country. Having grown disillusioned with what they perceived as widespread corruption amongst the GAA's hierarchy, the founding members imagined an organisation that would promote Ireland's national game of hurling through an ethos of absolute amateurism, with no exceptions. This ethos was to be bedrock of the HAI, its USP in a world where the very heart of modern-day sports was subverted by commercialism. A philosophy to be trumpeted across the globe.

With this idealistic revolution in mind, the date of its foundation was carefully chosen. It was symbolic. A new beginning. A new beginning on the same day the GAA celebrated one hundred years in business. The centenary year of its unchallenged monopoly.

Now nearly forty years on, the revolution was almost complete. Across all meaningful platforms, the GAA was about to be overtaken. In recent times, this rise in fortunes was credited to the talents of Mr Ade Fagan. Not least by the man himself. He considered himself the organisation's driving force. Had positioned himself as its top man. Marie always found herself drawn to such men. And such men were drawn to her.

The relationship they had cultivated over the past four years was the reason Marie didn't have to pay 'an arm and a leg,' like everybody else. Not to mention the other perks. The complimentary VIP passes, the corporate box, the expensive meals. In fact, just the other day he had invited her to dinner in his favourite restaurant in Oldcastle, Jude's. An exclusive establishment that he made a point of frequenting at least twice a week, as he had openly boasted over dessert.

"Why shouldn't I?" he had asked, his chin wobbling above the red napkin folded neatly into the collar of his grey Charvet shirt. Gauging her with a beady-eyed look, his fingers belied their stoutness by dexterously working the tip of his spoon around the edges of his tiramisu. Clearly determined to savour every morsel, he restricted himself to chopping off titbits at a time, then with practiced economy, slipping them into his waiting mouth. The way his expectant lips parted always reminded her of a pouting goldfish. "You see, it doesn't cost me a penny. All paid for by the Oldtown District Board."

For a man who fancied himself as the ultimate alpha male, at least politically, his voice must have secretly irked. It had an almost feminine, nasal whine. The fact that his once thick, dark hair was receding at an alarming rate, and his body had run to fat wouldn't inspire confidence either. Still, the power he held served as a great convincer. Buttressed, of course, by the calculated distraction of his finely stitched three-piece suit.

Marie knew Ade had been the director of the administrative arm of the local HAI for two consecutive terms before moving up the ladder to take charge at national level. Now, having cemented his place as president of one of the country's biggest national sporting organisations, it was clear that, in his mind, he deserved some special treatment. That he had earned it.

"But I'm seldom here with such beautiful company," he added between quarter-spoons, his bloated lips smacking irritatingly and robbing the compliment of its desired effect. It was then she decided that no matter how hard he tried, or how expensive the wine brought to the table, those bloated lips would be getting nowhere near hers. Not this time.

Now, as she watched the man's hooded coat disappear down an alleyway, she pushed all thoughts of Fagan aside. She had experienced a sudden chilling certainty that this hooded man was the crackpot that had sent her the little delivery. But who in God's name was he? And why follow her here, to the garda station? To demonstrate that he was fearless? That he was untouchable? And that she was the opposite? That he could get to her no matter where she went?

She stood staring after him for a moment longer until she was certain he was gone, then she quickly negotiated the remaining steps and entered the relative safety of the station. The foyer was empty but a young garda was attending to paperwork behind the reception counter. Contrary to the overweight cliché she was expecting, this guy looked slim and muscular beneath the shirt of his Garda uniform. He was tall with broad shoulders, skin as brown as a nut. 'Phil Lynott eat your heart out,' she thought admiringly, the urgency of her predicament momentarily forgotten. She instinctively took a moment to settle her appearance then walked directly toward him and deposited the tattered box she was carrying on the counter.

"Excuse me, young man," she said in a brisk tone, "but I need to see Detective Lyons right away. It's urgent."

"Ok, I'll be with you in a minute."

"Now would be better," the woman replied, then added, "My name is Marie Cox," as if expecting some sort of acknowledgement. The young garda looked up from his work but otherwise gave little reaction. Clearly irked, the woman continued a little more sharply, "Could you please inform Detective Lyons that I'm here?"

Having been assigned reception duty since his arrival at the station, he was getting used to dealing with pushy customers. The lady that had suddenly appeared in front of him definitely had the air of being one of those, in more than just attitude. She was tall, elegant, and expensively dressed. Her straight hair was shoulder length and blonde, but from a bottle he guessed, and despite the excessive make-up, she was certainly attractive. Even beautiful. Though this beauty was somewhat allayed by her rather severe demeanour. In the tightness around the eyes, he noted, and in the slight downturn to her otherwise luscious mouth. He smiled to himself. She reminded him of one of the hens his mother kept back home in Mayo. A real looker – a perfectly formed Brahma with an array of colour in its sleek feathers but a right bitch to the others. Constantly pecking them and grabbing their food. He decided the next time he ventured home he'd christen that chicken Mrs Cox. If indeed, the fox hadn't already paid them his yearly visit.

"I can, certainly," the young Garda replied calmly. "What should I say it's in relation to, Mrs Cox?"

"It's Miss Cox," the lady corrected, her blue eyes narrowing impatiently. "And it's in relation to a private matter." The young officer noticed her cast an anxious glance toward the street as if she feared being overheard.

"I see. Unfortunately, I'm not inclined to disturb the detective without some details. He's a busy man, as you can imagine." When he's hasn't popped out the back for a top-up, he added in his head.

"What's your name, young man?"

"Garda Danny Owens."

"Well then, Garda Danny Owens, seeing as your so adamant, you can tell him it's in relation to this." Welcoming the opportunity to be rid of it, she shoved the box across the counter and directly through the slot in the glass partition that separated them. "I received it this morning. Came back from my morning walk to find it on the threshold of my apartment."

"I see," the young Garda hesitantly reached for the offering. "It's not a bomb, is it?" he smiled innocently as he turned his attention to the rectangular box, crudely wrapped as it was in old newspaper. The newspaper had been split along the edge of the lid making it clear to the young Garda that the box had previously been opened. He also noted a blotchy red mark had stained the newspaper just beneath the cut. After a questioning glance at Miss Cox, he slowly lifted the lid.

From behind the glass, Marie Cox watched him closely. First, his eyes – a strange mix of green, brown, and blue, squinted as if unsure what they were seeing. Then they widened so fast, she feared they would pop out of his head. She couldn't say that he turned pale exactly, but his brown skin did blanch noticeably as a look of horror spread across his chiselled features.

"It's a hand," he gulped, and a bead of sweat appeared on his brow.

****

The office of Detective Richie Lyons was behind the furthest door of five along the hall. Up to now, Danny had no reason to venture any further than the first, which was the station's bathroom. He would have preferred if it had stayed that way. Having only spoken to the detective briefly on two occasions – the first of which, the detective had appeared far from sober – the young Garda had no reason to discount the consensus in the station that portrayed him as cantankerous at the best of times. This was far from the best of times.

Only that morning, Detective Lyons had returned from a week of enforced leave, having given a drug dealer a bit of a hiding in his cell a few months earlier. "Seemingly he had drink on board at the time," one of Danny's colleagues explained. "A bit of a habit with him you'll find. So rumour has it, the Super gave him a choice – walking papers or a drying-out clinic. I saw him going into the rehab centre myself and he wasn't looking at all happy about it so it must be true." The colleague clearly enjoyed sharing his titbit of juicy gossip. "I also heard he's failed a psyche exam, so they put him on enforced leave while they decided what they were going to do with him in the long term."

Apparently, no decision on his future had yet been made, therefore since his return, he had been practicing solitary confinement in his office.

Normally, the young Garda would have considered it the height of rudeness not to knock before entering another's domain, but he was so flustered by the idea of walking into the lion's den with the grotesqueness he carried that all protocol fell by the wayside. Afterwards, he would chastise himself for being so unprofessional. In that moment, balancing the box in one hand, he turned the handle of the door with his free hand and entered without a second thought.

Surprised by the sudden intrusion, Detective Richie Lyons eyed the door from where he was hunched over his desk. He was in the process of writing up a report on an attempted burglary case he had been working on prior to his enforced absence. The report was hand-written as were all the reports he filed. He hated computers. Didn't trust them. Despite countless assurances from more tech savvy colleagues, he feared that if the damn thing crashed, all his hard work was gone down the swanny. Resenting reports, to begin with, he had no intention of facing into one for a second time.

As if realising he'd just barged right in, the young Garda paused momentarily at the door, looking sheepishly over the tatty box he was carrying. Hesitantly, he approached the desk. As he did, he detected a mixture of stale odours in the room – alcohol and cigar smoke being the predominant offenders. Clearly the detective had yet to adjust to the smoking ban, even though it had been in law for years. And he wasn't even bothered to hide his drinking, which suggested his forced vacation had done little to mend his ways.

Lyons watched the young Garda approach but said nothing at first. He pulled his reading glasses down low on his nose and studied the intruder over the thin metal rims. Though his craggy face didn't show it, he secretly welcomed the interruption having developed a headache from pouring over the paperwork. Exacerbated the headache, he corrected, for the pain in his frontal lobe had already existed. It was a permanent affliction these days.

Sighing, he removed his glasses and rubbed the bridge of his broad nose with the tips of his thick fingers. If he had his way, all admin duties – form-filling, filing or recording of any sort – would be the remit of young Gardaí like the one standing in front of him now. They had to start somewhere, after all. Relieving the stress of an overburdened senior officer like him was as good a place as any.

"I must get that changed," he observed eventually, his voice every bit as craggy as his appearance.

"What, sir?" Danny asked nervously.

"The sign on the door that says barge right on in. Don't bother knocking cause the old man that works here is as deaf as a coot and won't hear it anyway. And he doesn't believe knocking first would be the mannerly thing to do cause he's so damn senile that he has forgotten what basic manners are about."

"Sorry sir…sometimes, I can be like a goat with an open gate…" the young Garda mumbled awkwardly.

"And anyway," the detective continued as if not hearing the amusing analogy, "even if he were neither deaf nor senile, it is universally recognised that a door is just a decorative addition to a room and not a functional one, so what would be the point of knocking on it in the first bloody place?"

"I'm sorry, Detective Lyons." The young Garda found just enough composure to quickly apologise. "I didn't knock because..." He hesitated as he glanced down at the box in his hands.

A goat with an open gate... Detective Lyons allowed himself a brief smirk which slowly faded on noticing how uncomfortable the young man standing in front of him seemed.

"You didn't knock because you wanted to surprise me with some doughnuts, is that it?" he offered.

"Not exactly, sir."

"Ok then, if not doughnuts, what have you got there?" His thick eyebrows furrowed as he tried to figure what possible relevance a paper-covered shoebox could have for him. "Shoes?"

The young Garda shook his head. "It's a hand, sir."

"A hand?" Detective Lyons set down his pen and ran the tips of fingers through his scraggly beard. The beard was a relatively recent addition and had yet to fill out. Still, he liked the cloak of it on his face, even though sometimes it itched like hell. After a moment of contemplation, he sat back in his chair and took a good look at the young man's expression. Did he just say a hand?

"What's your name, son?" he asked testily, thinking he'd nip the little prank in the bud. The young man was obviously taking the piss. Some practical joke collectively arranged with his colleagues on the front desk. It wouldn't be the first time the new recruits had tried to play a trick on the more mature members of staff or vice versa for that matter. A battle of wits had developed at the station between the rookies and the old guard which the detective found tiresome. To make it worse, neither side seemed likely to win it anytime soon.

"Danny, sir," the young man replied nervously, forcing Detective Lyons to admit he was playing it well. He certainly didn't look the joking type. "Danny Owens."

"Owens!" Lyons repeated obviously struggling to reconcile the traditional Irish name with the not so Irish complexion. Danny was well used to the quizzical reaction.

"Yes, sir. Danny Owens."

"What do you think of this, young Danny Owens?" he asked. Aiming for a distraction that might cause the young jester to drop his guard, he proceeded to recount the details of the report he was completing. "A young drug addict with previous broke into a house in one of the wealthier estates on the outskirts of the town with an eye on taking some jewellery. Unfortunately, one of the rungs of the ladder he used was damaged so as he was making his way out of the house, the rung gave way and the gobshite fell off the ladder, fracturing his hip on landing."

"Sounds like he got his just desserts, sir." The young man still looked nervous as hell.

"Yes, but here's the rub. He's now suing the owners of the house for leaving a faulty ladder within such easy reach of the public. His solicitor argued there should have been a sign stating the ladder was faulty and therefore dangerous to use. Ridiculous as the claim might be, the lout will most likely win the case. What do you make of that?" Detective Lyons shook his head at the idea of it.

The young Garda glanced at the box while an anxious tongue flicked out to lick his lips. "I think it's ridiculous, sir."

Standing close to him now, Danny noticed the detective had a jagged scar on his right ear and another on the index finger of his left hand in which he held the glasses. 'The man doesn't only look like a bear,' Danny thought, 'he looks like he's wrestled one. Probably won too.'

"In my day if you fell, you fell, and it was your own fault. Not somebody else's. If you fell off someone else's ladder with a fistful of their jewellery in your pockets, the very least you deserved was a fractured hip. A broken neck mightn't have gone astray either. And a kick up the hole." He sighed before adding to himself, 'Or a good beating, for that matter.'

"The world has gone to pot, sir," Danny agreed. He shifted on his feet but didn't look as if he was about to crack. The façade of nervous innocence remained.

"Yes, it has, and old-timers like me are left writing up goddamn reports on it. Now, young man, as you might have guessed I have it up to my eyes with young pups codding the system so let's have it. What's really in the box?"

"Sorry, sir, but it's exactly like I told you. It's a hand. A severed hand. A lady from one of the papers just brought it in."

At once, Detective Lyons sat upright in his chair. His eyes narrowed as he studied the box, his expression growing ever more serious. "What lady from what papers?" he asked while running agitated fingers through the coarse hairs of his fledgling beard.

As if on cue, the woman suddenly appeared at the door. Danny sighed internally. He had invited her in behind reception and asked her to wait in the small interrogation room opposite the bathroom. Yet here she was, as cheeky as a pet pig.

"Miss Cox," Detective Lyons declared in surprise and with obvious displeasure. Danny couldn't tell if he was more upset by the sight of the woman herself or the brash manner of her entrance.

"Detective Lyons," Miss Cox replied with an air of haughtiness as she strode confidently toward his desk, her long legs outlined beneath the thin fabric of the floral dress she wore and accentuated by a pair of red high heels. "It's good to see you again."

Not wishing to look incompetent in front of his superior Danny managed to tear his eyes away from those shapely limbs and step forward to bar her path. However, the detective stayed him with a quick shake of his rugged head.

"No point closing the door when the horse has bolted," he sighed. "I'll take it from here."

On reaching the desk, Miss Cox cast a dismissive smile in Danny's general direction. "Sorry, but I couldn't wait any longer. There's somewhere I need to be."

"A match, I presume?" Lyons offered wearily while sitting back in his chair in what Danny judged a defensive pose.

"Yes. The hurling quarter-final is on. Very important game, as I'm sure you're aware. Oh, I know what you're going to say. Backdoor nonsense that you wouldn't watch it if it was in your rear garden." She smiled coyly. "And you, who used to love hurling, Richie,"

Without taking her eyes off the detective, she directed her next comments to Danny. "By all accounts, he could have been one of the greats, you know. If his heart hadn't got in the way. Or was it the drink?" she smiled devilishly. "No, that came later, didn't it?"

Detective Lyons ignored the dig, but Danny noted more than a hint of annoyance cross over his face.

"Take a seat, Miss Cox," Lyons instructed firmly.

"Thank you," she replied, "but I'll stand. As I said, I've got somewhere I need to be."

"Don't we all," replied Detective Lyons pointedly. "However, if the item in this box is what our young Garda here claims it is, then I'm afraid you'll need to reschedule."

"Oh, it is, Detective, I assure you." Miss Cox's tone suggested she was finding the whole thing tiresome. "I simply arrived back from a walk and there it was, waiting for me on the threshold of my apartment. In that tatty box. Delivered like the milk." Her emerald eyes seemed to focus in on Lyons. "Don't you see, it must be a mistake," she stated. "I can't believe it was meant for me."

Lyons unblinkingly returned her stare then pursed his lips as if trying to make sense of this sudden turn of events. Finally, he glanced at Danny before nodding at his junior colleague. "You can leave the box."

Danny was glad to hear it, so he quickly placed the box on the desk and turned for the door. As he did so, Lyons eyed Miss Cox for a moment before sliding the box across the table until it was directly in front of him. A concerned frown creasing his thick forehead, he slowly lifted the cardboard lid to peer inside. Despite his years of experience, he instinctively recoiled at the gory sight that awaited him. It was indeed a hand, just as the young Garda had stated. The fingers of which were curled in the shape of talons, grey and stiff with rigour mortis.

"What?" Marie Cox asked dryly. "You don't trust me, Richie?"

To Danny's ear, the heavy sarcasm did little to hide the fear in her voice.

Chapter 3

The first stop Britney and Fiona made after leaving Stacey Rourke's house was at the building site where her missing husband worked. The site being conveniently located near Emmet's Hill on the outskirts of town prompted Fiona to suggest they call there on their way back to the station. However, the words were barely out of her mouth when she seemed to have a change of heart.

"What if Halley calls in?" she asked, casting a look of concern at her friend. "He won't be happy to see you gone from that desk."

"We informed dispatch, didn't we, which makes it official business?" Britney replied, then shrugged in response to the unconvinced expression that lingered in Fiona's eyes. "I bet you Flynn has already told him anyway and took pleasure in it. But to be honest, what that poor lady is going through trumps anything Halley could throw at me."

"Deep down she really believes he's dead, doesn't she?" Fiona observed. "Do you think she could have done something? I mean, did you smell the bleach?"

"You think she cut him up and buried him under the floorboards?" Britney gave a shake of her head. "I got the impression she was hiding something, but I don't think it's that. No, that woman is timid as a lamb. I think cleaning is just her coping mechanism. But I do understand her concern. Let's hope we can prove her wrong. For her and for those poor kids. Did you call the hospital?"

"Yep, before I called dispatch. No one even remotely matching his description was admitted in the last week. No record of him being arrested either. At least not recently."

"Recently?"

"He was arrested a few years back for assault. Nothing came of it, but dispatch found a note in our files."

"Good of Stacey to keep that to herself," Britney replied as she drove. "Perhaps those little hurling arguments weren't so silly after all."

"Yeah. And I spoke to the hardware. Jim Rourke was a regular customer alright, but he didn't call that day. And they haven't seen him since. Maybe the poor woman has a right to be thinking the worst."

"Maybe," Britney acknowledged sombrely.

The building site was set more than a hundred yards in off the road but was easily spotted due to the large machinery and piles of displaced earth that dotted its landscape. And, of course, the thick mud on the makeshift lane that led inward. At the entrance, a large sign told Britney the site had received planning for forty-two residential dwellings, two office blocks, and a crèche. Another Emmet's Hill, Britney thought as she drove in. More brown envelopes, no doubt. Then suddenly she slowed down causing Fiona to throw her a quizzical glance.

"McBride Construction," Britney explained with a nod toward the sign. "Remember that vandalism complaint that landed me on desk duty."

"The one you accused Flynn of trying to bury?"

"That's the one," Britney replied as she drove on. "Looks like I might get another chance to figure out why."

She found the site office located in a large parking area to the front of the development, surrounded by a fleet of grimy cars, vans, and trucks. Even though the surface was temporarily covered with rough stone which crunched under their car tyres, the parking area was every bit as muddy as the road. With Fiona keen to preserve the sheen on her religiously polished brogues, Britney parked the squad car next to a white builder's van, in a spot as close to the office as possible. The pair then gingerly walked the short distance to the office door. The look on Fiona's face suggested she would have much preferred a piggyback.

The office was set up in a rectangular prefab building which was sitting approximately two feet above the ground on pillars of concrete blocks. Similar blocks also constituted a set of three steps necessary to facilitate the climb to the door. The door was ajar, inviting Britney to lean in. Doing so, she found the cabin occupied by a tall man wearing a high-vis vest and hard hat. He was leaning over a makeshift desk which was overloaded with sheets of drawings and paperwork, some of which threatened to spill over onto the soiled floor.

"Hello," she called to get the man's attention. When he glanced up from his work, she almost fell off the step. She knew him. Well, kind of. She'd met him at a party that Fiona had taken her to a while back. They'd chatted briefly and had even kissed, but it had been a wild party and they'd gotten separated somehow. At least that's what

Britney had told herself afterwards. She'd thought of him once or twice since but never expected to see him again. Yet here he was, and for the life of her, she couldn't remember his name. Though the kiss…the kiss she would never forget. Gathering herself, she cleared her throat then smiled with just the right amount of apology. "Sorry to bother you, sir. My name is Sergeant Britney Kent. I'm here with Garda Fiona O'Malley."

The man nodded, a mixture of surprise and recognition crossing over his ruggedly handsome features. He removed his hard hat and pushed back the thick lock of brown hair that had strayed down over his eyes.

"When I saw the Garda car driving in, I wondered if I did something wrong," he said evenly but his tone was betrayed by the slightest smirk tugging at the corners of his mouth. His extremely kissable mouth. "Sometimes, it's so hard to tell."

"I'm sure you were perfectly innocent," Britney replied in the most professional tone she could muster considering a blush was rising from her toes. "But there are a couple of things you could help me with. First of all, I'm following up to know if you're happy with the outcome of the vandalism complaint logged with the station?"

He shrugged. "Young lads from town as it turned out. Just out to get some kicks. We told the detective we weren't interested in pressing charges."

"Detective Flynn, was it?"

"Yep, that's him. Did a good job, as far as I'm concerned."

"Glad to hear it." Britney couldn't tell if he picked up on the fact her tone belied her words. If he did, he let it pass.

"You said two things?"

Now, Britney nodded rather solemnly. "A man who works here has been reported missing. Jim Rourke."

The expression of concern she received in reply seemed genuine. The man folded the paperwork he was studying and set it aside, then moved out from behind the desk and stepped forward.

He was in his late twenties, Britney judged, and as tall as she remembered him, with wide shoulders and a broad chest. But it was his eyes she recalled most clearly of all. Even from the doorway, she could see they were a penetrating shade of blue. She also happened to note there was no sign of a wedding ring on his finger but admonished herself for the thought that followed even as it formed. They were here to investigate a missing person, not trawl for dates.

"Jim's missing?" The man sounded nonplussed. "I thought he was just off sick. He went home early one day last week." He paused. "Or was it the week before last? I'm not sure."

"Friday week," Britney provided. "But unfortunately, it appears more serious than that. I mean he never made it home. You haven't heard anything from him since then, have you?"

"No, not a word. His crew are still working their contract and are ahead if anything, so I didn't give his absence much thought."

"Ok. Could I have your name for my records?" Britney asked, keeping her expression unreadable. "And, also, could I have the names of everyone else who works here."

"Well, my name is simple enough to remember. It's Bob," he arched an eyebrow pointedly but softened the look with a smile. A knowing smile. With a hint of shyness too, Britney thought. "Bob Harris. I'm the foreman here." As he spoke, he moved closer until he was standing directly in front of her. He acknowledged Fiona's presence with a polite nod, but otherwise, his gaze remained focused on Britney, a playful twinkle in those searing blue eyes. Despite the seriousness of the inquiry, Britney's heart skipped a beat.

"The rest will take a little time to get together for you. Perhaps if you give me your number, I can send them on when I'm done?"

Now Britney felt the heat rise in her face and unconsciously raised her hand to her blemished left cheek. Her eyes flitted away for a moment, long enough for her to take a breath. And remind herself she was the one wearing the uniform.

"Thanks," she managed, "but I'll collect them on the way out, if that's ok? In the meantime, could you tell me where I'd find Brian Farrell? I'm told he works for Jim."

"Yes, he does, Sergeant," Bob replied, his tone business-like. "He's Jim's main carpenter. A good lad."

He pointed toward a row of houses to the right of the cabin that were currently under construction. "You'll find him at the back of those. The house at the end, I think."

His eyes met Britney's once more. "If you need anything else, just ask."

"We will, but for now thanks for your help." Conscious of the amusement in Fiona's demeanour, Britney deliberately emphasised the plural. It did little to appease the teasing smile on her colleague's lips. Or the devilment in her eyes. Britney wasn't at all surprised when halfway down the makeshift steps Fiona ribbed her with a playful nudge. "Hot or what?"

"He's ok, I suppose," Britney replied coolly, their shoes once again crunching on the gravel.

"Ok? He's a hunk. What's more, I got the impression you two know each other?" Fiona's sculpted eyebrows raised with the teasing question.

"We don't. Why?" Unable to look Fiona in the eye, Britney was grateful to reach the car.

"Because he was clearly flirting with you, Brit," Fiona continued as they got in. "Subconsciously then, which is even better."

"No, he wasn't. And even if he was, we're on a case."

"So, you're admitting he was then?"

Britney shook her head in exasperation then started up the car as if to say that was the end of the discussion. However, Fiona wasn't letting her off the hook that easy.

"He even asked for your number, I noticed."

"In a professional capacity."

"And those eyes. The way they bore into you. I was even hot looking at the two of you." The flush now burning up Britney's cheeks made Fiona laugh.

"Just shut up, Fiona," Britney instructed sharply but the secretly pleased smile that followed only served to encourage her colleague.

"Brit and Bob sitting in a tree,

K…I…S…S…I…N…G!"

Whether she was aware of it or not, Fiona had hit the nail on the head and by the time they exited the makeshift carpark, Britney had broken into a giddy laugh herself. Then Britney thought of Stacey and her mood dampened. It just didn't feel right to be laughing and joking when that woman was in such a miserable state. It felt as if they were cheating her in some way and, God knows, she would be cheated of enough if her husband didn't come home.

****

They found Brian Farrell working on the roof of the very end house in the development. On hearing his name being called, he finished nailing the rafter he was holding in place then climbed down the scaffold and turned off the generator that was growling noisily in the background. He didn't seem quite as surprised to see a Garda on-site as Bob the foreman had been.

"Is this about Jim?" Mr Farrell asked on watching them approach.

"Yes," Britney replied. "His wife Stacey has reported him missing."

Brian slowly nodded as he removed his safety helmet. "I thought she might." He was a stocky man, with weathered skin and receding hair. He looked to be in his mid to late thirties.

"You don't think she should have?"

"Oh, he's certainly missing. But is it anything worth reporting?" He shrugged. "I doubt it."

"Why do you say that, Mr Farrell?"

Brian Farrell glanced around at the other men on the crew who had downed tools and were now keeping a close eye on what was transpiring. Several of them unashamedly eyed up the two women, with most of those eyes lingering on Fiona. It was nothing Britney hadn't experienced before. Being blessed with barley blonde hair, Michelle Pfeiffer looks and a body to die for, Fiona could turn heads, even in the unflattering lines of the Garda uniform. And she could keep them turned. Yet, she was single, something which Britney found hard to credit but, unfortunately, could readily relate to.

"To start with, it has to be someone outside of work, right?" she lamented to Fiona over a glass of wine one evening.

"Damn right," Fiona acknowledged. "Workplace relationships just aren't worth the headache. If it doesn't work out the whole thing goes tits up, pardon my French."

"Both before and after," she added with a cheeky smile. Britney couldn't help but laugh as she took a sip of her wine.

"That leads to the issue of a girl in uniform, doesn't it?" Britney continued in a more sober tone. "Some men just can't see past it, can they? I mean some of them are so damn cowardly it frightens them while others are the total opposite, aren't they? They find it a bloody turn on."

Fiona readily agreed. "It's not the uniform, Brit. It's the fact that they can have power over someone in authority. That's the thrill. That's what turns them on. I bet that Detective Flynn would be one of those if he wasn't a cop himself." She gave a distasteful shake of her head. "Speaking of Flynn," she said, growing suddenly serious. "He really has it in for you, Brit. I mean, I see how he watches you."

Britney nodded. "I know. As I told you before he doesn't like being challenged by a woman. Especially one who has turned him down."

"You mean he's hit on you?" Fiona asked, sounding surprised.

Britney nodded. "More than once. That's why I try and avoid any work dos. When he gets drink in him, he's not inclined to take no for an answer. How about you?"

A deep frown marred Fiona's otherwise perfectly smooth skin as she shook her head. "Not hit on exactly. More like undressed me with his eyes. Trouble is, I think all men are like that. Deep down. At least to some degree."

Then she smiled as a thought struck her. "Ben, on the other hand…"

"He is good-looking," Britney admitted, "I'll give him that. And fit."

"Ah come on, Brit," Fiona exclaimed. "He's more than fit."

"He's gorgeous!" they both intoned at once. With that they clinked their glasses and laughed.

Now, as she watched the leering eyes of the builders, Britney wondered if all men were indeed the same, as Fiona had suggested. Had her father been like that? Definitely not. Was Bob? She really didn't think so. His eyes were too honest. Too genuine. She found herself recalling how she'd thrilled like a schoolgirl under his gentle gaze when the frustrated voice of Brian Farrell brought her back to the job at hand.

"Ah, come on, boys. Back to work," his plea loud enough to carry to the scaffolding. "Just because Jim's not here doesn't mean we're on a holiday." He turned back to Britney, "Can we talk in your car?"

"By all means."

She opened the passenger door for him before getting back into the driver's seat. As he sat in beside her, she picked up the healthy aroma of a working man – sweat and sawdust and petrol fumes. It was a strong smell, but she didn't find it offensive. Quite the opposite, in fact. It reminded her of hugs shared with her father in the evenings after he came home from work. He too had worked in construction. Fiona, who now sat in the back didn't seem to find the smell quite so pleasant. She turned up her nose and let down the window. Britney laughed to herself. Fiona preferred men with soft hands and aftershave. Like the last man she went out with – a primary school teacher from Carlow. "He smelled so good," she told Britney, "that I suggested I carry him around in a bottle."

"Look," Brian said getting straight to the point. "I don't know what Stacey told you, but Jim can tend to be a little erratic. He has ups and downs, if you know what I mean? When he's up, he's the best guy you could meet but when he's down, there's no talking to him. He does his own thing and to hell with everyone else."

"You mean, he's done this kind of thing before?"

"Not exactly. At least not for quite as long. But now and then he goes off the radar for a day or two. Sometimes whole weekends."

"What about the day he went missing? Was he up or down, as you put it?"

"He seemed fine that day. Perhaps a little quiet. But otherwise, fine."

"Do you think he was worried about something?"

"Jim's always worried. He's that kind of fella. Things can get to him, and he finds it hard to let go."

"In what way?"

"Take the HAI, for one thing. He hates that organisation. Refers to it as the 'Hog All' association. Especially hates its president...what's his name?"

"Ade Fagan," Fiona offered from the rear seat.

"That's the one. Had some run in with him years ago over player welfare or something and hasn't let it go since. Claims he's nothing but a money grabber."

"Anything more recent?"

"Like what?"

Britney shrugged. "Any chance he's having an affair?"

Brian shook his head adamantly. "No. He would never cheat. Not on Stacey, not on anyone. But sometimes he drinks and when he drinks, he disappears into his own little world."

"So, you're saying he's just gone on a bender...perhaps an extended one this time?"

Farrell shrugged.

"He's been under a lot of pressure lately with the business. Especially since that incident a few months back."

"The vandalism?"

"Yes," Brian replied while shaking his head in dismay at the memory.

"Some wankers broke into the site one evening when we were gone and pulled down half the house we'd erected. Cut rafters, knocked walls. Generally wrecked the place. Caused thousands of euros worth of damage. Set us back months on our schedule so we had to work extra hours just to catch up. I thought it was that shower of thugs that are going around targeting businesses, but Jim took it personal. Suggested it was someone targeting him specifically."

Britney shot a quick glance at Fiona through the rearview mirror.

"The foreman said it was just teenagers looking for kicks?"

Brian shrugged. "Jim didn't think so. Especially after finding that hurley left behind at the scene. We found a steel bar too, but it was the hurley that got Jim all riled up. Claimed they were taunting him with it. Personally, I think he was being paranoid but in the heel of the hunt, he was the one paying for it."

"When did that happen?"

"June, I think."

"His wife never mentioned it."

Brian gave a quick shake of his head. "I don't think he would have told Stacey. Didn't want to worry her. Not on top of all the other problems he was having."

"Oh?"

"Yeah. Insurance is a big issue. The premium is gone through the roof and he's not sure if we'll get cover this term. And then, of course, he can't work like he used, not with those knees of his. So, he has to employ an extra carpenter to cover for him."

Britney glanced back at Fiona who nodded in understanding. If he was under such pressure, then it was plausible that he might have decided to take a few days away from it all. But leave the kids like that? She didn't think so. On the other hand, the pressure might have gotten too much for him. Overwhelmed him. And then God knows what he would have done.

"If it was a case of him needing some time, where would we be likely to find him?" Fiona asked.

"One of those early pubs in The March, I'd have thought. But I've tried all the usual haunts."

"And no one has seen him?"

"No."

"Any friends he might hole up with?" Britney wondered.

"Lots of them. A man drinking in The March always has friends. At least until he runs out of money."

"So, you really think he's just drunk somewhere, and he'll reappear once he sobers up."

"I think so, yes."

"Did you tell Stacey this?"

"Yes. But she doesn't think he'd do that to her and the kids."

"But you do?"

"Look, I've known Jim a long time. He's a good guy but sometimes he needs to break away from it all. There was this one time he went drinking and ended up in Barcelona with some guys he'd just met. Didn't come home for a week. And then there was that time he sauntered off to America for a year. All that was before he was married, though."

"Has he ever done anything like that since he got married?"

"No," Brian admitted, "but that doesn't mean he didn't feel like it sometimes. Marriage can be a tough station for some men." With that, he opened the door. "Sorry, but I've got to get back to work."

Britney glanced over her shoulder at Fiona as if to enquire if she had any further questions. She didn't.

"I hope you're right about this, Mr Farrell," Britney said as he got out of the car. "A young family is depending on him."

Brian Farrell paused, "I know, Sergeant. And more importantly, so does he. He'll turn up."

Britney might have nodded but she wasn't convinced. Neither were Stacey Rourke's little children, judging by the look she had seen in their eyes.

As Brian walked away from the car, she rolled down the window. "One more thing," she called out. "Did any of your guys borrow his van lately, for nixers perhaps?"

Brian shook his head.

"Not me anyway. Doubt any of the other guys did either. We work six days a week here. Believe me," he added wearily, "it's enough."

****

Danny Owens glanced at his watch as he returned from walking the reporter as far as the street. She had remained in Lyons' office for over an hour.

"Must have chattered like a magpie, sir," he said to Lyons who awaited his return by the reception desk. "Did she shed any light on why she ended up with someone else's body part?" After getting rid of the box, he had downed a couple of Alka Seltzers but still the thought of it made his stomach lurch.

"Claims she has no idea."

"You believe her?"

Lyons' lip curled. "I believe no one. You shouldn't either. Not in this job."

"I certainly agree with you in this case, sir. Something tells me that woman has more secrets than British intelligence." Danny glanced at Lyons who was in the process of extracting a cigar from the box that had earlier rested on his desk. "She's kind of famous, I take it."

"You could say that. She's a well-known reporter. But even better known as a woman around town. What do they call them?"

"A socialite, sir. Although I could think of less flattering name for her. Sorry for letting her barge in like that."

"Not your fault. The great Marie Cox thinks the same rules don't apply."

"Seemed like you were acquainted, sir?"

Lyons ignored the question.

"I proposed twenty-four-hour protection. She brazenly asked for you. I offered a female officer."

"Good, because she stuffed a card with her address and phone number into my pocket on the way out. Told me if I ever got tired of police work to give her a call because she'd have no problem finding a position for me." He shook his head. "She's some piece of work. Randier than a puck goat, I'd bet and twice as brazen."

'And more slippery than an eel,' Lyons added to himself. "She declined my offer," he stated out loud. "Was adamant she could take care of herself."

"Stubborn too, then. Or stupid."

"Arrogant might be the better word. I just hope it doesn't come back to bite her in the ass."

"I've a feeling she might like that, sir," Danny suggested with a smirk.

"Very true," Lyons replied, his dark eyes now sizing up Danny.

"What's your name again, son?" he enquired. Up close Danny could see evidence of the heavy drinking that Detective Lyons was notorious for – red, blotchy skin beneath the scraggly beard, bloodshot eyes. Broken capillaries on the nose.

"Danny, sir. Danny Owens."

"Daniel," Lyons said as if having misheard though clearly, he had not. He pursed his thick lips thoughtfully.

"That's a good Christian name. An interpreter of dreams I believe. Ok, Daniel. Tell me about Miss Cox arriving with the little present she brought us."

Actually, Danny had been christened exactly that – Danny. Not Daniel. He hated Daniel. Always had. Daniel was his father's name. And though his mother might have loved the man Danny could never forgive him for leaving her in the lurch.

Danny considered correcting the detective but at that moment it didn't seem to matter. Not compared to a severed hand in a box. He shrugged uncertainly. "There's not much to tell. I was only with her a few moments before I brought her into you."

"Brought her in? I got the impression she barged in," Lyons's expression remained unreadable. Finally, a twinkle of amusement challenged the darkness of his eyes. "As I said, not your fault. Tell me the rest."

Danny looked at him blankly.

"How did she arrive? Did you see anyone with her or lurking around outside? Did she look scared, etc.? Come on, it's not rocket science."

"Oh…" Danny paused to consider his answer, fighting not to let his anxiety show but wilting under the older man's forbidding stare. Right then he wished he'd taken up the apprenticeship his uncle had once offered him. Fitting pipes would be so much easier than this.

"Come on, man. We haven't got all day."

"Well," Danny began uncertainly, "I'm not sure how she got here but I suspect she walked some of the way as she was a tad out of breath when she arrived, and I noticed her face was flushed beneath the makeup."

Lyons nodded, but otherwise, his grizzled features remained unmoved. Was it a nod of approval? Danny wondered or was the man simply acknowledging what he was surely already thinking – this chap is a useless buffoon, letting a member of the public just walk into the heart of the station like that.

"Go on," Lyons urged.

"She was alone. At least, I didn't see anyone hanging around outside or follow her when she left. I think she took a taxi."

"You think?"

"Well, she crossed the road and headed in the direction of the taxi rank, sir," Danny added quickly.

Lyons nodded dispassionately once more. "Ok."

"She let on she was more annoyed than upset. More put out than scared. If it was me, I would have been as scared as a cat on hind legs and made sure everyone knew it."

"So, what does that tell you, young Owens?"

"That she's a cold bitch, sir. And there's probably any number of people who would have happily sent her that little surprise."

"And what else?"

"That she has her suspicions about who's behind it but doesn't want to let on."

"Because?"

"Because she's involved in something untoward, sir. Perhaps a sordid affair of some sort. Or worse."

"Exactly, young Owens," Lyons replied in the tone of a teacher appreciating his student's efforts. "Not just a pretty face then?"

"Then again, it could be something as simple as loathing, sir. I mean I've only just met her, and I feel like sending her something vile myself."

Now Lyons' face cracked with what Danny could only presume was an amused smile. It didn't last long. "What else did you garner from her visit?"

'That you have some sort of personal history with Miss Cox,' Danny thought, but kept the thought to himself. "That you have your work cut out, sir," he replied instead.

Lyons nodded while pensively pursing his lips. "Not just me, young Owens. As reward for your astute observations, I'm going to give you a chance to get out of that silly uniform. I need a driver and you're it."

Danny Owens kept his expression neutral. If any other detective had offered him the chance to jump in on a big case, he would have been over the moon, but he wasn't keen on getting involved with a man widely considered a loose cannon.

"Thanks for the offer, sir, but..."

"To start with, get forensics on the phone," the detective ordered, completely ignoring Danny's attempted objection. "We need a team down here now to go over that hand. And I mean now. And call the Super. We'd better fill him in on what our lady friend delivered. But Daniel..."

"Yes sir?" Danny noted there was now a determined glint in the older man's dark eyes. Again, he was hit with the image of a bear. One waking up after a long winter. Alert now and hungry. But Danny detected a wariness about him too. As if the bear sensed danger.

Was it due to the surprise visit of Miss Cox? Or because there was some crazy out there chopping off people's hands? He couldn't tell.

"Leave the details to me."

With that, Lyons turned on his heels and headed for the main exit.

"I'm popping out for a while," he informed Danny, speaking over his shoulder. "If anyone is looking for me, tell them I'm gone to see a man about a dog."

"Yes, sir." Danny struggled to keep his tone deferential. He didn't have to be a rocket scientist to know what this was code for. Before reaching the door, Lyons paused to set light to his cigar. He couldn't even wait until he was outside, Danny thought, imagining two fingers to the establishment rising up on the puff of smoke. Along with his fledgling career.

"A driver," he huffed to himself. 'More like a patsy to hide behind while you're off getting pissed.' As he returned to his desk behind reception, he wasn't sure whether to laugh or cry.

****

On leaving the station, Marie Cox passed off by the taxi rank and turned right towards the bus stop a hundred yards further on. She loathed taking taxis. Walking, even the short distance to and from the bus stop, was what helped preserve her figure. And her figure wasn't something she could afford to lose. She reached the stop just as the bus that would drop her within walking distance of her apartment arrived. She quickly hopped on, but before taking a seat she scanned the faces of the other passengers. Women, children, young men – all dressed in ordinary, everyday clothes. None wore a hooded coat, or even remotely fit the image she had lodged in her head. She breathed out a sigh that she hadn't even realised she was holding and took a seat near the front of the bus. As it pulled away, she once again wondered who would be targeting her and why? Was it someone at work? Surely not. A sportswriter, even one as talented as herself, just doesn't attract that sort of attention. Either from the public or from her colleagues. Although she did have some serious bust-ups over the years, she could think of none that would warrant this level of gruesome. Not even close.

Therefore, it had to be connected to her moonlight activities as she liked to term them. Somewhere along the line she'd pissed somebody off. Somebody she knew. The elaborate disguise suggested as much. That long coat and deep hood had served to completely hide the man's features, prompting her to presume she must have, at the very least, seen him somewhere before. Otherwise, why the need for such an elaborate concealment? Unless it wasn't chosen for concealment alone. With its dark, almost gothic appearance, that hooded coat certainly stood out. Drew one's eyes. Instilled a certain level of wariness. Of fear.

But who would go to such lengths to frighten her? It clearly wasn't the boss, so who then? One of the lesser shareholders? Suppliers? Subordinates perhaps? She didn't think so, simply because she drove profits and when it came to profits, they were every bit as protective as she was. One of her contacts then? Or high-profile customers? Neither option seemed reasonable. The men she knew had little reason to hide from her. In fact, it was quite the opposite. They longed to be seen with her. Craved her attention. Craved it so much that they'd buy a €200 bottle of wine just to keep her sitting at their table. Sometimes even that wasn't enough… Then it hit her. One thing and another added together until it all made sense… The slimy bastard…

She cursed loudly, prompting some of the other passengers to glance in her direction. Was he that sick? She wondered as she forced a reassuring smile to placate the quizzical look on the face of the woman sitting next to her. Would he really go to these lengths just because she didn't sleep with him? He was certainly the possessive type, but psychotic? He had tried his best over the years, even gone as far as purchasing for her a foreign property but she had never been able to bring herself to close that particular deal. Had he finally decided he had enough of her leading him on? Was this payback? If so, what sort of a freak was he? And why a hand?

The route from Swords Garda station to her apartment was approximately a five-minute bus journey. It led her down Bridge Street, past Swords Tower, and on towards St Colmcille's Park. From the bus stop there she had a short walk to St Colmcille's Crescent, the upmarket estate where her apartment was located. It was shorter still if she cut through the narrow alleyway which led from the main street to the estate.

After hopping off the bus she found herself picking up her pace as she turned off the street and down a shortcut toward the rear of the development. A steady look behind confirmed she was alone, yet the narrow confines of the alleyway made her uncomfortable. The concrete walls were above head-height, and the route was intermittently cut with T-junctions which fed neighbouring estates. Finding herself peeking around the corner of one of these she cursed the fact that she hadn't bitten the bullet and taken a taxi.

To take her mind off her fears she took out her phone and punched the number of the only man she could think of egotistical enough to follow her. The number rang out, triggering a further litany of curses. While waiting for it to go through to his mailbox she fumbled in her bag for her keys just to have them at the ready for when she reached her door. She found them just as her associate's pathetic whine invited her to leave a message.

"Fagan, you sad, miserable, cowardly, piece of shit," she spat as she took a right turn in the alley, "if you're fucking following me, I'll cut your teeny, weeny little balls off and stuff them into your mouth like brussels sprouts at Christmas."

"Ooh, nasty…" the menacing voice came from directly behind her. "Is that what they call imagery in your line of work?" The tone was taunting. Belittling. Terrifying.

Marie Cox froze. It was the same muffled voice she'd heard at the station. Part of her thought she recognised it, but she couldn't be sure. Not distorted as it was. The only thing she was sure of was that the deep, manly voice didn't belong to her long-suffering suitor.

Suddenly the hooded man moved closer, right up behind her and now her survival instincts kicked in. She made to run but the high heel of one of her red-soled Louboutin's twisted beneath her and she fell, the phone flying from her hand to shatter on the concrete. Sensing the man reach for her, she drew a breath to scream. But with the rag in the hooded man's hand suddenly placed firmly over her mouth, she couldn't even do that.

****

Moments of enlightenment, true enlightenment, can often occur during times of extreme stress. That was certainly the case for Marie Cox. She was about to die, and that realisation had put everything she valued into perspective. The truth was she had valued nothing. At least nothing worth valuing. All the money, all the prestige, all the social climbing, amounted to a mouthful of spit when a crazed man stalked you in the darkness.

She was wrong about something else too. She wasn't strong as she'd always prided herself on being. She was weak. Weak and cowardly and afraid. So afraid that she had pissed herself. As she huddled in the cold, dark room, she wondered where the man had disappeared to. He was close by, she could sense it, but she couldn't quite pinpoint him in the gloom. It didn't help that her head was all fuzzy. She was pretty sure he had drugged her when he'd put that rag over her mouth. The sudden wooziness allied to the headache she'd experienced on waking was evidence enough. Along with the nausea in her stomach.

Gagged and bound by a thin cord that looped round her ankles and wrists, running up her back to her neck, she was effectively hogtied. At first, she had struggled against her binds but soon learnt that with every little movement the cord constricted further round her neck and threatened to cut off her oxygen supply. In other words, if she didn't remain still, she would choke herself to death.

With the offending cord securely tied to what felt like a forklift pallet she lay on her back next to a long wooden box. On the ground next to the box, she saw a large, crumpled shape. When her eyes adjusted to the dark this shape registered as looking alarmingly like that of a body. An inanimate body. The deep shiver that ran through her then was caused by far more than just the unnatural cold.

Forcing the terror from her mind she tried to figure out where she was. Some sort of abandoned warehouse, she decided. It was certainly cold enough. But where? She had awoken sometime earlier to a sensation of the earth moving only to pass out again and now everything was still. She had no idea how much time had passed since she'd been taken or how far she'd travelled.

Was she still in Dublin? In Ireland even? The idea gave her pause for thought. Perhaps, in considering high-profile clients, she had been looking at this backwards. Perhaps she'd been taken just as she knew others had been. Those on the lowest rung of humanities ladder, the kind that would hardly be missed. The kind that had been taken in her name, handpicked for profit. Was this a lesson to show her what the other side of the coin felt like? Or had the boss turned on her, after all? Decided to get rid of her by delivering her into the very hands that they secretly dealt with. Had the buyer now become the commodity?

Whatever the case, it gave her hope. Hope that this crazed man mightn't kill her after all. At least not straight away.

"I've heard you received journalism awards," the man leaned down out of nowhere and spoke directly into her ear, his breath warm against her cheek. "For articles like that one in which you vilified that poor referee, no doubt. Couldn't spot a foul if it had feathers on it." He snorted. "Not the most original headline but then you're not the most original of individuals, are you? I mean that referee was an easy target. And cowards like you always focus on easy targets."

The man's voice remained muffled, and she could see now from the corner of her eye that the reason for this was the kind of thick neck gaiter outdoors people wore to protect against the elements. Pulled up from around the man's neck, over the bridge of his nose, it covered most of his face. The deep hood that he wore dropped low over his forehead, and consequently, only the area around his eyes was visible. And a hint of his greying locks, barely discernible in the dark.

"And that's the reason I've taken you. The reason I focus on you now."

The man stood then edged around until his shadow hovered in the space directly in front of her, his deep-set eyes watching her intently, every bit as dark and cold as the room they hid in. For the briefest of moments, a flicker of light danced in their irises, and she sensed she had seen them before. But eyes alone were so hard to recall. Even the most remarkable diamond required a visual setting to make it complete. To make it memorable. Yet given a chance, she felt sure she would remember. But in this presumption, the great Marie Cox was also wrong. Because both her remembering and forgetting would soon be over.

"You see, I've been watching you. You and your cronies. And I know all your secrets. All about your illegal little side-line. Being a top sportswriter is a great cover. Isn't that true, Madame Cox?"

Though thrown by his obvious insight, she tried to focus on the voice. It was deep and gravelly beneath the gag of the thick gaiter. Like the eyes, she found herself wondering if the voice wasn't vaguely familiar. In her woozy mind something stirred. An image. A face. It emerged and disappeared. Emerged again. But her fear ensured she couldn't hold onto it. Or worse. Refused to accept it.

As she desperately clutched that twig of recognition, he leaned down to gather strands of her hair, coaxing them together with his work-hardened fingers, almost like a hairstylist would when suggesting a new style. But he had far from the considerate hands of a hairdresser, so as he worked, he tore strands of hair from her head causing her to flinch, a movement which drew the stroke of his fingers to her cheek. 'Now it begins,' she thought but soon realised his strange grooming of her was a perfunctory act – meeting a necessity, not a desire.

He was simply pulling the hair back from her ears. But what in heavens name for?

"Peroxide blonde," he stated. "Isn't that what they call it?"

She sensed that sneer again.

"False, like everything else about you."

He completed his strange task, then produced a piece of nylon string from his coat pocket. With a grunt, he stooped low until his face hovered directly over hers then he reached behind her head and tied the clump of gathered strands into a ponytail.

"As I said, I've been watching you. Reading up on you. And I've come to the conclusion that you are what they call a self-centred bitch." This close, she picked up on the smell of stale alcohol and cigarettes. And got a better look at the man's eyes. Slowly, the image seemed to come into focus in her head, until it became a tangible face, at once both aligned and at odds with the eyes she stared into. For where once those eyes were kind and gentle, they now looked possessed. Twisted with a deep hatred. She gulped. The dark intensity of their stare told her this wasn't business. This was personal.

Suddenly, she screamed, wailed through the gag in her mouth. The blow had come out of nowhere, the cudgel catching her square on the kneecap and shattering it into a dozen pieces. It was delivered so fast that she couldn't see exactly what he used, but guessed it was a bar or a club. Possibly a baseball bat, concealed earlier no doubt under his long coat. Now, as her screaming faded, she registered the dull wooden clunk as he discarded the implement onto the floor.

"It's bad, isn't it?" the man said, his tone anything but concerned. "That's why paramilitaries use kneecapping as their go-to punishment option. All sorts of nerves in the knee, you know. One blow delivers a lifetime of damage."

He wasn't lying. The shock came in waves and feeling herself go weak, it took all her strength not to pass out. Then the pain came, the most unbearable she had ever felt. In the throes of the agony that followed, the cord constricted, and she came within millimetres of ending it all.

"You treat people like they are little toys, specifically put on this earth for your amusement. For your pleasure." The words were critical, but his voice remained emotionless as if reciting a pre-rehearsed statement. Not spur of the moment but something he had long dwelled on. "You play with them for a little while then throw them away, don't you, Miss Cox? As flippantly as someone might throw away a butt of a cigarette or a chewing gum wrapper." As he spoke, his left hand, large and life-worn, disappeared under his coat and a moment later reappeared clasping a knife. A long knife with a wicked looking serrated blade.

In protest, Marie Cox gestured with the only part of her that was free to move – her head, short sharp movements that spoke volumes. Her body tensed on the ground, her limbs straining against the ties. Even if she wasn't securely bound and her mouth wasn't stuffed with thick wadding, it would have been all she could manage. That and to wet herself again.

"As long as you get what you need, you don't give a damn about others, do you, Miss Cox?" The man continued, "Of course, you don't. You're a high-flying reporter. An award winner. Ordinary people are beneath you. Ordinary people don't matter." He snorted disdainfully. "Perception is all that matters. Guided by the story you contrive." He gave an irritated shake of his head. "And the story has to please the masses, hasn't it, Miss Cox? No point writing a story that doesn't please the masses."

"Well, this is going to be the greatest story of all, and the only person it's going to please is me." As he spoke, he held the large, serrated knife in front of her face. Twisting it playfully in his hand, he allowed the sharpness of its edge to catch what little light the room offered. And to capture Marie Cox's attention. Her eyes widened as she watched it rotate in front of her, flickering menacingly in the semi-darkness. Behind the gag she pleaded with him, calling his name but it came out in little more than muffled grunts. The man ignored her. He dropped to the floor and set his knees either side of Marie Cox's body, straddling her. He leaned forward, determined to see every vessel of fear in those once supremely confident eyes.

Up that close, Marie found the stench of alcohol unmistakable.

"You need Dutch courage to do what you do, you fucking coward? Can't get it up…is that it? Or can't keep it up," she spat the words through the gag while beneath the thin fabric of the floral dress, she attempted to spread her long, elegant legs. It was performed as a provocative act, designed to taunt him, to distract him, to encourage him to make a mistake. A mistake that would give her a thin edge. A chance. When it came to men, those legs had always been her most reliable weapon. Not this time. This time they failed her when she needed them most. And not because so much pain flooded through her dramatically swollen left knee that she almost passed out but because the man didn't even notice.

His reply told her as much. Told her that she was all out of chances, and the pain was only going to get worse.

"Did you like that hand I sent you?" he asked with an indifferent air. A tone so cold that the room itself seemed to shiver. She knew then that he had no intention of raping her. He had no interest in her that way whatsoever. That had been her last hope. That he would untie her and assault her, and in his throes of unsanctioned pleasure, leave himself vulnerable.

But he wasn't here for sex. Sex wasn't going to save her anymore. With that realisation, she closed her eyes and began to mumble an incoherent prayer. Even muffled as it was, the man understood what she was doing. With impending death, it was a human being's default reaction. No matter what their religion. Their beliefs. The certainty of fear was the greatest creed of all.

"Do you think God will listen to a bitch like you?" He shook his head. "I don't think so. I think he has enough to do, what with all the starving children in the world, all the diseases, and natural disasters. Why would he worry about an unnatural disaster that the world would be better off without?"

He ran the knife across his thumb until blood flowed. "This knife is my Excalibur," he explained. "My sword of retribution." He paused and when he spoke again it was almost to himself. "My route to atonement."

On the precipice now, Marie abandoned prayer and returned to what she knew. Prayer was unnatural to her, but fight. Fight, she understood. In her mind, she clawed and bit and screamed at the man, laughed at, and belittled his ignorance in her head. Derision was her go-to defence, had always been, and was now the only one left to her.

'Excalibur was never a sword of retribution, you uneducated dolt. It was a sword for the righteous. To be drawn only by the divinely appointed heir of the great king, Uther Pendragon. And that's not a sword. It's a goddamn kitchen knife.'

"But before I finish my work," the man continued, testing the sharpness of the knife once more, "I must tell you why you were chosen. You see, a young person came to you once. Came to you with a story. A good story. An honest story. It was a human-interest story. But you wouldn't listen. You dismissed it without a thought. Dismissed that person as a whinger, in fact. Humiliated the individual in the same way the others had. Created a perception for the masses."

"Oh, I'm sure that's not the only person you've humiliated in your life. In fact, after watching you for the last while, I'm certain of it. It's your MO, isn't it?" he continued. He held the knife in front of her eyes then casually removed the gaiter to reveal his face. A face so twisted with hate it made it almost unrecognisable to her now. "Well, this is mine," he purred.

Catching her by the scruff of the neck he forced her into a sitting position then shoved her backwards until her back was propped against the wooden box. She whimpered but he ignored her as he reached for her right ear with his big hand. Gripping it in his thick fingers, he roughly pulled the lobe away from the side of her head until her ear stuck out at a right angle. Then he raised the knife in his left hand. With her hair pulled back, there was nothing to interfere with the blade, meaning it would be an easy task. One clean cut. He sliced downward with the knife. Blood spewed over his hand and onto Marie Cox's face, down her neck and over her ample breasts, staining the front of her floral dress as it flowed.

She screamed into the gag but even to her it sounded little more than a sonic fart carried from a million miles away. She writhed, kicked, and strained but the man ignored her, his eyes instead gauging the efficiency of the cord as it served the purpose he intended. Then, he casually turned his attention to the other ear. And her blood spurted anew, once again running down her neck and into her bosom. It wouldn't settle there, but would keep on running, until urine wasn't the only liquid ruining her favourite shoes.

In the cold darkness of his sanctuary, the man allowed himself a satisfied smile. Torture came surprisingly easy to him. As did killing. The difficult part had yet to come when the trick would be to get in and out while avoiding the ever-judging eyes. But then he was becoming an expert at deceit too.

Taking the letter out of his pocket he dipped his finger in the blood. "Please forgive me?"

****

To add some veracity to her excuse of popping out for lunch, they decided to stop into a nearby fuel station which housed a small coffee shop called Bun'n'Bean. It was your typical roadside café with plastics seats and microwaved dinners, but at least the coffee was far superior to that at the station.

As they sat waiting on their order of paninis and coffee, Britney couldn't help but smile. The extent of the evidence Fiona put forward left Britney with little choice but to admit that she was right. Bob Harris had been flirting with her. Not in any sleazy kind of way as was the penchant of the likes of Terry Flynn but subtly, in a shy schoolboy kind of way.

"Sometimes not so subtly," Fiona pointed out with a wicked smirk on her face. "And he's no schoolboy, is he? Those were working man's muscles I saw." She leaned forward onto her elbows as if she was about to share a confidence. "Makes you wonder about the muscles we couldn't see, doesn't it?" Fiona laughed at Britney's expression, her perfect teeth lighting up her equally perfect face. The kind of face people usually only see staring back at them from the illusory lights of a big screen. "Ah don't be so coy, Brit. I know you're thinking that too."

Just then the waitress arrived with their lunch. Britney was never so glad of a distraction. Although it wasn't enough of a distraction to stop her own thoughts from teasing her.

After speaking with Brian Farrell, they had driven back to the site-office as arranged to pick up the list of all the workers employed on site. As promised, Bob Harris had the list ready on a neatly printed A4 sheet.

"I've put my phone number on the end, in case you need anything else," he said when Britney popped her head back inside.

"Thanks, I appreciate that," Britney said, her tone a tad more appreciative than she intended. She couldn't help it, not with the way those blue eyes lingered on hers when he handed over the list. Not studying her but seeing her. Really seeing her. Scar, gap toothed smile, the works. She met his gaze and for a moment his eyes flitted away only to return at once, like a wary swallow probing for a place to nest. So cute, she thought, as he offered his hand for her to shake. Her instincts had been right. He was a proper, genuine man. And with genuine hard-earned muscles too, Britney noted as she appreciated the strength of his grip. Not those protein inflated things so many men liked to flaunt these days.

"Nice meeting you again, Sergeant," he said then nodded toward Fiona. "You too, Garda…"

"O'Malley," Fiona finished with a knowing smile. She didn't bother extending her hand. Even while addressing her, the man's eyes had hardly strayed from Britney's nor was his hand letting go anytime soon.

Britney sensed that too, keenly aware of the extended physical contact. His grip was firm yet gentle, his considerable hand wrapped like a protective mitt over hers. This time, despite her best efforts, the flush reached her cheeks. Part of her didn't want to let go either. Not ever. Still, she pulled her hand away then folded the sheet of paper and held it up as if it were a wand that would break the spell.

"If you think of anything else, you can ask for me at the station." Her voice felt fragile, as if it could break at any moment. "It's Sergeant Kent," she reminded him, then turned to leave.

"Sergeant Britney Kent," Fiona piped up before she'd managed a second step.

Bob nodded appreciatively. "Ok, Sergeant Britney Kent."

Britney kept walking so she wouldn't be betrayed by the wide smile that involuntarily lit up her face.

Now, as they finished up their lunch and sipped the coffee that actually tasted like coffee, that impish look was back in Fiona's eyes.

"You've got to admit it's true Brit, I could almost smell the hormones in that cosy office of his. You've got to ask him for a date. I mean, it would be a crime not to!"

Britney shook her head as she hid behind the rim of her coffee mug. "I can't. He's part of a case. Anyway, a lady doesn't do that sort of thing."

"Nonsense," Fiona retorted. "Women ask men out all the time. Things have changed, Brit. Don't have to wait for a leap year anymore. And anyway, until we're officially told otherwise, there is no case, just an abandoned woman overreacting. So, if you don't ask him out, I'll arrest you myself."

"You're the one fascinated with his muscles...why don't you ask him out?" Britney knew her reply was a weak effort at passing the buck but with Fiona so determined to rib her, it was the only line she could come up with.

"I have a boyfriend," Fiona replied quickly.

"Yeah? Since when?"

Fiona smiled enigmatically. "Since last weekend, actually."

"So, that's why the eyes were hanging out of your head this morning, then. Who is he...come on, I want all the gory details?"

"Not a chance...you're only trying to turn this on me. But it wasn't me that stud was flirting with, was it? If it had been, I wouldn't think twice – boyfriend or no boyfriend. I'd be in that office checking out his muscles right now. But it's you, he wants, Britney. He made that perfectly clear."

In one way, this was the part that pleased Britney the most. He hadn't flirted with Fiona. Not once. In fact, he had barely let on to notice her. Not that Britney was jealous of her friend but sometimes she couldn't help feeling like a weed wilting in the shadow of a rose. But during the encounter with Bob, she had felt different. The spotlight had been hers. And she hadn't wilted. She had held her ground. Met his gaze. And discovered that even though she mightn't be Michelle Pfeiffer, she could still be a leading lady in her own right. It wasn't that good-looking men hadn't flirted with Britney before. They had, but usually on night's out while wallowing in a belly full of beer. She had even dated one or two of them, but surprise, surprise, none had turned out to be quite the prince charming she was looking for. But Bob hadn't been like that as far as she remembered. He'd been sober, respectful. She'd been the one drunk. The one hiding. And now…well, she could certainly picture him being a prince.

"Well, are you going to ask him out or what?" Fiona smiled devilishly from across the table. "And come to think of it, what did he mean by 'nice to meet you again'?"

Cursing under her breath, Britney gave an exaggerated shake of her head. Fiona could be a right pain in the ass when she wanted to be. Still as she took the last sip of her coffee, she couldn't deny the giddy feeling in her stomach. However, that feeling soon faded at the thought of returning to the station. And not only due to the prospect of having to face into the calculating stare of Detective Flynn.

"One for the road?" Britney asked with a hopeful glance at her colleague.

"Only if we can talk more about Bob," Fiona replied. Though Britney threw her eyes up to heaven, it was a price she was willing to pay.

Chapter 4

It was just after three thirty p.m. when the voluntary groundsman at the Ballyfeud hurling club looked up from his work and, not for the first time since his arrival, stared in the direction of the changing rooms. 'Was somebody up there?' he wondered. Somebody who shouldn't be? They had been a little late today, himself and his colleague, Timmy, but had still made sure to close the gate on arrival. They always did, whether coming or going. Therefore, the gates were still closed yet he couldn't shake the feeling that someone else was in the grounds, watching him. Deep down though he knew that wasn't the case. It was just his mind playing games on him. All day he'd been on edge, even more on edge than he had been since Stacey had informed him that she'd reported Jim as missing. Fearing him badly hurt or worse. Now, his nerves had almost reached breaking point.

He glanced around, looking for Timmy who he had last seen marking the lines at the furthest end of the field. Timmy was also a volunteer groundsman at the club and being a dedicated member like himself, spent at least three nights a week there. Not to mention weekends.

The two of them aside, the grounds usually remained empty on the evening before a game and that was the way he liked it. With no one around to bother them, the pair could really get stuck into their work. Cut the grass one final time, line the field, secure the nets. It was tedious work sometimes, but in general, Alan loved it. He loved the smell of the burnt petrol from the mower mixing with the sap of the freshly cut grass, loved it so much that he sometimes wondered if he was an addict, a junkie of some sort, a 'rustic glue' sniffer. He loved how the pitch looked after it was cut, flat and smooth and only begging to be played on. He especially loved it once the space was defined by the crisp, white lines he and Timmy created with the lime marker. The side-lines, the end-lines, the square – all the divisions that made up a hurling field. Straight as a die, they were, and perfectly measured. It was a question of pride – individual, fraternal, collective. He'd bet there wasn't a better pitch in the entire country. Now, as he stared toward the changing rooms, all of that was invisible to him. Jim was on his mind and a hundred and one scenarios played out in his head. How could he ever come to terms with the fact that his only son was gone?

"Timmy," he called out. "I think there's someone up there in the changing rooms. Can you see anything?"

In response, Timmy raised his hand to shield his eyes from the afternoon sun and peered towards the one-storey building. He could see nothing untoward except perhaps the outline of a shadow inside the away dressing room.

"It's probably just kids, Alan. They've been hanging around here a lot lately. Even broke a damn window yesterday." Suddenly realising the weight of what Alan might be thinking, he added, "I'll go check."

"Good man," Alan replied. Timmy thought he could detect a note of hope in his colleague's voice. Apprehension too.

"Tell them they can use the second field if they want to play but they're not allowed in the changing rooms. I don't want to have to clean them again."

"Will do." Timmy set the last of the flags down where he was standing and as he began to cross the field, he wondered if it really was Jim up there in the shadows, as Alan was no doubt hoping. His son having come back safe and sound, but sheepish. Embarrassed by all the pain he had caused. It would not be the first time he had upset his father, nor the last, Timmy felt certain.

Alan chewed his lip as he watched Timmy make his way up the side-bank that hemmed in the pitch then across the parking area towards the changing rooms. In his mid-forties, Timmy was still a young man and was able to cover the ground quickly. Suddenly, though, he stopped in his tracks as if he had walked into an invisible wall.

"Al…" he called out, sounding alarmed, while at the same time removing the flat cap he wore on his head and holding it in front of him as if worshipping at mass. Or mourning at a funeral.

"Yes."

"I don't think it's kids," his voice was strained now as he wrung the cap nervously in his hands.

"What do you mean?" Alan asked, his heart skipping.

"I mean you better come see, Al. You better come quick."

Alan dropped the pegs he was holding then darted across the field and up the bank as Timmy had just done. Being a good bit older than Timmy, it took him a tad longer to cover the ground. Consequently, he was almost out of breath by the time he caught up with his colleague.

"What is it, Timmy?" he asked between gulps of air. "What the hell is so wrong?"

"Look," Timmy's voice wavered as he pointed toward the partly ajar doorway of the second changing room. Alan noted Timmy's hand was shaking. "In there."

Alan's deep grey eyes followed to where Timmy was pointing but his eyesight wasn't what it used to be. He was forced to squint as he peered past the door into the shadows. Still unable to register what had Timmy so shaken, he took a step closer to get a better look.

"I can't see anything..." he began, then paused as his brain caught up with what his weary eyes were seeing. "Oh my God," he whispered as he moved closer. In the shadowy room, he could just about make out a figure hanging from a cord attached to the light fitting in the ceiling. He stepped closer, his breath catching in his throat. Now, he could clearly see it was a man.

Timmy remained where he was, frozen to the spot. He found it hard to even look. "Is it... Is it your boy, Jim?"

Alan shook his head and slowly breathed out. "No, thank God," he sighed, then instinctively began to bless himself but midway through the act he lowered his hand as if suddenly conscious of what he was celebrating. It may not have been his son hanging there but a man was still dead. A closer look told him it was a man he knew.

"I think it's Donie Cullen," he informed Timmy. "But I don't think he killed himself."

"What? Why?" Timmy's weathered face had turned a sickly shade of pale.

For a long moment, Alan stood silently by the doorway his eyes fixed on the gruesome sight in front of him. The rope, the blood, the legs dangling inches from the ground. But most of all he couldn't take his eyes off the stump – the man's left arm was missing a hand. Below the stump, the dark red blood pooled on the sheet of newspaper set on the floor. His eyebrows furrowed. It is not dripping he thought to himself. The stump is not dripping. Then he bowed his head and once again blessed himself, but this time, with the consecration of a soul in mind, he completed the act. "Because I don't think he chopped his own hand off."

****

When Britney and Fiona finally returned to the station, they found the office to be a totally different beast from the one they had left earlier. Prior to their departure, there had been a work-like, yet relaxed atmosphere preserved by the relatively muted sounds of a normal day, but as they returned through the Garda entrance at the rear of the building, they could sense that something major was afoot. The place was a hive of activity with phones hopping, Gardaí engaged in animated discussions and orders being bandied about. In the time they had been absent the main office had been transformed from a dreary bureaucratic hub into a major incident room where all their colleagues now seemed to be working feverishly.

'Shit, they've found Jim Rourke's body,' Britney thought as she stood at the door. Suddenly an image popped into her head of breaking the news to a heartbroken Stacey and those two little children whose eyes had been so full of fear and uncertainty. She forced the thought away.

"What's going on?" Fiona asked of their colleagues as they moved deeper into the warzone.

"We've got a body," Ben replied without looking up from his computer.

"Is it Jim Rourke?" Britney demanded while passing by his desk en route to her own. She still had paperwork to finish and now she also had a report to write. A report that may have suddenly taken on far more significance.

Ben glanced up, a quizzical look on his face. "Who?"

Britney paused. "Jim Rourke. The man that's missing. We called it in earlier."

Ben shook his head. "It's someone named Donie Cullen. Found hanging in a hurling field out in Ballyfeud."

"Suicide?"

"Don't think so. His left hand was chopped off."

Fiona pulled a face. "Christ, that's gruesome," she said. "Had he a wife?" She shrugged at his wry smile. "It's always the wife."

Ben snorted. "He had a wife. But we don't think it was her. It's a strange one. Eerie. Like something out of a

Stephen King novel." Instead of elaborating any further, he nodded toward the front of the room. "And Halley's here. He's on the warpath."

Britney glanced to where Ben directed and to her dismay saw Superintendent James Halley talking quietly to Detective Terry Flynn. The Super was a thin man, medium height, with short grey hair; always pristinely presented in his Superintendent's uniform, complete with jacket, epaulettes, brass buttons, and cap. Now, his tanned face bore a thunderous expression.

"Shit," Britney said, and quickly slipped into the seat at her desk, hoping the movement wouldn't catch Halley's attention. And vainly hoping that Halley hadn't noted her absence. A moment later Fiona did the same.

Too late. The Super had spotted them.

"Where the hell have you two been?" he barked as he broke away from his conversation with Terry Flynn. "Sergeant Kent!" His eyes seared into Britney's, as she was the highest in rank of the pair. "I thought I'd put you on desk duty to relearn some of the basics, Sergeant."

Like not thinking for myself you mean, Britney felt like retorting. "Needed some fresh air, sir," she replied instead. She considered explaining about the suspected missing person but held back. He would blow his top if he discovered she was out working a case against his express wishes, especially now with all this new commotion going on around them. A murder in a hurling field. Who would have thought it?

"Fresh air! It took half the day to get fresh air. You got the lungs of a sperm whale?"

The Gardaí closest to Britney glanced up from their desks, struggling to hide the amusement on their faces. Terry Flynn watched with a satisfied smirk.

"No, sir," Britney replied hesitantly, then cast an apologetic glance in Fiona's direction. Her colleague was sitting at her desk with her head down, as if focused on the paperwork in front of her, clearly not wishing to draw attention to herself. Britney couldn't blame her. She was on the lowest rung of a very high ladder.

"Well, what took you so long, then?"

Britney noted that the veins on Halley's neck were bulging. Never a good sign.

"Come on, Sergeant, I'm waiting."

Feeling herself wilt under the pressure of Halley's grilling Britney deciding it would be best to come clean. "I got a call about a missing person, sir. I, we were taking a statement from his wife."

"Whose wife?"

The missing person obviously, Britney replied in her head but out loud she said, "A man by the name of Jim Rourke." She glanced around the room. "When we came back, we thought that's what this was all about."

"Well, you thought wrong, Sergeant..." Halley barked. "This is a murder enquiry. Meaning we need all hands on deck and not running around after some fly-by-night." He paused as if a thought struck him then looked at her questioningly. "Jim Rourke, you say?"

"Yes, sir," Britney replied hesitantly, unsure now where Halley was heading, but acutely aware of the sinking feeling in her stomach.

"Living in Emmet's Hill?"

"Yes, sir."

The Super, with his back turned on her, was now directing his question to Terry Flynn. "I heard that name before. Isn't he the lad who used to hurl one time?"

"It certainly is. Kind of went off the rails, if I recall," Terry glanced at Britney, his smirk still lingering, openly taking pleasure in her discomfort.

'What a prick,' she thought.

The Super gave an exaggerated nod. "I thought so. Drink, if I remember correctly and possibly drugs. Gone missing more times than Wally." He shook his head in dismay then cast a look of irritation in Britney's direction. "That's not a missing person, Sergeant Kent. That's a pisshead on a goddamn bender." As he spoke, his voice rose by several octaves until the latter was a shout, resulting in all the heads in the office popping up to watch the exchange.

Britney, feeling certain that Rourke's absence couldn't be so flippantly explained was about to object but thought better of it. Even though all her instincts told her that Jim Rourke was genuinely missing, she had to accept the possibility that she was wrong. Stacey Rourke had never mentioned anything about a drinking problem, but Jim's employee Brian had alluded to some trouble in his past. Perhaps Brian was right, and he'd just needed to let off some steam. Still, Britney wasn't convinced. It just didn't feel right, but she was around long enough to know that now wasn't the time to debate the point. Not when Halley had veins bulging in his neck.

"So, while you two are off playing Tonto and The Lone Ranger," Halley continued, "we've got a body strung up like a side of beef out in a goddamn hurling field. And in case you don't quite get it, it's nothing as straightforward as a missing person or a suicide. It's a goddamn murder. A bloody gruesome one at that. So, you keep your ass at your desk," he ordered, "and do your work. We'll discuss the consequences of your disappearing act when this is done." He glanced around the room, eyeballing anyone who had the nerve to look back at him. "That goes for everyone!" he bellowed. "Get to work. This is a murder investigation, so, for God's sake, investigate."

He returned his attention to Detective Flynn.

"Terry, as discussed, you and Joe head this up. Start with his immediate family then spread it out from there. We need to know who would want this man dead. The elusive Sergeant Kent can assist with the legwork."

Britney cursed under her breath. Behind Halley's back, she could see Detective Flynn's eyebrows raise suggestively at the mention of legwork. His sick mind was never out of the gutter.

"That is, of course," Halley added with a pointed look in Britney's direction, "if she hasn't another lost puppy to go chasing after."

The shake of Britney's head was barely perceptible.

"Good. Then someone get these Gardaí up to speed on all that has happened in their unauthorised absence and put them to some goddamn use. We've a murder to solve."

"I'll personally see to it," Detective Flynn assured, his salacious grin revealing a row of nicotine-stained teeth.

Chapter 5

When the call came around midday from Detective Lyons requesting Danny pick him up outside a pub on Main Street, the young Garda was actually relieved. He'd spent most of that morning gathering background information on Miss Cox and was starting to feel like he was a three-legged calf wading through mud. It seemed any number of people would have liked to cause the notorious Marie Cox distress. As follow up, he began compiling a list of possible suspects – acquaintances, colleagues, neighbours – with a view to eliminating as many as possible, one by one. It was proving just as difficult a task.

Main Street was in a tough part of town, something that wasn't lost on Danny as he pulled up outside the Sheep's Head Tavern half an hour later. Glancing around, he saw most of the neighbouring buildings were in a dilapidated state while the Tavern itself was a dingy little place with bars over the windows and a steel-plated front door. It had the look of abandonment about it yet focusing on a hole in one of the dirty windows, Danny could clearly spy customers inside. All things considered, Danny wouldn't have been surprised if the hole had been caused by a bullet.

Glancing around, he saw no immediate sign of Detective Lyons. Was he inside getting pissed? It hadn't sounded like it on the phone, but Danny wouldn't put it past him. Reputations were built on consistency, after all. He waited another minute or two but then, growing impatient, he took his phone out of his pocket and prepared to dial the personal number the detective had earlier used to call the station. As he did so, he let the car roll forward a couple of yards, braking gently once he could peer around the corner. He spotted Lyons standing in the shadows of an alcove, engaged in what looked like a heated discussion with another man.

While he could clearly see Lyons' side profile, the stranger had his back to him. Danny could tell that he was tall, almost as tall as Lyons with similarly broad shoulders. But where Lyons was bulky, this guy was extremely thin, bordering on gaunt. Dressed in a hoodie and a pair of dirty jeans, the man sported a pair of brown boots instead of the runners Danny would have expected to complete the look. Middle-aged, Danny guessed by the set of him, although he couldn't clearly see his face. Certainly, worse for wear. A pimp or druggie? Whoever it was, Detective Lyons didn't look happy. He was aggressively shaking his head while the man facing him gesticulated as he spoke. Their words certainly appeared heated. As Danny watched, Detective Lyons gave one final shake of his head then with a resigned air, took what looked like a wad of cash out of his pocket and handed it over. On receiving it, the man immediately took off in the opposite direction from the car, hobbling slightly as he turned down a side street and disappeared.

For a few moments, Detective Lyons stood and watched him go before finally glancing in Danny's direction. Spotting the car parked up on the kerb, he made his way over but as he did so, he glanced back over his shoulder as if to make sure the man had gone. He appeared flustered but then between the beard and his naturally ruddy complexion, Danny found it hard to tell.

"Friend of yours, sir?" Danny asked through the open window.

"They call him Snake. He's my street ears," Detective Lyons replied as he hobbled to the passenger side of the car and opened the door. "What young kids like you might refer to as a Confidential Informant. Helps me out from time to time. Asked him if he'd heard of any gang banger who'd recently lost a hand. He hasn't but he'll keep his ears open."

Using the door as support, he lowered his large frame into the passenger seat then rested for a moment with his feet sticking out onto the footpath.

"Whatever you do, don't take up hurling," he groaned. "Leaves you with nothing only a bad back and dodgy knees. And no one will give a shit."

Danny huffed at the thought. "No fear of that, sir. Not much hurling in Mayo."

"Not much football either from what I see. Except with the ladies… Maybe ye should put them out against the Dubs."

Danny allowed himself a brief smile at the dig.

In recent years, the men of Mayo had been beaten in every GAA All-Ireland they'd played in, and more often than not had been beaten by the Dubs. They had been so misfortunate it had become a bit of a national joke with people suggesting they were cursed. The women, on the other hand, had won the All-Ireland numerous times.

"Perhaps they're minding themselves," Danny replied. "Don't want to end up broke-up like you."

"I didn't win any All-Ireland's and I'm still this way. That's what happens if you get injured in that organisation. They just toss you aside like a piece of shit. Then bring in the next clown that'll run around like a damn racehorse for them." After another groan or two, he swung his legs into the car then reached into his shirt pocket and pulled out the box of Hamlets. His hand shook noticeably as he eased one out, in fact, trembling so bad that it took him two attempts to slip the slim cigar between his lips. Twice that to crank the wheel of a Bic lighter with his thumb. Finally, he managed to set the cigar alight then took a long puff that he seemed to draw all the way to his toes. After a moment of rumination, he released the smoke out the side of his mouth.

"This used to be a decent neighbourhood," he commented while glancing around in dismay. "Now it's riddled with drugs."

Danny detected more than smoke off his superior's breath. He hadn't seen the detective since he'd walked out of the station to 'see a man about a dog.' No prizes for guessing where he'd spent the time. 'Hair of the dog' in the Sheep's Head Tavern was as close to a canine as he'd come, Danny was betting.

"Everywhere you turn, there are addicts, like that lad I just met. Buying or selling or stealing whatever they can just to get their next fix. Has the whole world fucked up! But they're just the symptom. The real problem is further up the ladder."

"The suppliers," Danny offered. "The Gangs."

Detective Lyons shook his head.

"Just another symptom. I'm talking about the governments. The businessmen. The banks. Those fuckers control everything. They could put these gangs out of business in the morning if they really wanted. But they don't because half of them have invested in companies that profit from 'crime prevention' while the other half can't survive without snorting powder up their noses. Then there's the auxiliary beneficiaries – the prison service, the media, even the daily newspapers. If it wasn't for drugs, they'd have nothing to write about. Half of them would close down in the morning if they hadn't a drug war to report on. No. Drug business is something governments can't afford to get rid of, so every day, more and more kids' lives are ruined because they're unwittingly controlled by those white-collar bastards." As he spoke, his eyes glinted angrily. Drifted away a bit. "Innocent young kids whose whole futures are destroyed. Turning to crime. Prostitution." He shook his head vehemently and Danny thought he heard the sound of teeth grinding. "It's another damn cancer and something has to be done to stop it."

This was about as much as Danny had heard from him in a single discourse in the entire year he'd been at the station. Also, about as passionate a tone as he'd heard him use.

"That why you got transferred to the drug squad, sir?" Danny asked.

"Yep."

"But you were in homicide, right?" He knew Lyons had been a homicide detective prior to his well-chartered fall from grace. Had been demoted as a rap on the knuckles is what Danny had heard. No prizes for guessing what earned him the rap.

"Twelve years. And I know what you're thinking. Drug squad is a step backward. Hasn't quite got the same sheen to it. But despite what those arseholes in the station say, I requested the transfer. As I said, drugs are where it's at for me." He smiled bitterly, revealing a row of slightly uneven and stained teeth. The price of too many cigars. Ale too, no doubt. "Those bastards thought they could bury me under paperwork for the next eighteen months but the irony of it is that now I have a hand in both games. A severed hand arriving by post... It stinks of gangland. If I hadn't been in the office when Miss Cox called in, God knows whose lap the case would have fallen into. Now that it's in mine, I have no intention of being their bird in a cage."

"But I've found nothing tying Marie Cox to that particular industry," Danny pointed out. "No history of drug use. No links to suppliers. No association with criminal gangs. However, I did find plenty of people who despised her. Her work colleagues' descriptions of her range from manipulative and egotistical to obnoxious and calculating while her immediate neighbours suggested she had a different man in her apartment for every day of the week.

The old man I spoke to said her carry-on bordered on criminal. But as far as drugs go – nothing."

"Not on the face of it, I bet." Lyons replied dismissively. "But that's why we're checking up on all her contacts. It's called shaking a tree, young man. And don't forget the business she's in is riddled with drugs. "Must be, considering all the shite they write."

"Do you think we should pay Independent News a visit then, sir? See what her colleagues have to say face to face." He glanced across at the detective. "One of her colleagues mentioned that Miss Cox isn't due in the office today so it might be a good chance to shake that tree a little more, sir. Perhaps loosen an apple or two."

Detective Lyons allowed himself an amused smile at the riposte then lay his head back on the rest and closed his eyes. Exhaling a puff of smoke, he suddenly looked tired, every bit the jaded detective faltering towards retirement.

"We could walk, sir. It's only down the road."

"I know where it is," Detective Lyons replied pointedly, his eyes remaining stubbornly shut. Danny started the engine.

****

Independent News would normally be a hive of activity with over fifty staff members spread out over three large offices, but on this occasion, it was manned by weekend staff only. After arriving just before lunchtime, the pair spent the best part of an hour interviewing those who worked closest with Miss Cox. They found the sentiment was generally the same as Danny had garnered by phone. However, they found no suggestion of drug use on Miss Cox's part or of any interaction with local suppliers. And though her colleagues clearly despised her, none stood out as hating her enough to send her that gruesome little present. From what Danny could tell, they simply struggled with her demanding personality, especially the men in her life, as was often the case with overbearing women. At least in Danny's experience.

"However, her demanding body was another story," the droll voice of one of her male colleagues – a rather crude man named Fred who had a phony smile and greased-back hair – informed them with a conspiratorial wink. Neither Lyons nor Danny was in the conspiring mood.

"Have you heard from her today?" Lyons asked wearily.

Fred shook his greasy head. "She called yesterday but I missed it. I was hoping to see her at the game. We usually make a night of it afterwards, if you know what I mean."

Danny found his suggestive smile sickening.

"Did you see her at the game?"

"Not this time. As I said, I missed her call then I got distracted with another lady-friend."

"Which took up the rest of your evening, I suppose." Lyons' brusque tone stated he wasn't waiting around for an answer.

"He was some ass," Danny commented as they later left the office building through a large glass door and descended a set of stone steps toward the car. Danny had parked just around the corner from the three-storey building, leaving only a short walk along Rathbeale Road. Still, he wondered if Detective Lyons could manage to step this one out.

"I've seen more class hanging out of a cow's tail, sir. If that's what our Miss Cox is surrounded by, it's no wonder she's the way she is," Danny said.

"Well, if you lay down with dogs," Lyons replied, continuing with the animal analogies that Danny seemed so fond of. A farmer's son for sure, he decided, while at the same time wondering how a young man with obvious African heritage spoke with an accent that wouldn't be out of place at the Ballinasloe horse fair.

"But she's a beautiful woman," Danny objected, "and it's not like she doesn't know it. Why associate with someone like that?"

"Because Danny, for people like Marie Cox, sex is a bargaining tool. Used to gain whatever advantage they can." He took an extended draw of his Hamlet. "It's a means to power," he explained, releasing a sharp puff of smoke through his nostrils as he spoke. "And she's not one bit concerned who she hurts as long she gains that power. That slimeball in there thinks he's the smart one." Lyons shook his head. "She'd eat him up and spit him out. Just like she'd do with you if she got her hands on you."

"Not a chance. I'd rather stick my head into an ants' nest." Danny glanced at Lyons, his curiosity getting to him. Along with his growing concern about conflict of interest. He decided to chance his arm. "What about you, sir?"

"Me?"

"Yes, you and Miss Cox, sir?"

Lyons stopped suddenly in the middle of the street and turned to look at Danny. His eyes furrowed and his mouth bore a thin-lipped expression. He looked as if he was about to say something, then abruptly changed his mind. Instead, he took another drag of his cigar while his eyes studied his colleague.

"Too much of an oil painting for me, son. I prefer my women natural." He smiled evasively but Danny noted the slightest twitch in the corner of his eye. What was he hiding? Was it something his superiors should know about? Surely if it were, an experienced detective like Lyons would put his hand up, even if he was a bit of a maverick. Reminding himself he was only the gofer, he pushed his concerns to the back of his mind.

"Ok," Lyons continued in a business-like tone, "we have a woman who is either envied or loathed by her peers. Envied for her good looks and perceived position in life, loathed for her ambition and determination to make it to the top no matter what it takes, correct?"

Danny nodded. "Yes."

"In fact, she is so ambitious and self-absorbed that after delivering a severed hand to a Garda Station, her immediate concern is to make her way across town and be on time to report on a match. We know this because I read the report in this morning's paper. Quite a good report it was too. A talented lady our Miss Cox. Extremely so, considering she must have missed at least the first half of the game due to our little chat, yet she was able to write in detail on exactly what occurred."

"She must have stolen or copied somebody else's report?" Danny speculated.

"Perhaps, but it's most likely she had someone else doing the writing for her." The detective puffed the cigar thoughtfully. "I'm guessing our creepy friend, Fred. In return for the promise of favours, of course." He moved further along toward the car.

Following after him, Danny pointed out, "Either way, she is handing in somebody else's work and claiming it as her own. That's plagiarism."

"Hardly a huge crime in the scheme of things," Lyons observed.

"That's true, sir," Danny agreed. "But it does show she is more than willing to bend the rules." He paused just as they reached the car, his kaleidoscopic eyes widening as a thought struck him. "That could be the reason for the severed hand, sir?" he said excitedly. "A warning. To use only what is written by her own hand and stop stealing other people's work."

Detective Lyons eyes studied him tolerantly. "It could be, but I don't think so." He leaned up against the car, his elbows resting on the roof, tendrils of smoke rising from the failing cigar. "Writers don't tend to cut off other people's hands over plagiarism. They're wordsmiths, therefore, they take a more progressive line. They sue."

"Like that drug addict with the ladder."

"As I said, progressive. But back to the point. I really think this is far more sinister than simply stealing somebody else's notes, young man." He looked across the car at Danny. "This is personal. Something like this always is.

About something sordid in her past, I'd bet." He tossed the cigar and stubbed it out with the toe of his shoe then folded himself into the passenger seat, groaning as he lowered himself down using the grab handle. "What else did you unearth regarding her background?"

Danny reached into his shirt pocket and pulled out his notebook. He flicked to the relevant pages and scanned the notes he had taken. "She went to school in St Mary's, an all-girls school then went to college in UCD. Started working at Independent News straight out of college."

"Any association with criminals, perhaps in the form of former boyfriends, girlfriends, school pals?"

"None that we could find. No black marks against her name whatsoever. Squeaky clean apart from being a bitch. But she does seem to have access to quite a bit of cash. Has over a hundred thousand in one bank account and nearly eighty in another. Not to mention several properties, a credit union account, a post office account, and an account with some foreign bank that we are still trying to access."

"Traced through all the correct channels, of course?"

"Yes," Danny replied, while smoothly buckling his seatbelt. "No problem getting warrants when a severed hand is in the evidence room."

"Good. The last thing we want is for her to start a crusade in the paper. What with all this new data protection crap and all. Did you check if she's ever written an article about criminals or localised crime?" Detective Lyons asked, probing a different angle. His seatbelt not closing quite as smoothly as his colleague's, drew a frustrated curse from his lips as he struggled with it. Probably close to reaching its extension limit, Danny guessed, even though the man was carrying little excess weight.

"Not since her internship," Danny replied. "After that, it's been sport all the way."

"What you're telling me is there's no reason to think that whoever sent her this hand was a known criminal or had any ties to organised crime."

"No, sir."

"Then we are left with the people we've interviewed so far. Are we certain none of her peers could have been so provoked by her demeaning attitude to leave a severed hand at her door?"

Danny shook his head. "She mightn't be the most popular woman in history, sir, but she's no Atilla the Hun."

"Atilla the Hun was a man!"

"Sorry, sir, Maggie Thatcher then. She's no Maggie Thatcher. So who would be bothered to send her a warning like that?"

"Why do you keep presuming it's a warning?"

"What else could it be, sir?"

"It could be proof that a certain deed was done, or it could just be a mistake, like she claims. Maybe meant for someone else."

Danny looked at him then nodded thoughtfully. "Like they just got the wrong address, you mean?"

"Possibly. That's certainly what Miss Cox seems to think."

"Or," Danny offered with enthusiasm, "it could be a beginning, like in that film Seven. The one with Morgan Freeman and Brad Pitt."

"A beginning?" Detective Lyons asked dubiously. "Of what?"

Danny shrugged. "I dunno. Some sort of cult killing?"

"You were right the first time, you don't know," Detective Lyons replied pointedly. "And if it pans out anything like that film, you don't want to know. So, let's just focus on what we do know and then try and figure out where the hell this hand came from. And more importantly, who it belongs to." He glanced at Danny questioningly. "Did you put it up on the national database?"

"Yes sir. Nothing so far."

Lyons sighed in frustration. "Anything back from forensics?"

"Oh yes, sir. Sorry, I meant to tell you. The hand is male just as we suspected. From a man in his early sixties. Judging by the condition of his skin, he wasn't an office worker, but not necessarily overloaded with physical work either. Perhaps he worked in a factory or as a foreman of some kind."

"So, not the type that Miss Cox would be bothered to associate with. Anything else?" mused Lyons.

"Yes, the severing of the hand was done recently. The low level of coagulation suggests as recently as this morning. However, the temperature of the body part allows for a window of forty-eight hours."

"Two days?" Detective Lyons pursed his lips. "If that's the case, the man is most likely dead by now from shock or blood loss, unless he has gotten proper medical attention. Did you check all the hospitals and clinics as I asked you?"

Danny nodded. "No sign of a one-handed man."

Lyons produced the box of Hamlets and the Bic lighter from his trouser pocket. Pulled another cigar out and slotted it between his lips with those shaky fingers.

"I think we have to pay a visit to Miss Cox. And this time we're going to get some straight answers."

Danny turned over the engine. "Easier to get a cow to squirt pasteurised milk into a bucket, I'd bet."

Chapter 6

"Shit, Joe," Detective Flynn grumbled, as they made their way back to the station. "This case is going to screw us up for weeks. Months maybe. The last thing we've time for right now is heading up a damn murder investigation."

"I know," Joe agreed, "but look on the bright side, Terry. You've got pretty little Britney as your gofer. Waiting on you hand and foot."

Terry smiled at the thought of it. "Tidy little bitch, ain't she, despite that little scar of hers. Compact. But thinks her shit smells sweeter. By Jesus, I'm going to prove her wrong, Joe. Make her scream til she likes it. Can't say I didn't warn her, there'll be no KY for that bitch."

Joe laughed. Not because he found it all that funny but because that's just the way it was. Had been from the very first day they worked together, a little over six months ago now. Terry made the wisecracks. Joe did the chortling.

Terry was right about one thing though. This case was going to eat into their personal time. Burglary, petty theft, assault – those kinds of cases suited them down to the ground. Simple and straightforward. Most of the time they had a clear lead to follow. Open and shut, more often than not. Or simply shelved. Murder, however, was an altogether different matter. And this was no ordinary murder. Joe wondered if he'd be able to stay focused on his more pressing task.

"Do you think this is some sort of psychopath we're dealing with, Terry? I mean, who cuts off a hand, for God's sake? And before the poor bastard was even dead."

"Foreigners do," he shrugged. "Eastern Europeans, Orientals. Tipperary people." Once he was finished smiling at his own humour, he shook his head. "Nah, I think somebody killed that man for one of the usual reasons but then tried to make it look like there was some other, more sadistic motivation. My money is on the eldest son. He's a dodgy bugger if ever I saw one. Toby, if I remember correctly. I believe the locals call him Tinker."

They were on their way back from questioning the family of Donie Cullen, a chore which, to their dismay, took up most of their day. Mr Cullen was survived by his wife and three children, two boys and a girl but despite questioning them for hours, they had nothing only Terry's hunch to work with. Joe knew all too well that Terry's hunches were usually based on his own dislike of someone and little else. In other words, they were the opposite of concrete. Quicksand more like. Although he had to agree that Toby did look dodgy as hell, what with that shifty smile and being unable to maintain eye contact for any length of time during questioning. Couldn't see a solid motive though. Not yet, but it was early days.

The victim himself was well known in the community having lived in the village all his life. He worked as a foreman in the local brick-making factory along with being a worker's rep there. He had also been a former director of the hurling club. Therefore, he was well known amongst his peers. But was he well-liked or well-respected? Joe was doing the job long enough to know that the three weren't mutually inclusive. That was something they would have to dig into. Do that and motive usually followed. Joe had his money on an affair. He'd sensed something amiss when he spoke to Cullen's wife.

"Ok, the son could be dodgy," Joe admitted. "but we're still going to have to interview the wider family and all the neighbours."

"No, we're not," Terry objected. "We've got enough to do with that new order coming through. Anyway, I'm heading up the investigation, remember. So, it would be remiss of me not to delegate. I think an important job like that would be right up the street of our Busty Britney, don't you?" He smiled to himself. "After all, Uncle Harry did say she should do the leg work."

Joe chose to ignore the fact that by constantly using the first person, Terry obviously didn't consider him as a joint lead in the investigation even though they were partners of equal rank. Truth was, it suited Joe to play second fiddle. If they solved the case, he would share in the credit, perhaps not equally but enough to keep him in clover for a while, but if, and more likely when the shit hit the fan, Terry would be the one out front in the firing line. Joe might take a hit or two, but he would survive and for the time being that was all that mattered. The game they were playing was all about self-preservation.

"I thought you had different leg work in mind?" Joe said, his eyebrows raised suggestively. "But you're damn right. Why bark when you have a dog? And come to think of it, it mightn't be a bad idea to start training that new girl in as well. I think she has a certain potential." Now Joe offered a salacious smile, although the leer didn't quite fit with his face. "And I don't mean at barking!"

"Perhaps, but Fiona is certainly no dog, Joe. She's juicy as a peach. Although, there are some doggy things I wouldn't mind doing with her. Shit," he groaned and leaned back in the seat. "Even thinking about it is giving me a hard-on."

"Pity about you," Joe said. "You're not the only one looking at that little tease every day. Unlike you, though, I don't have someone waiting at home to take the edge off."

"Oh, I thought you told me you were married?" Terry asked. It was said casually, but Joe could feel his partner's eyes on him, gauging his reaction. Watching for a mistake. Even though he'd had Terry's back during a number of tough deals lately, Terry still hadn't completely accepted him. Probably never would.

Joe shook his head. "Was," he answered coolly. "Been divorced a year and a half. Best year and a half of my life."

"She still living in Cork?"

"Yup. And still a bitch."

"Tell me about it," Terry snorted. "The longer you're with them, the worse they get. And the less damn fucking attractive. Truth is, I haven't shagged Tina in months. Just can't feel the love, you know what I mean? In fact, I'd rather shag that dog of a Filipino that cleans the floors in Fat Tony's."

"Greasy Gabby? Now, that would be a new low, even for you, Terry!"

"Oh, you've no idea how low I can go…" Terry replied with an unexpected edge to his voice. "So, you wouldn't want to cross me. Capeesh?" A deadly look drifted across his face, and almost as quickly, it was gone. Suddenly he laughed uproariously and reached across to slap Joe on the thigh.

"Speaking of Fat Tony's, fancy a burger and chips for lunch?"

"Sure," Joe replied with a nervous chuckle. "And while we're there I might have a go at the cleaner myself. Any port in a storm, isn't that what they say?"

"So, two burgers, two chips, and one HOT DOG!" Terry declared with a cackle. He turned the car and headed in the direction of the chipper. A few moments later they pulled up at Fat Tony's and Terry hopped out. He disappeared inside for about ten minutes and when he returned, he was carrying two bags packed with burgers, chicken nuggets, and chips. A half-smoked cigarette was hanging from his lips.

"On the house, I presume," Joe said, having learned from early on that Terry seldom put his hand in his pocket in this city. Food, drink, tickets to HAI matches – whatever Terry needed, he got and usually gratis. It was a 'quid pro quo' kind of arrangement. They looked after Terry and if they ever had any trouble, Terry looked after them. One call was all it took. One call and the perceived transgressor either got a good beating or was arrested on some trumped-up charge like drug possession or drunk driving. Joe had witnessed it first-hand.

"Isn't everything?" Terry winked as he handed the bags in through the window. "Think of it as local policing at its best."

"Oh, I'm not complaining," Joe assured. "I'll take whatever they give me. God knows this job doesn't pay enough without something to sweeten the pie." He took the bags and rummaged through them as he checked his order. "Speaking of something to sweeten the pie, a drink would be nice."

"Jeez…" Terry swore. "That dirty greaseball screwed me again. I told him the last time I'd kick his ass if he ever tried that shit. It was no nuggets the last time," he grumped. "Now it's no fucking bevvies." He spat out the cigarette then turned back toward the restaurant. "No one short-changes Terry Flynn," he swore as he went. "Not for so much as a fucking cola."

Joe laughed as he watched him disappear back inside. "Capeesh," he said to himself. Who the fuck did Flynn think he was? The Godfather?

Knowing that putting manners on Fat Tony might take Flynn a while, he decided to use the time alone to sort some things out. He rooted out his phone and dialled the number he was told to use. Waited for the man to answer. There was a new consignment on its way. The big one. Preparing for it was his job in all of this. As he contemplated waht lay ahead he played ping pong with his cheeks.

****

116

The weather was about to change. Danny could see it on the horizon – dark clouds moving in from the Irish sea carrying the threat of rain. The heat of the past week was slowly giving way to the chill that was more in keeping with the time of year. He could feel winter hovering like an expectant vulture in the air.

"You're driving like you just waxed the damn car," Detective Lyons grumbled as he took an impatient draw of the cigar he held between his thick index and middle fingers. The cigar looked no bigger than a cigarette in his huge hand. Between the large frame, the unkempt hair and beard, and the ever-present cigar, Danny had a sudden impression of programs his mother used to watch when he was a kid. He imagined Lyons as some sort of a cross between Grizzly Adams and Columbo. Now that he was sporting a grey rain mac, the image was complete. Lyons ingested the smoke, held it momentarily then blew it out the window in a sharp puff.

"I thought all you young guys were boy racers," he whined as he threw an impatient glance at his watch. It was close to two p.m.

"Believe it or not, sir, they train all that out of us in college," Danny replied. "You know, public safety and all that." Even though Detective Lyons had rolled down the window, the pungent odour of the cigar was filling the car, forcing Danny to open his own window and draw in a deep breath. Almost instantly, he regretted the move. The Dublin air wasn't much better than what Lyons was breathing out. Worse even. Acrid, sticky, stink. He'd never get used to it. At times like this, he really missed home.

The woods to the rear of his house. The heather-filled hills overlooking them. The fresh salt air drifting in off the Atlantic to fill a man's lungs with freedom. A heavenly place, if only there was work to be had. Someday, he'd get stationed back there. Someday.

"To hell with public safety!" Detective Lyons growled. "No one has heard from that woman since she left my office and she's not answering her goddamn phone. What, son? Do I have to spell it out for you?" He glanced at his watch for the third time in minutes, then shook his head. "I should have insisted on sending an officer."

"Not your fault, sir, she wasn't having it. Anyway, there could be any number of reasons she's not contactable."

Detective Lyons cast him a sceptical look and was about to respond when his phone rang. One glance at the number told him it was the Super. He let it ring.

"Aren't you going to answer it, sir? It could be Miss Cox!"

"It's not. It's the goddamn station. They get kind of nervous when I go out on my own. For some reason, they think I might go off on the piss."

Danny heard the phone ring out and shortly afterward a message beeped through. Detective Lyons ignored that too.

"They do that a lot, sir? Check up on you, I mean."

Lyons forced a humourless smile. "I'm an embarrassment, haven't you heard?" Then he shook his head and drew aggressively on the cigar. As he blew the smoke out the window, he mumbled to himself, "Closed more cases than the lot of them put together, yet they insist I do a goddamn psych exam. Then they rig it so that I look like something out of The Shining." He puffed what was left of his cigar then tossed it out the window. Glancing in the side mirror Danny saw it hit the asphalt in a shower of angry sparks.

"Turn right here and then a left at the next lights," Lyons ordered. "Five minutes no more!" It was an instruction rather than a statement.

Danny did as Lyons directed then took the next left onto Bridge Street and directly past Swords Tower. He judged he should easily make it to the address he had for Miss Cox within the five minutes. Still, he kept his foot down until Lyons pointed out the entrance to the estate which contained Miss Cox's apartment block. Pulling into the left lane he turned off the main street onto the narrow drive which led to the gated entrance. The gates were open, allowing him to drive through, past rows of townhouses on either side, and follow the road until it curved deeper into the estate. The houses here were larger than the ones at the front with bigger gardens and extended space between them.

"Not cheap around here," Danny observed as he drove.

Spotting an engraved stone plaque set into the nearby wall, Danny slowed to check the name against the one he had been given. They had reached St Colmcille's Crescent.

"Go on," Lyons urged, "over there." Without hesitation he pointed toward a large red brick apartment block standing on its own at the rear of the estate.

The drive narrowed, funnelling them towards the single, two-storey building beyond the rows of houses. There were cars parked either side of the drive making it even narrower again and he was forced to slow to navigate past a delivery truck, the rear corner of which protruded quite a distance out into the street. Abandoned more than parked, Danny observed as he pulled wide to avoid it. Some people just didn't give a shit. He should have slowed then but because of Lyons' demand for urgency, he found himself driving faster than he would have. Suddenly, a man appeared from behind one of the cars forcing Danny to swerve and hit the brakes hard. The man dodged to his left, only avoiding the car by mere inches but kept on running, not even pausing to remonstrate. Getting a brief look at him Danny saw that he wore a long raincoat with a deep hood that covered his face.

"Shit," Danny cursed, throwing a sharp glance at Detective Lyons, "I nearly killed that gobshite."

The detective didn't seem to hear. His eyes were on the sideview mirror watching the man disappear in the opposite direction, his expression suddenly grave.

"Pull in on the kerb over there. And when we get inside, keep your eyes and ears open, your mouth shut."

"Christ, sir!" Danny swore, instantly alarmed by the sudden change in the detective's tone. "Do you think that man came from Miss Cox's building?"

"Could have. He certainly came from that direction."

Swinging the wheel sharply toward the kerb, Danny parked the car and hopped out. Detective Lyons took a little longer, but he was closer to the building. Abandoning the car, they made a dash for the front entrance where Lyons located the buzzer for Marie Cox's apartment and pressed it firmly. He waited a moment but there was no answer, so he pressed it again, even more impatiently this time, holding the buzzer down for a longer time. Silence.

"Something's terribly wrong," he warned. "I can feel it."

Danny felt his heart pick up its pace, "Do you think that's our guy? The one who delivered the hand?"

"Not sure," Lyons replied, "but something's lit a fire under his ass."

"Try the button beside it," Danny advised. "I think I was speaking to them earlier. An elderly couple if I remember correctly. Only themselves and Miss Cox on that floor of the building. I got the impression they hadn't much time for their neighbour."

Selecting the button on the intercom with the name 'Brown' scrawled across it in blue pen, Lyons pressed it. A male voice answered almost immediately. Elderly. Danny recognised the slight tremor as that of the man he had been speaking to earlier.

"This is the Brown residence," it declared in a clipped tone. "Can I help you?"

"You certainly can," Lyons replied while leaning toward the speaker. "My name is Detective Richie Lyons. I need to gain access to this building."

"Have you ID?" came the reply. A tad haughty, Danny thought, reinforcing the impression he got earlier, an impression confirmed with the pointed statement that followed.

"This is an exclusive building."

With an impatient sigh Lyons proffered his ID number but still the man hesitated.

"Look, Mr Brown," Lyons suddenly barked through gritted teeth, droplets of spittle raining down on the polished steel of the intercom. "I'm here about a possible disturbance in your neighbour's apartment. I think she may be hurt or worse. So, open the damn door or I'll knock it down and take you in for obstruction!" As he spoke, his voice steadily rose until the latter was close to a shout.

Almost instantly a buzzer sounded practically begging one of them to push on through. Danny duly obliged and they were inside. Lyons headed straight for the stairs, belying the aches in his limbs by taking the steps two at a time.

"She's on the next floor. Apartment 101," he called back to Danny who, caught by surprise by his sudden dash was now several steps behind.

"Don't tell me you run like you fucking drive," Lyons growled as he neared the top.

Two more steps and Lyons found himself on top of the landing, glancing left and right for Marie Cox's door. Danny alighted a moment later to see Lyons, his face flushed and struggling for breath, make his way cautiously toward the desired entrance.

Immediately Danny's heart sank. The door was ajar.

"Stay behind me and for God's sake, don't do anything stupid," Lyons ordered. On reaching the door he shoved it further open then loudly declared the presence of Gardaí.

"Hello? Miss Cox. Are you in there? It's Detective Lyons."

There was no answer, prompting him to repeat the question.

"Miss Cox. Are you in there?" Again, he was met with silence, so he swung the door inwards. That's when he detected the smell. It was faint but hung in the air like a warning. He had smelled the odour before. Far too many times. A mixture of copper and ammonia with a sweet undertone. Blood and faeces. Death was in the air.

He took a deep breath through his mouth, then cautiously entered. Danny, his nose twitching, moved in behind, watching his colleague's back as he had been trained to do. Deep down inside, he felt like a little boy in a strange place, too scared to let his father out of his sight.

The hallway through which they entered was wide and minimally decorated – the walls painted white with cream tiles on the floor. Framed prints of abstract art hung at head height. Three doors led off the hall, each fashioned from dark walnut, two of which were now closed. Lyons took the third which led into a large sitting room, again decorated in the contemporary minimalist fashion. White walls, pale flooring. A large, dark settee with voluminous cushions adding splashes of colour.

There was no sign of Miss Cox. Manoeuvring around the settee which held centre stage in the room, Lyons headed for a double doorway through which they could see the corner of a polished chrome kitchen table and a matching chair. The chair sat away from the table as if it had recently been in use.

"Miss Cox are you here?" Lyons called out but again there was no answer. They stepped further into the room then suddenly Lyons stopped in his tracks. Danny, finding the tension close to unbearable, very nearly collided with him. Glancing at Lyons he noted a dark expression cross his colleague's face. He warily allowed his eyes drift to where Lyons was staring. It took a moment to register what they beheld. A further moment still to make sense of it.

"Son of a bitch," he exclaimed finally, his eyes widening in horror. "Is that...?"

Lyons nodded. "Yes," he replied dejectedly. "It's Marie Cox. Or what's left of her." After a moment he drew his eyes away and turned to Danny. "I'm starting to think you were right, young man." Danny thought he detected fear in his colleague's voice. He licked his lips. His mouth was dry.

"About what, sir?"

"That hand really was only the beginning."

Danny nodded dumbly while he continued to stare upwards, his mouth open and his eyes wide. He'd never seen anything like it. And in that moment hoped he never would again.

Both of Marie Cox's ears had been severed. With her previously flowing hair now tied back in a ponytail this savagery was one of the first things Danny noted. That and the more obvious fact that she was hanging by the neck. The strangulation cord attached to an elaborate chrome light fitting erected as the centrepiece of the ceiling. A focal point. Certainly that now. The cord, coloured blue and white originally was now stained with streaks of red. The same red that stained Miss Cox. It was everywhere. On her face, down her dress. Pooled on the tiled floor beneath her. A stark contrast with the neutral decor. Her sterile kitchen had become her personal abattoir. Painted shades of death.

In the midst of it, she dangled. Stiff and lifeless, her blue eyes now bulging out of her head, her smooth complexion no longer a healthy glow beneath her makeup, but putrid. Purple. Purple overpainted with that deep shade of red. The mutilation hadn't killed her. She had been starved of air. Not a good look. Ultimately, Danny observed sadly, the beauty that she seemed to trade so flippantly was something that had abandoned her.

Beauty too had abandoned the floral dress – the same one she had worn to the station. Dishevelled and bloodied, it hung on her body with the grace of a sack cloth, no longer accentuating her figure but betraying it. Even the most celebrated physiques droop and sag in death. Its colour too, proved a traitor, stained as it was in the vividness of blood, faeces and urine, a trio of shades that highlighted the body's weakness.

Projecting below the discoloured hem were those long elegant legs – the weapons she had unveiled at the station. Not so elegant now, though still clad in those exotic high heels. Stiffly spreadeagled, both limbs were streaked with blood, but it was the left that was especially grotesque. Its knee was a misshapen lump, purpling skin stretched over a joint swollen beyond recognition. Whoever did this had tortured her first.

Danny had never seen a dead body before. Not outside of a funeral. Thus far avoided it in the line of duty. But the stillness of the milieu before him left little doubt that this was one. Miss Cox was dead. The fox had come to take her after all.

As Danny stood transfixed, Detective Lyons moved further into the room, stepping carefully so as not to disturb the crime scene. Making for the blood that pooled on the floor beneath Marie Cox's dangling red shoes. When he reached it, he bent down and sampled it with the tip of his finger.

"That's strange," he mumbled to himself as he reached up and placed his hand flat against the lower part of her calf.

"What's strange sir?" Lyons' remark brought Danny out of his reverie.

"Well, the blood has yet to coagulate, but the body is cold to the touch."

"If the blood is fresh sir…" Danny threw a desperate glance at the window, "that mean we just missed the killer."

Lyons nodded. "He walked right into our lap, and we let him go. It was almost as if…" He shook his head as if to dismiss the idea before it formed.

"It was almost as if what, sir?"

"I think it was quite a coincidence that he walked right out in front of our car when he did. Don't you? It was almost as if he was taunting us. Daring us to catch him."

"We still can, sir," Danny replied with more desperation than confidence. "He's only minutes ahead of us." He made a dash toward the door, but Lyons caught his arm.

"Leave it, son. He's long gone," Lyons said. "Could be anywhere by now."

But Danny had the bit between his teeth. He pulled clear of Lyons and darted out the door. Bypassing the elevator because it would prove too slow, he took the stairs two and three steps at a time.

"For God's sake, leave it!" Lyons shouted. "You've no backup." His warning fell on deaf ears.

Within moments Danny had exited the building and was sprinting down the drive. In the short time they had been inside the building the weather had changed dramatically. Now, it was lashing rain, resulting in Danny instantly getting drenched, his sports jacket of little value in the downpour. And he had scoffed at Lyons' Columbo coat.

On reaching the rows of cars where he had first spotted the man, he stopped to get his bearings then took off in the direction that he judged the man had been heading. Following the curve of the drive, he spotted the opening to a narrow alley that ran between the houses. Bordered as it was by concrete fencing, Danny guessed it was a pedestrian route designed to give the residents a short cut from the estate to the main road. Judging this to be the most likely option he took off down the path at a sprint, the soles of his shoes tapping a desperate rhythm on the wet asphalt. He jumped over a large puddle then flung himself around a ninety-degree corner so fast that he bashed into the concrete barrier opposite.

A moment later he found himself breaking out onto the main road. Cars and buses flew by in the rain, their tyres causing sprays of mist to rise from the street. On the footpaths, pedestrians rushed back and forth, hunched against the driving rain with their jackets, jumpers or shirts pulled up over their heads in vain. Soaked to the skin, they were. Those with greater foresight strode with umbrellas aloft but cursed the state of their shoes. It all contributed to the perfect hiding place for a man already dressed in rain gear. Could he have planned this? Danny wondered. Timed his kill with the rain. No way, surely.

Glancing desperately left and right, while wiping the water out of his eyes with the back of his hand, he started to believe the man had done because he could see no sign of his quarry. Then throwing one final glance in the direction of town, something caught his eye. The distinctive hood. It bobbed in the distance appearing every now and then between the many other hoods, hats and brollies that occupied the footpath.

"Hey!" Danny shouted instinctively as he took into a sprint. "Hey, you!" The man instantly glanced over his shoulder having somehow heard the shout above the raucous combination of rain and traffic. His movement was a tad stiff, Danny thought, giving the impression of an older man. Broad, relatively fit looking, though the long dark coat he wore could hide a multitude. As did the hood and scarf. Or was that a beard?

On spotting Danny, the man shouldered some nearby pedestrians out of the way and took off running. He ran with a funny gait, with his left arm held tightly by his side as if hurt or, perhaps, he was carrying something secured against his body. Whatever the case, it definitely hampered him and despite what Lyons' thought, Danny could move when he wanted to. Like a lightning bolt, in fact. With each stride he gained significant ground, despite the treacherously slippy footpath. Or perhaps because of it. The man ahead didn't seem as sure-footed.

For that basic reason, Danny felt confident he would catch the man within the next fifty yards. Single-handedly apprehend the man that butchered Miss Cox. The thought spurred him on. But just as he was getting within reach, the man swerved to his right and with timing that belied his sluggishness, he hopped on a bus which had just pulled away from the kerb, then he squeezed sideways through the closing door and disappeared. Danny chased after the bus, slamming his fist on the baggage door to alert the driver but the bus failed to stop, the driver either not registering the racket above the driving rain or choosing to ignore it. Whatever the case, the vehicle began to pick up speed and, to Danny's dismay, slowly but surely put distance between himself and his quarry.

Soon Danny was left behind and there was nothing he could do only lean on his knees and catch his breath while his murder suspect was being carried away to safety. And dry now too, with Danny left demoralised in the torrential rain.

When he finally got his breath back, he pulled his phone out of his soaking trouser pocket and called the station to report what had happened, instructing them to have the bus checked at the next stop. However, he was pretty sure it was a wasted call. Once out of sight, the suspect could simply hop off at the first opportunity then dump the coat and disappear into the rabbit warren of the Dublin back streets to become just another soaked jackeen.

****

The walk back took Danny a lot longer than he'd imagined – almost twenty minutes, his shoes squelching with every step. He had run quite a distance and for little or nothing as it turned out. When he finally made it back to the upstairs apartment, he found Lyons in the hallway, checking the exterior door for signs of forced entry. He didn't look surprised when Danny returned empty-handed. Or soaked for that matter.

"Stay out in the hall," he instructed as he eyed Danny disapprovingly. "I don't want you dripping all over that crime scene."

"I nearly caught him, sir," Danny objected.

"To use your parlance, son, nearly never milked a cow. But let's hope you at least got a look at his face because there's nothing to go on inside apart from the body. Well, did you?"

Danny shook his head sending some drops flying from his curly black hair, one of which hit his colleague in the eye.

Lyons was tight lipped as he wiped it off.

"I got a brief look at him, sir," he said between deep gulping breaths. His legs might have stopped but his heart was still racing. "But not close enough to make out anything specific except the hooded coat. And some sort of scarf." He shrugged uncertainly. "Maybe it was a beard. I couldn't be sure with the rain."

"If it was, it was fake, I'd bet. Add in the long coat and it makes a pretty good disguise. Anything else?"

"Not really. A middle-aged man or older, I'd guess by the go of him. But he's definitely our man because he took off running the minute he saw me," Danny paused. "Do you think he planned on the rain, sir? I mean, I couldn't spot him for ages with the other coats, brollies and all? If it hadn't rained, he would have stood out like a sore thumb, sir."

"Possibly," Lyons replied. "If so, that would make him very organised indeed. To torture and kill someone, yet time it exactly right for the rain to disguise his getaway… But then, it could be just a coincidence. I mean, I wore a coat because I listened to the forecast this morning. That doesn't make me anymore clever than most people." He glanced at the sopping Danny and smirked. "Except maybe you."

"Very funny, sir."

Lyons snorted a laugh then his expression grew serious again as he pursed his lips. "Anyway, tall with a hooded coat and beard is not much to go on but it's all we've got for the moment. Apart from that severed hand and whatever we can get from this mess. There's no sign of forced entry so what does that tell us?"

"Miss Cox either knew her attacker or he bluffed his way in," Danny suggested. "Or maybe he waited until she was opening the door then pushed his way through, which might be the more likely scenario, considering what he was wearing."

"Or," Lyons added, "he subdued her at some stage outside her apartment, disabled her in some way and took her key. Then dragged her inside and got to work. Whatever the case, he's a cool customer. Was probably watching her for a long time, logging her movements. Perhaps even sourced the code for the building." He sighed. "I was a damn fool to let her just walk out of the station in the first place. Should have insisted on sending an officer."

"You couldn't have known, sir. Not for certain."

"Couldn't have known. A severed hand wasn't warning enough! What do we need? A trail of fucking breadcrumbs?" He ran his hand over his beard in frustration. "Ok, shut down this entire building. It's a crime scene until forensics say otherwise."

Just then an old man popped his head out from the apartment next door. He was rake thin with wispy hair and large liver spots on his face. Mr Brown, Danny presumed.

"Is it safe to come out?" he asked in a frail voice. Danny could see an elderly woman peeping out from behind him. She was the image of her husband, making him wonder if people really did take on their partner's traits after a lifetime of living together.

"No," Lyons replied bluntly. "I want you to remain inside. But first I have a few questions."

The old man hesitated, halfway in and halfway out the door.

Lyons flashed his badge as he approached him. "That ID enough for you, sir?"

The old man seemed to wither under Lyons' glare. He nodded but said nothing.

"Good," Lyons' reply was dripping with sarcasm. "Now did you see anyone suspicious hanging around here earlier?"

Once again, Mr Brown shook his head. "Like I told that young man that called earlier, we keep to ourselves. We don't want any trouble." He began to inch back inside.

"What about yesterday or the day before?" Lyons asked, his firm tone pinning the old man to the spot. "In fact, did you see anyone bothering her anytime recently?"

The old man smiled wryly. "No more than usual. There were always people in and out of there. When I say people, I mean men. Coming and going like it was one of those bordellos. My wife reckons she's one of those women who sports a fur coat but no knickers." The deep frown that followed clearly displayed his distaste. Allowed a bit for his wife too. Then in an enquiring tone, "Is Miss Cox ok?"

Lyons ignored the question. "Anyone specific?"

"As I said, we keep to ourselves." The old man smiled dismissively then made to shut the door, but the woman pushed past him to stick her nose out.

"I might have seen someone," she admitted in a conspiratorial tone, "yesterday morning when Miss Cox was out walking." As she spoke her eyes darted up and down the hall as if checking if the coast was clear. She kept her voice low for fear of being overheard. "She got a delivery. Very poorly presented. The gift I mean. Not the man. Although he was poorly presented too."

"Is that so?" Lyons replied, with a glance at Danny. There was a stirring in his dark eyes. Perhaps she saw the killer. But could she describe him? That was always the worry. Even Danny knew eyewitnesses were notoriously unreliable. Elderly people even more so, for obvious reasons.

"Can you describe this person for us, Mrs Brown?" His intensely dark eyes zoned in on the old lady's face. Watching for any hint of exaggeration or even deceit, Danny guessed. It was not unheard of for an elderly person, feeling isolated and alone or thrown on the scrapheap and forgotten to make up a story or add feathers to a tale just to get some attention. In fact, the latter went for all people as far as Danny could see. Loneliness is a powerful emotion. Right up there with love and hate. Living alone himself, Danny had his own experience of it.

"Well, it was just a peek, mind. I was concerned when I heard footsteps. I wouldn't like you to think I was nosy, you know?"

Danny smiled thinly at the comment. Conveyed as it was with such sincerity, the woman clearly believed herself innocent of any possible charges of snooping. Just a concerned citizen. However, Danny bet a fly couldn't shit in the building without her knowing about it. Next to her, Mr Brown tutted, clearly unhappy that she had felt the need to stick her head out at all.

"Not at all, Mrs. Brown," Lyons encouraged. "We all see things from time to time. Even if we try not to."

The old woman threw a 'told you so' glance at her husband then smiled in agreement. "Actually, I didn't see all that much because he had his back to me, and he wore a long, hooded coat," she shrugged apologetically then looked at Lyons as if appreciating his unusual size for the first time. It seemed to stir a memory in her. "But he was tall. And broad," she added with renewed enthusiasm, her beady eyes lighting up now with the idea she was conveying crucial information. "Kind of like you."

Lyons threw a sideways glance at Danny as if to acknowledge what Danny himself was thinking. It was the same man. The one he had chased. He returned his attention to Mrs brown and smiled encouragingly. "That's very helpful, Mrs Brown. Now, this is important." His pause was designed to add gravity to his next question. Danny noted the lines around his eyes contract in anticipation. "Did you by any chance see his face?"

The old woman pursed her thin lips then shook her head. "As I said, he had his back to me," she smiled apologetically. "Sorry."

"That's ok, Mrs Brown," Lyons assured, albeit in a frustrated tone. "You can't win them all. Thank you for your time."

She glanced at Danny. "My, you are wet, aren't you?" Her eyes lit up again. "Were you chasing someone?"

With that, the old man shooed her away from the door. "I presume that will be all," he said. It was a statement, not a question. This time he did disappear inside and quickly shut the door behind them.

At once, Danny heard it lock. He couldn't blame the old man for being wary, not with all the hullabaloo. And it wouldn't have helped to have a bear of a man like Lyons staring him down. I bet the poor man was sorry he ever mentioned the word ID. To make it worse, he didn't yet know the details of what had occurred across the hall. Imagining was often worse than knowing. Although in this case, Danny doubted it.

"The old man's not going to be much help, sir," Danny observed. "Same way on the phone. Like pulling hen's teeth. But the woman?"

Lyons wasn't in total agreement. "Nosey as fuck the pair of them, I'd say," he replied. "And they know far more about Miss Cox than they are letting on. Better let things settle down a bit but afterwards I'll want detailed statements from the pair of them. Especially about the visitors the old man mentioned."

"Ok sir," he glanced at the entrance to the apartment. The door was still open. "What do we do now, sir?" he asked somewhat anxiously. The mutilated body of Miss

Cox hanging just yards away made him distinctly uneasy. And he could really do with a change of clothes.

"Now, young Daniel, we wait for forensics. I called them when you were out chasing our ghost. Called for a team to secure the scene, as well, if that helps." He shook his head at the look of relief that passed over Danny's sodden face. "What? You afraid you're going to shrink?"

With little more to do before forensics arrived, Lyons took the opportunity to check the message on his phone. On reading the text he immediately swore. The Super hadn't been checking up on him after all. Beckoning Danny with the inclination of his head, he moved away from Browns' door.

"They've got a body with a missing hand," he informed his young colleague. "In Oldcastle."

"Oldcastle? That's almost an hour and a half from here, sir. Do they think it's a match to what we've got?"

"No tests done yet to confirm the match but it's a male. Left hand cut off pre-mortem. And…"

"And what?"

"And he was hanged by the neck just like our Miss Cox."

"Shit, sir! It has to be connected. Do you think we're dealing with a serial killer?" Danny wasn't sure how he should feel. Personally afraid, professionally excited. He settled on a bit of both.

Lyons ignored the question. "There was one other thing. The victim's left kneecap was shattered. Premortem as well."

"Torture?" Danny wondered, recalling the state of Miss Cox's left leg.

"Possibly," Lyons agreed, rubbing his hand through his beard in frustration. "Or a punishment. But whatever the case, it looks like we're dealing with some sort of crazy. A crazy who takes great pleasure in pain."

He sighed. "Stay here. I'm going to the front door for a smoke."

"Yes sir," Danny replied although the look on his face told Lyons that the last thing he wanted was to remain alone in the building with a dead body hanging inside the door, and nothing except the Browns for back up.

"She is dead," Lyons reminded him as he began to descend the stairs.

"I understand that, sir," Danny replied but his expression remained unchanged. Taking the ever-present pen out of his soggy shirt pocket, he used it to pull the door closed.

By the time back-up and forensics arrived, Lyons had smoked a full cigar and could have ignited another while Danny had damn near taken up smoking himself. There hadn't been sight or sound of the Browns since they locked the door. Danny wondered whether they would ever find the courage to step outside again, once they were informed of what had happened across the hall. Standing there alone was a surreal feeling. Life and death separated by the width of a door. By the thickness of a cord, in Miss Cox's case.

Once he'd instructed the backup Gardaí to secure the scene, Detective Lyons led forensics upstairs to the apartment. Both himself and Danny watched from the doorway as the experts got to work. And work they did. It was Danny's first time to witness a forensics team in real live-action and he found himself fascinated by their level of diligence and attention to detail.

On Lyons' request they initially focused on the area immediately surrounding the body – the floor, the ceiling, the light fitting. To start with, they photographed the individual areas from every perceivable angle, to ensure that absolutely nothing was missed, or later disturbed. Next, they combed these areas for fibres, hairs or other trace evidence that might offer a lead to the investigation. Then they began dusting for fingerprints. It was only when they were confident that they had preserved every last shred of evidence in the immediate vicinity, that they cut down the body and carefully placed it onto a gurney which waited just inside the door. With that done, they turned their attention to the rest of the apartment. Watching the body being lowered, Danny blessed himself. Admittedly he hadn't warmed to Miss Cox but even the devil himself couldn't have wished to see anyone end like this. No one deserved to be butchered in such a fashion. It was inhuman. Seeing her bloodied and distorted features up close made his stomach turn.

"Judging by the amount of blood staining her dress, the ears were cut off premortem?" Lyons mused as he studied the corpse now being slipped into a body bag. The person who had clearly taken charge of the forensic investigation, a small man with thick glasses and wispy grey hair, had finally given them the green light to re-enter the apartment. His name was Peter Holmes, the state pathologist. Lyons had earlier informed Danny he had gotten to know Holmes well over the years as a very accomplished and thorough individual. Danny sensed the respect was mutual.

"I'd say so," Peter agreed. "But…"

"But," the detective interjected with a knowing smile, "you can't confirm or deny until you have completed your post-mortem."

Peter nodded. "You know me too well."

"And I'm guessing you can't confirm or deny that it was the ligature that killed her?"

He offered a rueful shrug. "But given the level of petechial haemorrhaging, I would certainly lean towards asphyxiation as the cause of death. However, there are a couple of things I can confirm with some certainty. Judging by the onset of rigor mortis in the jawbone and neck, but the eyelids remaining relatively flaccid, I'm guessing she's dead a couple of hours at most. The low level of coagulation of the blood on the floor supports this. However, the body temp suggests it could be longer. Also, the level of bruising suggests that her kneecap was shattered premortem. With a blunt object like a club or bat. A steel bar maybe. And whoever cut her, took the ears with him, probably as a trophy," he admitted.

"Or a gift," Lyons mused quietly then glanced around the relatively undisturbed room. It bothered him that the chair pulled away from the table was blood-free. If it had been used during the murder as its position suggested, it would be stained in some way, surely. "Did it happen here or somewhere else?" he asked. He could see no sign of a struggle.

Holmes shrugged. "Hard to tell. There's certainly enough blood to suggest it happened here but the body temp does bother me. He could have staged the scene, I suppose. Preserved the blood from earlier to make this scene look authentic. But why do that?"

"To buy himself time," Lyons replied pensively then nodded gratefully. "Fair enough, Peter, you've done what you can. Once you have the rest of the i's dotted, fill me in, ok?"

"Will do, Richie." Then he cast Lyons a quizzical look. "I thought you were finished with homicide. Moved over to drug squad?"

"You thought right. But only a fool would think the two departments were mutually exclusive. And I've never considered you a fool, Peter."

Holmes smiled at the compliment, but the expression quickly faded as he glanced at the blood that had yet to be cleaned up off the floor. "Sometimes I wonder… Do you think she was involved in drugs?"

Lyons shrugged. "Isn't everyone these days…on something or other?"

"Too true." He shook his head sadly, turning to leave but paused mid-step. "I also heard you were tied to your desk from now on. You gone rogue on them again?"

Lyons smiled. "Just doing my job, Peter, you know how it is. Anyway, this case just landed in my lap."

"The hand you sent us. I heard." He smiled knowingly. "And now that it has, you're like a dog with a bone."

"Something like that…til I catch the bastard!"

Peter nodded as if to say he understood it would be exactly like that. And God help whoever tried to take the bone off him. He glanced towards Danny who was standing alone near the window, looking like a wet rat. A wet rat that was a little green around the gills. "That your latest side-kick?"

Danny, his face drawn, was now leaning up against the wall holding his stomach.

Lyons followed his gaze. "Yep."

"A little wet behind the ears, ain't he?" Holmes smiled. "Pardon the pun. Where did you pick him up – in the Christian Brothers?"

"More like pre-school," Lyons snorted, "judging by the way he drives! Good kid, though."

"Well, do me a favour. Take the kid back to wherever you found him before he spews up all over my crime scene."

Chapter 7

~

When Stacey Rourke first heard a body was found, she almost gave up the ghost herself. She was certain it must be Jim. Who else could it possibly be? Hanging in the changing room of the club he used to play for? Even when she heard reports it was an older man, she couldn't let go of that fear. They could easily be mistaken. People never looked the same when they were dead.

It was only when Jim's father, Alan, got a chance to call to see her the evening after his gruesome discovery that she felt reassured. Alan had done his best to set her mind at ease over the phone, but she needed to read the truth in his face before she could allow herself to relax. At least as much as she could with her husband missing.

"It's not him," Alan assured her. "It's a man from the Ballyfeud club. A HAI man that we all knew. He was treasurer of the club back when Jim was playing."

"And you found the body?"

"Yes, me and Timmy Dunne."

"Oh lord. That must have been horrible." Looking up at Alan from where she was sitting, she asked. "Did you think it was…"

Alan gave a shake of his head. "Not for a moment. Jim wouldn't do that to you and the kids, Stacey."

"Why is he still missing then?"

Alan hesitated, clearly struggling to find an answer, the pause drawing a heavy sigh from Stacey.

"Thanks for letting me report it, Alan. I needed to. I couldn't take it anymore." Her eyes were welling up as she spoke.

"I know, Stacey. I know. It wasn't fair to ask you to wait until now. I just thought…"

Stacey shook her head. "You thought he'd come back by himself. Like I did. But he's gone too long. It's been almost two weeks and now it will be all over the papers. I'll never forgive him, Alan."

"You will, Stacey. You'll have to. If you don't, the children never will."

She shook her head in despair. The poor girl looked completely lost. Broken. Alan knew that even if Jim was found alive, she wouldn't come back from this. How could she?

"What's the poor man's name?" she asked after a moment. "That man you found?"

"Donie Cullen."

"Was he married? Had he children?"

"Yes. Two boys and a girl. All grown up. His wife's name is Mags."

With a shake of her head, Stacey started to cry. Alan sat down next to her and put his arms around her. He had strong arms. Reassuring arms. Just like his son. Yet if a man hadn't strength in his heart, strong arms counted for nothing.

"They must be in a terrible state," she sniffed.

"Yes," Alan agreed. "They must be. But at least they know."

Stacey nodded sadly. "I realise it's a terrible thing to say, but I wish I knew. I can't take it anymore, Alan. Not knowing." It was a lie, of course. She knew. Deep down where terrible truths find a place to hide. Alan could read that on her face.

"Sssh, Stacey, please don't cry," he said, his eyes welling up at the doubts pricking like thorns in his mind. "You've got to be strong for the children. We've all got to be strong for them."

But Stacey didn't seem to hear.

She just stared at some imaginary spot on the kitchen wall. Not imaginary, Alan realised. It was the spot where the photo of Jim and Stacey used to hang. That nice lady cop had taken it, Stacey had informed him over the phone. She was going to find Jim, she promised. Alan wasn't holding his breath.

"If I know Jim," he said, fixing his stare on his daughter-in-law, "the last thing he'd want is for you and the kids to continue suffering. I'm sure it will be all over soon, Stacey."

"I hope so, Alan. I hope so," she gripped his arm tightly.

"Oh Alan, where could he be?" she looked at him pleadingly, her eyes now ultra-focused. Seeing him. Seeing through him. And he through her.

Alan shook his head despairingly. "Wherever he is, may the Lord God help him."

****

Britney had little intention of giving Detective Flynn the chance to personally see to anything, no matter what declaration he'd made to Superintendent Halley. Two days had passed, and she still bristled over that suggestive little remark.

With both anger and frustration spurring her on, she insisted that she had full access to the crime report with a view to familiarising herself with every aspect of the case. In truth, there wasn't much to read. The file only consisted of a few pages outlining the discovery of the body, a couple of witness statements, and a preliminary forensics report. She did find statements from the next of kin but none from the wider family or from those dwelling in neighbouring properties.

To Britney's eye, the report was sorely lacking in detail and sloppily composed but she didn't expect much more from a team headed up by a buffoon.

With that shoddiness in mind, she logged onto the crime database to ensure the details of the case had been uploaded onto the interdepartmental data sharing system. To her surprise, she found this task had indeed been completed. Probably by Triona, their IT marvel. Certainly not by Flynn. Whatever the case, it was a step in the right direction. Now all stations nationwide would be aware that there was a murder investigation underway in Oldcastle, and that the victim was missing his left hand. While she was logged on, she decided to check if there was the discovery of a severed hand anywhere in the country. To her great surprise, she found such a case. It had been uploaded the evening before, in a station in Dublin. Swords of all places. A severed hand found in Swords. There was an irony in there somewhere.

Surely Flynn would have been informed of this discovery by now, yet there had been no mention of it in the report. Again, this didn't surprise her, even though it should have been one of the first things any semi-competent detective would have updated. A severed hand and a body amputated from the wrist. It wasn't rocket science to put two and two together.

She shook her head. Flynn wasn't just a creep. He was also a liability to the case. Too busy worrying about getting his rocks off that he couldn't even take care of the basics. It was clearly true what everyone said – he wouldn't have gotten past training college if it wasn't for his uncle Harry holding his hand.

Concerned they may not yet have been contacted officially, Britney picked up the phone and dialled the number for the station in Swords. After a moment it was answered by a Garda who sounded jaded, as if he had pulled a nightshift and was long overdue to finish.

"That's the case Detective Lyons asked the super to assign him to," the Garda told her after she had explained the reason for her call. "Been upgraded to murder."

"You mean you found a body to match the hand?" She couldn't help feeling disappointed at the coincidence. Two bodies missing a hand was surely a million to one.

"Not exactly. We found a body, but it wasn't missing any hands. She was missing her ears. I believe you guys have the body to go with the hand?" he paused. "We filled Detective Flynn in on all this. Do you not talk to each other down there or what?"

Britney felt stunned. Again, there was no mention of this in the report. "Sorry, yes we do. I was just a little confused. Could I speak to Detective Lyons please?"

"Unfortunately, no," the Garda replied. "He's out of the station at the moment but I'll make sure he's contacted."

"Immediately?" Britney urged.

"Yes. I'll do it now before I finish."

Britney thanked him and was about to hang up but found herself wondering how much effort the Garda would really make. Some of her colleagues could be very protective of their personal time and were loath to do anything above and beyond. This one sounded particularly apathetic and if the end of his shift was due as she assumed, then she wouldn't be surprised if a scribbled note on a post-it was the extent of the effort he made. Bearing that in mind, she requested Detective Lyons full name and number. It would be much easier to call him directly once she got things straight in her head. When the Garda hesitated, she reminded him it was a double homicide they were dealing with and if he didn't cooperate, she'd insist the Garda track down this Lyons fella himself, right away. Britney could almost picture him looking at his watch. A moment later he duly obliged.

Returning her attention to the report her attention was caught by the section referring to the sheets of newspaper found at the scene. Though the originals remained with forensics the report did state they were sports pages from the Independent News. Again, apart from the date of issue and page numbers, no real details were provided. The file did contain a photograph of the bloodied newspaper as it was found, placed directly beneath the hanging body. Her instincts told her this was significant but for the moment she couldn't fathom how.

While pondering this she kept reading and it was then that she spotted an entry that was undoubtedly significant – the name Rourke. The body of Donie Cullen had been found by two groundsmen at the hurling field, one of which was a Mr Alan Rourke. Britney was taken aback by this. It couldn't be a coincidence surely. How many Rourke's were there in the locality? Not so many, she was willing to bet, to negate the possibility that this Alan Rourke and the missing Jim Rourke were somehow related. After all, hadn't Stacey told her Jim Rourke once hurled for the Ballyfeud club. Clicking the keys, she inserted the name of Jim Rourke into the database hoping to find a positive link to Alan Rourke but found no such information currently available.

Feeling frustrated, she sat back in her chair contemplating the significance of a possible connection between the two names. Despite Halley's adamant stance, perhaps she had been right, and Jim Rourke was genuinely missing and not gone on an extended bender which seemed to be the popular theory. Missing, and somehow linked to this murder case? She debated calling Stacey Rourke to confirm the connection, but a disturbing possibility popped into her head and gave her pause for thought. In the unlikely event that the skeleton of a theory churning in her brain proved to be the case, then that poor woman had more than enough on her plate.

She knew that by right she should pass her theory on to Detective Flynn, but she wasn't about to do that. Not after their last confrontation when he mocked her 'amateur efforts' at playing detective regarding the vandalism case. "If you want your name in lights, Kent (his pronunciation deliberately leaning toward a U instead of an E), do the exam. Otherwise leave the serious stuff to the big boys."

No, she wouldn't be telling Detective Flynn anything. Anyway, even if she wanted to, there was no sign of him. Himself and his side-kick Joe were gone again. Had been gone all morning. Not that she was complaining. Their absence gave her the freedom to follow up on what she considered a genuine lead without anyone looking over her shoulder.

"I'm going out for a while," she told Fiona who was stationed at the desk directly across the aisle from her. "You want to tag along?"

Fiona barely looked up from her paperwork. "Can't. I'm swamped with stuff here."

"Doing Flynn's work for him again?"

"Exactly. File this, Fi, file fucking that, Fi," she sniffed. "He thinks I'm his personal fucking secretary. In fact, he just handed me the completed autopsy report on the Cullen man. Told me to go through it and inform him of anything notable before I leave."

"I was wondering when that was going to arrive. Anything of interest?"

"A few things. Cullen's hand was amputated pre-mortem, as we know, by the combination of a hatchet or cleaver, and a serrated blade. Possibly a kitchen knife. It also seems he was strangled before being hanged. By a thin cord or string. Maybe a twine of some sort. The rope used to hang him almost disguised the mark of that original cord but not quite."

"Strangled before being hanged? Now that's interesting. Perhaps the killer wanted to look into his victim's eyes." Britney said. "Watch him die. Up close and personal." 'But why hang him afterwards?' she mused to herself. 'Why the double whammy?'

"Could be. And maybe he liked to hear his screams. Might explain the amputation?"

"And the shattered knee," Britney agreed. "If that was the case, he'd need somewhere private, like a warehouse or something. To ensure his work wasn't disturbed."

"Or somewhere out of the way. Isolated," Fiona suggested. "Either way it would have to be somewhere he could come and go as he pleases."

Britney nodded as she mulled this over. She glanced around looking for Triona Maguire. Garda Maguire, the inhouse IT marvel, was middle-aged with a settled look topped off with a pair of tortoiseshell glasses but there was no sign of her right then.

"When Triona comes back would you ask her to do a search for abandoned buildings. Isolated farmhouses, cabins, warehouses, that kind of thing. And get her to check street and motorway cameras. This man gets from A to B somehow. And gets there quickly, considering what he does in between."

"Should I pass it by Yabba Dabba Doo?"

Britney smiled at Fiona's use of the nickname. "Not if you can help it. Speaking of Flynnstones, did he hand in anything resembling progress on a suspect?"

Fiona shook her head. "Doesn't seem like it from what I'm reading. Looking at the son, I think, but doesn't seem to be a whole lot to back it up. Apart from the lad being a bit of a tramp, by all accounts." She shrugged. "It's early days."

"Anything on our missing man's phone?"

"Still off, I'm afraid. Which is not a good sign, I know," she quickly added in a conciliatory tone on seeing the frown that crossed Britney's features. "Anyway, forget all that for a minute," she urged, her eyes twinkling playfully. "Where are you heading? Off to meet your building site boyfriend for a romantic lunch?" she smiled cheekily. "Followed by a little roll in the hay!"

Britney shook her head in mock weariness. "Just need some fresh air. I won't be long." She didn't like lying to Fiona but thought it better for Fi to know nothing than be considered complicit in her unauthorised absence if Halley happened to pop in.

****

Alan Rourke's house was located approximately twenty minutes outside the city of Oldcastle, but it took Britney almost twice that to find it. Only minutes after leaving the town behind, she found herself surrounded by green fields, rolling hills and overhanging woodland. The roads were narrow. They twisted, turned, and cut back on each other so frequently that for a while she completely lost her bearings. The rain that had fallen the previous day still dampened a surface that was muddy to begin with, causing the car to skid several times as she negotiated the tight bends. At times, her heart was in her mouth as the hedgerows drifted too close for comfort.

Eventually though, after stopping to ask directions from a lady out walking a rather large and vicious looking dog, she found the dwelling she was looking for.

It was a modest house, compared to the others that kept it company along the road. A white, pebble-dash bungalow with a small tarmacadam yard at the front in which a white transport truck was parked, its rear partially blocking the entrance. The name QUINN FOODS was printed on the sides of the white truck in large, red letters. This tallied with what she had read in the report about Alan Rourke working for a food company. At least Flynn had gotten that much right. Parked next to the truck was a grey Nissan Micra, up in years but in pristine condition.

She parked directly behind the truck, then checked for any sign of a dog – the overgrown beast she had spotted on the road had her on high alert. After thoroughly scanning the yard, she decided the coast was clear. She climbed out and cautiously stepped her way to the front door. As she approached it, she noted both the house and the yard were neat and tidy with a pair of potted plants purposefully placed either side of the doorway to add a welcome splash of colour.

The door opened on the second knock and Britney was greeted by a small, grey-haired woman with tired, sad eyes, whom Britney judged to be in her early to mid-sixties.

"Oh, hello Garda," the woman said, her head inclined in surprise. "Can I help you?" Britney noted a hint of trepidation in the woman's voice. The unexpected sight of a Garda uniform at a person's door tended to have that effect but the woman's dour appearance suggested there was far more to it on this occasion. Britney's senses sharpened.

"Hello, I'm Sergeant Kent from Oldcastle Garda Station. I'm looking for Alan. Alan Rourke."

"Alan's my husband," the woman replied. "He's not long back from work. Delivers to restaurants, you see, so starts early. Can I ask what this is about?" There it was again. That strain in her voice. Now matched by a flicker of desperation in her sad eyes. "Is it about our Jim?"

Britney's heart leapt at the mention of the missing man's name. Her instinct had been right. Alan and Jim Rourke were related. 'Our Jim' clearly suggested father and son. It might mean nothing but then again it might mean everything. Britney composed herself. Now that the link was made, she had to tread carefully.

"Yes and no," Britney replied evenly, conscious of the strain the woman was obviously under. She was surely going through the same hell as her daughter-in-law. Possibly worse. It was her child that was missing after all. The son she had given birth to. Britney's heart went out to the poor woman. "I just want to ask Alan some routine questions concerning his discovery at the hurling field on Saturday."

"Oh, I see," she sounded deflated.

Britney sensed she would have welcomed any news about her son then, good or bad. With missing persons, the not knowing was always the worst.

"I think he spoke to detectives about that already."

"I know," Britney smiled reassuringly. "I'm just doing follow up. It won't take long."

The old woman glanced over her shoulder hesitantly before relenting. Britney wondered if she was checking the house was tidy enough for an unannounced visitor or subconsciously seeking affirmation from her husband. She seemed the meek sort.

"Yes, yes, of course. Come on in." The lady stepped aside, allowing Britney to enter then pointed down the hall towards a door at the end.

"He's in there. Watching *The Chase*, I shouldn't think."

"Oh, I love that programme," Britney replied enthusiastically. "The Beast is my favourite."

"Mine too, although Alan loves Frosty Knickers," she forced a weary smile then turned and shuffled in the direction she had pointed, gesturing for Britney to follow. When they reached the door, she paused. "My name is Vera by the way," she said and held out a petite hand for Britney to take. As she accepted it, Britney judged it fragile and cool to the touch. Timid in its grip.

"Hi Vera, as I said, I'm Sergeant Britney Kent."

"Sorry for being so guarded earlier," Vera continued apologetically, "but Alan just hasn't been the same these last few days. Not since Jim disappeared."

"I understand. It must be extremely difficult."

"It is. He's never been gone this long before."

She looked at Britney with imploring eyes.

"I'm sure he'll be fine, Vera," Britney lied, noting the old woman's comment in her head.

Vera nodded slowly. "He will, won't he?" The reply was automatic, but Britney could tell that deep down the poor lady didn't believe the words out of her own mouth. Like her daughter-in-law, she feared the worst. Perhaps even something worse than death?

After a gentle knock, Vera opened the door and led Britney into the sitting room where they found her husband, Alan, sitting with his back to the door. Even though the weather was warm for October, he was warming in front of a coal fire and wearing a heavy jacket which appeared to be part of his work uniform. Contrary to what Vera presumed, he wasn't watching *The Chase* but instead was watching a hurling video that seemed homemade and somewhat dated. Engrossed in the TV as he was, he barely glanced over his shoulder.

"Alan, there's a Garda here to see you," Vera declared once she drew close to him. "A sergeant from Oldcastle." As she spoke, she lay a familiar hand on Alan's shoulder. Reassurance or warning, Britney couldn't tell. On spotting Britney's uniform, he sat up in surprise, then removed his glasses and set them aside on the table.

"Oh, hello," he said hesitantly. "Ahm, come in." He stood and pointed to the seat opposite him. "Hope the fire's not too hot. I know it's mild out, but a cold has gotten into my bones lately."

"It'll be fine, I'm sure," Britney replied as she took the seat offered. "Better hot than cold."

"Can we get you anything – tea, coffee, something stronger?" Recognising the faint slur to his words, he cast a sheepish glance at the tumbler of what looked like whiskey on the table. "I normally wouldn't but…" Like Vera's, his voice also sounded strained.

"I understand," Britney assured him. "It's a difficult time. But I won't join you, thanks." She ensured her tone was business-like. "In fact, I don't plan on keeping you long. As I was telling your wife, I just have a few follow up questions." She glanced at Vera who nodded, then smiling hopefully at Britney, quietly left the room.

As she did so, Britney subtly appraised Alan. He was tall and well-built and quite attractive for an older man. His grey hair was cut short, and his face was clean shaven except for the sideburns that ran about a half inch below the lobes of his ears. He seemed younger than Vera by a number of years although Britney suspected that, even in the short time he'd been missing, the absence of her son had aged Vera substantially more than it had her husband. It was plain to see that Vera was a worrier. What, she wondered, was Alan?

He reached for the remote then turned down the TV as he returned to his chair. Dressed in work clothes and a pair of worn brown boots she didn't see him as a fragile sort. He had a robust look about him. But then a heavy burden of worry can change people.

"That's an old one," Britney observed, nodding toward the video which was still playing on the screen. "All-Ireland Final?" As she proceeded to sit down, she took a notebook and pen from her side pocket and set it on her lap.

Alan shook his head. "Just some old clips of my son playing from when he was younger. I haven't looked at them in years. That's Jim with the blue strap on his leg."

Alan had a deep, well-worn voice that kind of reminded Britney of Kris Kristofferson, one of her father's favourite singers. She had often listened to *Sunday Morning Coming Down* while having breakfast with him of a morning. Thinking of her father gave her a pang in her chest. He was dead five years now, from a heart attack, the doctor said. But the doctor was only half right. His heart had been broken long before the onset of any illness. She would never forgive her mother for that.

"Looks like a fine player," Britney observed even though she'd be the first to admit she wouldn't know one end of a hurley stick from another.

"He was," Alan agreed. "Far better than I ever was even with..." He shook his head then hit the off button on the remote and the TV monitor obediently flickered out as if to say that's the end of that discussion. Returning the remote to the table, he fiddled around for a moment in the manner of a man looking for something he'd misplaced then seeming to realise what he was doing he stopped.

"Sorry," he said, "I used to smoke. So did Jim, in fact. We gave them up at the same time. Back when the ban came in." He shook his head. "Jesus, that was sixteen years ago and I'm still having the craving."

"Stress will always find the weakest point in your defences," Britney observed. "Ice-cream is my thing. Went to town on it when I was in training college and put on two stone. Took me two years to get it off." It was a trivial remark, but she hoped that sharing a confidence would put him at ease.

Britney was glad to see Alan smile in acknowledgement.

"God tests our strength by putting obstacles in our path," he said. "Sometimes we don't even need obstacles. The human race is weak."

"That's certainly true," Britney agreed then leaned forward in the chair, debating in her head whether she should pose the question that was just begging to be asked. While considering this, she glanced around the room. It was neat and cosy, solidly furnished – the couches comfortable but dated, the carpet worn, especially the patch directly under Alan's boots. Britney saw little to suggest even a modicum of wealth. It was a modest room designed and decorated by modest, working-class people.

Dotted along the magnolia-coloured walls were family photos from varying stages of its development, with Jim invariably standing in the middle of the picture and flanked either side by his mother and father. In one he was a little boy with curly blonde hair, in another a gangly teenager, his hair by then darkened to the sandy shade it would remain. At least until the grey started to appear, as portrayed in the picture she had taken from Stacey's house. In general, the photos depicted the Rourke's as a happy family, but Britney knew you could never really tell from photos. To her left were a couple of pictures of hurling teams, the players sporting blue jerseys – the local team colours, Britney presumed. In one, she spotted Jim standing at the back of the group with his arms folded across his chest. In the other, he was kneeling at the front. In both, he looked focused. Ready for battle. Proud.

Apart from these photos, there was a picture of the latest pope whose name she couldn't recall and sitting on the TV was a statue of Madonna and Child. Clearly, a religious household, she decided. Yet, according to Stacey, Jim didn't even go to Mass. 'An act of rebellion?' she wondered.

As she was about to return her attention to Mr Rourke, she noted a rectangular shaped spot on the wall, next to the team photos, which was slightly lighter in colour than the rest of the room, suggesting a frame had recently been taken down and never replaced. She wondered if this might have been one of Jim on his own. She could see no pictures portraying him as a mature man. Perhaps they could no longer stomach to look at him? She thought, while also wondering if perhaps they were conducting a search of their own and using a photo for identification purposes.

Deciding to strike while the iron was hot and perhaps catch Mr Rourke off guard, she flipped open her notebook and asked her question.

"Is Jim weak, Alan?"

A look of what Britney recognised as shame crossed over Alan's face for the briefest moment before it was gone. However, Britney had been watching for the reaction and noted it.

"I thought you were here to ask about Donie Cullen?" he accused.

"I am," Britney replied evenly, "but I'm also here about Jim. As I'm sure you're aware his wife, Stacey, has declared him missing." She fixed her gaze on Rourke's and held it. "Is he missing, Mr Rourke?"

Alan's intense brown eyes flashed angrily, and his fist clenched in frustration, but he forced his voice to remain calm as he sat forward in the chair. "Yes, Sergeant, Jim is missing. We didn't want to make a big deal about it because it wouldn't be the first time he left without a word. But he's never been gone this long. Not since the children."

There it was again. The suggestion that Jim still tended to go missing sometimes. Why had Stacey played that down? Britney wondered. Perhaps she was embarrassed. Or perhaps, as she stated, all that errant carry-on had happened prior to their marriage and with it now being in the past, Stacey simply wanted to leave it there. But then why did both Alan and Vera allude to it now? And earlier Brian Farrell? A smokescreen to buy him time?

"Can you think of anyone who would want to hurt him?"

Alan Rourke shrugged then turned to stare out the window like a man unwilling to face a truth. "Jim had his enemies; I'm not going to deny that. He got into a lot of trouble with the hurling and stuff. Got a name for being a bit of a prima donna so some smart asses gave him a hard time. But that was all behind him. He has Stacey now. And the kids." As he spoke, a shadow crossed over his face only to disappear just as quickly.

"Then if he's not hurt, where do you think he is, Mr Rourke?"

Now Alan glanced down as he nervously ran his hands up and down his thighs. When he looked back up again, he was unable to meet her gaze. "I wish I knew, Sergeant Kent," he said finally. "I wish I knew."

"Ok," Britney said, deciding not to push it, but now feeling certain that Rourke was hiding something. She made a quick note to reflect this in her book.

"Let's talk about Donie Cullen. What connection had he with your son?"

Alan shook his head. "None. At least no more than anyone else in the club. You see Donie Cullen was the treasurer of the club for a number of years. Jim was a young player at the club during that time. That was about the extent of it."

"Did their paths cross for any other reason?"

"No. At least not that I know of." He sat further forward in the chair until now he was perched on the edge of the seat. "Look, if you're somehow trying to tie Jim to this murder, you're crazy. The only person Jim ever hurt was himself, but he got over all that once he settled down with Stacey and the kids."

"Sorry Alan, I don't mean to upset you. I'm just trying to get a handle on things. It's routine."

With that, Alan sat back and seemed to relax a little. Gripping the glass in a robust left hand, he knocked back what was left of the whiskey then set the glass back on the table, wincing as he swallowed the fiery liquid. Britney got the impression he wasn't normally a drinker. Not a whiskey drinker anyway. Sensing that if she pushed too hard on the topic of his son, Rourke was likely to close up like the proverbial clam, Britney tried a change of tack.

"There was another man with you when you found Mr Cullen's body."

"Yes, Timmy Dunne. He helps out in the field."

Britney compared this to the name in her book which she had copied from the case report. It matched.

"Did either of you notice anything strange before you discovered the body?"

"Nothing strange exactly but I thought I saw some movement around the dressing room. We thought it was just kids, but Timmy went to make sure. That's when he spotted Donie's body."

"So, technically it was Timmy that discovered the body?"

"Yes, I suppose so. When he first saw the body, he thought it was Jim." Alan shook his head. "I knew it couldn't be because Jim wouldn't do a cowardly thing like that, but Timmy Dunne never thought much of our Jim."

"Oh?" Britney's eyebrows raised. "Why do you say that?"

Alan shrugged. "He was always saying Jim let the club down. Too lazy to train and stuff like that."

"Stuff like that?" Britney pushed.

"He considered Jim a troublemaker. A prima donna," Alan sighed in frustration then shot her a pointed look. "Maybe you should ask him why he didn't like my son?"

Britney met his eyes for a moment. He used the past tense, she noted. Didn't like, not doesn't like. Does Alan Rourke already believe his son is dead? Perhaps dead to him.

"Ok, I will," she nodded her head reassuringly. "Now, back to the discovery of the body. Did either of you see anything else?"

Alan shook his head. "Look, I went over all this with those detectives."

"I know, Mr Rourke," Britney forced a reassuring smile, "but as I said I'm just following up. Now, where were you and Timmy Dunne before the movement caught your attention."

"I was fixing the nets on the goals. Timmy was marking lines on the field. There was a match fixed for the next day."

"Had both of you a clear sight of the changing rooms?"

"Yes."

"Any idea then how someone dragged Mr Cullen into the room, killed him, hung him up and cut off his hand without either of you hearing or seeing anything?"

Britney watched Alan closely. She had deliberately mixed up the sequence of events. The hand had been cut off pre-mortem, not post, something which anyone involved with the crime would surely have been aware of, but Alan didn't so much as blink. He simply shook his head.

"None," he replied thoughtfully. "That puzzled me too. There is a second door to the rear of the building but even so, it would have taken the killer quite a while to do what he did. And he had to have come in through the main gate. Still, neither of us noticed a thing." He shrugged. "But then we were a good distance from the changing rooms."

"Could you see the gate from where you worked?" Britney asked.

Alan paused to think about that. "No, actually. The changing rooms block the view. Maybe Timmy could see. But it's impossible to see the gates from where I was."

"And I presume they weren't locked?"

"No. We only lock them when we're leaving. But they were closed."

"Who arrived first?"

"We arrived together. I usually pick Timmy up, but Vera was very upset that evening, so to gain a little more time with her I asked him to call for me. We closed the gate once we were inside. It's a habit."

Britney nodded. That was as she expected. The pair came to work on the field and closed the gate behind them. According to the Garda report, it was also closed when the first Gardaí arrived. Still, working down on the field as they were, anyone could have driven in past Alan and Timmy unnoticed and driven out a few minutes later, reclosing the gate. She made a note of these details before moving on to her next question.

"Could it be possible that the body was there before you arrived?"

"No. We always clean the dressing rooms first thing. They were empty."

"Did you lock them after cleaning them?"

"No. We leave the doors open a little to let some fresh air through."

"So, it would be fair to say that whoever did this knew in advance that the gates might be closed but the rear door would most likely be open?"

Alan nodded pensively. Threw a wary glance at Britney.

"What I'm trying to get at Mr Rourke, is that whoever did this was clearly someone who knew the run of the place."

"Probably," Alan agreed reluctantly, "but an awful lot of people know the run of that place." The latter was added a touch defensively.

Britney nodded then offered a smile hoping to encourage Alan to relax. He had opened up a little with the less personal line of questioning, so Britney decided it was time to cut a little closer to the bone once more.

"Jim would know the run of the place, wouldn't he?"

Alan's face instantly clouded over. He looked at her as if she had just stabbed him in the back. "No more than anyone else involved in the club," he retorted. "We have over two hundred members."

Britney made a show of adding another note in her little book. There may be two hundred members but at the moment, she was interested in only one. She hesitated before asking the next question as she sensed Mr Rourke was reaching the end of his tether. "What was your relationship with Jim like?"

Alan sighed impatiently then let his eyes drift out the window again as if the sight of the sergeant was getting too much. "It was good," he replied eventually. "We had a good relationship. Oh, we had ups and downs like any father and son but nothing we couldn't deal with. He was always a good boy, despite what people might say."

Britney noted a hint of bitterness in his latter words but let it pass. "And what was his relationship like with Donie Cullen?"

Now, Alan puffed his cheeks and stood up.

He had enough. Britney cursed silently. She had pushed too far.

"Look, if you ask me, some crazy killed Donie Cullen. Some nut job that should be in the mad house. Or else the husband of one of those women he was shagging."

"You mean Cullen was having an affair?" Britney replied as she stood to face him. There was no mention of that in the report.

"An affair? That's a joke. He used to run around like a bloody tomcat in heat. Known to have a couple of kids on the wrong side of the blanket."

This was news. From what she had read, the son Toby was the deviant. Like father, like son, she supposed. Still, she didn't think this was a crime of passion. Not of the sexual kind anyway. However, she pursed her lips as if considering this new possibility.

"He may very well have had a number of women on the go, Mr Rourke, but it does leave us with an obvious question. If he was killed over an affair, why hang him in the dressing rooms of a hurling field? And not just any hurling field but the same hurling grounds you happen to be caretaker of. And why cut off his hand?" If the killer was a disgruntled husband, Britney reasoned, he'd surely cut off something more telling. The same applied to a disgruntled wife or lover.

Alan shrugged. "I've no idea."

"But you do see the problem I face?"

"Yes," he glowered at her. "You think Jim killed that man and hung him in the dressing room for me to find. To in some way punish me for some ill-treatment or other. And now Jim is on the run."

Britney remained silent for a moment, allowing the possibility hang in the room. As she watched him closely, Alan Rourke closed his eyes and ran a hand over his face in obvious frustration. When he opened them again, his expression had turned cold. "I'd like you to leave now, Sergeant. Please. Before I say or do something I'd regret."

Britney nodded reflectively. Thanking Mr Rourke for his time, she pushed herself out of the chair. As she exited the room, she glanced around to see him following close behind as if to make sure she left. He remained on her heels as she turned down the hall, hunting her silently, like a towering shadow, the soft tap of his boots on the tile not the only hint of his presence. The anger emanating from him was so palpable that she felt glad to reach the door.

There, next to a holy water font, she noted another picture hanging, the colour of this one faded with age. It consisted of two men standing side by side and smiling broadly. One of the men, whom she didn't recognise, was dressed in a fisherman's waterproof coat, secured at the waist with a length of twine. The deep hood of the coat was pulled back from his face as he proudly held up a large fish for the camera. The other man, clearly a younger Mr Rourke, was holding a pair of fishing rods and a net. He had a calm air about him and certainly looked happy then. Casting a furtive glance in his direction, Britney noted he looked a completely different man now. She couldn't blame him for that.

Having caught up with her, he reached past her to open the door and she got a whiff of the sweet whiskey he was drinking. And the smokes he claimed himself and his son had given up.

The meaning of the open door was clear, but Britney stubbornly ignored the backhanded invitation. Having spotted no sign of Vera on the way out, she asked that Rourke thank his wife on her behalf. Then apologising for the interruption, she assured Mr Rourke they were doing their best to find his son. The grunt she received in return told her he wasn't impressed. With that, she stepped outside but paused one last time to ask for Timmy Dunne's address. Alan Rourke glowered at her for a moment before nodding toward the photograph of himself and the other man.

"That's him there in the photo you were looking at. His wife left him some years ago after his son was injured in an accident, so he'll be on his own. If he's not at home, he'll be gone fishing."

Having imparted that bit of information he followed up with the address, then closed the door in her face. It was a discourtesy that didn't bother her. She had gotten what she came for, and more along with it. Far more. She passed out by the truck and quickly got into her car, then sat back and tried to put her thoughts in order. If her reading of Alan Rourke was right, then his son Jim was more than just a missing person. Of that much she was certain. As she turned the key, the engine struggled to turn over, kind of like the predominant thought in her head.

Was Jim Rourke a terrified witness or a cold-blooded killer?

****

The turnoff to Timmy Dunne's house was ten minutes further along the road. He lived at the end of a long, narrow lane in a small, white-washed cottage, with a slate roof, a red half-door, and small up and down windows. Though in need of some attention, the house was as cute a building as Britney ever did see. With some structural repairs and a touch up of paint here and there, she could easily picture it being the photo of choice on any Irish tourism brochure or website. It was typical of those select images which, over the years had drawn Americans in their droves to the Irish countryside in search of their heritage – a quaint cottage, a horse and cart, an old woman in a shawl weaving a basket. In this case, however, there was no horse and cart or any sign of an old woman. In fact, she could see no sign of anyone at all as she approached.

At the front of the cottage, there was a small gravel yard that ran down the side of the house. There, semi-disguised by an overgrown hedge, was an old Ford Cortina that looked like it had seen better days. Beyond the car, the gravel continued, leading to what looked like an untidy back. Though still charming, it was clear to see that lately, the place had become starved of a woman's touch. Would the man appear the same? Britney wondered as she drove in over the crunching gravel then parked her patrol car just inside the entrance.

When she got out and looked around, she had a sudden sense of unease. Although only ten minutes from the Rourke's, the property carried a greater sense of isolation, enclosed on three sides as it was by scrub and overhanging pine trees. The narrow lane that she had just navigated seemed to be the only obvious entry. Judging by the lane's neglected appearance – overgrown hedges and thick grass sprouting between rutted wheel tracks, there was little reason to believe the place was regularly visited by anyone apart from its owner, and Alan Rourke of course. Nor were there any neighbouring houses visible from where she stood.

'Should I be here alone,' she wondered. 'If something happens, I'm totally screwed. I could scream but I'd be heard by nothing only squirrels.' Dismissing the feeling as paranoia, she pushed the negative thoughts away. She only had a few questions and then she was out of there.

"Hello?" she called while moving toward the house. "Anyone home?" She reached the door and knocked. No answer. She then took a moment to peer through a pair of grubby front windows, one either side of the door, but saw no sign of life inside.

"Hello," she called again, louder now as she left the windows and moved to the side of the house to make her way out the back. She was halfway down the gable end by the time she could see past the building to the end of the half-acre haggard that constituted the rear of the property. She spotted several broken-down cars strewn about under the trees along with an assortment of spare parts. There was no sign of anything that constituted a garage, so she guessed the man fancied himself as a bit of a grease mon-key in his spare time.

"Hello." A hint of trepidation had crept into her voice.

The thick trees blocked out the light to such an extent that the haggard was a haven of mottled shadow. Peering from light into shade Britney had to squint to see clearly.

After a moment, her eyes adjusted allowing her to spot a man there, working in the shadows beneath a small lean-to building located at the base of a broad pine tree. He was wearing one of those distinctive bucket hats that outdoorsy people wore to keep off the rain.

Britney stopped short of the shadows. "Timmy? Tim-my Dunne?"

On hearing her voice, the man stopped what he was doing and turned around. When he spotted Britney, he held up a hand and waved her over then reached for his mouth and removed the cigarette he was puffing on, flicking it with his thumb, sending it flying into the grass to die. As she got closer, Britney could see he was indeed the fisherman she had earlier noted in the photo on Alan Rourke's wall. Along with the hat, he was also wearing a leather apron and was holding a long knife in his hand. According to Fiona's reading of the Medical Examiner's report, one of the instruments used to amputate Cullen's hand was a large knife with a serrated edge. This knife had a serrated edge, she noted uneasily, perfect for sawing through flesh. The next thing she noted was that the brown apron the man was wearing was streaked in blood. It was a sight that stopped her in her tracks.

"Is everything ok, Mr Dunne?" she asked, warily. She was suddenly conscious of the fact that she was totally unarmed. She found her utility belt uncomfortable while driving, and though it went against all good practice, tended to remove some of the bulkier items meaning her baton remained in the car. The security of a gun was way beyond her pay grade.

'Shit,' she thought, 'no one even knows I'm here. He could cut me up and eat me for lunch and no one would be the wiser.'

Stepping out from under the roof, Timmy Dunne seemed to draw the shadows with him before stalling as he noticed Britney's reaction. His eyes followed her stare down to his apron then after a moment he smiled sheepishly on realising how he must look.

"All's good, Garda. Just gutting a few fish." He had a flat accent, typical of the people of the area. "They're legal

I swear. Caught by my own rod down at the weir. I have a licence if that's what you're after?"

Britney relaxed a little, silently chiding herself for being such a, well, such a Britney. "Do you fish often?" Again, using small talk to make him feel at ease. Herself too.

He shrugged. "I hit the river once, maybe twice a week. Sell what I catch to the restaurants in Oldcastle. Get a good price for it too if I have it skinned and gutted."

'So, you're pretty damn handy with that knife, then,' Britney mused to herself.

"As I said, I have a licence."

"I'm sure you have, Mr Dunne but I'm not here to check your fishing licence. I'm just here to ask a few questions about your discovery of Mr Cullen's body. My name is Sergeant Kent."

On hearing her explanation, he put the knife down next to an open bottle of stout that stood on a small table sheltering under the lean-to then he wiped his hands in some old newspaper that lay close to hand on the table. "Ok. But I don't know what I can tell you that I didn't tell the others." His hands now clean he tossed the paper into a bin located just outside the lean-to then picked up the bottle of stout and took a slug. "Seems like you lot have a left hand that don't know what your right is up to half the time." Once he had spoken, he seemed to realise the pun in his words. "Sorry, I didn't mean anything smart by that." His apology was accompanied by a wry smile which suggested he enjoyed the pun all the same.

As he spoke, Britney tried to get a read on the man. He wasn't quite as tall as Rourke and leaner, yet the thick galoshes and apron he wore gave the impression he was broader than he looked. She couldn't see his hair beneath the low sitting hat, but he was unshaven, his stubbly beard shadowing his florid face with shades of salt and pepper. Like the house, he could benefit from a woman's touch.

Her first impression was of a simple, pastoral man, living a simple, pastoral life. And living it alone now that his wife and son had gone. Harmless enough, surely. But then history is littered with psychopaths and serial killers that had seemed harmless enough. Seeming harmless actually gave them an edge. People tended to feel at ease with such individuals and let their guard down, the notorious Ted Bundy being a case in point. How many victims had he to his name? How many had paid the ultimate price for their misplaced trust? Still, no matter what way she looked at it, she couldn't see Timmy Dunne slicing anything more than the fish he caught in the weir.

"It's just some follow up," Britney explained, then proceeded to ask similar questions to the ones she'd previously put to Alan Rourke. The answers he provided were more or less along the same lines. "According to Alan, you arrived at the grounds together. Was that the case?"

Timmy nodded. "Yes. Alan was running late so I tipped over in the Cortina and picked him up. This thing with Jim has him out of kilter."

Britney had her notebook out again, making note of his replies. "On arrival you got straight to work?"

Timmy Dunne nodded.

"And who cleaned the changing rooms?"

"He took one. I took the other."

"Who took the one in which the body was later found?"

"I did."

"And you saw nothing unusual, obviously?"

Timmy shook his head.

"Alan neither?"

"Mentioned nothing to me. The only unusual thing I saw was the side window. It was broken the day before," he shrugged. "Probably just kids."

Or the killer paving the way, Britney thought. "I presume both you and Alan have keys to the building?"

He nodded. "Along with certain members of the committee."

"What about Donie Cullen. Did he have a key?"

"Could have had." He shrugged. "I'm only the help."

"I see." Not that it mattered. If the body wasn't there when they arrived, then it had to have been delivered sometime between their arrival and the time Timmy Dunne discovered the butchered remains. Whoever did it must have timed it perfectly to get in and out without being seen. And they must have nerves of steel, Britney concluded.

To pinpoint Dunne's exact positioning during the approximate time of the event, she asked, "I presume you were within sight of Alan Rourke at all times?"

Timmy pursed his lips and shrugged. "Not all the time. I went to the toilet at one stage. And a while after that the lawnmower broke down, so Alan went to the storage shed for a replacement belt."

"How far away is that shed?"

"The furthest end of the grounds." Seeing the calculating look on Britney's face, he gave a rueful shake of his head. "But I know what you're thinking. I wasn't out of his sight long enough to do what was done to Cullen. I mean, to hang him up and butcher him like that must have taken time. A lot of time."

Not if he was already dead and butchered, Britney thought, and the light fitting manipulated to suit the killer's purpose. The report had stated that the fitting had been unscrewed and the rope tied to a timber joist. Gaining entry to prepare this could explain the reason for the broken window. Would Dunne break a window if he had a key? As a decoy perhaps?

"I couldn't do that anyway," Dunne continued dispiritedly. "Hard enough to gut a fish."

"I'm sure you couldn't," Britney agreed routinely. However, she had noted that he referred to the dead man by his last name which gave the impression he had not been too fond of him. Still, she felt it was a moot point. The more she thought about it the more she was convinced it would have been nigh on impossible for either himself or Alan Rourke to magically produce Cullen's body, hang it from the light fitting and stage the scene without the other noticing.

Unless they were in it together, of course. She dismissed this idea almost as quickly as she thought it. They were simple men, leading simple lives. And even if they wanted to kill Donie Cullen, why stage the scene at the field? It only served to drag them into the investigation. And what possible connection could either of them have to the Dublin murder? She shook her head. They mixed in completely different circles to the deceased reporter. No, there had to be a third party involved, she reasoned. Someone who had planned this down to the last detail. And with connections to both victims.

Britney asked some further questions she thought pertinent to this line of enquiry, all the while noting the answers in her notebook. Timmy soon grew weary of the interrogation, something he made clear when answering in a rather blunt tone. "No, I have no idea how the killer could have gotten in and out without either of us seeing him, but he must have. Otherwise, Donie Cullen would be still alive, wouldn't he?"

"I suppose he would," Britney readily agreed. Despite her benign impression of the man, she wasn't about to start arguing the possibilities with someone who chopped up fish in a shed at the end of his garden. With a serrated knife. Though coincidental, as she now believed that to be.

"Yes, he would," Timmy asserted. "Not cold as ice like he was."

"You mean you touched him?" Britney asked in surprise. She hadn't read any reference to that in the report. Just that both his and Alan Rourke's fingerprints had been found in the changing room but that was to be expected. They had reason to be there on a daily basis. The omission bothered Britney. If something as significant as an individual being in contact with the murder victim's body was left out, then what else was missed? Any detective worth their salt would have highlighted the possibility of transference. What if a hair was found on the body or something as simple as a fabric thread and it later came to light that it belonged to Mr Dunne?

"Yes. Didn't disturb anything, mind. Once I got over the shock I went in and checked for a pulse. But he was as dead as those fish I've been gutting."

"Did Mr Rourke also touch the body?"

Timmy shook his head. "Don't think so. Not sure if he even went into the room. He just stood there staring. Staring and praying. Lord have mercy on his soul, he kept saying. It could easily have been his son, you see. In fact, I thought it was at first. I honestly thought it was Jim."

"Alan mentioned that," Britney acknowledged, now focusing on Dunne's weathered face. "He said you don't think much of his son. Is that true?"

Timmy hesitated. Glanced back at the half-gutted fish on the table. When his grey eyes returned, they were hard to read. "It's not that I don't think much of him. It's just a hurling thing. He could have a bit of an attitude when it came to training, you see. I thought he was always letting the other players down. Doing his own thing. Disappeared to America one season, leaving us high and dry. Even considered himself too good to pay the club membership. Then he went and gave it up altogether even though he was still young. We might have won the Club Championship if he'd played. Gone down in history."

"So, it's nothing personal then?"

Timmy shook his head dismissively. "Nah. Just hurling is all."

"In Oldcastle that could be deemed as very personal."

He forced a smile. "Perhaps, but apart from that, I've nothing against Jim Rourke."

Britney was pleased to note he used the present tense.

With that he turned away and picked up a sharpening stone and began to hone his knife.

Britney got the message.

She left him then to meld back into the shadows and return to the slicing of his fish.

****

Her route back to Oldcastle took her past the hurling field, and with her mind full of questions, she decided to take the opportunity to stop and survey the scene.

The gates were closed but remained unlocked giving clear access to any investigating team that wished to enter. They were, however, wrapped in crime-scene tape to ward off any nosy parkers. She removed the tape, opened them, drove in, got out and walked around the grounds. She noted the positions of the doors to the changing rooms and where the groundsmen claimed they were working. Gauged their viewpoints in relation to the gates, the shed, which was quite a distance away, and the back door of the changing rooms. Satisfied their story held true, she turned her attention to the interior layout of the building. Finding the door locked she was forced to peer through the broken window. Standing on tiptoe she could see the changing rooms shared an internal hallway giving access to shower cubicles and the back door. With the building facing down onto the field, the back door was actually facing the road. And the gates.

After due consideration, she concluded it was possible. Difficult but possible. Someone could have entered unnoticed. However, to pull it off, the perpetrator must have had comprehensive knowledge of the grounds. Or perhaps used Donie Cullen's knowledge?

She returned to the car, and though a further delay risked incurring Halley's wrath, she drove the short distance to the Cullen's neighbourhood with a view to following up on an omission she had noted in the case report. Interviewing the victim's neighbours was the kind of tedious chore Flynn would do anything to avoid which explained why it had been put on the long finger. Believing that one way or another, she would eventually have been landed with the job, and most likely from the confines of her desk, she spent the next two-hours interviewing neighbours, family and friends of the deceased man.

As sometimes can be the case with rural communities, they proved a tight-lipped bunch with little light to shed on the investigation. By her fifth interview, she had become wearily convinced she was doing little more than dotting the i's and crossing the t's. That was until she popped into the local shop to pick up a late lunch comprised of a tuna sandwich and a can of Sprite. She needed the sugar rush. If the rest of the neighbours proved reticent, the heavy-set shopkeeper did enough talking for the lot of them. Britney wasn't complaining, especially when the lady happened to recall spotting Jim Rourke's van at the field a week or two before the killing. Perhaps on a recon mission, Britney reasoned, her outlook perking up no end.

"How can you be sure it was his van?"

"He used to pop in here after practice back in the days when he was playing, two or three times a week, for a coke and a sandwich. It was definitely his van. I remember wondering if he was coming back playing again. He might be getting on a bit, but we could do with him," she said while she spread a thin coat of light mayonnaise on a slice of spelt bread, as per Britney's instructions.

"You know it doesn't bear thinking about," the shopkeeper continued in a more philosophical tone, "and that's why I didn't say anything before. But those two hated each other, you know. Jim Rourke and Cullen."

"Is that right?"

"Oh yeah. Sworn enemies they were. For years. In fact, they'd a right bust-up awhile back outside the pub next door. The shouting and roaring kept me head off the pillow." She paused to glance questioningly at Britney. "Salad?"

Britney nodded. "You hardly know what it was all about?" she was about to ask but the shopkeeper got there before her.

"I heard it started with the son, Toby. A right troublemaker that one. Always needling the young Rourke chap. Usually about hurling. By the time it was over, Toby had a black eye for himself, and the father had been landed on his arse. Not that I was complaining." She wrapped the sandwich and placed it on the counter next to the Sprite. "Four euro fifty," she smiled dutifully.

Britney paid then thanked her for her help and turned for the door.

"I know it's terrible what he did but part of me wouldn't blame Jim Rourke, you know," the lady called after her as she left. "Them Cullens opened their mouths once too often, if you ask me."

As she got back into her car and headed for home, Britney was more convinced now than ever that scumbag or not, Toby Cullen had nothing to do with his father's death. Nor had any of his neighbours. Unless the shopkeeper talked him to death.

Chapter 8

Once he made it outside of Peter Holmes' office in Dublin's central hospital, Danny took a moment to compose himself. Placing his head on his arms, leaning over the roof of the car, he drew in a deep breath and let it out slowly. Thankfully, the heavy weather that caused the rain of previous days had moved on, leaving the evening air cool and fresh. Then again if it was still raining, he mightn't have noticed.

"Jesus," he said, "we're dealing with an animal."

Holmes had once again gone over the details of the killing, confirming asphyxiation as the cause of death, but not from being hanged. "I would expect to see fracture of the upper cervical spine if she had died from hanging. Therefore, I think Miss Cox had been strangled beforehand," he informed them while drawing their attention to a tiny piece of nylon fibre he'd uncovered embedded in her neck. It matched the fibre used to tie her hair. He'd also found traces of trichloromethane in her blood. "Chloroform to lay people," he explained. Which might support the idea that she was killed elsewhere.

"No, not an animal," Lyons replied as he followed Danny out through the door, leaving the morbid sight that was Marie Cox's frigid body to the attuned senses of Holmes and his forensics unit. "A psychopath possibly, or a sociopath. Either way, the man we're after is controlled and organised. A controlled and organised sadist."

Danny nodded. "Sadist, yes. I can see that. But controlled and organised?" He shook his head. "He's a butcher. He butchered that poor woman."

"Yes, he did. But I think everything he did was for a reason and not just for the pleasure of the act itself. He's taking whatever he cuts. Just like he took that hand. Inflicting pain is part of it, but to cause pain is not the end goal, I don't think. At least not the only end goal." Outside at last, Lyons lit up another cigar, the stench of it carrying on the breeze and very nearly making Danny's already tested stomach heave.

"What is the end goal, then? To deliver what he takes to some other poor unfortunate, then butcher them as well?" He shook his head in dismay. "Jesus. I hope not. I hope this is the end of it." But even as he wished it, Danny knew that wouldn't be the case.

"Not just any poor unfortunate," Lyons surmised. "I think they were chosen for a reason. Just like the murder scene was staged for a reason. Therefore, they must be connected – Miss Cox and the man in Oldcastle. And by more than a severed hand." He looked across at Danny who had moved round to the driver's side of the car and opened the door. "You look like you could do with a stiff drink. I know the perfect place. The Sheep's Head. It might be a different world but it's only a few streets away."

"Shouldn't we go back to the station first, sir?"

"We should," Lyons acknowledged. "But we're not going to. I need to think. And I do my best thinking with a beer in my hand. Anyway, if I brought you back to the station looking like some sick puppy again, they'd have me accused of child abuse as well as everything else." He puffed the cigar. "I take it you do drink?"

"Yes, sir."

"There you go then."

Danny wasn't about to argue. After what he'd experienced over the last few days, a stiff drink was exactly what the doctor ordered. Maybe two.

Standing outside the Sheep's Head Tavern Danny was even more convinced the hole in the window was caused by a bullet. He could clearly see the circular profile where the projectile had entered causing a football-sized area of glass directly below it to crack. Roughly positioned at head height, Danny wondered if the projectile had hit its target. He couldn't recall hearing about a shooting on Main Street but then it wouldn't be the first gunshot on the North Side to have gone unreported.

Up close the tavern was every bit as grubby as it had previously appeared from the car but once again, he could see plenty of customers inside. On reaching the steel front door, they found it closed with no handle readily apparent to open it. However, Lyons seemed to expect this. He located a buzzer fixed to the wall next to the doorjamb and pressed it. Then he waited.

"There's a camera inside," he explained. "Watching us right now. To keep us pigs out," he stated, "and the protestants. They really hate protestants."

"Then what about a black pig?" asked Danny. "Who also happens to be a protestant?"

"They shoot them," Lyons replied casually with a pointed glance at the hole in the window, "but seeing as you're with me…" he added dryly.

After a moment or two the door buzzed open, inviting them in. Lyons entered with Danny hesitantly following behind, wondering what kind of place Lyons was dragging him into. Was it a drug haven? Or an IRA haunt? Perhaps a mixture of both seeing as how the New IRA had started dabbling in the drug business. Seemingly, dealing was how they were financing themselves these days; something, it was reported, that turned the stomachs of the older, more idealistic republicans.

Once inside, the door clicked closed behind them bringing to Danny's mind The Eagles hit lyrics, *you can check out anytime you want but you can never leave.* Glancing around, he wondered if there was a back door out of the place or if that was barred up as well.

"You look almost as green as you did earlier," Lyons remarked.

"Not my usual kind of place, sir," Danny replied, as he glanced around, distaste clearly displayed on his face.

The bar was dimly lit and smelled to Danny of a sickly mixture of body odour, stale beer, farts, and cigarette smoke, kind of like Lyons' office, in fact. As if determined not to restrict the pollution to the olfactory, it was noisy too with sports commentary blaring from a telly which hung from a steel bracket above the faux-mahogany bar. The crowd that gathered in front of the telly was surprisingly large for a weekday, especially considering the state of the place. It was as close to falling down as a building could come, Danny reckoned, without actually caving in. Warped floors, plaster falling off the walls and a ceiling that bowed so low in places he could almost hit his head off it. Beige was the dominant colour whether that was because of the natural tone of the paint or the fact that it was tarnished by the thick smoke that hung in the air, Danny couldn't tell. 'No wonder Lyons liked the place,' he thought. The concept of the smoking ban hadn't seeped quite this low yet, either.

"It's not exactly The Ritz," Lyons agreed, "but they serve the best pint in town."

"I bet you can get more than a pint, sir," Danny remarked throwing a wary glance at a group of men drinking close to the bar. Some in tracksuits and runners, some in working man's clothes, they all had a hard, inner-city edge about them. Their beady eyes were watching Danny even as he watched them. The shaven headed man standing closest to Danny had an angry scar running down his face. He looked like he'd carry out a hit just for the fun of it. Wouldn't think twice about chopping off a hand.

"Yeah, peace," Lyons replied. "No one gives a shit who you are in here as long as you're getting pissed like the rest of them. Which suits me fine. But there's also information to be had. The kind of people who drink in here keep their ear to the ground, so if there's a drug connection to that severed hand, someone'll know about it. They'll talk too because they know me. Trust me. At least they would if you could take that disgusted look off your face and pretend you fit in."

"Fair enough," Danny replied, kind of liking the idea. It was almost as if they were undercover.

"What's the real story with the camera, sir?"

"This used to be an IRA bolthole. If they spotted someone that they didn't trust at the door," Lyons allowed himself a smirk, "like, say a black protestant, they'd refuse to open it. The new owners kept it on to use if the Gardaí ever decided to raid it for after hours." He inclined his head. "More or less obsolete after I started drinking here, something for which they show their appreciation from time to time." He tapped his temple as if to say, 'using my brains, son.'

"And the hole in the window?"

Lyons shrugged. "I never claimed to drink with angels. Just relax and keep your ears open." He glanced toward the bar. "Pint of Guinness? Or are you one of these new-fangled gin types?"

"Guinness is fine."

The barman was a short thin man with a beak-like nose and eyes that watched everything reminding Danny of a bird of prey. Not an eagle but a kite or a kestrel. He had a large tattoo of a Celtic cross on his neck and more ink running down his bony arms. His t-shirt declared, 'I don't do cocaine, but it smells amazing.' He didn't look all that pleased to see Lyons but then he didn't look all that displeased either. His avian features were that hard to read. Perfect for the place he was in.

"Back again, Richie?" he said as he approached Lyons. "I thought you'd have enough of it after last night. You were here this morning too, I heard."

"Yeah. Needed a cure. And now I need to take the edge of. Had a hell of a few days."

"I heard there was a murder alright. You involved in that?" Benny smiled unashamedly on realising how his question sounded. "In the investigation, I mean."

Lyons sniffed at the joke. "You could say that. Did you hear anything else?"

Benny shot a glance at the men at the bar then shook his head. "Just that it was pretty gruesome. Usual?"

Lyons nodded. "Make it two. With a large whiskey."

Benny pulled the Guinness then left them on the counter to settle as he turned to fill a measure of whiskey from an optic fixed to the wall behind him. Once full, he set the whiskey down in front of Lyons. It had barely touched the countertop before Lyons enveloped it in his big hand and knocked it back. Danny could almost see the tension ease on Lyons' face as the fiery liquid hit the spot. Setting the glass down, he paid Benny for the drinks who then topped up the pints and set them on the counter alongside the empty whiskey tumbler. As he did so, a quiet word passed between them that Danny couldn't quite hear over the noise of the TV. However, he did spot Benny's nod even if it was barely perceptible. Without another word, Benny turned his attention to the next customer while Lyons casually picked up the pint in front of him as if nothing of note had just taken place.

"Cheers," he said to Danny. "Get that inside your shirt."

Danny found himself smiling wistfully. "That's what my step-father used to say," he said as he raised his glass. "He was a Guinness drinker too."

"Was?"

"Yeah. He passed away three years ago. Sixty-nine years old and running like a Nissan when suddenly, he just keeled over. My mother's still alive, though. Thank God."

"Family support is important," Lyons agreed, "especially in this line of work. Relationships too, although they can be tough. Any girlfriend on the scene. Or fella?" He shrugged. "You just don't know these days."

"Not at the moment, sir. Girlfriend, I mean," Danny added quickly. It was ridiculous he knew but for some reason he could feel himself blushing. Perhaps because it had been so long since he'd had a girlfriend, he wasn't sure himself anymore.

Lyons didn't seem to notice. His eyes were scanning the back of the room. After a moment he pointed to a table near the rear of the bar, the only one available that Danny could see. Possibly because it was near to the toilets, which, he presumed were even less aromatic than the rest of the place.

"It's away from the telly," Lyons observed, "so, at least we'll be able to hear ourselves think." Without waiting for a reply, he enveloped his pint in his huge hand, then headed off in that direction. Again, Danny had little choice but to follow. That, or fall prey to the glowering patrons.

As he passed by the TV – the only item that looked modern in the entire place, Danny saw that the game being played was a replay of a drawn hurling match from the previous weekend. Dublin vs Wexford. The small crowd that had gathered in front of the TV were quite animated especially when it came to abuse for the referee. He was clearly a bastard, a dick, and every other degrading classification a person could think of. As were all belonging to him.

Danny was working his way past the group, holding his pint of Guinness aloft to avoid overly exuberant arms, when he noticed a gaunt man perched upon a high stool near the door, seemingly watching the match, yet aloof from the others. He was wearing a grubby hoodie and jeans, and a pair of thick-soled brown shoes that had seen better days. His attire could be interpreted as a direct representation of the man himself, him being gaunt, unshaven and with his eyes sunken in his head giving him a hunted look. Was it the tall man he had seen Lyons with previously? Danny thought so.

Once they'd settled at the table, they each took a couple of slugs of stout and let it ease down. Moments passed before either spoke.

"So," Lyons said, his expression remaining as serious as usual, but Danny noted a playful twinkle in the man's eye. It was the most relaxed Danny had ever seen him. "Back to your boyfriend?" Danny sensed the detective wanted to enjoy his pint without talking about the case. That suited Danny just fine.

"Funny, sir," Danny replied dryly then took another gulp of his beer. He decided to turn the tables. "Have you anybody, sir? A wife?" he asked. Then, tongue in cheek, he added, "Or a husband maybe?"

Lyons snorted derisively, but at the same time his eyes narrowed, emphasising the lines in his forehead.

"Call me a homophobe if you want but I believe in Adam and Eve. Not Adam and Adam." As if to underline the point he took a long draw of stout then reached into his jacket pocket and withdrew the packet of cigars. He pulled one out and lit it without so much as a guilty glance around.

"As you might have guessed, they don't give a shit about rules in here," he said when he saw Danny eyeing the cigar.

"That's why you fit in so well, then, sir?"

Lyons snorted a laugh just as a roar went up drawing his attention to the telly. "You know I used to hurl once, back in the day." He took a puff of the cigar.

"So, I believe, sir. Heard you were good too."

Lyons ignored the compliment. "It was a different game from what those fellas play. It was a man's game then, first time hurling and pure stickwork. You had to win your own ball. None of that running into space shite and expecting someone to pass it to ya. And it was tough." He allowed himself a wry smile at the memories. "In my day, a player was only sent off for aggravated assault or murder."

"Sounds like fun," Danny observed dryly. "Might explain the state of your knees."

Lyons shrugged. "Yeah, I took a few belts in my time, but that's the way it was then. No physio like these days. That's one thing that's changed for the better, I suppose. The rest," he curled his lip in distaste. "It's a running game now. If you get the ball, you run with it. Or you pass it to someone else and they run with it. Run, run, run. That's not hurling. That's relay racing. In proper hurling you let the ball do the work and stand toe-to-toe with your man. Not run away from him every chance you get." He took a slug of his pint. "It was the best game in the world, but they've ruined it now. I suppose it reflects the way the whole country has gone."

It occurred to Danny that Lyons seemed as comfortable in himself as he'd ever seen him. Certainly, far more talkative than normal. Was it the familiar surroundings or simply the fact that he had a beer in his hands? And another few in his belly from that morning if Benny was to be believed.

"Anyway," Lyons continued, "the point is, I used to hurl. And yes, I was good. Got a call up to the Oldcastle District team when I was nineteen."

"I didn't know you were from Oldcastle, sir?" Danny replied, making a mental note of this hitherto concealed coincidence. If that's what it was?

"Born and bred. But I haven't lived there in years in case your mind is starting to work overtime."

"Not at all, sir." Danny replied quickly. "I was just wondering if you made it?"

For the life of him he couldn't recall having heard of an Oldcastle hurler called Richie Lyons.

"Did I make it?" Lyons repeated the question as if asking it of himself. "Yes, I made it. Oh, not as a hurler, mind, so no point racking your brains. I had a girlfriend at the time, you see. She left for Belfast to study, so I packed it in and went with her."

"You spurned the chance to play inter-district for a girl, sir?" The incredulity was evident in Danny's tone. While the GAA used individual counties as divisions the HAI had divided its members into districts. A district call up was considered quite a big deal.

"Not just any girl, young man. The girl. The only girl that mattered." He finished his pint and gestured to Benny, who was working the floor collecting glasses.

With a nod of acknowledgment, Benny finished wiping a table then returned to the bar and began to pull another brace.

"I hope she was worth it, sir. I mean that's an awful lot to give up for a girl."

Lyons' nod was barely perceptible. His eyes seemed focused on some invisible spot ahead of him, and though his ruddy face remained unreadable, Danny was aware of a sudden sadness in the man.

After a moment, Lyons blinked. "Not just any girl. And yes, she was worth it. I mightn't have any medals to brag about, but I spent twenty-eight years with the most beautiful girl I'd ever seen." He took a puff of his cigar and released it slowly, like a sigh. "And I don't regret one minute of the time we spent together. Regret a lot of other things, mind. But not that."

Danny was taken aback by the detective's candour. He found this version of Lyons surprising and bordering on likeable. And what's more, Danny could see Lyons meant every word he said. It was in the eyes. His mother had always said that. 'If you wish to know a man's truth from a man's lies, don't look at his face. Look at his eyes.' She'd smile ruefully after reciting her little mantra. 'Should have heeded my own words. God knows, I looked into your father's eyes long enough.'

Lyons took a slug of his drink, his eyes drifting away again. "You know, the day I met Molly it was her birthday. She was celebrating in one of the bars I used to go to when I was first stationed in Dublin. When friends dared her, she got up on a table in the middle of the pub to sing *Brown-Eyed Girl*. It was her favourite song, you see. She was forever humming it to herself." He smiled at the memory. "She couldn't sing a note, bless her, but God was she beautiful. Raven black hair that cascaded down her back. Beautiful green eyes. A smile that I couldn't take my eyes off." He paused, then gave a rueful shake of his head. "Even after all these years that's how I still see her. Dancing on that stool with that brilliant smile on her face."

Now, Danny welcomed a drink. My God, this man has a heart after all. "Are ye still together, sir?" Danny rued the question even as he asked it. He felt his heart sink as he realised too late what was coming. He should have known. God knows he'd been told often enough. Many said it was the reason Lyons drank the way he did. Way to go, Danny. Great attention to detail.

"In a way. Molly died of cancer two years ago," he puffed his cheeks then slowly released the breath. "Two years ago, next week, in fact. But I still talk to her every day."

"I'm really sorry, sir," Danny's apology sounded inadequate, even in his own ears, so he floundered for something else to add. "Any family, sir?"

It had been a topic of debate around the station. Lyons had been transferred several times before arriving at Swords the previous year as an addition to the drug squad. Apart from him being widowed and having a penchant for drink, no one seemed to know much about his personal life.

Lyons shook his head, and that faraway look was back in his eyes. "Kids just didn't happen for Molly and me." He sighed. "And now she's gone and…" he hesitated as if he was about to add something else but took a long drag of his cigar instead. "Shouldn't be that way though," he finally said, almost to himself. "Not if the doctors had done their damn job properly."

A long moment of silence followed as Lyons reflected on whatever was on his mind. When Benny arrived down with two more pints, Danny felt relieved that the tension was broken.

"Enjoying the match?" Benny asked as he placed the beer on the table. He caught Lyons' eye and gave a terse shake of his head. Lyons acknowledged the message with a nod.

"I wouldn't look at it if it was in my back garden," Lyons replied loud enough for anyone close to hear. "They've it ruined with all those touch-me-not rules and black cards. You'd get a card now if you looked sideways at someone. And as for that back-door nonsense. You lose a game, yet you get another chance, and another, and another. It's a joke. Like playing swords with sticks. You might get your ego a little bruised, but we all know no one is really going to get hurt, don't we?"

"Not like in your day, eh Richie?" Benny asked, winking conspiratorially at Danny. He'd obviously heard Lyons' rant before. "A man's game then."

"Damn right. Those players nowadays wouldn't go to bed with the light off. And as for the size of the pitch – you could turn the titanic on that field in Gaelic Park."

"Does that not make it better, sir?" Danny asked. "More room to show off their skills?"

"If they had skill, they wouldn't need all that room," Lyons replied dismissively. "That's the whole point of skill. It comes to the fore in the tightest situations. Nowadays, it's just a game of running away. If your marker is tougher than you – run away. If he's stronger than you – run away. If he's a better reader of the game than you – run away. Even a headless chicken can run, for God's sake." He shook his head disagreeably then took another long draw of his beer. "It's called hurling for a reason. From the verb to hurl. Meaning to impel something with great force. Not tap it from one player to another. It was invented as a replacement for war. Not a game of hide and seek. They've sanitized everything in this country to the point that cowards can become the new heroes. And for what? To sell it to fucking Sky. More plundering bastards. Isn't that right, Benny?"

"Damn right. Soccer with sticks if you ask me. We're more English now than the bloody English themselves." He shook his head in disgust. "What would all our martyrs think? The likes of those that died on Bloody Sunday. They turn in their graves is what. And all to suit an audience that don't have a clue what they're damn well looking at. I blame that fucking president… What's his name?"

"Ade Fagan."

"Yeah, that bollox. He's interested in nothing else only lining his own pockets. Doesn't give a shit as long as it's making money for him and his cronies. Sold the whole thing down the river for advertising revenue." He picked up the empty glasses off the table.

"He thinks he's above it all, but he'll get his comeuppance someday."

With Benny heading back to the bar Lyons turned his dark gaze to Danny. His eyes, though a tad bleary were still sharp. Watching. Looking. Appraising.

"Come to think of it, you're a bit of a contradiction yourself, Daniel. An Irish, black protestant? And a cop. How does that happen?"

"Well, I'm not really a protestant, sir, but I am the rest, I guess. A bit of a piebald really." The latter was stated unashamedly. "My mother is from Mayo," he explained, "but she went to train as a nurse in London. There she met a Nigerian doctor with whom she had a brief fling. She said it was love but if it was, it was one way. Nine months later, I was born in a maternity hospital in Hammersmith and two months after that my mother returned with me to Mayo where I grew up as the one and only black boy in the small town of Ballinrobe. Never met my real father but heard he went back to Nigeria. As it stands, I am now the one and only black Garda in Swords Garda Station."

"Hell of a journey," Lyons observed. "You could just as easily have been abducted by nuns and buried in the backend of a field somewhere. That's what they did to black babies, you know."

Danny nodded. "That's why my mother never got me christened."

"She was dead right, 'cause that church is only a shower of thieving bastards." Lyons replied but now he seemed distracted.

A moment later Danny could see why. The gaunt man he had seen sitting at the door was now passing by on his way into the toilet. He looked in their direction but gave no sign of recognition. Neither did Lyons. Still, a silent acknowledgement seemed to pass between them. Danny was sure now that it was the same man he'd seen earlier. Lyons' snitch. His CI. It was clear to Danny that the barman, Benny, was another.

Soon after, the man returned from the toilet, and left the bar. But this time Danny got a good look at his face. And at the tattoo of a redheaded snake on his neck. He found himself wondering how the man would have looked in a long coat and hat. He was still wondering it when Lyons pushed himself away from the table with a grunt.

"I'm busting for a piss."

****

It was dark by the time the cab dropped Lyons at his house. He hardly noticed the rain as he wobbled toward the door then fumbled in his pocket for his keys.

'Young Danny's a good lad,' he thought when watching the cab pull away. A bit naïve, like all rookies. Innocent, which suited Lyons. He counted himself lucky it had been Danny and not a more seasoned Garda that had been on the desk when Miss Cox had brought that hand in. Although the chap was sharper than Lyons had first given him credit for. The look of recognition that had crossed over the lad's face when Snake passed out to the toilet was unmistakable.

He didn't say anything, just watched, but Lyons could see his mind working overtime again. Putting two and two together. He didn't ask about Cox either, even though those questions were also written all over his face. As they had been since the beginning. That's why Lyons had brought him for that little chat in the bar. To get a feel for how he was thinking. A gallon of beer later he was little the wiser.

And now as he was being carted away in the cab, the young Garda was watching him. Lyons could feel it. Although he couldn't see him clearly in the rain, he could sense the chap's eyes on him. On the house. It had been a mistake to bring him here, Lyons admonished himself, as he found the right key then felt the door click open. You've got to be more careful, Detective. People are looking. Watching. Waiting for you to slip up.

He pushed open the door but still, he paused before stepping in out of the rain. He needed a moment to steady himself and to try and get his head right. There was more tormenting him than Danny's suspicions. More than the drink. He didn't want to go inside. He hated going inside these days. A house wasn't a home anymore. This one nor the last. Not since Molly died. All it was for him now was a concrete box. A painted concrete box. And a cage for that person he didn't recognise anymore.

She was in there still. He could see that but then how could she not be? Securely locked away as she was. He stepped back from the door and let the rain wash over him as he looked up. It drenched his hair and ran down his face, over his eyes and cheeks. Melding with the tears that trickled through furrows of crow's feet to run off his beard. He could see the light on in her room and her shadow as she walked past the window. He was pretty certain Danny had seen that too. Yes, it had been stupid of him to bring him here. A mistake. Or was it? Perhaps, deep down he wanted to. Needed to. If another man could only see, could only understand his torment.

There she was again. Lingering now. Back and forth. Back and forth. Hungry. Like a tiger in a cage. She was no more suited to a cage than he was. Feeling the familiar anguish overwhelm him, he leaned momentarily for support against the blue Merc that he kept parked next to the door. A car he could ill-afford to keep on a copper's salary – the tax alone was well out of his price range. Then again, the same could be said for the three-bedroom house he was about to enter. Looking from the outside in, some people would say he had it made but they hadn't a clue. No one had. He took a deep breath and shrugged then pushed himself away from the car and returned to the door. The rain now stinging his eyes, he tripped over the threshold and practically fell into the hall. Clumsily. Noisily. If he hadn't realised it before, he now knew he was far too drunk for the usual confrontation. That would have to wait until the morning. For now, he just hoped she was one step closer to acceptance. That they were one step closer.

****

As he stumbled into bed, Danny cursed his stupidity. Even in college, drink had never agreed with him. At least, not with the African half of him. All he ever gained were gaps in his memory and a hangover from hell. And bouts of the dt's if he really went to town. Though equally disturbing, that wasn't what he experienced now. At least he didn't think so.

The sight of Miss Cox lying mutilated in the morgue was still in his head, lurking behind his eyes, only now his head was spinning, and his stomach felt even worse than it had when he'd first seen that damn hand. He knew now he wouldn't banish the sight of the mutilated Miss Cox no matter what he drank. If ever. But there was another image there too. The image of a ghost. Drifting back and forth behind the curtains of Lyons's gable end window. Danny tried to focus on the image, recall if it had been real but everything was a blur in his fuddled mind. Still, as his head hit the pillow, he saw the long hair of a girl.

With her hands pressed against the windowpane. As if begging him to stay.

****

Detective Lyons awoke to the sound of the phone ringing somewhere way off in the distance. His head was thumping as he sat up and tried to pinpoint the intrusion. Finally, he discovered it was coming from his trousers that lay crumpled in a heap at the far side of the bed. Groaning at the darts of pain in his temples, he leaned across the bedcovers and dipped his hand into the front pocket, eventually finding the device buried amongst a fistful of change.

"Hello," he groaned as he held it up to his ear.

"Detective Richie Lyons?"

It was a female voice. Young. Business-like. Full of energy. Exactly what he needed right then. Shit.

"Yes?"

"This is Sergeant Britney Kent in Oldcastle Garda Station."

"Britney?"

"Yes. Britney," Sergeant Kent replied impatiently. She felt like asking if he had an issue with that, but she'd a feeling she'd get the same nonsense she always got. 'Never thought I'd hear of a cop called Britney or, the only Britney I ever heard of was on the radio…' "Like the singer," she stated, deciding it better to bypass the bull and cut to the chase.

"Ok, Sergeant," Lyons replied as he glanced at the time on the phone. It was nine thirty a.m. He hadn't even had his first piss yet and he was already late for work. With anyone else, this would have been grounds for further reprimand, but Lyons knew the powers that be had all but given up on trying to straighten him out. They'd made it clear they were counting down the days until they were well rid. The feeling was mutual. But he had his task to complete first.

He pushed himself up on the side of the bed and cleared his throat. "How can I help you, Sergeant?"

"We hear you're missing a body up there."

"Well, we have one, but yes, you're right, we're missing another." While he spoke, he tried to clear his mind. Britney Kent, she'd said. He'd been expecting Detective Flynn. As he pondered on the significance of this unexpected development, he ran a reluctant tongue over his lips. His teeth. The inside of his mouth. He was used to the furry feeling after drink. Didn't mean he liked it.

"We found a body to go with your missing hand, Detective," Sergeant Kent continued. "Or didn't you get the message."

"Oh, yes…yes," Lyons replied as it all started to come back to him. Even he could tell his words sounded like those of a kid with too much candy in his mouth. "In Oldcastle! Your man is missing a hand. Our hand." A dart of pain shot through the space behind his eyes, and he groaned automatically.

"Are you ok, Detective?" Sergeant Kent asked hesitantly. "You sound a little, er, distracted." Was he on the toilet while he was talking to her? It sure sounded like he was having a crap. That was all she needed. Another pre-historic pig to deal with.

"It's nothing. Just a bit of a cold." In truth, Lyons felt like puking his ring up. Again, it was a routine feeling. It would pass he knew. He took a deep breath. "We've got a hand and a body. In fact, you should have heard about it on the news by now. The body is that of the sports reporter, Marie Cox."

"Didn't get to see the news but, I've heard of her. Remind me again, what paper does she work for?"

"The Independent News. She also happens to be the one who found the hand."

"Found?" Britney asked as she mulled over this unexpected link to the newspaper discovered at the Ballyfeud murder scene. It suggested that the particular page of the paper they found had been placed deliberately.

"Received, would be a better way of putting it. It was delivered to her apartment."

"Sounds like we've got a lot to talk about," Britney observed.

"Yeah, seems like someone's making sure of it," Lyons replied. "Who's running the case at your end?" He was well aware it wouldn't be a sergeant.

"Detective Flynn. He's, ahem, he's a bit of an arse-hole, if you don't mind me saying."

Flynn. Just as he thought. But who the hell was this Sergeant Kent? And why was she the one ringing him?

"He suggested you just send us anything you've got relative to our end, but I think it would be far better for us to meet in person. Me and you, I mean. I've got some ideas on the case that he's not necessarily agreeing with."

Lyons nodded hesitantly to himself. Now he understood why she called. Flynn had developed a bit of a rep as the kind who'd use a sledgehammer to convince a square peg it fit into a round hole.

"I presume you've passed that with your superiors?" Something told Lyons she hadn't.

"Of course," she lied. "Told them Flynn couldn't run a case if it had wheels on it." Britney was all too aware of the dangers of disparaging a senior Garda, but she wasn't about to let him railroad her on this one. Not after the fishy way that vandalism case was handled. She was pretty sure something had been swept under the carpet but as yet didn't know what. Now, Flynn was ignoring a direct link to a murder case which just happened to be linked to the vandalism as well. Linked by Jim Rourke.

'Of course...not!' Lyons corrected in his head but let it pass. Feeling himself coming around at last, he stood and began to pull on his trousers, struggling to get one leg in while using his free hand to balance on the side of the bed. His head spun and sweat beaded on his forehead. His stomach rose to say hi to his tonsils.

"But you could?"

"Yes, I could," Britney replied without hesitation.

"Ok. Sounds like you're the one I need to talk to," Lyons had a feeling no matter what he said, he wouldn't shake her off.

"Are you up to date on the case?"

"Yes."

"Then suggest a time and place and I'll be there."

"Tomorrow at ten?" Britney replied instantly.

Lyons hesitated. That wouldn't work. He had appointments to keep.

"Sorry, I'm up to my neck with the case here so tomorrow and the day after are out. How about the morning after that at ten?" He couldn't for the life of him recall what day it was.

Three days? Britney shook her head despairingly. At the rate the killer was going another person could be dead by then.

"Ok," Britney reluctantly agreed. "I'll call back to arrange a place. In the meantime, let's hope the killer has no immediate plans!" She hung up.

With the line dead, Lyons stuffed the phone back into his trouser pocket and finished getting dressed. He quickly went to the bathroom and splashed some cold water over his face then towelled himself dry. As he did so, he caught a glance of himself in the mirror. His eyes were baggy, his jaw saggy, and his cheeks were the colour of a dead mouse. Even he had to admit he looked washed up. That was the reason he had started to grow the beard. To hide. From himself as much as from anyone else.

He tore his eyes away from his drawn reflection, opened his fly, then manoeuvred himself in front of the toilet bowl to enjoy his first piss of the day. It was surely sad when pissing became one of the great pleasures in life. Once that dubious pleasure was over, he slowly made his way across the hall and braced himself for the inevitable. There would be absolutely no pleasure in the confrontation. But making up, that would be worth it. It always was.

Taking a breath to clear his head, he stopped at the door to the room and knocked. There was no answer, which was no surprise. And no deterrent. He simply waited for a moment before knocking a second time.

"Morning," he called. "Are you awake?" Once again, he was greeted with silence, but he didn't let it upset him. He was used to the routine. "I'm coming in," he warned, "so, please behave." Even as he said it, he knew the request was a waste of breath. No matter how he asked, she would only behave if she chose to. It all depended on what mood she was in. Or if the drug had worn off.

He gave her another moment then turned the key which protruded from the lock – kept there to be handy in case of emergencies and opened the door.

"I'm coming in now."

Assailed by the same heavy silence, he stepped inside and closed the door behind him, locked it then deposited the key safely into his trouser pocket, next to the phone. The girl was lying on the bed, curled up in the foetal position as if to protect herself from him. This was nothing new. It was all part of the game. The dance. Not to be taken personally.

He moved into the room, stepping softly on the balls of his feet as if stalking her, his dark eyes focused on her, watching for the faintest hint of movement. Even with her left leg shackled as it was, she could be swifter than lightning and catch him off guard. She always judged it to perfection too, waiting until he was a foot from the bed before she lunged. That way there was enough slack on the chains for her to reach him.

Though a necessary evil, he hated restricting her. He had deliberately set the chains up that way, with limited freedom. Just enough slack so that she could look out the window if she wanted to but not enough to reach the door at the opposite side of the room. Yet, it didn't stop her trying. He did consider the use of chains as cruel but binding her in steel was the only option. He had learnt the hard way that she could bite through even the thickest of rope. Had done on several occasions and havoc had ensued. The first time he applied the chains, she had broken her teeth. Consequently, that was the last time she'd bitten. The chains at least.

She always went straight for his throat too, with arms outstretched and claws bared, screaming like a banshee on a wild winter's night. Mostly, he caught her just in time.

This time she got within inches of his face. If she had gotten any closer, she might have ripped his eye out or sunk her teeth into his jugular. Or made for his ear again. The last time she'd almost bitten it off, but he had managed to shake her loose just in time. At least in time to save enough for the doctor to sew it back together again. When the doctor had enquired, he'd explained the occurrence away as a hazard of his job, just as he had done previously with the bite marks on his hand. It was a story he couldn't keep telling.

Now, as he wrestled with her, he gripped her stick-thin arms tightly and forced her back onto the bed, pinning her down until the paranoia-infused strength faded out of her and she was forced to give up the fight.

Then he deftly produced a syringe from his pocket and stuck it in the stringy muscle of her upper arm. Forced the plunger with his thumb.

As her eyes dilated, he leaned in and whispered in her ear. "Who am I?"

She shook her head from side to side as if desperate to get the image out of her head.

"Who am I?"

"You're my…"

"Who am I?" he asked once more, trying to be both gentle and forceful at the same time. He needed her to say it. To hear it from her lips. It was for her own good. And his.

"You're my Daddy," she muttered, sounding thick-tongued, her eyes faltering as the drug took hold, but suddenly they refocused as if seeing him for the first time and her head shot up. "You're my big, strong Daddy." This was louder, said in a sneer. Her lips twisting with hate.

He ignored the disdain. Instead, he smiled and rubbed the sweat from her brow, pleased that she had found the words. He knew she'd smell the alcohol on his breath as he leaned close and kissed her forehead, but it couldn't be helped. It was part of him now.

"Good girl. Now, let's take the chains off and see if we can get you undressed."

He spoke softly but inside he braced himself for what was coming. The real struggle. Setting his jaw, he prepared for the emotions that would inevitably course through

211

him. They were almost impossible to control. But that wasn't his fault.

Two days, he reminded himself.

He'd better get to work. There was far too much to do.

****

The hooded man set his glasses on his nose then picked up the bloodied ears and carefully placed them on the cotton-wool wadding. The deep redness of the gory appendages created quite a contrast with their pristine white setting and would, therefore, be quite a sight for the recipient. This was intentional of course. His art demanded maximum effect. Blood and gore would give him that – a telling combination; the sight of which horrified most people, though it never bothered him. He was used to blood.

In his line of work, you had to be.

Miss Cox's ears had been quite petite, a fact which, the man was fairly sure, she had been proud of. For him, the size of the ears was quite irrelevant in his grand scheme, but it did make them easy to package. Easier than that hand anyway. Sitting atop the cotton wool, they fit snugly into a large matchbox which then could easily be wrapped and slipped into the pocket of the long coat he had bought especially for his work. Packaged and ready for delivery.

He had left the earrings in place. Even though they looked to be expensive, they were of no interest to him. He had no requirement for trinkets. That was the whole point. Her kind of people valued trinkets above all else. Above the decent and fair treatment of their fellow human beings. But they had pushed too far and now he had no choice but to push back. To teach them. To teach the world. All he asked for was the strength to complete his mission. With that in mind, he closed his eyes and recited God's prayer. Its mantra brought him peace.

Then with his package safely tucked away in his coat, he taped up his sleeves and trouser cuffs before opening the door on his little makeshift workshop and heading out into the world. He was worried he'd be missed on this occasion because he would be gone a while longer than any of his previous little sprees. His MO would be different too. He didn't like changing things, but he wasn't prepared to rely on anyone else to make his little delivery. It had to be made in person but there was no way he could make the journey twice. Such an extended absence would only add to her pain. So, just this once, the time of delivery would also become the time of the kill.

He could live with that. It wasn't an exact science, after all.

Chapter 9

Sitting at a table in Frampton's restaurant, Britney struggled to keep her nerves in check. She had arrived early for her midweek date, a decision she was now regretting because it gave her far too much time to second guess what she was doing. Was she making a mistake? Would seeing him be regarded as a conflict of interest? After all, Bob was a witness in a case. Not a very important witness, perhaps, but still a witness and even one date with a witness could be construed as misconduct. She was so worried that she hadn't even confided in Fiona.

The problem was, she couldn't help herself. It was as if he was a drug and after that accidental reunion her craving had been reignited. Now she was hooked. That's why when he had called her out of the blue, she'd felt her heart leap. Now, she was every bit as nervous as she had been when closing her eyes for her very first kiss. A lifetime ago, with a boy whose memory was fading in her mind but would never be completely forgotten.

She could barely remember the last time she had been on a proper date either. Her previous relationship had lasted three years and even though there were early signs that it just wasn't working, she had clung to it like a struggling swimmer to a buoy. Plodding along from one argument to another, dismissing each fresh disappointment as just a blip. When the end finally came, it was a massive relief. She couldn't see that being the case with Bob. That's why she'd been tempted to follow Fiona's advice and call him. He'd just got there first.

As she waited, her mind wandered back to the investigation. She hadn't been exaggerating when she'd inferred to Lyons it was a mess. Flynn and sidekick Joe hadn't been in the office long enough for it to be any other way.

Over the past few days, they were steadily coming and going but never staying long enough to have a proper team meeting or to share information in any meaningful way. They were either out of their depth or their minds were elsewhere. If the latter was the case, she couldn't fathom why. After all, what could possibly be more important to a detective than a murder investigation? Especially one that he himself was heading up. Come to think of it, the only time Flynn ever seemed interested in anything relating to police work was when dealing with the media. He made sure to be present for all press conferences. Present, front, and centre. Then he'd fill them with a heap of shite about the progress they were making. Regarding this case, there was no progress as far as Britney could see. There was barely an investigation. At least not from any coordinated point of view. Hopefully, her meeting with Lyons would change all that. However, after speaking to him on the phone, she had her doubts about that too.

Arriving just before eight p.m., Bob Harris was punctual which Britney marked down as a good sign. He was dressed casually in jeans and a t-shirt, which were just about tight enough that she could see his muscles rippling as he walked. Now that he was out of his foreman's attire, he was even better looking than she remembered. Taller, broader, more handsome. Her heart skipped a beat at the sight of him. When he spotted her, he waved, before bestowing that shy but contagious smile as he walked over. She almost melted at the puppy dog look on his face.

"Good to see you again," she said with a nervous smile of her own while secretly hoping she hadn't made a fool of herself during their original encounter. She stood and awkwardly offered her hand, which he took, but then leaned over and kissed her cheek. That cheek. The one she'd spent all evening trying to tone with concealer. However, if she had expected initial contact to be awkward, it wasn't. Quite the opposite. It felt exhilarating. The proximity of his lips, the smell of his aftershave. The feel of his skin against hers. It was how she had remembered it. All scars were forgotten.

"Good to see you too," he replied. "You look wonderful."

She welcomed the compliment. She'd spent hours getting ready. Fixing her hair and her makeup. Swapping one dress for another until she finally decided on what dress to wear – a black number, not too muted but not too sexy either. She didn't want to give the wrong impression.

"Thanks. You don't scrub up too bad yourself. Although I must admit, I am a bit partial to a high-vis and a hard hat." In her mind, she was shaking her head and screaming. Why did I say that? I hate when men say that kind of thing to me.

"Just a high-vis and hard hat?" he quipped light-heartedly, but almost immediately followed up with a level of honesty that impressed her loads. "Actually, it was a close call. I don't have much more in my wardrobe, to be honest, apart from old boots and some rain gear, and I didn't think they'd be appropriate," he smiled disarmingly. "I decided if a beautiful girl is willing to go out with me, she deserves an effort. So, I went out and bought these. I hope they're up to scratch."

"They're perfect," Britney replied sincerely. "Absolutely perfect."

The date couldn't have gone better, at least right up to the end. But it was the end that counted. The meal was wonderful and the music in the background was every bit as intoxicating as the wine, but without the right company, it all would have been lost on her. In truth, she couldn't have imagined spending the evening with anyone more wonderful. The conversation flowed from the start, shifting seamlessly from one topic to another, at once both engaging and light-hearted. She found him funny and sincere, and genuinely interested in what she had to say. She honestly couldn't remember having enjoyed herself quite as much, even when recalling that embarrassing first meeting. Though he was too much of a gentleman to say it straight out Britney got the impression she had been every bit as drunk as she remembered, so she quickly moved the conversation along. They initially skirted around any talk of work, but with Britney's curiosity honed by recent events, she couldn't help herself. Even as she asked the question, she feared she was opening a can of worms.

"Have there been many attacks on the site?"

Bob shook his head. "Just the one. Security had been asleep in his hut. It won't happen again."

Britney could see by the determined glint in his eye it wouldn't. "And how did you find Detective Flynn? Did he deal with it ok?"

"Couldn't have been more helpful to be honest. Very professional." He raised his dark eyebrows. "Why?"

Britney shrugged. "Just not his biggest fan to be honest." She should have stopped there but with the wine flowing and feeling as comfortable as she did in his presence, she found herself confiding details about Flynn that would have been best left alone.

"That's bullying," Bob observed. "Pure and simple. And if he's coming on to you like that when he's pissed, that's sexual harassment. I can't believe nothing is being done about it?" he declared incredulously.

Britney shrugged. "He's the Super's nephew. Anyway, he's just an asshole. I can handle it."

"The point is you shouldn't have to. If that kind of thing happened elsewhere, even on a building site, the place would be closed pending a full investigation," he shook his head in frustration. "The fucking cops are more corrupt than the rest of us."

"Not all cops," Britney pointed out defensively.

"Sorry," he agreed. "Not all. But the ones at the top certainly are. Like that case with the whistle-blower. They went to town on him." He shrugged. "Power corrupts and absolute power corrupts absolutely."

"That's true," Britney conceded. "I know the Gardaí had its fair share of bad apples, and scandals, but I think we are doing a decent enough job here in Oldcastle."

"I suppose so," Bob replied with a slightly cynical smile. "In fact, I'm pretty sure the majority of men in the town would readily agree with you."

"What's that meant to mean?" Britney asked, a little puzzled.

"Come on," he replied in a vaguely sarcastic tone. "You must know about the pop-up brothels?"

Britney shook her head. "I've heard rumours, but you hear those in every town."

"These aren't just rumours. They exist. They're the talk of the canteen every Monday morning. The lads get texted the location and make a beeline for the place once the pubs close. Seemingly they rotate between premises. A different location every weekend." His expression grew serious as he looked at Britney now. "Meant to be a cop running it all." He informed her then sat forward as if to gauge her reaction. Did she really not know?

"That's a fairly serious accusation," Britney replied eventually. "Any names mentioned?"

It was Bob's turn to shake his head, "No. No one really cares. Not when they're getting their rocks off as they put it. But from what I hear, it's a cop based in Dublin."

"You seem to hear a lot. Some might think you have hands-on experience."

"Nope. Just telling you what the guys are saying. Personally, I like the gentleman approach – to converse with women, not pay for them."

"Well, that's good to know," Britney replied evenly then finished the glass of white wine she had ordered. The date had taken a turn she didn't care for. She had hoped it to be a break away from work but because of her own big mouth work was now all she could think of. Pop-up brothels in Oldcastle. And run by a cop? How come she hadn't heard about any of that back at the station? Surely someone would have picked up on it. If Bob was right, then every randy dog on the street seemed to know about it, for God's sake. The more she thought about it, the more she decided Flynn knew as well. A hound-dog like him had to.

Bob too could sense the mood had changed and something his father used to say suddenly came to mind. 'A wrong word to the wrong woman and suddenly a kiss on the cheek becomes a slap on the face.' Yet there was one more question he just needed to ask. "Any news on Jim Rourke?"

Britney took her time answering. "I can't talk about a case. Not even that one."

"I wouldn't ask but the guys on the site are getting worried," Bob explained, "especially after what happened to that poor man out in the hurling field." He paused for a moment, giving time for an answer but clearly none was forthcoming. "In fact, we're all worried. And some of us are afraid. Especially with that other story all over the news as well. That reporter lady. It seems to me they are all connected. That reporter and the HAI man and Jim Rourke."

"How…" she began then stopped herself. "I can't discuss any of that."

"But I'm only asking because…"

Britney shook her head once more. "I can't Bob. I'm sorry." Now she knew the date was a bad idea. She swore to herself. "I shouldn't have come here. It was against my better judgement."

Taking some cash out of her purse, she set the notes on the table to pay for her share of the meal then stood and picked up her coat. "I'm sorry Bob, but I'd better go. There are just too many conflicting things going on at the moment."

"Ok," Bob replied as he hesitantly stood to face her. "I understand. I don't necessarily like it, especially not a second time," he admitted, "but I do understand."

If Britney felt guilty about this, she refused to let it sway her. She simply nodded then turned to leave.

"Sorry for pushing it, Britney," Bob called after her, "but everyone is worried."

She stopped a yard from the table and turned back. Just then, she spotted Fiona sitting at a table across the restaurant. A good-looking young man was sitting opposite her whom Britney presumed was the boyfriend she had alluded to. They were sipping wine but had yet to order any food. Perhaps feeling Britney's eyes on her, Fiona looked up. On spotting Britney, she waved hello, then noticing Bob at the table behind Britney, she smiled and gave a big thumbs up, the smile slowly fading when she saw the dejected look on Britney's face. Britney forced a thin smile in acknowledgement. So much for keeping the date under her hat. Hopefully, she could trust Fiona to be discreet. If not, the whole station would know, and Flynn would have her rightly by the short and curlies.

With that appalling thought in her mind, she turned her attention back to Bob. "I know. I'm worried too. We all are," she said, then took a moment as she tried to sort through what was troubling her. As far as she was aware, the only connection to all three cases that she knew was in her head. There certainly had been no connection made public. It hadn't even been accepted by the lead investigators, for God's sake. What was Bob? Some sort of super sleuth? Perhaps he could read her mind? She doubted it. She could barely read it herself.

"Now, I have a question for you."

"Fire away," Bob replied calmly.

"What makes you think they are connected? These two murders and Jim Rourke? Most people think Jim is just gone walkabout."

He shrugged. "Maybe. But if it was me, I just couldn't take off and leave those two kids he has behind. Could you?"

Britney already knew the answer to that. She'd rather die first.

****

At four thirty p.m. the following evening, Doctor Phil Carmody, a partner at The Oldtown Medical Clinic decided he had enough of patients. He instructed the secretary at the clinic that he was finishing for the day. There were four other doctors in the clinic, and any patient waiting to see him could be transferred over to a colleague. Whether they liked it or not, he was in the mood for golf and some stupid kid with tonsillitis or an over-sensitive mother with migraine wasn't going to stand in his way. The secretary made note of his instruction and in return, she reminded him of the little present that someone had left for him at reception earlier that morning. A small box rather crudely wrapped in newspaper with the doctor's name scrawled upon it.

"Is it a gold bar?" he asked with his usual disdain while closing the apps he had been using and shutting down his computer. He knew if he hurried, he could make the five o'clock tee off time and be in the nineteenth before it got dark.

"Well, it's a bit light for a gold bar but I'm sure it's far more valuable than that," his secretary sighed, while holding the tip of her pointy chin. "Remember, Doctor, it's the thought that counts."

'Yeah right,' thought the doctor as he turned his nose up. The last present he'd received from a patient had been a pair of cheap cufflinks that had looked tarnished even as he took them out of the box. Or what about the second-hand watch he had received from the old woman whose husband had died right there in his surgery. As if the likes of him would go around wearing a dead man's timepiece. No, he'd far prefer if they kept their trinkets to themselves and paid his callout bills on time.

"Yes, Madeleine, you have told me that before. I'll tell you what. You open it and if its anything nice you can keep it. How's that?"

"Fine by me, Doctor," Madeleine replied coolly. "Enjoy your golf." She dropped the little present into her bag to take home for later then got to work reallocating the rest of the doctor's patients. His colleagues wouldn't be happy, she knew, and neither would the poor people that came to him for healing. They'd have quite a wait before they'd be seen and, as usual, they would take out their frustrations on her. She'd be run off her feet for the next two hours at least. 'Enjoy your golf,' she repeated to herself, any inkling toward magnanimity drained out of her. 'May you fall into a hole and never come out.'

Once he had dealt with the secretary, Doctor Carmody grabbed the leather duffle bag which contained his golf attire then slung his expensive cashmere coat over his arm and exited through the rear of the building, making his way to the parking bay reserved for the in-house doctors. There his latest Mercedes was waiting. On his way to the car, something did twig with him as odd. Two things in fact, but he was too busy imagining the banter in the clubhouse to let whatever it was bother him. He should have let it bother him. If he had, it might have saved his life.

The first odd thing he noted was the car parked next to his. It was a battered looking saloon car, Japanese or one of those working-class types that he wouldn't be seen dead in. Nor any of his qualified colleagues either, for that matter. Yet there it was, parked in the reserved area of his clinic. Bold as brass. As if it belonged. The second thing, which would later register with him, was that, despite its appearance, he recognised the car. He had seen it lately. Several times. Outside his house and near the golf course. It stuck with him because it was a real rust bucket that sounded like it was on its last legs. And he had gotten the impression the driver – a rather serious looking man with dark, deep-set eyes, was watching him. Soon he would learn the reason why.

As the doctor neared the car, he pressed the unlock button on his key fob then heard the loud beep as the doors clicked open. The man hunkered in the shadows close to the car heard the exact same thing but still, he waited. He had been watching the doctor. Doctor Carmody was a man of habit. And of refined tastes. He always carried his ultra-expensive tweed coat over his arm which he then carefully laid out across the back seat. Laid out with far more consideration than he had shown one poor unfortunate, who had been entrusted to his care. He would place the coat lengthways across the seat then smooth out any wrinkles in the fabric. To accomplish this, he would have to lean into the car which, to the satisfaction of the man watching, he now did.

Just as the doctor was extracting the final crease from the tweed coat, the hooded man struck. He leapt out from behind the rust bucket and bundled the doctor onto the back seat of the Mercedes. Then he wrapped one arm around the doctor's neck and with the other hand, held the laced cotton wadding to the doctor's nose. Oh, he could have opted for a stun gun or some other new-fangled apparatus, but he was old school when it came to technology. Even ordering the chloroform online had proved taxing and he'd nearly bitten his nails to the quick with the stress of waiting for it to arrive. Still, it was the safest option.

It would only take a brief moment for the chloroform to do its job he knew but still, he was well aware that for that brief moment, he was at his most vulnerable. He was half in and half out of the car, and even though the parking spot the doctor had chosen as his own was next to the wall of the building, it was also closest to the door so clearly visible to anyone entering or exiting the car park. The man just hoped his luck held, as it had up to now. Twice already, he had very nearly been foiled before the event. Once at the hurling field when he had to get in and out of the dressing room without being noticed – quite an achievement considering he had to hang a man in between, and again outside the police station when he had interacted with Marie Cox. It had been a risky indulgence he knew and if she hadn't been so arrogant, she would have left the station with protection. If she had done that, she would be alive now. But she'd liked to think of herself as an independent lady and on home she went. He had gladly followed. Later, set up the scene so that it told the story he wanted it to tell, then got out of there.

Oh, he had been tempted to stay a little longer with Miss Cox just to watch her dangle simply because he had grown to detest what she stood for, but he was glad now he had stuck to the plan. Otherwise, the game he was playing would be over. Almost before it had begun.

The doctor was stronger than his age suggested, but he was no match for his assailant. He was certainly no match for cotton wadding loaded with enough chloroform to stop a racehorse in mid gallop. Stop, but not kill. This detail, the man had been very careful to get right. He didn't want the doctor to die without knowing why. The man held on tight until the fight went out of the doctor's limbs, and he collapsed onto the back seat, inadvertently undoing all the effort he had put into his precious coat. Then the man quickly dragged him from the Mercedes and unceremoniously dumped him into the backseat of the Toyota he had purposefully acquired for the occasion. A banger of a thing that he'd brought across the border a little over a week earlier. It had fake tax and insurance certs and no cashmere for the doctor to lie on, only an empty coal sack and some discarded tools. Perfect for the job, he thought then made a mental note to empty the car before he disposed of it.

Once he had the doctor safely inside, the man stuffed him down into the footwell behind the front seats and covered him, first with his precious coat then with the coal sack. Finally, he closed the door of both cars. Feeling assured the doctor couldn't be spotted, he discreetly checked for any signs left behind by the struggle. He saw none. Satisfied, he hopped into the driver's seat of the Toyota and drove out through the main exit with the hood pulled low down over his eyes. He knew the incident would be caught on camera and that the Gardaí would review it in detail. It didn't matter. The doctor would be long dead. And anyway, he had been careful to keep turned away from the camera so that no one would recognise the man dressed in the long, deep-hooded coat, and waterproof boots.

Chapter 10

Approximately a half hour after Doctor Carmody was bundled into the back of the car he considered so beneath him, Britney's shift ended. Instead of going home she decided to pay The March a visit. The March was the public square, located in the city centre, directly in front of the castle. It was called The March simply because that was where the Norman family who had built the castle centuries earlier paraded their armies. Now it was the city's entertainment hub with every second building having been converted into a restaurant, pub or late bar.

Though she had been feeling tired all day and a little down, she was desperate to dig further into Jim Rourke's whereabouts. On a hunch, she had checked out the boarded-up apartments at the front of the Emmet's Hill estate but had no joy. The empty buildings remained secure with no sign of forced entry whatsoever. If Rourke was hiding out, it wasn't in one of those. It had seemed too easy, she had to admit.

As she drove in the direction of the March, she reflected on what had her feeling so tired – her disastrous date with Bob Harris, of course. She had been tossing and turning all night over it. She had said too much, she knew that. The wine was partly to blame but not solely. She had genuinely liked him, liked him a lot, and that had encouraged her to talk more than she should. Dissing Flynn in public wasn't very professional but now in the cold light of day that wasn't something she regretted. What she did regret was how the date ended. Her first decent date in years and she'd run home like Cinderella. She hadn't even had the presence of mind to leave behind a damn shoe. Perhaps that was a good thing.

Although it was clearly only natural curiosity and concern for a missing colleague, Bob's questions had made her uncomfortable. He was just too close to the case. Afterward, he'd texted to apologise for being such a nosy parker. She'd briefly acknowledged receipt of it but had left it at that. Now that the case was escalating, the last thing she wanted was to be accused of being a leak. Worse still, a leak that couldn't keep her legs together. Flynn would have a field day with that. Still what Bob had told her about the brothels was interesting. If there was some sort of shady goings-on in the city, she knew Flynn would be involved – head, neck, and heels. She decided that once this case was closed, she would make it her business to prove it. If not before.

With that ambition spurring her on, she parked the car on the edge of The March hoping to kill two birds with the one stone – learn more about the brothels and perhaps uncover a clue to the whereabouts of Jim Rourke.

Many of the pubs in The March were high-end establishments, but it also housed some that were well known as early houses, accommodating all-day drinkers. Having learnt from his colleague, Brian Farrell, of Jim Rourke's historical tendency to go on drinking binges, Britney felt it would be worth calling to those bars to see if there has been any sign of the missing man over the past week. Someone might have seen him. Might have even been drinking with him. Perhaps all her Christmases would come at once and she'd find Jim Rourke in a drunken stupor in a corner of one of them. She wasn't holding her breath.

It was early evening and the rain from previous days had passed off, so the sun was still shining when she wandered into the square. Apparently, there had been a match in Fenian Park, the HAI grounds located just a short walk from the main street. With the crowd spilling out from the stadium, the bars on this side of town were busy. It took only a brief investigation in the first two bars to determine there wasn't sight nor sound of Jim Rourke. Nor had there been. She had expected as much. However, she did catch sight of Terry Flynn hanging out towards the rear of the second establishment. He was in the company of a heavyset man Britney had seen interviewed on the telly. Ade Fagan. The President of the HAI. The pair had obviously met up for the match and she was willing to bet that Flynn was now having a night out on the HAI expense account. He liked his drink, Flynn. Especially when he was getting it for nothing. Although Fagan himself didn't drink, he had a reputation of been *flaithúlach* when it came to entertaining his cronies. With the organisation's chequebook, of course. Making a mental note of the connection, Britney quickly moved on, glad that Flynn hadn't spotted her. Confident too that Fagan wouldn't be caught dead in the next bar she was heading to and therefore, would keep Flynn out of her hair.

It was on the third bar, a dated looking establishment called Bernie's, that she pinned her hopes. Apart from being one of the most popular drinking haunts in the town, Bernie's kept irregular hours and just as irregular customers. It was also known as a republican stronghold. When Britney entered the bar, a rebel song was pounding out from speakers over the door and many of the revellers, mostly drunken young men, were boisterously singing along.

On the wall to the left of the door was a painted mural depicting a man in a balaclava standing beneath the slogan *Tiocfaidh Ár Lá* while brandishing a gun in one hand and a hurley in the other. Dotted along the wall, either side of the mural were framed posters depicting the heroes of the 1916 Easter Rising, one of Bobby Sands and further along, one of Michael Collins. The drinks counter ran along the wall opposite.

Once her uniform was spotted, elbows began to nudge, and eyes to wink. Soon the conversation died to a murmur. In the hush that followed, the music sounded even louder than it had before. A moment later, that died down too until you could almost hear a pin drop. Seeing the wary look on the punter's faces, she cursed the fact that she hadn't changed out of her uniform. Uniform meant on duty and on duty to those watching her, generally meant trouble for someone. And that meant shut mouths all around.

A quick scan of the bar told her that she'd have to keep looking for Jim Rourke but confirmed the presence of the other person she wished to see. Bernie Madigan.

The eponymous owner, rumoured to know more about the underground in Oldcastle than almost anyone else in the city.

However, having interviewed her previously regarding a rather nasty fight outside her establishment, Britney knew that getting an honest word out of her edgeways could prove tougher than soliciting a confession from even the most hardened gangland criminal.

Bernie was an elderly woman, with wiry grey hair, beady eyes, and a round hump on her back. She had a reputation of being meaner than an alley cat, tough as Sheffield steel, and sober less than half the time. She was now perched on a stool at the end of the bar, next to a skinny man of similar age with a protruding chin and frog eyes. A half-finished pint of ale sat in front of her.

"Wha? Is the music too loud for ya?" The squawk came from Bernie's husky, worn-out voice. It was well known Bernie had little time for the Gardaí after they rescinded her licence a few years earlier for persistent breaches. "Or have ya come 'ere to have a bit of fun?" She made a show of glancing around at her clientele. "I'm sure there's plenty here who would like to get their hands on that lustrous hair of yours!"

Her statement was met with cackles of laughter.

"Dibs on being first," the frog-eyed man said. He grinned displaying a row of broken and rotten teeth. "Maybe we can have a little dance first? Just to get to know each other, if ya know what I mean?"

Though Britney didn't show any reaction, he nudged Bernie and roared with laughter. He was so drunk that he very nearly fell backward off the stool in the process.

Some of the men closest to Britney laughed too but when she cast them a withering look, they quickly turned and stuck their noses in their beer.

"Tempting as that may sound," she said dryly, "I'm not here for a date." She walked further into the bar, only halting when she was within yards of Bernie Madigan.

"Can we speak in private?"

Bernie took a slug of her pint.

The frogman piped up again. "It'd be more in your line to be out catching that killer," he declared. "The one that's cutting up people instead of comin' in here botherin' folk like Bernie. But you cops are all the same. Checking car tax and insurance is all you're good for. You couldn't catch the Ebola virus if it was crawling all over ya."

Britney didn't so much as look in his direction. "Well, Bernie?"

"Maybe," she shrugged. There was a devious sparkle in her eye as she spoke. "If you give an old woman a laugh and let your hair down first. Make like the Wella ad."

"My hair is staying as it is, Bernie," Britney replied, "but your licence mightn't be if you don't give me what I need. And you won't get it back so quickly this time."

"Ooh! Threats!" her skinny sidekick called out. "And from such a pretty little thing. But little does she know, eh Bernie?" He nudged her again then followed up with a wink which was so blatantly obvious that it couldn't have been more inanely comical. "Tell her, Bernie," he urged in a slurred voice. "Tell her about Flynn."

Britney decided to chance her arm. "If you mean Flynn getting your licence back, I already know about that. Who do you think does his bloody paperwork?"

"I'd say you do a lot more than his paperwork," the man sniggered. "I bet he likes cat-licking that little scar of yours." Britney resisted the urge to raise her hand to her face, but raising it to his, might be a different matter. She relished the thought of a good slap sending those oversized eyes of his bouncing off the walls. Unfortunately, she didn't get the chance because she wasn't the only one getting sick of hearing his voice.

"Will ya shut up, ya plank," Bernie barked as she studied Britney closely. "What do ya want?"

"I'm looking for Jim Rourke?"

"Jim who?" She held up a hand to her ear as if she hadn't heard.

"Jim Rourke. He used to drink in here, Bernie," Britney fixed her with a stony stare to show her that she wasn't in the mood for messing about.

Bernie watched her for a moment, squinting out at her through a lazy left eye. Finally, she shrugged. "Rourke the stook," she sneered. "You know what a stook is, don't ya?" she asked, then immediately answered her own question. "It's a thick gobshite. A stupid bollox. That's Jim Rourke, for ya. Hated everything to do with Oldcastle, just because he got dropped from the hurling team one time. Always dissing it, so no one has much time for him around here." She glanced around the bar and received many a nod in return.

"We ain't seen that man here in years. Thank God!" Frogman called out. "Not since we won the last All-Ireland. He got a bit of a thumping after that cause he couldn't keep his big mouth shut. A little bit like you."

If Jim Rourke did indeed get a thumping, Britney was of the opinion Skinny Frogman wasn't the one dishing it out. At least not on his own. The impression she got of Jim Rourke was of a strong and fit individual, certainly too much for this loud-mouthed soak to handle.

Britney returned her attention to Bernie who shrugged.

"Rourke's married to some poor unfortunate, I hear. With kids. One a those that's supposed to have turned over a new leaf. But for me, once a gobshite, always a gobshite." She said the latter loudly then glanced around before leaning closer to Britney and speaking in a more reserved voice, "I already told all that to Flynn…so, what do you really want?"

"You told Flynn?" Britney asked casually. "He didn't even tell me he was coming down here." She shook her head in feigned disgust. "If he'd only keep us minions informed, I could have saved myself a trip."

"He wasn't 'ere," Bernie replied. "Not due til the end of the month, as all you thieving bastards well know. But that partner of his called me up the other day asking the same questions."

Now this was interesting. Were they taking Jim Rourke's disappearance seriously after all?

"So, is that why you're really here?" Bernie asked, "Or is Flynn trying to squeeze me again?"

"Nah, all good on that front," Britney quickly replied, continuing the charade. Already she was developing a clear picture of what kind of game Flynn was playing and it wasn't by the book, that's for sure. It didn't surprise her. She'd always understood Flynn played by his own rules and had suspected shagging junior colleagues wasn't the only reason he had been moved on from his previous post. Yet she had never been able to confirm the level of his corruption. She sensed now she just might do exactly that. "I'm just looking for information."

"Hm," Bernie grunted. "An expensive commodity round ere." A sly smile tugged at the corners of her mouth and Britney could imagine the cogs in her brain turning. "I'll tell you what, young lady. You take me on in a game of pool and if you win, I give you all the information you want. But if you lose, you let down that lovely, thick brown hair of yours for all these gentlemen to run their fingers through," Bernie's devious smile broadened, showing more gums than teeth.

Britney gave a brief shake of her head, her ponytail swinging as if to add emphasis. "Not a chance, Bernie. I've heard about you playing pool. Let's just say your approach to the rules is every bit as selective as your hearing."

"She's right there, Bernie," Frogman piped up enthusiastically. "It's like that posh Dublin one said when she was ere – you wouldn't know a foul if it had feathers on it." With that, he roared with laughter once more and slapped the bar in delight but quickly quietened down when Bernie cast him another of her withering looks. Were they a couple, Britney wondered? They certainly acted like one. She glanced from one to the other. Yuck, she thought as the image that popped into her head made her shiver.

"What Dublin woman?" Britney asked, in a conversational tone, but now watching them both intently, having picked up on Bernie's silent warning.

Bernie shook her head. "Don't know what that eejit is talking about," she replied dismissively. "All we ever get in here is cadgers and scroungers. Oh yeah and gobshites." She threw a loaded glance at her partner. "We get loads of them."

Frogeyes immediately dropped his head into his pint. It was easy to see who was wearing the trousers. And abundantly clear that to get Bernie's tongue to loosen up would take a bit of persuading.

"I'll make you a deal." It was Britney's turn to barter. "You give me what I need, and I'll have a word with Flynn. I'm sure we can do something about your overheads, if you know what I mean. If you don't give me what I need, mind, I can do the opposite."

"Don't arrange that with no one but Flynn," Bernie objected. "So, how would you do anything about my overheads?"

"Come on, Bernie, let's not play games. Everyone knows what Flynn thinks about when he's not thinking of money," she smiled suggestively. "And in case you haven't guessed, I'm closer to Flynn than most."

Bernie eyed her suspiciously through that lazy eye as she tried to figure out if Britney really had the kind of influence at which she was hinting. Her nod was barely perceptible.

"You're certainly his type," she admitted. "Young and feisty. Although on first impressions, I thought you'd have more class. Then again," she shrugged, "people used to say that about me too." She then lowered herself off the stool and attempted a twirl which proved far more clumsy than elegant. "Classy bird, eh!" she said then cackled her gummy laugh.

"Yes, Bernie. A real movie star," Britney replied sardonically. The landlady might have been petite, but she was no Audrey Hepburn, that's for sure.

"Good answer," Bernie acknowledged dryly, then suddenly business-like, she took a step closer to Britney and leaned forward to whisper into her ear. Despite the unpleasantness of the woman's appearance, Britney stood her ground. "Now, how about you come in the back? My friends here might be half pissed but they have ears like elephants. And memories to match." Without waiting for an answer, she turned and headed for a door to the rear of the bar.

Britney eagerly followed. Already Bernie had confirmed what Britney had suspected for a long time – Flynn was running some sort of extortion racket. The question was how big a racket was it? And did it extend into the sex trade? As she passed from the seedy bar into surprisingly elegant living quarters, she felt a thrill of excitement. The next few minutes could be the most important of her career.

A half an hour later, Bernie was all talked out and Britney was back on the street. She immediately called Fiona's mobile.

"I have him, Fiona," she exclaimed when her friend answered.

"Have who?"

In her excitement Britney didn't even hear Fiona's reply.

"From what I've heard today, I think I can get enough on Flynn to warrant a criminal investigation. All I need is to get one or two of his other targets to talk."

"What targets, Brit? What have you got on him?"

Britney couldn't blame her colleague for sounding confused. Or wary for that matter. She took a breath then quickly filled her in.

"Jesus," Fiona exclaimed, once Britney had finished. "You're telling me we won't have to put up with his leering eyes any longer." Britney could sense the relief in her voice.

"Yes," Britney replied. "By the time I'm finished with him, he'll be sharing a bunk with a 220lb gorilla in the biggest lonely-hearts club in the country. He'll know all about leering eyes then. And grubby hands too."

"Sounds like karma," Fiona admitted.

"Damn right!" Britney agreed and couldn't help but smile as she hung up. However, her smile soon faded when she considered the fact that she was no closer to finding Jim Rourke. Where the hell was he? And what, if anything, was he planning to do next?

As she contemplated this, she realised she was starving so decided to drop into Fat Tony's for a takeaway. A good curry was called for. Fiona's diet of paninis only went so far.

****

The man waited patiently for the doctor to come to. It had taken a little longer than the others but that was of no matter. He was back on schedule and time was now on his side. Oh, they were probably missing the doctor by now, those few that cared, or perhaps not. His golf buddies would have long given up on him and would be more than halfway through their round, their minds starting to turn to pints and whiskey chasers. Or perhaps some of those fancy gin cocktails they all seemed to love these days. Before teeing off, they might have called his mobile once or twice – in fact, he'd heard it ring several times in the doctor's pocket and ignored it, but that would be about the extent of their concern.

The people in the clinic may have noticed his car still parked in the reserved bay but that by itself wasn't unusual. It was common knowledge that sometimes he left the car overnight while carousing on the town with his particularly starchy white-collar friends from the solicitor's offices across the way. There was also the time that his wife picked him up on their way out for a fancy dinner, therefore the car in the bay wouldn't ring any alarm bells. Not yet.

The man had been watching the doctor as he had been watching the rest of them. Creatures of habit the lot of them. Bad habits in the main. Selfish habits. The doctor every bit as bad as the rest. Perhaps worse. But not for long more.

When the doctor came to, he did so with a cough and a splutter and nearly choked on the thick wadding in his mouth. His head was pounding from whatever drug he had ingested, and his heart was racing even though he hadn't moved a muscle. Once he got his breath back, he tried to sit up but couldn't. In fact, he could barely shift his weight. His mouth wasn't the only thing that was tethered. His hands were tied securely behind his back and his ankles were attached to a large plastic pallet by a thin cord. On the pallet sat a long rectangular box that even to the doctor in his bewildered state, looked worryingly like a repository for the dead.

Instinctively, he fought to pull free but soon realised his struggles only served to tighten the cord which looped round his neck, effectively constricting his windpipe, millimetre by millimetre. With the trachea having only a diameter of approximately twenty-five millimetres to start with, even the slightest movement was one he could ill afford. With this realisation, the disorientation he had felt on waking quickly gave way to panic.

The man sitting opposite him watched him closely through the disguise of the semi-darkness. Fear was what the man was looking for. Fear was what he thrived on. In this case, he was looking for the kind of fear that the doctor had so flippantly inflicted on others with his indifference. His apathy. The man felt pleased when he saw it mirrored in the doctor's eyes, a furtive ember in the half-light which was the extent of illumination allowed by the nature of his containment.

"You won't remember me," he said after a while, "but I dealt with you once, a while ago now. Back when you cared for someone who was dear to me." He snorted derisively. "Cared for, might be the wrong choice of words. In fact, it is certainly the wrong choice of words. There was no real caring involved. People like you just don't care, do you?"

Doctor Carmody vaguely recognised the voice, though, for the life of him, he couldn't place it. But he could clearly sense the bitterness in the man. Could feel the resentment emanating from him. The doctor attempted to reply but the wadding stifled his efforts to such an extent that he sounded like he was trying to talk underwater.

With a sigh, the man impatiently ripped the tape off the doctor's mouth.

"I do care," Carmody objected breathlessly after spitting out the obstruction. "I have always cared. For me, my patients come first."

"For you, you come first," the man abruptly cut him off. Even though they weren't sitting face to face, Doctor Carmody could sense the man was a drinker. He could smell it off him. A drinker with a screw loose. More than one screw loose, he corrected himself. And not an educated man, he judged by the glimpses he got of him.

Unkempt and crudely dressed. A man that perhaps could be swayed by an erudite voice.

"I'm sure I can help you," he said, "if you tell me why you are doing this. Is it money you need?"

"I don't need your kind of help," the man replied between gritted teeth. As if to underline that statement of independence he raised some sort of thick cudgel over his head and brought it crashing down onto the doctor's left knee. The doctor screamed then jerked and writhed against the ties that bound him before finally falling into an oxygen deprived stupor. The man let him go, just set aside the cudgel, then loosened the cord and patiently waited. He knew from experience that pain would bring the doctor back to him soon.

Some moments later he noted the doctor's grey eyes flutter open. The fear they contained had intensified. No longer an ember. Now a full-blown flame.

"Hurts, doesn't it?" he said in the same weary tone he had earlier used. The same tone but slightly different, the doctor sensed, even in his depths of agony. Weariness now mixed with resolve. The tone reflected as certainty in the man's eyes. Certainty of death. The doctor at once understood that he was looking into the dark eyes of the crazed killer he'd heard about on the news. A man he knew, he now realised. Through hurling, from years before but still recalled well enough to jog a memory. What he couldn't understand was why him. What had he done to deserve this? He was a doctor, for God's sake. A pillar in the community. He had earned respect. Deserved it.

"It's all the nerve endings you see. The knee is one of the most complex joints in the human body. A tapestry of bones, ligaments, and tendons, and of course, the aforementioned nerve endings. But I don't need to tell you that, do I? You're the doctor."

The doctor showed no sign of hearing him, but he had. He had heard every word. And he knew then he'd been wrong. This man was far more educated than he had given him credit for. And far more dangerous.

"Did you like my present?" the man asked. "I hope so. I worked hard on it. Or should I say them? Anyhow, I have another present for you now."

As he spoke, he reached under his coat, and when his left hand reappeared it was holding a knife. A long, dangerous-looking knife with a jagged edge. On seeing the knife, the doctor instinctively began to struggle against his bindings, which in turn reduced the opening in his trachea to the point where he had to gasp to breathe. Rapid, pain-ridden gasps. Still, he struggled, the cord drawing so tight that he suspected his blood flow must have been cut off at the wrists because he could feel his hands going numb. Or was that the cold? He felt so cold. He shouldn't be this cold, not yet. He hadn't been cut as far as he knew. He wasn't losing blood. He glanced down. His shirt was open to the waist but otherwise, he remained fully dressed. A half-open shirt didn't explain the chill he was feeling. He glanced around. Where was he? In some sort of warehouse? Or freezer? Because of the shadows that hovered around it was too dark to tell. Too dark to tell anything except that he was completely alone with this crazy person.

"I'm going to give you the present of sweet release," the man continued with a wicked smile, "but not before you understand the truth of why I'm here."

So, he told him. He told him exactly who he was and why he was there. Explained why the doctor had been chosen. But still, the doctor couldn't understand. His eyes betrayed he hadn't registered a thing suggesting he couldn't even recall the incident. Or, for that matter, the person involved. This incensed the man, so for dramatic effect he rubbed his thumb along the edge of the knife then nodded satisfactorily at the blood that he drew. He'd done a good job honing it.

"Everyone knows that a doctor must swear an oath," the man continued. "The Hippocratic Oath, I believe it is called. On swearing it, they undertake to treat the ill and the injured to the best of their ability. But people also know that doctors are human. And humans can be cruel. You're a cruel man," he accused. "A heartless one, some would say. Well, I'm going to take the core of your cruelty. I'm going to take your heart."

With that he reached forward and pulled the doctor's shirt further back from his chest. Felt round with his fingers for where the heart would be.

"You're the doctor," he reminded Carmody once more. "Am I close?" Then he shrugged. "It doesn't really matter. Your heart won't be used again. I wouldn't wish that on anyone."

With that he plunged the knife deep into the doctor's flesh, then twisted and slowly began to cut, allowing the serrations to do as intended. Though the doctor's windpipe had effectively closed, he found sufficient air to howl a series of terrified objections.

"I too swore an oath," the man said, ignoring the doctor's screams. "The difference is I intend to keep mine."

All the while the doctor screams grew louder. Louder and louder until one final tug on the cord silenced everything, only moments before the knife got the chance. All that was left to the doctor was the infinite and hopeless scream of the damned.

In the blood that flowed, the man dipped his finger.

****

The doctor was found the following morning by a lady golfer named Breda who was playing the first round of the day at the Oldcastle Hurlers classic. Her ball had swung right on the eleventh hole of Oldcastle Golf Course, forcing her to follow it into a thick copse of trees. She cursed when she finally found it next to the roots of a large elm. Then swore loudly when she saw it was nestled in a sharp indent that looked to her like the print made by the heel of a boot. Boot or not, it would mean another shot if not two which she could hardly afford to drop. Her opponent was playing out of her skin, far better than her handicap would suggest and Breda was already two shots down. To make it worse, Breda couldn't stand the stuck-up bitch.

She glanced around but her opponent was nowhere in sight, tempting her to nudge the ball out into the rough and continue from there. But only for the briefest of moments. Breda was a lot of things, but she wasn't a cheat. With no choice but to take the dropped shots on the chin, she stooped down to retrieve the ball and that's when something landed on her neck.

Something faint, splashing like a drop of water, but thicker. Fearing it was a bird poo, she cursed and as she hurried to wipe it off, she straightened to peer upwards into the branches to shoo away the offending creature. The second drop landed on her upturned face, close to the edge of her mouth, tempting her tongue to involuntarily flick out and taste its distinct metallic tang. Scrunching her face in disgust she quickly wiped her mouth with her sleeve then studied the stain that had transferred to the white fabric of her windbreaker. She froze. It wasn't bird poo. Unless the bird was of some rare and exotic type she'd never heard of. Because this poo was deep red in colour and tasted of copper.

Chapter 11

Having arranged it for eleven a.m., Britney chose the Castle Café to meet with the detective from Dublin. Being housed on the bottom floor of one of the castle's guard-towers the café offered a clear view of the park and the woods beyond. Apart from this beautiful setting the café served the best coffee in town. It also provided outdoor seating which offered a relative but welcome level of privacy.

After the heavy weather of previous days, she was pleased that although clouds still lingered, the morning was generally bright with a promise of sunshine. She hoped it was a good omen for the meeting. So far, it had been a tough few hours for the force. The news of the murdered doctor had spread through the community like wildfire. The poor golfer that had found the body earlier that Friday morning was on a course of heavy sedation while the rest of the town's population were on high alert. First, a body found hanging in a HAI dressing room and now a second found hanging on the grounds of Oldcastle Golf Club. Both bodies were brutalised premortem and both crimes were obviously carried out by the same person. To make it worse, there was also the third connection – the body in Dublin, butchered and hung in the same fashion. All three victims were well known in their communities which meant the papers were having a field day, their literary knives well and truly out for the Gardaí.

Independent News, the paper for which Marie Cox had worked, was especially vitriolic, accusing the entire force of incompetence, indifference or both, and cited their collective failings as the reason for the alarming rise in gang warfare and vicious crime. They believed that Marie Cox would still be alive if the Gardaí were doing their jobs. Those other men too.

Britney wasn't sure if that was the case but what she did know was that the more sensational the headline, the more anxious the public grew. It was getting so bad that some people were afraid to leave their houses while others had taken to meeting in secret to plan ways of combatting the fear that was taking hold. There was a consensus amongst the more belligerent of these groups that if the police weren't going to stop this man, they would. Britney shook her head at the thought of that. The last thing they needed was a band of vigilantes roaming the streets. However, she had a feeling that things were going to get a whole lot worse before they got better.

With such pressure coming from the public, the station was even less appealing than normal. Several extra Gardaí had been called in from surrounding stations to help with the investigation, resulting in it being crowded, hot and boiling over with tension.

With personnel already on edge, the presence of a sweaty Detective Flynn didn't help matters. He was barking orders at anyone that moved, like a panicked general blinded by a cloud of smoke. The result was that people were running here and there but getting nowhere. The only good thing about the mayhem was it allowed Britney to slip out of the station unchallenged. It was an opportunity at which she wasn't about to turn up her nose.

As she had for the doomed date with Bob Harris, Britney arrived early and waited for a table at the end of the terrace to become vacant before she sat. While she waited, she sipped coffee and nibbled on a bun, watching people come and go. Joggers, sightseers, families on a day out. The castle attracted all sorts. As she watched, she saw Alan Rourke appear from the direction of the carpark, carrying a plastic crate filled with vegetables and chilled meat, clearly a delivery for the cafe. For a moment their eyes met, but her presence didn't seem to register with him. He looked lost. Forlorn. As if he had the weight of the world on his shoulders. Britney hoped this meeting would go some way to lifting that weight. For him, for Stacey, and for those two beautiful kids.

She had almost finished her coffee by the time the cavalry from Dublin arrived. As the hands of an ancient looking clock on the exterior wall approached eleven a.m., she spotted them coming through the main gates long before they reached the steps to the terrace on which she sat.

As they neared, she noted they were at the same time both older and younger than she had imagined. And rather eccentric, where she'd hoped for plain and simple. The bearded detective, with his long trench-coat and hobbling gait, had a kind of cut-throat pirate look about him – she actually found herself checking to see if he was sporting a hook for a hand. The brown-skinned young man that followed him was dressed maturely in navy slacks, a white shirt, and blue tie, but looked like he had yet to nick his face with a razor blade. So, this is what I get for reinforcements, she grumbled to herself. Long John Silver and one of the Jackson Five.

However, her attitude changed once they had made their way toward her table. After a quick scan of the patrons, the senior detective made a beeline for her as if he recognised her from a previous encounter. That, she knew, wasn't possible. They had never met before.

"Sergeant Kent?" he asked as he reached her table. She nodded and glanced around. "Yes. How did you know?" For once, she wasn't in uniform as she'd badly stained it the night before with the takeaway curry she'd picked up in Fat Tony's. Having gotten late home, she hadn't had a chance to clean it, and with her backup already in the wash, she was left with little choice but go to work in plain clothes and risk the wrath of Halley once more. Not sporting the tell-tale uniform, she couldn't think of any other signs that would have given her away.

The detective shrugged. "A young lady sitting alone."

She shook her head dubiously. "I'm not the only young woman here sitting alone." She had spotted two more while she was waiting. One in the furthest corner of the terrace working on a laptop and the other sitting near the steps reading a morning paper. She could quite easily have been either of those.

"True. But neither of the other two are deliberately sitting out of earshot of the other customers, and in a position where they can clearly see anyone coming through the gates, therefore giving them a heads up on their party's arrival. And neither of them is sitting in line with the steps where they can get a clear view of anyone entering and therefore, get a read on the kind of people they would soon be dealing with," he smiled. "This is the seat I would have chosen. Ergo, hi to you, Miss Kent."

She smiled appreciatively. Finally, a detective with an imagination. Things were looking up.

"By the way, I'm not quite as infirm as I appear. Just my knees. They groan after spending too long bent up in a car, but they'll be fine. In a while, I'll be running around like a gazelle."

"I'm sure you will," Britney replied sceptically. Up close she could see that he wasn't quite as old as she had first feared, yet he was no spring chicken. Judging by the furrowed brow and grizzled beard, she estimated him to be close to retirement age while his ruddy complexion gave the impression of an individual who was always hot, even in winter. Running around like a gazelle. Not a chance.

The younger man was good-looking, some would even say his ethnic features and chestnut skin elevated him to striking. He was above medium height and well built. He exuded honesty from his large eyes – a distinctive mixture of grey, green and blue.

"I'm Detective Richie Lyons," the older man said. "This is Daniel…eh…"

"Owens," the young Garda interjected wearily. "Danny Owens."

"Pleased to meet you, both," she replied as she rose halfway off the chair to take their proffered hands in turn. "Sergeant Britney Kent."

Lyons pulled up a chair opposite Britney. Danny sat to her right.

"Ok, now that the formalities are out of the way," Lyons said, "let's order some coffee. That M50 was almost the death of me. They're wrong when they call it the biggest carpark in the world. It's not a carpark. It's a fucking graveyard."

'Yeah, smelled like one too,' thought Danny, recalling the farts Lyons had released on the way down. Stank like someone had shoved a dead rat up his hole. He was killing himself with all that drink but didn't know it. Or maybe he did and didn't care. But now Danny appreciated an exquisite new aroma. The sergeant's perfume. Though subtle, it had a wildflower scent that reminded him of evening walks back home. Her scent wasn't the only thing he found distracting about her. Petite with fine brown hair tied up in a neat ponytail, she was certainly pretty, even in the wrinkled shirt and slacks that looked like they'd been thrown on in a hurry. She wore no makeup, not even to hide the slight, linear blemish that ran from the corner of her eye to below the curve of her left cheekbone. But with those eyes, she didn't need to. They were the focal point of her face, overriding everything else, even what others might perceive as flaws. Large and hazelnut brown, they boasted long, elegant eyelashes – the kind some women would pay a small fortune to have artificially applied. In this case, Danny could tell they were perfectly natural. In fact, it was this lack of embellishment that elevated Sergeant Kent from pretty to stunning, Danny decided.

As those eyes studied Lyons, they seemed both eager and wary at the same time, like a deer tempted to share the life-giving waters of a stream with an ageing bear.

Lyons didn't seem to notice her eyes on him. He was focused on getting served. With a wave of a hand the size of a pitching glove, he quickly caught the attention of a waitress donning a pink apron which had the image of a steaming coffee cup in the shape of a castle emblazoned on the front. The waitress proved both experienced and efficient, so it didn't take long before he was sipping contentedly from a steaming Americano. Danny noted his big hand folded around the mug in the same way he drank his pints of beer. Britney feared the stoneware would shatter in his giant left paw and wondered if a similar incident had caused the jagged scar that ran along his thick index finger.

A quick perusal of his younger colleague revealed no such war wounds, at least outwardly. His strangely tinted eyes however, displayed a level of weariness that belied his age. Opting for a strong cup of tea he took a long gratifying slug before setting it down on the table with a sigh. Britney chose to forego a refill of her coffee as her head was already buzzing. Instead, she flicked open her notepad and clicked the top of her ball-point. It was time to get down to business.

Just then somebody so unexpected walked up the steps that Britney nearly dropped her pen. It was her foreman, Bob Harris. To her relief, he didn't spot her straight off but walked up to the counter to browse the menu. After a moment he caught the attention of the girl serving and ordered a coffee and ham roll to go. He was obviously on a break as he was in his work clothes, but Britney still thought he looked every bit as tasty as any of the sweetest treats on the menu. As he waited for his order to be filled, he turned around and casually scanned the room, nodding hello to one of the other customers that happened to be glancing in his direction. Britney noted that, funnily enough, it was mostly the women present that happened to be looking up at him and suddenly she felt a wave of jealousy. It was ridiculous, of course, but she couldn't help it. No more than she could help breathing.

When his glance swung through the door and in her direction, their eyes immediately locked, and her heart leapt. His gaze was so intense, so vibrant that she couldn't look away, even if she wanted to. A moment later the serving girl broke the spell when she set Bob's order on the counter. Bob held Britney's gaze for an instant longer then turned to pay, reluctantly severing the connection. Still, Britney couldn't help but smile. It had only been a brief interchange, yet it felt as if an entire conversation had passed between them. Apologies. Understanding. Absolution. It was all there. All present in that briefest of moments.

As he turned to leave, he acknowledged her with a shy wave and a hopeful smile. She knew then that they would soon meet again. And that when they did, it would be no half-finished fairly-tale. Cinderella wouldn't be running off before midnight this time.

"That your boyfriend?" Lyons asked with a hint of humour. His lips tugged to the right and up, his eyes creased, but in a jolly way. For some reason, it made the scar on his ear more noticeable.

Britney felt her face redden. "Just someone I know," she replied a little too quickly.

"Just someone I know, doesn't make a girl blush like that!" Lyons remarked with rare humour lingering in his eyes. Danny couldn't help but feel for the sergeant. She'd obviously been caught off guard and was now doing her best to ignore the detective. She sat up in her chair and tried to compose herself, but Danny noticed that despite the colour in her cheeks, she was smiling.

For her part, Britney chided herself for acting like a lovesick schoolgirl in front of colleagues. Just then her phone beeped, and, in turn, the colour in her cheeks deepened. She instinctively knew it would be a message from Bob. Taking a deep breath, she tried to ignore it, but even though what she was there to discuss was life and death, she could hardly wait to read it.

"This is the situation from my point of view," she began, hoping her tone adequately declared it was time to move on. To herself as much as to her colleagues. "As you are aware, I am part of the team working on the case that this morning's papers have inevitably dubbed 'The Courier'…" Although the brunch rush was over, and the coffee shop was practically empty now she kept her voice low.

"Inevitably?" It was the young Garda who spoke. It was a naïve question, but Britney welcomed it as a sign they were now firmly focused on the case and not on her love life.

"Of course," Lyons replied, his eyes now dead serious. "Once they discovered that the cases were linked by the delivery of a hand, a handle like that was inevitable? Courier. Postman." He shrugged. "It mightn't be all that original but now that it's out there, we are all stuck with it. Forever."

"Exactly. And as I was saying, I'm part of the team working on this case, but unfortunately, I use the term 'team' loosely. The lead detective fancies himself as an untouchable and from what I can tell, his partner is little better." Corrupt too, she reminded herself but wasn't prepared to go into detail regarding that just yet. Not until it was concrete. "The rest of the Gardaí on the case seem to be floundering under their leadership. There is no proper sharing of information or, for that matter, anything that would resemble a team briefing. Just the lead detectives and their cronies. Us minions just get fed scraps. It's like we are all running around in the dark and no one has the sense to switch on the light." She looked to Detective Lyons first, then to the young Garda, Danny Owens. "That's why I'm here," she informed them, a glint of determination in her brown eyes. "I suppose you could say I want to switch on the light."

"That's fair enough," Lyons acknowledged, "but you must understand that we will have to liaise with your team-leader whether you like it or not. In fact, we are heading directly to your station once this meeting is over."

"I understand that, Detective, and I'm fully ok with it – not that I have a choice."

"There's always a choice."

"But there's also procedure," Danny reminded them quickly. Like them or not, rules are there to protect everyone. Black, white, rich, poor. He felt he was in enough trouble already without loading on more. Lyons had only returned to the station that morning and already he had him off gallivanting. Danny promised himself that once they got back, he was approaching the Super with his misgivings once and for all.

"Normally, I'd agree," Britney replied, "but on this occasion, I say to hell with procedure." She glanced at Lyons. "Do you know Detective Flynn?"

Lyons gave a brief shake of his head before glancing at his coffee. "Can't say I do."

"Well, apart from being on some sort of ego trip," Britney continued, "he is also the nephew of our Superintendent and I have a feeling that once he gets what he needs from you, he'll commandeer the entire case. Not necessarily to solve it, because I don't think he'd be capable of discovering who ate the three bears' porridge, but he'll be determined to control it. I've a feeling the last thing he'll want is outsiders poking their nose around on what he likes to think is his patch. If that happens," she shrugged, "God help us. We'll have more bodies than Dunkirk."

"What you're proposing is we liaise with this Flynn fellow just to be seen as meeting with our procedural requirements but at the same time, we run our own private little investigation behind his back?" Lyons' expression was inscrutable.

"Exactly. That way nothing can fall between the cracks. And at the moment, the cracks we're dealing with would make the Mariana Trench look like a bicycle-wheel rut."

"Fair enough," Lyons replied thoughtfully. "Kind of right up my street actually. Never did like that word procedure."

"I never would have guessed, sir," Danny replied wryly. Then feeling it would be best to start as they meant to go on, he addressed Britney with the truth of their position. "The detective's phone has been hopping all morning with our Super trying to drag him back to the office. You see, Sergeant, he's officially on desk duty." He could feel Lyons eyes boring into him now, but he didn't care. It was bad enough flouting the rules where the Super was concerned but even though he'd only met her, he felt this girl deserved better. He got the feeling she was depending on them. "The truth is that our position on this case is no more official than yours. It just landed in our laps."

"That may well be the case, young man," Lyons agreed, acidly. "But now that I'm on it, wild horses wouldn't drag me off."

"I know how you feel, Detective. Flynn tried to restrict me to desk duty too, but I'm not having it. Something stinks about the way this case is being run and I'm going to find out what."

"Strong words, Sergeant."

Britney shrugged. Perhaps, in her frustration she had said too much but it was the truth. She told him so.

"Now, that's a pair of balls," Lyons noted admiringly. He threw a dismissive glance at Danny. "You're free to go anytime you want, young man. So far, all you've done is chauffeur me around, meaning the only thing they could cite you for is driving like a girl. Oh yeah…and drinking like one!"

'Perfectly fine by me,' Danny thought. 'The sergeant is welcome to you, farts and all.'

"Ok, Sergeant Kent," Lyons continued, in a more business-like tone, "now that we've got the foreplay out of the way, if you show me yours, I'll show you mine."

Britney bestowed him with her best gap-toothed smile. If it was Detective Flynn who had said that she might have slapped his face, but now she simply returned her attention to her notebook and eagerly flicked through the pages. Time to get to work.

****

Despite the mayhem, Britney's extended absence didn't go unnoticed at Oldcastle Garda Station. After a series of unwarranted barks at the new guy Ben to take his finger out, Flynn signalled to Joe to have a quick meeting in his office.

"She's up to no good as usual, that Britney one," he said, once the door was securely closed behind them. "Gave her some paperwork to file then she snuck out the back, thinking I wouldn't notice. The last thing we need right now is a damn busybody throwing a spanner in the works."

Joe readily agreed. "Ok, we'll keep a close eye on her from now on, but I wouldn't worry too much about her. She's just a plodder trying to play at detective. And she's on her own so…" He paused. "Although herself and that new girl, Fiona, do seem to be thick as thieves these days." His eyes lingered on Flynn. "That could be a worry."

Flynn gave a pensive nod. "You think she's trying to get Fiona on side with a view to working together to gather evidence behind our backs?"

"Possibly. But even so, what harm can she do? Where can she go with a complaint? To your uncle?"

Flynn smiled cockily at that. "That is true. But still, we're not in a position to take any chances. Even if we were, I'd like to take her down a peg or two. She's getting too big for her boots. By the time all this is over, I intend to show her what happens when you cross Terry Flynn."

Joe nodded his approval, although he knew his partner's ruthless streak required carefully monitoring. The upcoming task demanded it.

"Is the consignment still on schedule?" he asked.

"Of course," Flynn replied. "All is going according to plan. And you're about to move up in the world. The boss thinks it's about time you cut your teeth, if you know what I mean."

"Ok. Just tell me when and where," Joe said, an eager smile spreading across his face. He was tempted to question the identity of this 'boss' that Flynn kept referring to but knew he'd get the same dismissive answer as the last time.

Flynn gave a brief shake of his head. "All in a good time, Joe. All in good time." His phone buzzed prompting him to dip his hand into his pocket and draw it out. "But for now, we've got immediate things to worry about. This Detective from Dublin."

"Lyons?"

"Yes, Lyons. I know him, we go back a bit. He's a stubborn bastard. Old school. The last thing we need is for Kent to be buzzing in his ear." He checked his phone and saw he'd received a message. "In fact, my sources tell me our little busy body is meeting with him right now."

"Shit," Joe swore. "Now, that could be a problem." He also knew of Lyons as a man not to be messed with. In fact, if he didn't know better, he'd mark him down as this enigmatic leader Flynn seemed so eager to protect. If, indeed, there was such a leader.

"It's being managed," Flynn said, "and as I said, I know Lyons from old. But he won't be coming on his own and I can't afford anyone digging too deep, especially not now. So, we take more than we give and have him leaving here thinking we couldn't find a fanny in a whorehouse." He smirked at his little bit of inhouse humour. "That way we can focus on the consignment. If that goes according to plan, we can stand back and let those Jackeens be the ones buried under this steaming pile of shit."

Joe nodded. "Ok. Do we mention Jim Rourke?"

"No. Not unless we have to. Kent thinks she's made a connection, and maybe she has, but she hasn't a clue about Rourke's connection to us. And that's the way we want to keep it. Otherwise, our carefully erected house of cards comes crashing down." He sighed deeply to release his pent-up frustration. Things were getting more complicated than he'd hoped. "As far as closing this thing goes, I don't care who's seen as doing the donkey work. But if it starts to look like it's going to pan out, we'll make sure to be in a position to take the credit. In other words, if it starts raining porridge, we're the ones standing there with the goddamn spoon. Capeesh?"

"Understood."

"By the way when Lyons is here, I do all the talking. You listen. Make a goddamn coffee if you want to. But whatever happens…" He fixed his eyes on Joe, his dark gaze penetrating. Joe couldn't decide if he saw a flash of fear or craziness in Flynn's eyes. "Whatever happens, my name has to be kept out of this," Flynn growled between gritted teeth. "Do you understand?"

Joe nodded. "No loose ends."

"Exactly."

****

"You've probably heard that since I was in contact with you there has been another development." Britney said. Apart from a small group of Spanish sightseers, the café was practically empty now, so they could talk a little more freely. "A body. Discovered this morning on the local golf course."

"Yes," Detective Lyons replied. "The station informed us on the way down. A doctor."

"Yes. A very prominent man in the Oldcastle community. So, the pressure is ramped up on all sides, meaning we don't have time to dilly dally." Reflecting on how he'd delayed their meeting by days, she cast Lyons a reproachful look, which he blatantly ignored. Water off a duck's back, she judged with irritation.

"So, now we've got three dead bodies," she continued. "All apparently strangers to each other yet somehow linked. We know without a shadow of a doubt they are linked because the killer has linked them. Yes, with his special delivery but also with his MO. They were all butchered, then strangled before being hanged, and all three had their left kneecap smashed. Yet as far as we can tell, there is nothing else to connect them apart from what I just mentioned. Am I right?"

Lyons nodded. "Two of them are here in Oldcastle but one of them is on my patch so, no obvious link there. The only thing we see that links our Miss Cox to your first hanging man is the left hand she received in the post. Just to be clear, forensic analysis has proven that it is Donie Cullen's hand, severed premortem. As yet, we can find nothing linking Miss Cox to the doctor."

Britney nodded thoughtfully. "And as yet, we can find nothing to link Donie Cullen to the doctor, apart from both of them residing in the same county. Mr Cullen wasn't a patient at the doctor's clinic nor was he a member at the golf course where Dr Carmody spent most of his spare time. In fact, I don't think Mr Cullen even played golf." She turned another page in her notebook. "We've checked their respective financial records and found no link there either, so, as far as we know, they weren't in business together. As it stands, they seem to be quite separate individuals."

"Had the doctor any link with the HAI club where Mr Cullen was found?" Danny asked.

It was a good question, but again the answer was a negative. "Not that we can tell," Britney replied. "Why would he? He's from a different parish, he would naturally support a different club. He certainly had some involvement in the HAI itself but," she shrugged, "who in Oldcastle doesn't?"

"True," Danny replied. "Even the detective here used to play for The Tigers at one time, back in the Dark Ages." He shook his head, still struggling with the revelation. "He gave it up for a woman."

Britney looked at Detective Lyons with renewed interest. "You played for Oldcastle?"

"Briefly," Lyons replied casting a look of annoyance in Danny's direction. "You've had colds longer."

Danny ignored the glance. "I looked him up. Seems Richie here wasn't half bad," he smiled cheekily. "Could catch swallows coming out of a barn, they said. If I'd had that chance, I would have taken hand and all. Certainly, wouldn't have passed it up for a girl!"

"Ah yeah, but your generation understands nothing about life," Lyons replied with a sniff. "You're all blighted by the need for instant gratification. Can see no value in the long game. But you'll learn," he cautioned. Now, a knowing smirk tugged at the corners of his thick lips. "If your big mouth doesn't get you in trouble first, that is!"

Despite the admonishment, Danny retained his cheeky grin as Lyons turned to address Sergeant Kent. "Just to let you know, I grew up here. Near Sycamore Row. So, I know this town pretty well."

"Oh," Britney pursed her lips, thoughtfully. "That's not far from the doctor's surgery. Did you know Doctor Carmody?"

Lyons shook his head. "I've been gone a long time."

"What about Cullen?"

Lyons paused. He could see the sergeant watching him closely, adding two and two, and no doubt coming up with five. Determined to nip the idea in the bud, he said, "Apart from recognising her as a sportswriter, I didn't know Marie Cox either until the day she walked into our station." Then added pointedly, "So there's no conflict of interest here."

Danny looked at him sharply but said nothing.

"That's good to know," Britney replied evenly. She had noticed the look from the young Garda but thought it best to let it pass. Then after a moment's consideration, she changed her mind. Even though this was a superior Garda she was speaking to, albeit from another station, she felt it was her duty to make certain. The last thing she wanted was to get caught up on a revenge mission because Lyons happened to know one of the victims and was on a personal undertaking to bring the killer to justice.

"However, it is a bit of a coincidence, you'll have to admit," she pressed. "A detective originally from Oldcastle having a case fall into his lap that brings him right back to his hometown." It was bad enough that she was running around behind the backs of her so-called team, but if it turned out that the detective she was liaising with had such a clear conflict of interest, it would mean the end of her career for sure. Even as she thought it, she realised how hypocritical it sounded. 'Britney! Have you forgotten Bob Harris, the witness you were ready to jump into the sack with?'

"Yes, it is a coincidence," Lyons insisted. "And that's all it is."

It was clear that the sergeant's barely disguised insinuation both surprised and annoyed him. Yet, Danny suspected Lyons couldn't help but admire the girl's audacity. The detective was right, she had more balls than most male Gardaí he knew.

Still, Lyons sat forward until they were close enough to each other they could arm wrestle. His expression was stony, and Danny could feel the tension rise a notch or two. Though the wariness remained in her eyes, Britney didn't so much as flinch under Lyons's stony gaze.

"What are you pussyfooting around, young lady?" he began a tad sharply. "Is it the idea that I intentionally inserted myself into this investigation? That perhaps I have some sort of personal agenda and that's why I'm here talking to you and not off playing golf, waiting for a position to open up in some retirement village. Perhaps I was having an affair with Miss Cox and I'm out to avenge her or, worse still, perhaps I'm the crazed killer everyone is looking for, so I cleverly put myself in a position to steer you all on a wild goose chase," he snorted as he sat back in the chair. "It's not the case, of course. Not that it would be such a difficult task."

Now, Britney sat back in her chair too. She fiddled with her empty coffee cup for a moment, then sighed. "Ok. Then why are you here and not playing golf with your cronies?"

Detective Lyons ran his hand through his beard, clearly disconcerted by the tenacity of the girl. "Simply because of rank alone, I am under no obligation to explain myself to you," he stated, "but I will anyway. I needed this case. I was resigned to filing paperwork for the remainder of my time until the most unfortunate Miss Cox came into the station. I happened to be the only detective present at the time and the highest-ranking Garda on duty. So, as young Daniel here so eloquently put it, I took hand and all, pardon the p…" he paused in mid-sentence, shut his eyes for a moment, and shook his head as if an idea had suddenly struck him. "Greed!" he exclaimed when he opened them again. He sat up in his chair, a sudden energy emanating from him. "It's greed!"

"What?" Danny eyebrows furrowed. He glanced at Britney. She looked just as confused by the sudden change of direction.

"Greed," repeated Lyons. "Don't you see. The severed hand. It symbolises his greed. Donie Cullen's greed."

"Of course," Britney sighed as she picked up his train of thought. She leaned forward in her chair, her expression now one of engagement rather than wariness. "And cutting off the ears?"

Detective Lyons shrugged. "What do you do with your ears?"

"You listen," replied Danny.

Lyons snorted. "Only when it suits, with you apparently." He was clearly still miffed about Danny's earlier disclosure. "But yes. You listen. In the killer's mind, Miss Cox may have refused to listen. To what, I don't know but I think whatever it was that she didn't want to hear, killed her."

Britney nodded, her enthusiasm gaining momentum. "And the doctor's heart was cut out because?" She left it hanging.

"The killer considered him cruel?" Danny suggested with eyebrows raised. "Heartless."

"Ok, I can buy that," Britney admitted. "But why send the hand to Marie Cox. As a warning? Or to frighten her?"

Detective Lyons shook his head. "I think both. But I also think it's more than that. I think he's leading us. From one to another. Joining the dots for us if you like. Perhaps time isn't on his side. Or perhaps he thinks we'd be too stupid to make the connection ourselves."

'I can think of at least one detective that would be,' Britney agreed in her head. 'Sidekick Joe making it two.'

"If that's the case, Marie Cox's ears should have been sent to the doctor," she pointed out, "but as yet no one has reported their discovery."

"Tell them to keep looking," Lyons urged. "They'll be there somewhere. In his house or in his car perhaps. But they'll be there." He nodded to himself as if to acknowledge his certainty. "This is personal, so he would have delivered them himself."

Britney was clearly in agreement.

"We've already checked with all the courier companies working in the area and none of them had a record of the address for either the doctor's house or his surgery. We then canvassed both neighbourhoods to see if anyone might have been seen hanging around or if there was someone spotted making a delivery but nothing yet."

"Again, keep on checking. You never know, someone could have spotted him without realising it."

Britney nodded then glanced from the detective to the young Garda. "What about Miss Cox? Anyone spot anything strange around the time she received the delivery?"

Danny gave a slight inclination of his head. "The old woman next door might have seen someone, but her description was vague. Just a man in a coat. And no courier deliveries registered for the area either. If he made the delivery himself, he must be one cool character. And very organised to obtain the building code then get in and out of the building without incident. At least the first time."

"The first time?" Britney looked from one to the other. Was she missing something?

"When he made the delivery, he means," Lyons interjected. He discreetly shot a cautionary glance at Danny then gave a brief shake of his head. "No one saw him on that occasion, except possibly the old lady as my young colleague explained. And I mean possibly. She's quite doddery. And, I got the impression, prone to exaggeration."

"A man in a coat is hardly an exaggeration?" Britney replied. 'Especially not, considering the evidence,' she thought to herself. Evidence she had yet to reveal. "Anyone else in the building."

Lyons gave a shake of his head. "The old woman and her husband live in the only other occupied apartment. The ground floor is currently vacant."

"Someone definitely saw our killer the second time, though," Lyons pursed his lips ruefully. "Unfortunately, she's now dead."

Britney eyes wandered from one to the other again then nodded. Forgetting it was empty, she picked up her coffee to take a sip but only got the dregs which, to her distaste, were cold and tasteless. It had been a touch watery to begin with. Just like the explanation she had just received. Lyons was obviously holding something back. She considered following up but decided to leave it alone for now. She didn't want to alienate these two as well. Instead, she jotted an entry in her notebook regarding the funny looks her two colleagues had just shared.

"Any evidence left at the scene?" she asked after a moment.

Lyons shook his head. "Nothing obvious. Just the body and the ligature. And the pool of blood, of course. However, we did find some crumpled newspaper in a bin. We think it was used to wrap the box the hand arrived in, but best of luck getting fingerprints off that."

"Newspaper?" Britney queried, her brown eyes focusing. "Let me guess…pages from the Independent News?"

Lyons eyed Britney, obviously impressed. "Yes, as a matter of fact. It was some sports pages from an old edition of the paper. Apart from the fact that Miss Cox was the named reporter, it contained nothing significant. Only statistics and match reports. The kind of paper you'd use to wrap your fish and chips."

"We also found similar sheets of newspaper placed at the Cullen scene."

"Placed?"

"Yes. They were found directly under where the body was hanging. Soaked in the victim's blood."

"Interesting." Lyons remarked thoughtfully but didn't elaborate.

"Apart from the paper, forensics found little else at the scene." Britney stated. "No conflicting traces. No alien residues. How about your guys?"

"Same as that. The team came back empty-handed on everything including the nylon string used to tie Miss Cox's hair back. And the nylon used to strangle her, of course."

"She was strangled before being hanged then?" Britney asked, sitting further forward. "So was our guy. And with some kind of nylon string, you think?"

"More like a thin nylon cord, blue and white in colour. It left a deep mark in her neck which we didn't notice at first, concealed as it was by the heavy swelling."

"Our guy was strangled first too. Probably with the same type of string or cord. Is nylon a common item?"

"Very, so there no point trying to trace the purchaser of the cord. This type of nylon has many uses. Rope obviously being one. Then there's guitar strings, angling, clothes even."

On hearing his reply, Britney's eyes shifted causing Lyons to pause, but whatever she twigged, she kept it to herself. Deciding he couldn't blame her for playing him at his own game, he continued. "Forensics found no traces on it apart from DNA from Miss Cox. It seems our killer either got lucky or he knows what he's doing. I'm swayed towards the latter and guessing he's wiping everything down as he goes. Using gloves too and taping the cuffs of his clothes so he doesn't deposit DNA. Perhaps using Vaseline on his eyebrows."

"What if he's like you and has a beard?" Danny enquired.

"He'll shave it off."

"Or use some sort of facial covering," Danny replied, recalling the man he'd chased.

"Or he could be just killing them elsewhere," Britney suggested.

"Possibly," Lyons agreed, recalling Holmes' remarks regarding conflicting blood temperature. He decided not to share his thoughts.

"No sign of sexual assault?"

"No. Torture but no rape. So, no DNA there either, I'm afraid."

"Well, he did make a mistake with the doctor," she informed them. "Quite a big one."

"Did he?" Lyons asked, sounding surprised.

"He was picked up by the cameras in the parking area. We have a half-decent image of him abducting Doctor

Carmody. A tall man, six foot, maybe taller, driving a battered-looking Toyota Corolla saloon."

"Did they capture his face?"

"Unfortunately, not," Britney replied. "He was wearing a broad hood or hat which covered his face from the camera, and he had on a long coat which covered most of his body. Sound familiar?"

"The description the old woman gave," Danny supplied.

Britney gave a pensive nod. She was convinced she had seen a similar outfit before but for the life of her couldn't recall where. She threw a deferential nod in Danny's direction. "We do believe he was wearing some sort of facial disguise as well, but the footage was grainy."

"Sounds to me like he was prepared on all fronts. A long coat covers a multitude, in regard to both DNA and camera lenses," Lyons observed. "So, maybe not such a mistake, after all."

"The car can be traced. In fact, we are working on that now."

Lyons shook his head. "It'll be a black-market job. Probably brought in from England through the back door. No tax. No insurance. Chassis number ground off. No way of tracing it to any previous owner here."

Britney shrugged. "Maybe." It was still a possible lead, she was prepared to argue, but decided to move on. "This guy is working a tight schedule," she said after consulting her notebook. "I mean our body discovered on Saturday and your Cox woman on Sunday."

"And the hand delivered Saturday morning," Danny said. "He certainly gets around."

"But how? We haven't found that car on any motorway cameras between Dublin and Oldcastle so what does he use? Another car, a train, a bus, or what? And why the rush? Is there some deadline he needs to meet?"

"Or he is escalating," Lyons replied. "Which could mean there are bodies we don't know about yet."

Britney released a heavy sigh at that thought.

"Ok," she said, her voice subdued, "we have a basic understanding of his MO and a loose theory regarding his motivation," she stated in frustration, "but it still leaves us with three strangers. These people. What links them?" 'And what links them to Jim Rourke, she wondered but kept the thought to herself. She didn't want to cloud their thinking with her theories. Not before they had a chance to form their own.

"That, my dear, is the million-dollar question," Lyons replied. "It could be anything from praying at the same church to shopping at the same store… or it could be nothing at all. They could be completely random." He shrugged. "Just unfortunate enough to fit the killer's twisted criteria."

When he looked at Britney there was a shadow in his eyes. "Have you ever seen the film Seven?"

"Of course," Britney replied. "Brad Pitt!"

"Yes, amongst others," Lyons acknowledged, with, Britney noted, the usual derisory tone ordinary men seemed to reserve for discussions concerning the more beautiful specimens of their sex. Why did everything have to become a pissing contest?

"The point is, after receiving the hand, Danny suggested this might be like the film, Seven. Of course, I initially scoffed at the idea. But now I think he was right. In more ways than one. Apart from the killer displaying psychopathic tendencies and undisguised sadism, he is doing this for a reason. He is teaching these people a lesson. And at the same time, he is teaching us a lesson. The rest of the world. He won't stop until the lesson is learned. Or…"

"Or," Danny finished, his usually upbeat expression grim, "we catch him."

Britney sat back in the chair and pinched the bridge of her nose. On hearing the detective outline his thoughts on the kind of killer they were looking for, she suddenly felt she was in way over her head. She wasn't trained to catch psychopaths. It was way above her pay grade. She was trained to check for motor insurance and broken taillights. Perhaps investigate the odd burglary. Not chase psychopathic, serial killers. Yet, she knew she couldn't leave the investigation to Flynn and his sidekick Joe. It would be a massacre in more ways than one.

"There's another part to this," she tentatively informed the pair now sitting opposite her. "At least I think there is."

"Oh?"

"Yes. A man was reported missing late last week. Last Saturday to be exact. His wife called it in."

"Purely a coincidence, surely?" Lyons concluded with a wry smile.

"Touché," Britney replied dryly, recognising the reversal of sentiment from their earlier exchange. "But this next thing really is a coincidence. Too much of a coincidence in my view. The missing man's name is Jim Rourke. His father is Alan Rourke who just happens to be one of the men who found Donie Cullen's body. His van was spotted outside of the hurling field leading up to the murder and it was well known there was animosity between himself and Cullen. Also, according to our station log he was arrested a few years back for assault. Although no charges were filed, it still points to the fact that he may be capable of violence." She looked from one of them to the other, her expression expectant.

"And you think that this Jim Rourke is somehow involved. May even be the killer," Detective Lyons replied thoughtfully. "His bloodlust cultivated perhaps by a hatred for Cullen and a fractious relationship with his own father." He raised an eyebrow. "Abuse maybe?"

Britney nodded slowly, grateful that someone was taking her seriously. "Yes. He kills Cullen and positions the body in a place he knew his father would find it. As some sort of message perhaps. Or to taunt him." She shrugged. "But I've nothing to base my suspicions on except what I just told you."

"And you're thinking he's not missing," Danny mused. "He's in hiding."

"Exactly."

"Who reported him missing?"

"His wife."

"Any chance this Rourke fella is dead, and his wife is involved?"

"That's kind of like coming home and finding your house empty then wondering if the resident mouse ate your cat." Britney shrugged at Danny's quizzical look. "If you met her, you'd know what I meant. She's a nervous wreck. And he's a big man. Strong."

"Conjecture is all well and good," Lyons interjected impatiently. Once again, he picked up his cup like a tumbler and took a sip. Britney could tell by the curling of his lip that his coffee had gone cold too. "But apart from the fact this man is missing, what's the connection to Marie Cox. Or to the doctor?" he asked.

Britney shook her head ruefully. "That, I don't know."

Lyon set the cup down then sat back and sighed. "We're going around in circles here," he said, "and as a hurling manager of mine used to say, better to save your legs and let the ball do the work." He then paused as a thought struck him. "Speaking of hurling, I know that name. Jim Rourke. Did he hurl one time?"

"Yes," Britney replied. "Seemingly he lasted every bit as long as you did. Only he got distracted by drink, not women."

"A woman," Lyons corrected immediately, then mused. "I knew I'd heard that name before. Apart from the body found in the club rooms, perhaps there's a HAI connection in all of this?"

"Possibly," Britney replied, sounding unconvinced but willing to hear him out. "But in what way?"

"Money, of course. It's always a bone of contention in that bloody organisation. It's as crooked as the day is long, so it wouldn't be the first time someone pilfered the coffers."

"Cullen was a former club treasurer," Britney pointed out. "Supplied hurleys as well. Seemingly it was a bit of a running joke that when both his appointed jobs coincided, the number of hurleys the club used more than doubled."

Danny sat forward. "Then that would fit with that hand business, wouldn't it?" he said. "Maybe Jim Rourke is taking revenge on people who stole from the organisation he played for."

"Well hell, Daniel," Lyons threw a look of surprise at Danny. "I guess we might make a copper out of you after all."

Danny smiled at the rare compliment. But there was something else he was wondering about. If all this was about embezzling HAI money, what had the kneecappings got to do with anything?

He was about to pose those very same questions when Lyons glanced at his watch then pushed back his chair and stood. Still ruminating on his unspoken thought, Danny followed suit.

"We've got to get to the station," Lyons informed Britney. Dipping his hand into his pocket for his cigar box he nodded his appreciation. "For what it's worth, I think you're right. I think we need to find this Jim Rourke. If he's not the killer, then he could very well be another victim."

Watching them go, Britney felt a sense of relief. Finally, she had something to work with. Someone to work with. Sensing things were on the up she checked her phone and smiled. The message was indeed from Bob. 'You look great. So, if I promise not to talk shop, any chance I could see you again?' The text was punctuated by a smiling emoji.

Just then the waitress with the castle cup apron approached to tidy the table. "It's either a man or the lotto," she observed. "Cause there's nothing else on this earth can make a girl glow like that."

****

At two p.m. that same Friday, Detective Flynn welcomed Richie Lyons into his office as if hailing the return of a hero.

"Joe, this is the great man I was telling you about," he exclaimed after the detective from Swords had been directed to his door. "Richie Lyons, the hurler!" It was as much a statement as an introduction, as if having to introduce such a man should be deemed unnecessary. Smiling broadly, he stood up from behind his desk and moved toward the door with his hand outstretched. On reaching his visitor, he gripped Lyons's hand firmly and shook it with enthusiasm. "Been a while since I first saw you playing but I'll always remember that day in Thurles. What was it, 87?"

"85," Lyons corrected evenly. "A lifetime ago."

Danny could tell Lyons had little interest in revisiting his glory days. Perhaps because they reminded him of his deceased wife.

"Still, I remember it well," Flynn replied his enthusiasm not waning. He turned to address his partner who was leaning back on the ledge of the window to the left of the door. He had his legs crossed, and his arms folded over a stout belly. He looked to be approximately the same age as Detective Lyons but there was no hint of recognition on his face.

"Best centre-back in the business," Flynn declared. "Tough as nails and able to play as well. Had the pleasure of playing with him for a while."

His partner's nod was reserved. "Nice to meet you."

"Richie, this is Joe Murray," he said then added with an inscrutable smile. "My partner in crime."

"And this is Garda Daniel…" Lyons replied once again struggling to recall his young colleague's name.

Danny was starting to believe he was doing that on purpose just to annoy him. He allowed himself a wry smile. It wasn't that Owens was difficult to remember. *Perhaps I should start using my Nigerian name? See how he'd fare out with Okonkwo.*

"Owens," Danny provided eventually, deciding it best for all to remain with the more familiar option, then shook the hands of both Murray and Flynn. "Never played much hurling, I'm afraid."

"Neither did I," Joe admitted then leaned closer and winked conspiratorially. "Don't think Terry has a drawer full of medals either," he informed Danny, his voice softening but not enough that it couldn't still be heard across the room. "More of a hurler on the ditch."

Danny smiled in understanding. The large number of team photos on the walls of the office told him Joe was probably right. Several of the former Oldcastle Hurling teams and of individual players, but Danny couldn't spot the detective's face in any of them. There were a couple of photos of him playing golf though. By the look of his choppy swing, he didn't look like much of a golfer either.

"That may be," Flynn admitted, "but I know a good one when I see one. And there wasn't much better than this man here." Again, he smiled ingratiatingly towards Lyons.

The detective just shrugged and mumbled a simple, "Thanks."

Flynn nodded toward one of the team photos on the wall. "There he is, third from the left. The one with the shoulders."

Danny turned to look at the photo and smirked to himself. In it, Lyons looked baby faced, beardless but with curly brown hair falling down to his shoulders.

"Look like you couldn't harm a fly, sir."

"Believe you me, that look was deceiving." Flynn assured. "Different game now of course. Faster. More skilful, I'd say."

"I wouldn't necessarily agree," Lyons' reply was automatic.

"I'd say everyone else would," Flynn argued, "and everyone can't be wrong!"

"They said that about the church too," Lyons pointed out wearily. "Burnt heretics at the stake for their opinions. Look where that got us."

"I suppose," Flynn snorted dismissively.

Danny could tell Lyons negative attitude toward the modern game bothered him. 'You should hear what else he has to say on the subject,' he thought, now closely studying the caption beneath the photo Flynn had drawn their attention to. He had spotted his colleague's name amongst the list of players, but it wasn't Lyons name that held his attention. It was the surname of another man a few spaces over. A name that he had only recently heard. He was pondering the possible significance of this when Flynn diverted his attention with a change of tone.

"Anyway, back to the present," the detective said as he returned to his seat behind the desk. The earlier congeniality now dispensed with.

"You're here to compare notes on The Courier case?" he said while leaning back in his chair. Somewhat defensively, Danny thought.

"Yes," Lyons replied. "We believe we've got a body with similar injuries to those of both your victims. And we've got the hand from your first victim. It's being transferred to your county mortuary as we speak."

Flynn pursed his lips. "So, I've heard," he replied eventually. Pushing further back in his chair he studied Lyons coolly for a moment as if to say, 'this is my office. You're on my patch.' "Do you mind if we talk privately?" His tone was guarded as he shot a glance in Danny's direction.

"You don't consider your office private?" Lyons asked dryly.

Flynn's answer was a lazy smile. "Only when I'm in it alone. Perhaps not even then."

For a moment, the two men stared at each other, but Danny couldn't tell what was passing between them.

Finally, Lyons turned and nodded to his younger colleague.

At the same time, Joe Murray received a similar message. "Come on," he said as he pushed himself away from the window and made his way toward the door. "I'll get you one of our world-famous coffees."

"World-famous?" Danny asked with a dubious smile.

"Yeah, because it doubles up as brake fluid."

"Must be a station thing," Danny replied as he followed the grizzled detective out the door. "Because it sounds just like ours."

The meeting was relatively brief, lasting a little over twenty minutes which was a welcome relief to Danny because one cup of the hot liquid that the station pawned off as a beverage, was more than enough. Referring to it as brake fluid was a compliment. From now on he'd stick to tea.

While they waited for the private meeting to end, Detective Murray led Danny to a table near the coffee machine and they took the weight off.

"Seems like your partner has some trust issues," Danny observed when they sat. "Or does he want to keep all the hay for himself."

Murray smiled at the comment. "He can be a bit of an ass, alright," he confided as he casually studied Danny, trying to reconcile the dark skin with the bogger accent. Sounded like west of Ireland. "But he's one with a vicious kick," he carried on. "I've learnt to keep my mouth shut." He took a sip of his coffee while he eyed Danny. The smile disappeared. "And so should you."

Danny detected an edge to Murray's voice. Was it a warning? He snorted dismissively. "Don't have to tell me, I just do what I'm told."

"Well, pass it onto Kent. She has no idea what she's messing with."

Danny could feel the tension fill the air.

"Between you and me, if she keeps meddling, she could find herself seriously hurt or worse."

As the detective watched him, Danny stared into his coffee for a moment. Swirled it in the mug. Finally, he looked up at Murray and nodded. "I'll tell her."

"You be sure to do that, son." Murray took a sip of his coffee then suddenly his expression lightened. "Ballinrobe, right?"

Danny nodded. If he was impressed with the accuracy of the detective's guess regarding his heritage, he didn't show it. He sipped his brake fluid and studied Murray over the rim of the mug, just as Murray had studied him. The detective had kind eyes, an honest, almost droopy face. Kind of reminded Danny of a Labrador he had as a pet once. Rusty. But Rusty's life was short-lived. Because that innocent-looking brown Lab turned out to have a savage side. He'd bitten Danny when Danny was only seven and for that, had to be put down.

****

It wasn't just the smoke of Lyons' cigar that bothered Danny as they left the station and headed back toward Dublin. The silence was like a vacuum sucking at his thoughts.

Keen to inform Lyons of his little interchange near the coffee machine, he made a couple of efforts to broach the subject, but the detective seemed in a world of his own. He was puffing smoke like a train but seemed unaware the pungent odour was filling the interior of the car because he had failed to so much as crack his window open. Rolling down his driver's side window, Danny wondered what could possibly have been said in the office to have Lyons this bothered. Had he been threatened too?

"Are you ok, sir?" Danny asked as he eased past an articulated truck while moving into the fast lane. They were on the motorway heading back toward Dublin with the needle of the speedometer hovering a couple of kilometres above the speed limit. It was as much as Danny would allow himself even though Detective Lyons had made him a promise on the way down to Oldcastle that if he got home before the rush hour traffic, he could have the evening off.

"I can think of better ways of getting my kicks than sucking on car fumes," Lyons had said by way of mitigation.

'Or on your Guinness farts, sir,' Danny thought but kept that to himself.

"Kent is right," Lyons replied eventually. "The investigation is a mess. They seem to have no tangible leads and Flynn didn't even mention Rourke as a possible link to the case. Worse still, they don't seem nearly as focused as they should be." He sighed. "Did Murray say anything to you?"

Danny nodded. "I think he warned me off, sir. He certainly wants Sergeant Kent to keep her nose out. In fact, I'd go as far as to say he threatened her and wants me to pass on that threat."

"Threatened! How?"

Danny quickly filled him in.

"Interesting," Lyons replied thoughtfully. "There's something not right with those two. Did he say anything else?"

Danny shook his head. "Just small talk after that. What I don't get though, is how did he know about our meeting with her?"

Lyons shrugged. "Oldcastle is a small town." He puffed the cigar. "For his part, Flynn didn't say much either. Titbits about the case, as I said. Made him look incompetent more than anything else. Kept trying to steer the conversation back to hurling." He paused. "Either our friends Detectives Flynn and Murray haven't a fucking clue and are trying to disguise the complete balls their making of things," he thought out loud, "or…"

"Or?" Danny asked.

"Or, they have something to hide. Something that's worth threatening people over."

"Some sort of cover-up, sir? Perhaps Flynn knows the perp…" Danny paused as he worked this new possibility through in his head. "Or worse still, what if he is the perp?" He carried on in a more animated tone. "I saw some golfing photos on the wall. One of them said it was taken at Oldcastle Golf Club. That could link him to the doctor…"

"Woah!" Lyons interjected. "I think you're getting a little ahead of yourself, son. Been watching too much Law and Order." He shook his head. "I saw those photos too but by themselves they mean nothing. Only that he plays golf. Everyone who thinks they're anyone plays golf these days. A long drive is a fucking badge of honour."

"Driving for show, putting for dough, or so they say," Danny remarked then threw a sideways glance at Lyons. "Why don't you play? I mean a lot of ex-hurlers take up golf, don't they?"

"Because as a druggie asshole so succinctly put it to me once, I'd rather shit on my hands and clap," Lyons replied dryly, then ignoring the amused smile on Danny's face, returned to their immediate concern. "No, if he's hiding something it probably has nothing to do with the case at all. It's probably just some inhouse thing. Although she didn't come right out and say it, I got the impression from Sergeant Kent that he's a bit of a bully when it comes to the female Gardaí. What if it goes further than that? Nothing like an accusation of sexual harassment to kill your career. Perhaps that's what he's trying to hide."

"Murray would have to be in on it too, sir," Danny pointed out.

"Predators always hunt in packs, son."

Danny nodded. It seemed plausible. If sexual harassment was endemic in the small station, a big case like this was the last thing Flynn would want. Too many elements from the outside shining a light on their cosy little arrangement – reporters, cameras, impartial detectives like Lyons. It would be almost inevitable that their dirty secret would be outed. Especially if Sergeant Kent was working to expose it behind the scenes.

"I have to say that even in the short time I met him, I didn't like Flynn," Danny admitted. "Didn't like Murray either. So, I could see something like that going on."

"Flynn is a piece of shit," Lyons agreed. "And he's one of those hurling groupies. I hate hurling groupies. And I hate golfers. Especially ones that stink sweeter than a perfume stand."

"You hate everybody from what I can see, sir," Danny replied. Then realising what he'd said, he added sheepishly, "if you don't mind me saying, sir."

Lyons' expression was unreadable as he studied his cigar. "Not at all, Daniel. And I don't hate everybody. Just the people I meet. I like Flynn less than most."

"He likes you though. Obviously thinks of you as a bit of a hero since playing with you back in the dark ages. I thought you told Kent you didn't know Flynn?"

"I don't remember playing with him," Lyons replied, somewhat evasively. 'Not the only person you didn't remember playing with,' Danny thought, but kept it to himself.

"He might have been a sub," Lyons admitted, "but I don't think so. Full of shite, I'd say. Anyway, while we're on that line, what did you make of Sergeant Kent?" Lyons asked.

"I liked her," Danny replied. Then shook his head when he saw the knowing smirk on Lyons lips. "Not that way, sir. Although she is a looker for sure. No, I liked her as a Garda. She seems straight and genuinely driven to find the right result. And she shoots from the hip as you discovered."

"She certainly does," Lyons agreed. "But I fear she sees conspiracies in everything. And is a bit quick with her judgements." He glanced at Danny. "Did you see what she wrote in that notebook of hers? I'm half blind without my reading glasses."

Danny took a moment before shaking his head. "Her hand kind of covered it." He shrugged as he drove. "Probably just some follow up notes about the case."

"Well, whatever it was, she clearly didn't want either of us seeing it," Lyons remarked then pursed his thick lips. "A girl like that could land herself in a whole lotta trouble. Especially if she keeps the wrong company. Which she's certainly doing with Flynn and Murray."

"Then I should definitely pass on that warning, sir?"

Lyons nodded. "You can give her one from me too. Tell her to be careful because if the game she's playing turns sour, we can't protect her."

Danny nodded sombrely, wondering if Sergeant Kent had any idea what she'd gotten herself into. Because for his part, he certainly hadn't.

After Lyons little cautionary note, they sat in silence for a while, lost in their own thoughts. Danny found himself thinking of Marie Cox. Her mutilated body was never far from his mind. With his thoughts thus occupied, Danny hardly noticed they'd reached the outskirts of Dublin but now with the traffic starting to slow, he eased down a gear.

"Why didn't you tell Sergeant Kent everything, sir? Like the fact that you knew Miss Cox?" It was a concern he couldn't ignore any longer. "And the fact that we saw the killer?"

Lyons didn't answer at first. He kept looking out at the traffic rolling along beside him, the closest being a red Honda with a male driver. The driver, a youthful man with a shaved head, earrings and a large tattoo of a red-headed snake on his arm, was clearly irritated by the unwelcome eye contact, so he threw a challenging glare at Lyons before revving the Honda and easing forward out of his line of sight. Lyons mumbled under his breath, his eyes narrowing as he kept following the car for a moment longer. Finally, he dragged his gaze away and popped open the ashtray, stubbing out his cigar.

"You know the killer could be passing by in any one of those cars," he stated. "He could be looking in at us right now. Would you recognise him if he was?"

Danny glanced at the passing strangers while at the same time trying to remain focused on the car slowing directly in front of him. Picking a killer out of all those faces would be like trying to locate a weed in a field of thistles. "No, I wouldn't," he had to admit.

"Exactly. That's why I didn't mention us seeing the killer. Because we didn't. We saw a man in a long coat and hat. Nothing else. Yes, he was most likely the killer, but we don't know that for sure." He offered a wry smile. "He might just have been spooked by the sight of Ballinrobe's version of the caped crusader chasing after him. Anyway, I'm not sure how far we can trust the sergeant just yet. Trust too easily and it can come back to bite you, so I always think it best to hold a little back in a situation like this. That's my piece of advice for you, Daniel. Trust no one and you might just make it to sergeant."

"But you did know Miss Cox?" Danny wasn't about to let him close the lid on that so easily.

Just then the tattooed driver that Lyons had been eyeing, cut across into their lane but at the same time, the traffic slowed dramatically forcing the Honda to swerve and come to a sudden stop directly in front of them. Danny had no choice but to hit the brakes hard, an action that sent Lyons flying into the dash. He barely got his hands up in time to save his face walloping off of the glove box.

"Son of a bitch!" he cursed. He flung open the door to toss the cigar then cast off his seatbelt and hopped out of the car, the pain in his knees suddenly forgotten.

"You stupid bastard!" he bellowed as he strode toward the Honda. "You stupid, druggie bastard!" All around him the traffic had started moving again, the minor incident having passed unnoticed with the majority of commuters. But Lyons seemed possessed. On reaching the car, he banged on the window, bellowing for the occupant to open it. Even from where he was sitting, Danny judged the young man didn't look nearly as brazen anymore. He looked decidedly cowed, but still he refused to open the window even a fraction. Danny couldn't blame him judging by the look of fury on Lyons' face.

After a moment, the traffic in the lane next to them started to flow freely but the cars directly behind Danny were held up by Lyons' antics.

"It's meant to be the fucking fast lane not a bloody parking bay!" a driver shouted while leaning heavily on the car horn.

Feeling embarrassed, Danny rolled down his window and leaned out.

"Come on, sir. Leave it," he called but the detective refused to heed him.

Instead, Lyons banged on the 'druggie's' car once more, this time on the side of the door. So hard that he left a noticeable dent.

"Open your window, you delinquent prick!"

With Lyons failing to declare himself as a Garda, the man obviously presumed this was just a case of some arsehole with road rage. He revved the car and with the lane now open in front of him, he got out of there as quick as he could. 'Rightly so,' Danny thought.

Clearly fuming, Lyons remained standing in the middle of the motorway, watching the car drive away while all around him the world moved on. He ran his hands through his hair, cursed loudly once more, before finally returning to the car.

"Those bastards are the scum of the earth," he pronounced as he sat back into his seat. "They think they can do what they damn well like."

"It was just the traffic, sir," Danny objected. "Not his fault."

Lyons shook his head and Danny heard teeth grind. "Druggie bastards are all over the place."

Danny didn't reply. Judging by the seething look on the detective's face, he decided it best to say no more. They drove in silence for the next few miles, Danny reflecting on what he had just witnessed. It had unsettled him a little if he was to be honest about it.

"So, where do we go from here?" he asked eventually. He was referring to the case but could just as easily have been mulling their future as colleagues. Lyons clearly didn't see an issue with his behaviour.

"I think you should help the pretty sergeant look for this Jim Rourke," he said simply. There was no reference to the incident, no sheepish tone. No apology. He then carried on in that same neutral voice. "He must be out there somewhere. Start by tracking down everyone he knows or has been in contact with over the last few months. Check phones, computers, bank statements, and find out where he's been and who he's been talking to. Initially, I thought this was somehow gangland related, but Benny's adamant it's not, and if anyone would know, he would."

Danny nodded. "Fair enough."

"I'm going to dig deeper into the victim's careers, their habits, their finances but especially their private lives, so I might be out of the station for a day or two."

'What's new?' Danny thought sarcastically, but part of him was glad he'd be free of the detective for a while even though the damn Super would undoubtedly be on the warpath again, with Danny left to face the music. Was Lyons determined to get the pair of them sacked or what? What was it the Super had said about him the last time? 'More time off than the bloody government.'

Up ahead the traffic had almost slowed to a stop as they came to the Red Cow Roundabout. Lyons swore under his breath, drawing a sarcastic glance from Danny.

"Looks like car fumes will be the only kicks you'll be getting any time soon, sir."

"Use the hard shoulder," Lyons urged. "That's what it's there for – emergencies."

"I wouldn't class getting your arse planted on a bar-stool as an emergency, sir," Danny replied pointedly feeling all the frustration he felt regarding Lyons' behaviour and his own situation boil up. "You have a problem, sir, you know that." The minute he said it he knew he'd overstepped the mark, but he didn't care. Though clearly an extremely capable detective, Lyons' drinking was out of control. In turn, he was out of control. The way he drank was bound to affect his judgement and what had happened with the Honda driver only served to underline that.

Lyons looked at him sharply. "Careful where you're stepping, young man," he warned acidly.

Danny shook his head. He wasn't prepared to back down. Not until he'd said his piece. "I get why you drink, sir," he said as understandingly as he could. "It's to fill the void your wife left. But I'm sorry, we're dealing with a psycho and I'm in way over my head. The last thing I want is…"

Lyons' anger returned instantly, his dark eyes flashing dangerously. "My wife is none of your concern," he growled menacingly.

'Perhaps you shouldn't have told me about her then, sir. Or can't you remember?' Danny thought to himself then conceded outwardly. "Maybe not, sir. But, understanding the kind of man I'm working with is. After all, it could mean my life."

"What? You're concerned my drinking might get in the way of me doing my job?" he snorted. "Rich coming from a rookie from the backend of nowhere who, to use an analogy you might grasp, couldn't find a bull in a field full of sheep."

It wasn't so much the insult that stung as the way it was delivered. With meaning. Despite his best efforts, Danny must have let that hurt show on his face because Lyons' intensity soon relented. "Look, I'm sorry, Daniel," his tone was now softer, controlled. Almost like turning on and off a tap with him, Danny noted. Irate one minute, composed the next. Yet, the more he studied Lyons, the more he detected the anger still lurking beneath the contrite air. "But, despite what you think you see, I'm one hundred percent focused on what I've got to do. And I'm damn good at it. What's more, I wouldn't be worried about getting hurt if I were you. This killer has no interest in us. He has an agenda. And he's going to stick to it."

With Lyons seemingly convinced in his assumption, Danny nodded. But for some reason, he didn't feel all that reassured. "One other thing," he said.

Lyons' eyebrows raised.

"My name is Danny. I was christened Danny. I grew up as Danny. So, EVERYONE calls me Danny. Not Daniel." In his opinion, Danny was cool. Daniel a good-for-nothing pompous ass. Especially when Lyons said it.

It was the detective's turn to nod. "Fair enough." As he spoke, he pulled a pen and notebook out of the inside pocket of his coat then scrolled through his phone until he found what he was looking for. It took him a while, his fingers like elephant feet on the buttons. "Here's the number the sergeant called me on," he finally said, his tone business-like once more. He scribbled on the notebook then pulled out the page and handed it to Danny. "The warning would sound better coming from you."

Danny took the number. He knew what Lyons meant. If the warning came directly from the detective, she might think he was just another high-ranking male trying to muzzle her and consequently she'd dig her heels in. From Danny, it could be interpreted as nothing more than it was – a junior colleague looking out for her safety.

A moment later Danny pulled up at the corner by The Sheep's Head.

"Call me if you need me," he said as Lyons heaved himself out of the car. "Otherwise, I'll see you back in the station, sir." 'Whenever that will be,' he thought to himself. Glancing around the outside of the dingy bar he saw no sign of the thin man.

****

Glad to see the back of Lyons for a while, Danny headed straight for his local gym, BodyBurn. There, he worked out hard for an hour in the hope of clearing his head. He'd a feeling he'd need all his wits about him in the coming days. When he finished with the irons, he spent some wind-down time between the jacuzzi and the sauna, then showered and headed for home. On his way, he inevitably thought of Marie Cox hanging from the light fitting but quickly shoved the image from his head and allowed it to be replaced by one of Sergeant Kent. Sergeant Britney Kent. She was certainly beautiful in an understated way but what made her even more attractive was the fact that she didn't seem to realise it. Or if she did, she had no intention of trading on it. Unlike the murdered reporter.

Danny was sorry Marie Cox was dead but guessed she had more than earned her enemies. Sergeant Kent on the other hand didn't deserve any. Not from what Danny had seen. He found it hard to think that anyone, especially a member of her own station, would wish her harm. Yet, she was in a tough grind. Knee deep in a major investigation with a corrupt and incompetent lead and no one to turn to but himself and Lyons. A pair of total strangers. And one of those strangers acting like a primed bomb. It was clear Lyons was bitter over his wife's death. From cancer, he had disclosed in the bar. A rare form of cancer.

To make it worse, the cancer was curable if it had been found in time. But it wasn't. And now he was trying to drink himself to death.

Ten minutes later, he pulled up outside the building in which he lived – an old townhouse on one of the less sought-after northside streets that had been divided into four flats while hardly being large enough for two. He parked next to the kerb and pulled out his phone to dial the number Lyons had given him. It rang out. Apart from passing on the warning, he had hoped to reassure the sergeant that he was there for her, that she had someone watching her back. Perhaps knowing that, she might sleep a little easier. On the other hand, perhaps she'd sensed it was him phoning and had deliberately ignored the call. Even though he was conscious not to let it show, she may have sensed his attraction to her earlier and seeing the strange number decided to ignore what she may have judged to be the opening advances of a junior Garda with a silly crush. If that was the case, he couldn't blame her. The more he thought about it, the more he was convinced that what Lyons inferred about sexual harassment at her station was true. With such a seedy cloud hanging over her, he was fairly sure the last thing she needed to worry about right then was another male Garda checking her out rather than doing his damn job. The call continued to her message box. Conscious of those concerns, he spoke in the most professional tone he could muster, leaving his name and number, and a brief message for her to call him back.

His flat was on the second floor of the partitioned building, meaning he had to climb a rickety stair to reach his door. The stairs creaked with each tired step, reminding him that once something becomes worn, it remains like that forever. Like Detective Lyons. The way he acted in the car was worrying. Even more so than his drinking. Sensing his superior was a man on the edge, Danny just hoped he wasn't dragged over with him.

On entering his cramped flat, Danny made his way directly to the narrow galley kitchen which seemed more squeezed than fitted into its allotted space. There he rustled up a tuna and mayo sandwich which he scoffed down in three bites and washed down with a glass of ice-cold milk. His hunger appeased, he plonked himself down on a moth-eaten couch to watch some TV but found himself flicking from one channel to another. With the light fading outside, he gave up on the attempt at distraction and made his way to the tiny bedroom that no one had seen yet but him. It was neat and tidy with the bed made, something that had become routine to him since his mother instilled the desire for neatness in him as a child. Now, every morning, he made the bed automatically.

Removing his phone from his pocket, he lay it on the battered bedside locker, one of the few pieces of furniture that had come with the place. Left behind no doubt by the last occupant because he couldn't imagine his churl of a landlord being so benevolent. Despite the locker's shabby appearance – it was hand-painted a dark brown with the paint cracked and peeling, and the door hanging at an oblique angle – Danny had been glad of it at the time of moving in. One less cost for him to bear.

His movements weary, he stripped down to his blue boxers. Discarding the blue shirt in a wash basket at the end of the bed, he slipped the navy tie onto the wire neck of a clothes hanger and overlaid the similarly coloured jacket. Then he checked his trousers for stains and finding none, he added that to the lower rung of the hanger. Finally, he draped the entire ensemble over the door of his IKEA wardrobe, leaving it ready for the morning. Wearing the same uniform more than two days in a row was offensive to his nature, but on a young Garda's salary, needs must.

With his clothes neatly arranged, he brushed his teeth and hit the hay. His last thoughts were of Sergeant Kent and the note she had made in her little book. It wasn't something he was proud of, but he had lied to Lyons about that. The truth was even though she had tried to conceal it, Danny had managed to get a glimpse of what the sergeant had written. At first, what he saw disturbed him but the more he thought about it the more he understood her assessment. And admired her insight.

She had scrawled the name – Detective Richie Lyons across the page followed by a large question mark.

It seemed Sergeant Kent's instincts were to distrust the crotchety detective. As he lay in the bed, Danny had to admit her doubts only echoed his own. He hoped, for all their sakes, those doubts proved unfounded.

****

Around the time Danny called, Britney was at home curled up with her cat and had just opened a nice bottle of wine to wash down a dinner of prawns and pasta. The wine was a reward for a pleasing day's work. By the time she had returned to the station, Flynn and Sidekick Joe were gone out somewhere, so she took the opportunity to write up all she had uncovered and email it to Fiona. She sent everything through their private emails because she didn't want to take the chance that details of her enquiry would fall into the wrong hands, namely Flynn's. It was early days yet and although she had a starting point, her witness wasn't overly reliable. That meant the main focus over the coming days would be to collect concrete evidence, something which had proved elusive up to now. However, she was confident that with Fiona's help, they would get what they needed. The thumbs up she received once Fiona spotted the email served to bolster that opinion.

Flynn's time was running out, she could feel it. Still, she was well aware that even with the necessary evidence, it would be far from smooth sailing. An internal investigation would split the station but the public one that would inevitably follow could split the force. She would be labelled a troublemaker and a whistle-blower. Perhaps branded a backstabber and a turncoat. However, the biggest stumbling block she could foresee was Superintendent Halley. If she wanted to make a case, she would have to go through him first. She could only hope that his involvement wouldn't validate the theory of blood being thicker than water. If that proved to be the case, she wouldn't hesitate in approaching a higher authority in the form of Garda Commissioner Wilson.

Now, as she relaxed in her sitting room the radio played in the background as it always did. She liked music in the house, had done ever since she was kid, way back when her mother used to dance with her to songs by Elvis or Old Blue Eyes himself. Before she left them in the lurch, that was. And marked her for life, in more ways than one.

The music soothed her to such an extent that she seldom switched the radio off. A house without music was a house without a soul, her mother used to say – one of the few things to come out of her mother's mouth that Britney agreed with. Wine, on the other hand, was something she didn't indulge in all that often, but it did help her relax, while Salem her cat comforted her far beyond any boyfriend had ever done. She hadn't had many. Two long term boyfriends and some flings that didn't get very far. None of them were all that serious. And none of them had the kind of effect on her that she'd experienced in the short time she'd known Bob Harris. Not even close.

He sent a shiver down her spine. In a good way. A very good way. Even thinking about him now, she felt her heart beat a little faster and her body stir. That awakening part of her regretted her decision to walk out on their date but the sensible part of her, the part that continuously struggled to rule her heart, knew it was the right thing to do. Yet who cared about the right thing? No one, as far she could see.

"Take what you can and to hell with the consequences. Isn't that the way of it?" she said to Salem as she gently stroked his back. "The way us humans operate. Have operated from the beginning of time. Destroying poor innocents like you and the world they live in with this 'have it now and pay later' approach." She shook her head. "Someone has to take a stand. Otherwise, depraved people like Flynn and this Courier have won." She took a long sip of wine. For her part, she was determined not to let that happen. Making a stand started by doing the right thing. That was why she kept ignoring her phone.

He was determined, that's for sure. It had rung three times already, once off a different number. That was when she silenced the ring tone and shoved it to the end of the couch. Yet she could feel its persistent vibration, begging her to answer. She should have pressed decline on that first call, she knew that. It would have sent him a clear message that she wasn't interested. But she couldn't bring her finger to hit the button. She was interested, that was the problem. Only for her job and the case she was on, she would be with him now. Holding him. Kissing him. Feeling him stir, just like she was stirring. She gulped some wine and tried to think of something else, something that would take her mind far away from the world she was living in but just as she thought she had found such a place, the phone vibrated once more. Insistent, suggestive, tempting. She wasn't sure if it was the wine or just her weak will, but this time when she reached for the phone, her thumb accepted the call.

"Hello," her voice almost broke as she said that one simple word.

"I need to see you," he replied without introduction. He didn't need one. He knew it and she knew it. Her racing heart went into overdrive at the sound of his voice.

"You don't give up easily," she replied while trying her best to keep her voice neutral.

"No," he admitted, "not on something like this. Not on someone like you."

She took a deep breath. She knew she wasn't thinking clearly. She knew the wine had lured her into a very vulnerable place and that any decision she made now would probably be regretted in the morning. And she also knew that he was smooth. Maybe too smooth. Yet she couldn't help herself. "Would you like to come over?" It was as if her mouth had taken on a power of its own, the words slipping out before she realised she had even considered them.

"Where are you?" he asked eagerly.

"I live in Clarnwood on the Johnshill Road. It's the second house on the right as you come into the estate."

"Ok. I know where it is. Give me ten minutes."

He hung up but it took a moment for what was about to happen to register. He was coming over.

Shit! Bob Harris was coming over.

She leapt off the couch and frantically began to tidy the house but it was in such a mess that it would need a team of cleaners to set it right so she kicked and tossed what she could out of sight then dashed for the stairs. If the house was a mess, she was even worse. Her hair was tangled and tied up in a bun that would look dated on a woman twice her age. She was dressed in a bathrobe that was built for comfort not a come-on, and a pair of puppy dog slippers that she'd kept with her through her teenage years, into college and beyond. Both items were covered in cat hair. Jesus, I hope he doesn't have allergies, she thought then screamed as she found herself standing in front of the mirror.

Five minutes, she thought frantically. Five minutes to turn a peasant into a princess. First, she dumped the robe then started on the makeup, something she reserved for special occasions. And for when she wasn't feeling too good about the mark her mother left. She applied the foundation as fast as she could, then wiped most of it off, manipulating what remained into something that would pass as embellishment. Dabbed on concealer, then some bronzer. One look in the mirror told her it was nothing Lisa Eldridge, Fiona's favoured makeup blogger, would be proud of, but on such short notice, it would have to do. That done, she released her hair and combed it out as she reached for a dress. The red one. Yes, the red one. Just as she pulled it over her head, she heard what sounded like a motorbike pull into her drive and a moment later the doorbell rang.

"Shit," she cursed as she caught herself in a tangle and almost fell over. She slipped the dress down over her gently curved hips and made for the stairs, holding onto the rail with one hand, fixing her hair and her dress with the other. She was out of breath when she reached the door but felt far more comfortable with her appearance than she had just a few minutes earlier. Taking a deep breath to steady herself, she opened the door and beamed a welcoming smile.

There he was, standing before her, dressed in a biker's leather jacket, a pair of jeans and a t-shirt. Directly behind him, a motorbike stood next to her service vehicle, its engine ticking as it cooled. A glint of humour danced in those piercing blue eyes.

"You look amazing," Bob Harris remarked with a glance directed at her feet. "Especially loving the slippers. Not sure if they go with the dress though."

Feeling a pang in her stomach Britney's eyes shot downward. "Shit," she cursed. Staring right back up at her were her worn-out puppy dog slippers. 'So much for Cinderella,' she thought, 'more like Bozo the Clown.'

She must have spoken out loud because when she looked up Bob was looking at her with an amused expression on his face.

"Nothing like a clown to break the ice," he remarked dryly, then simultaneously they both burst into giddy laughter. With that, Britney forgot about saving the planet. Forgot about Flynn and Jim Rourke. She even forgot about doing the right thing. The man in front of her was all that mattered. The man and the overwhelming desire that he roused in her. A desire clearly reciprocated. The humorous glint had disappeared from Bob Harris' eyes to be replaced by one of longing. Of need. Of desire.

Within moments he had her in his arms, kissing her hungrily, even more demanding than he had kissed her before. Both gentle and passionate at the same time. His probing tongue ravenous. His lips soft and sensuous. She responded in kind, then slowly backed away from the door and drew him with her, kicking it closed once they got clear of its path, almost certain to have lost her balance if not for his strong arms. First, they steadied her, then they began to explore her. Her red dress the only barrier between his flesh and hers. A hot flush coursed through her as his hands found their way beneath the hem of her dress and firmly cupped her pert buttocks, pulling her toward him. She backed away, not to tease him, but to lead him to the couch she had been sitting on only moments earlier, with only Salem and a glass of wine to comfort her. Oh, how quickly fortunes could change, she noted with a sigh. Outside, the world sighed with her, and as branches trembled a single autumn leaf drifted past the window. To and fro. Joyous in its fall.

****

With time off at a premium due to the ongoing investigation, the girls had fewer opportunities to go jogging than they had hoped. Determined to stretch her legs, Fiona suggested they meet at the castle woods on Saturday morning. Covering four acres, the woods were part of the castle's park which in turn was the remnants of a much larger estate. They contained imported spruce and pine trees, along with native specimens like beech, oak and ash, all growing together in perfect harmony. 'If only trees were people,' Britney thought, as they took the first steps of their early morning run.

Even though it was mid-October temperatures were still pleasant enough that they could wear shorts instead of a tracksuit. Britney's toned legs, being perpetually swathed in uniform slacks, welcomed the sense of freedom. They ran at a steady pace for half an hour before taking a break at a picnic spot secluded under a canopy of seasonally gold sycamore trees. With the broad leaves starting to fall, nature was weaving a carpet underfoot that was every bit as beautiful as any Persian rug. The sun was out again, fighting way above its weight for this time of year, yet there was a steady breeze that cooled the sweat on their bodies. The breeze smelled of pine leaves and wild mushrooms.

"Have you something to tell me?" Fiona asked Britney, a knowing smile tugging at her lips.

They had taken a break from running and were now resting on the trunk of a fallen tree, happy with their morning's workout.

Britney felt free for the first time in weeks. Free, happy and alive. She inhaled a deep breath of the wild-scented air and savoured the thrill that ran through her. A thrill borne out of pleasure. The pleasure experienced presently and the one her heart now revisited.

Having led Bob to the sofa, she had let herself fall backward but he held her as she knew he would, gently lowering her until she was safely resting beneath him. Then he leaned down and explored her with his lips, caressing her neck, her mouth, her cheek, tenderly kissing her scar. Embracing it. Honouring it. A soft sigh escaped Britney's lips and her heart fluttered, momentarily faltering like a caged bird suddenly free. Finally, it soared as she eagerly pulled him toward her, ripping at his clothes, he at hers. One by one, garments fell to the floor until only the red dress remained, riding high above her hips. She thrust forward, tempting him, teasing him with her semi-nakedness. Sensing her desire, he kissed her again, softly, suggestively. A moment later, she felt his body ease closer and in response, she thrust upwards to meet him. To urge him. To accept him. To experience him. She moaned as the hunger threatened to devour her and had to bite her lip to stop from crying out. Then, suddenly her breathing quickened and she found herself clinging to him as their bodies joined in perfect union, exploring, moving, existing as one. Cries of pleasure freely escaped her lips, but she didn't care.

Bob Harris was an ecstasy like none she had experienced before.

"Like what?" Britney asked innocently in response to Fiona's question. She was doing her best to remain expressionless, but it was proving a struggle.

"About what's put that twinkle in your eye?" Fiona's cheeks were flushed from the jog, but she still managed to look every bit as stunning as her surroundings.

Once again Britney found herself admiring her friend's undoubted beauty. But in no way envious. Not this morning. "What twinkle?" Britney replied evasively but try as she might she could no longer hold back the smile. When it broke free it lit up her face. "He called me," she finally admitted.

"Who? The foreman?" Fiona asked excitedly and leaned forward on the tree trunk.

"Yes, Bob Harris."

"He did more than call by the looks of you," Fiona said. "That bloom in your cheeks is not just from running." She smiled happily for her friend. "You're like the cat that's got the cream – pardon the pun."

"Fiona!" Britney exclaimed in admonishment.

"But you were with him, weren't you?" Fiona urged, keen to hear the gory details.

Britney allowed herself wallow in the memory. "Well, yes."

"When?"

"Last night. He called over and well, it just happened."

"You dirty dog!" Fiona replied. "You're a real dark horse, you know that."

Britney laughed giddily, recalling the night before and how natural the lovemaking had felt. Afterward, they had lain together, just holding each other and talking, and that had seemed completely natural too. Until the urge to give in to their passions swept over them once more.

"To be honest, I think I'm falling for him," Britney admitted. "I know I shouldn't say this, but he reminds me a lot of my father." The comment drew a look of faint disapproval from Fiona.

"I know I shouldn't think of him that way," Britney quickly acknowledged, "but he really does. My father used to work in construction too but it's not just because of that. I think Bob is honest and dependable like he was. I need that right now."

"So, Bob is dependable," Fiona repeated, her pencil thin eyebrows raised questioningly.

"And passionate," Britney smiled devilishly and raised an eyebrow in riposte. "So passionate!"

Now, Fiona did look impressed. She responded with a delighted giggle and extended her arm for a high five. "You go girl!" she exclaimed as their palms collided. "Let Flynn put that in his pipe and smoke it."

Britney readily agreed with the sentiment. "If that dirty creep ogles me again, I'll set Bob on him. See how brave he is when faced with two hundred pounds of muscle."

"Two hundred pounds?" Fiona smirked playfully. "I would have judged him at one-seventy. One-eighty, at a push." She raised her eyebrows once more. "From what we could see, that is. No wonder you're smiling like a Cheshire cat." She laughed momentarily at Britney's coy expression then her eyes grew serious. "You mention your father a lot, Britney. You miss him obviously?"

Britney nodded. She turned as if to admire the trees in front of her, but Fiona could tell that all she was seeing were memories. Painful ones.

"He used to work as a carpenter. Six days a week. All was good until Ma went off and left us for someone else. He was never the same after that. Still, he was always there for me. He had more integrity than any man I know. I think that's why I became a cop. I wanted to do something just as morally commendable as he was," she snorted. "See where that got me."

"Don't tar yourself with Flynn's brush, Britney. He doesn't represent what you aspire to be. There are good Gardaí and bad. Just like there's good and bad in every walk of life."

"Like my mother," Britney mumbled as much to herself as to Fiona. Fiona sensed this was something that really affected her friend. Perhaps what was driving her. Because she was certainly driven.

"You sound really angry about your mother? Is she still in your life?"

"Nope. Haven't spoken to her since she left. Fifteen years ago, now. We had a blazing row."

The question that Fiona followed with suggested Britney must have self-consciously touched her hand to her face.

"Is that how you got that mark?"

Britney's brown eyes blinked rapidly as she nodded "Yes. When she was upset, she had this habit of fidgeting with the rings on her finger. Rotating them inwards. That evening she completely lost it and when she slapped me, she caught me with the diamond of her engagement ring. I found out the hard way that diamond can cut like a utility knife."

"Oh my God! That's so sad, Britney."

"It was." Britney sniffed then offered a shrug. "But now I don't think about her much."

Fiona could tell that was a lie. A lie her friend desperately wanted to believe. After a moment Britney turned away from the trees. She forced a smile, but the earlier twinkle now eluded her brown eyes.

"What about you? That guy I saw you with the other night. Is it serious?"

"Nah," Fiona shook her head, her smile fading, "just a casual thing. Probably won't even see him again."

"That's a pity."

"Not really," Fiona replied dryly. "Miserable bastard insisted on going Dutch." With that, she hopped off the makeshift seat. With her shorts having ridden high while she was sitting, she shimmied her shapely hips as she pulled them back into place, laughing as a nearby jogger became so distracted by her provocative movements that he snagged his toe on a root and tumbled over. Clearly embarrassed he quickly jumped to his feet, shook himself off and kept on going without a second glance in the girls' direction.

Fiona's laugh was infectious and soon Britney was seeing the colour of the trees again, feeling the breeze. With her mother pushed to the back of her mind, thoughts of Bob again came to visit.

Inside, she was smiling as they finished their run.

****

Britney felt revitalised after their visit to the woods, and the shower that followed. On entering the station, she felt prepared for a busy shift, and for whatever Flynn might throw at her. With the victim count now at three, the team was coming under immense pressure to find a break in the case. Flynn had called a brief meeting outlining the direction he thought the investigation should take. It didn't surprise Britney that the link between Jim Rourke and his father was never mentioned, not once in the twenty minutes Flynn spent going over the various details. The main focus had been on the doctor.

Britney got the impression that Flynn considered the doctor's death more tragic than the others and solving it a far more pressing matter. It was a class thing, Britney knew. Flynn liked to see himself as rubbing shoulders with the elite. Ade Fagan, the HAI President, being a case in point. That's why the whereabouts of a nobody like Jim Rourke didn't interest him. It would, she believed, by the time this was all over. On finishing the meeting, Flynn called her aside. She was expecting some snide remark but for a change, Flynn was solely focused on the job at hand.

"You and Garda O'Malley look into the doctor's affairs," he instructed. "He's an important man in this community so tread carefully. But find me something that's going to lead us to his killer. I'm thinking a patient. One with a history of psychological troubles."

Britney nodded, her expression unreadable. She could recognise the validity of his thinking – not. A rogue patient wouldn't be a bad hypothesis if there weren't already two other victims to account for. She felt like screaming the latter but said nothing. She just smiled in acquiescence and turned to gather her phone off her desk. With Fiona in tow, she was more than happy to get out of the station.

Their first call was to the doctor's home where they met his wife of twenty-eight years. Her name was Mandy, a blonde, heavyset woman with a bloated face and glasses. She had the look of a drinker, Britney thought. Although she played the part of grieving widow to a tee – the requisite black dress, allied with the appropriate amount of sobbing. Britney got the impression that deep down she wasn't overly upset by the passing of her husband. Perhaps it was the fact that despite Mandy exuding all the correct noises, Britney noted that her expertly applied mascara had yet to run. At least not in a way that would match the level of grief she exhibited. Anyway, whether she was in genuine mourning or not, she could think of no one who would want to 'do that to her husband' – patient, or otherwise. As for a strange delivery, Mandy was adamant that no such delivery had been received.

It proved to be the same story at the doctor's clinic. After interviewing his colleagues and gathering as much information as was forthcoming regarding the doctor's patients, professional connections, and possible links to the other victims, they were no closer to making a breakthrough. Initially, the involvement of one particular patient had seemed plausible but under further investigation, it proved a dead end. Literally. So much for Flynn's theory.

To add to their frustration, they found no record of a parcel having been delivered to the surgery in the days leading up to the doctor's demise. However, the doctor's personal secretary was understandably off sick due to stress, meaning they couldn't close the book on that lead just yet. Making a note to follow up with the absent secretary, they left the clinic and headed towards the town centre in their service vehicle. That was when Britney checked her messages for the first time since the evening before. Gloriously occupied as she had been with her surprise visitor her phone hadn't been a priority, and her early morning rise for a jog meant she barely got a chance to look at the screen. Now seeing the message icon flashing, she presumed it was to remind her of the calls she had stubbornly but futilely ignored from Bob. A quick perusal of her message box told her that wasn't the case. Not entirely.

In the middle of those calls, she had received a voice mail from the sweet young Garda from Swords. Curious as to why he'd be contacting her at all, not to mention doing so out of work hours, she called him back right then. He answered on the third ring and got straight to the point, his tone not at all what she expected. No small talk. Brusque. Business-like.

"I think you are in danger," he explained, then informed her of what Murray had said. And Lyons too. Before he rang off, he assured her he believed in her and that if she needed anything, anything at all, she could just call. Though he was only a junior Garda with little influence, she found that reassuring to hear. The warning regarding Flynn, however, had sent a chill down her spine.

"That sounded serious," Fiona observed. "Everything ok?"

"I'm not sure," Britney admitted. "It was that young Garda from Dublin I told you about."

"Yeah, the innocent one," Fiona could see Britney's expression was troubled. "Is there a problem?"

Britney nodded pensively. "He called to pass on a threat he received from Flynn. Telling me to watch my back or else."

"That bastard," Fiona spat, pushing herself up in her seat, "thinks he can just go around threatening us like that."

Britney felt reassured that Fiona considered a threat received by one as a threat to both.

"We should report him Brit. We have a witness now. Someone from the outside."

Britney shook her head in frustration. "Like you said before, he'll just deny it. Anyway, from what I gathered the threat didn't come directly from Flynn himself."

"Then what do we do?" Fiona asked, sounding exasperated.

Britney only needed a moment. "As it stands, we're expected to do Flynn's legwork, aren't we?" When enunciating legwork her lip curled and she held up her fingers in inverted commas. "Appalling as that sounds, it authorises us to be absent from the station and to investigate, doesn't it?"

"Yes."

"Well, why not do exactly that? Why not use our time to dig into Flynn's little enterprise? Take him down on his own dime as it were!" Yes, she liked the sound of that. "Perhaps we will take The Courier down too." There was a determined set to Britney's jaw as she spoke. "The more I think about it, Fiona, the more I realise the two tasks aren't mutually exclusive. I saw Flynn's name amongst one of the doctor's files. He's a patient at the clinic."

"Not of Carmody's though?"

"No, but it's still a connection. They treated him for diabetes, something which doesn't surprise me considering how often he visits Fat Tony's." 'Probably getting fed for free too,' Britney thought to herself. "Anyway, it wouldn't be a leap to imagine he crossed paths with Dr Carmody on more than one occasion at the clinic. Probably played golf with him too at Oldcastle Golf Club." She paused to gather her thoughts. "And with Flynn being such a hurling fanatic, he would have known both Donie Cullen and Jim Rourke, perhaps more than just casually. If that was the case, he could be linked to three key individuals in the investigation, two of whom are dead, the third missing. As far as I'm aware, he never so much as hinted at any connection."

Fiona shook her head. "Not that I heard."

"Maybe it's no wonder he dismissed the absence of Jim Rourke as just an unreliable soak gone on a bender. In other words, nothing to see here. That might also explain his attempt to direct our attention towards some psychotic patient and therefore, away from him and his corrupt cronies."

"Ok, but what cronies? Joe Murray?"

Britney shrugged. "Murray's his partner, isn't he? The question is, are there any others? And if so, how high does it run. And have they become so depraved that they've gone from intimidation to killing people."

One thing she was certain of was Flynn hadn't counted on her level of diligence. He had expected her to ask some questions and check the doctor's records. Not those of his colleagues. Now she had a link.

Determined to find another one, they drove directly to Fat Tony's. The chipper was closed for business, but Tony was inside preparing for the evening ahead.

"Not you lot again," he growled on seeing the two Gardaí at his door. "Let me guess. Two burger meals to go. And on yours truly." However, his attitude changed on spotting Britney. "At least you pay for yours." His demeanour softened even further when Britney explained why they had called. "I have it up to my neck with that prick," he began and didn't stop there. "Taking so much free grub he should be fat as a fool. But then you can't fatten a mangy goat, can you?"

On leaving Tony's twenty minutes later, they drove through the town, looking for other business owners to grill. As the day progressed, they experienced varying degrees of success.

The October sun was well on its way to disappearing behind the city's grey slate roofs when they pulled up outside a small electrical shop on Main Street. The shop was one of the oldest family-owned businesses still surviving in the town centre, many of the rest having long given way to fancy bars, expensive boutiques, and the big conglomerates like Sports Direct.

"It's hard to believe that Flynn is behind all of this," Fiona said as they parked and got out of the car. "I mean I know he's a corrupt piece of shit, but a killer?" She shook her head in disbelief. "Why?"

"To cover up his illegal activities," Britney replied with a shrug. "Perhaps everything is starting to unravel on him."

So far, they'd visited ten businesses in the city and three of them had admitted that Flynn was extorting money from them under the guise of protection.

"The process is simple," explained a small man with glasses, grey hair and a copious belly hanging out over his suit trousers. He was the owner of a car business located on the second last roundabout on the city's ring road.

His initial reaction to their questions had been the same as all the other proprietors they had spoken to. Suspicion and reticence. But Fiona proved to have a disarming way about her. After a quiet word from her, the proprietor seemed to relax his guard a little and become more open to Britney's enquiries. Britney had to admit she was impressed with Fiona's capabilities. She'd make an excellent detective if she ever decided to go down that route.

"It all started when that notorious family of itinerants began targeting our businesses," the car dealer explained with a disgruntled expression. "You know the crowd I'm talking about. They've been carrying on for years. Anyway, they started breaking windows, harassing customers, stealing. They kept at it until it came to a point where we had no choice but to pay them off."

Britney's ears pricked up. The vandalism cases that had become so common?

"That's where Flynn stepped in. He turned the tables on the tinkers by targeting their halting site, burning caravans, confiscating their ponies, dealing out a beating or two. Oh, he didn't do it personally. He hired in muscle from out of town. Dublin, I think. IRA dissidents, some suspected."

Britney pursed her lips thoughtfully. That's why Flynn had her grounded to the desk. The vandalism cases were linked as she had suspected. Flynn linked them. Now it was possible he was linked to the IRA as well. And to The Courier case. That could be where the kneecappings came in. Kneecapping was often considered a favourite punishment of the IRA and for good reason. The knee being the most complex joint in the body meant one well-placed blow resulted in shock-inducing pain and irreparable damage.

"Then with the itinerants frightened off, he took the payments for himself?" Britney guessed.

"Exactly. Has been doing so ever since. That was three years ago. To be honest, I just can't pay it anymore."

Britney glanced at Fiona then smiled reassuringly at the worried looking man. "That's why we're here. To make sure you don't have to. All we need is for you to give us an official statement."

The man shook his head sharply. "I can't," he replied in a panicked voice. "He'll send those thugs in their vans after me." He turned to walk away. "You better find someone else."

"But we can protect you," Fiona assured.

The pot-bellied man's lips curled in a sneer. "You protect me? I don't think so."

Britney caught the cynical look he cast in Fiona's direction. 'Another fan of the Gardaí,' she thought sarcastically. Then a thought occurred to her. "When you say vans, what do you mean? Like construction vans?"

"Yeah. Seemingly the tinkers didn't know what hit them the first time. Thought it was just some crowd looking to buy cheap tools, so, they welcomed them with open arms," he smiled wickedly. "Got their comeuppance, didn't they?"

"Surely did," Britney agreed but her mind had drifted elsewhere. She was wondering if those raids were anything to do with why Jim Rourke had been lending out his van. And if Rourke had any connections to the IRA apart from drinking in Bernie's. Everyone knew the link between the modern-day IRA and criminality was blurred at best. The old guard had been a different kettle of fish. They had been idealists. Patriots. Fighting a just cause. But if this new brigade was dealing out beatings in Flynn's name, it was far from just. And had nothing to with republicanism.

Now as they entered O'Brien's electrical shop, they hoped to find the person who was strong enough to hold out against the tide of big business buyouts, would be also strong enough to stand up to Flynn and his thugs. If, of course, Flynn had targeted the shop. Turned out he hadn't. Most likely too small to interest him.

"But I did notice something strange goings-on around here," the owner, a grey-haired woman, admitted. She was a well-kept woman, tastefully dressed, with her hair tied back. She looked to be in her late sixties, perhaps early seventies but still quite pretty. Britney thought she must have been a real looker in her day.

"In that building over there to be exact," she pointed at a townhouse almost directly across from hers. Her accent was flat like all the locals, but it had a posh twang to it.

"Used to be a clothes shop but it closed down about two years ago and was turned into apartments."

"So, what strange things did you see?"

"About six months ago, a woman from Dublin took it over. Wanted to use it as a pop-up shop, I heard. Selling homemade confectionery and jams and such. They even had a lovely display. Set out the entire downstairs. The strange thing was it got an awful lot of customers for a jam shop. And most of them were men. Lots of them coming and going. But…"

"Let me guess," Britney interjected while reflecting on the Dublin connection. "Not too many buying jam?"

"Exactly. I got the feeling they were selling more sugar in that place than was in the jam, if you know what I mean. I made a complaint and all. Spoke to a lady Garda about it but nothing happened. At least no one called to see me."

She sounded extremely disappointed by this, and Britney couldn't blame her. After going to the effort of making a complaint, the least she deserved was a follow-up. Unfortunately, that was the way the public saw the force these days. The immediate focus seemed to be on bringing in revenue from traffic fines and public order offences with everything else put on the long finger.

"That was me," admitted Fiona. She turned to Britney, a rueful expression on her face. "I took the complaint, but I handed it over to Flynn. He said he'd look into it." She shook her head and shrugged apologetically. "I'd no idea."

"Flynn?" The woman cut in. "Is he that burly detective who goes around like he owns the place? Trying to look like something off The Godfather."

"That's him, why?" Britney asked.

"Because I saw him over there a few times. Once he went in with a girl. Seemed to be a young girl too. Far too young for him. When he came back out, he was on his own. He hadn't bought any jam either, for that matter."

"When did it shut down?" Britney asked but had already guessed the answer.

"Oh, not long after I made the complaint, I'd say. Thought the young lady here was after doing her job, after all."

"Then that was about two months ago," Fiona stated, looking a little abashed. "I'll have the exact date logged at the station."

The woman nodded. "That sounds about right."

"We could trace the name on the lease." Fiona suggested.

"It'll be Mickey Mouse, I'd say. Or Marylin Monroe." The old woman paused, her sharp eyes squinting as she took a closer look at Fiona. "Speaking of blonde bombshells," she said, "I can't recall the voice, but I do have a feeling I've seen you somewhere before."

Fiona shrugged. "Possibly. Been in and out of your shop once or twice. Bought a kettle the last time if I remember."

"Well, that would be it then," the woman replied. "Hard to forget a looker like you." She smiled. "Hope it's still working for you?"

"Boiling perfectly, thanks," Fiona replied with a gracious nod then turned to Britney as if to ask, have we anymore questions.

In response, Britney thanked the woman for her time and handed her a card.

"If you think of anything else, give us a call on this number. My name is Sergeant Kent, Britney Kent." She made a move toward the door.

"Just like the singer then?"

"Yes. Just like the singer."

"*Kiss me, baby, one more time*," the woman recited as they left, then with eyebrows raised she addressed Fiona, an inscrutable look passing over her face. "I bet the guys say that to you a lot."

Chapter 12

On Sunday afternoon a prayer vigil was held in Jim and Stacey's parish church, St Mary's Cathedral. Stacey had requested the local priest, Fr Michael Maher, arrange it so that family and friends of her husband could gather and pray for Jim's safe return. Once arranged, the priest suggested he inform the media to raise awareness of their plight and get an image of Jim out into the public arena. They also posted contact details in the hope that if there was any sighting of Jim, they would be notified.

Normally the phone number of the Garda Station would be the one handed out, but the Gardaí had yet to acknowledge that Jim was officially missing. It seemed that apart from the young Sergeant Kent, there was no one in the force willing to take his prolonged absence seriously. But even the sergeant's interest was dubious, in so much as it lay not in Jim's wellbeing but in the opportunity to lay the blame for a series of horrific murders at his door. With that foremost in their minds, the family decided that the details of his father, Alan, were the ones to be released. "God knows, Stacey has enough on her plate," was Alan's sentiment.

There was a huge turnout for the vigil. In response to Fr Michael's request, several reporters and cameramen did appear, local ones mostly but also a crew from national TV who promised to air the story on the evening news.

Along with the cameras, came the inevitable hangers-on and rubberneckers that media attention can bring but Alan Rourke also noted a lot of genuinely concerned people. At first, he had been opposed to the prayer vigil, but now he had to admit it was a moving sight. Neighbours, friends, colleagues – Alan recognised faces that he hadn't seen in years, all seemingly troubled by Jim's absence and all wishing his safe return. He knew that if his son was watching, he would wish to turn back the clock and be home with his family. Alan, however, knew both in his heart and his head that it was too late for that, even if Stacey wasn't ready to openly admit it.

Glancing around the congregation, he spotted all sorts of so-called important people present too. Politicians, priests, and agricultural reps – an array of community leaders gathered to 'pray' for his son. He even spotted the bloated figure of Ade Fagan, the President of the HAI, in muted conversation with local HAI rep, Shane Fitzpatrick. Fagan's son, David, stood behind the pair, appearing as a younger replica of his father. A little shorter and not quite as obese yet, but every bit as pampered. Most people would feel honoured by the presence of such high-profile figures, as Alan would have been just a couple of weeks earlier, but Jim always hated Fagan. In fact, the very sight of the 'smarmy hypocrite' made his blood boil. And seeing as this vigil was being held in Jim's name, Alan was tending to see things from his son's point of view.

No, they weren't there for Alan and his family. And they certainly weren't there for Jim. They only looked out for themselves. Fagan especially. Hadn't Jim developed a pain in his jaw over the years telling him so.

Having been elected HAI President four years earlier, Fagan had then ensured he became the first such president to be suitably remunerated, as he had put it himself in many a self-serving interview. In other words, he got paid for his services. And paid handsomely for a job he should have been honoured to do. With remuneration within the HAI a major bugbear of Jim's, he found that unforgivable. After all, wasn't that the reason they broke away from their counterparts, the GAA, in the first place, he maintained – because of the inequality they perceived in that organisation. "And now, there's Fagan blatantly flouting that golden rule," Jim argued, not long before he went missing. "A rule you, and thousands like you, abided by all your life, Da." It was true. Alan had. First as a member of the GAA and later, as one of the disillusioned rebels that formed the splinter group of idealistic revolutionists that, in 1984, went on to become the HAI.

"But like all idealisms, it's a crock of shit," Jim declared. "The likes of Fagan lines his pockets while people like you still offer their time for nothing. He's just laughing in your faces. Like he laughed in mine."

Though he hated to admit it, Alan knew it was true. And now it was rumoured Fagan even wanted the district stadium named after him. Fenian Park was to become Fagan Stadium. The announcement to be made on district final day. A day fast approaching. No, the president wasn't there for him. He was there for the cameras, the handshakes, the self-promotion. That was one of the reasons

Alan hadn't favoured the idea of the gathering. People like the Fagan's and Fitzpatrick turning up making a mockery of their pain. Turning the event into a circus. His son might have done a terrible thing, but he was no clown.

To his great relief, the gathering didn't become the farce he'd feared. It was brief, tasteful and well-directed by Father Michael who spoke kindly about the boy he had baptised. A boy who played hurling with such freedom, joy and natural ability, who grew up to become an even better husband and father. A good son. A man not without his personal trials and tribulations but a man who fought to overcome those problems and be a better man because of them. A stronger man.

Jim's good friend and work colleague, Brian Farrell, also spoke to the gathering. He briefly referred to Jim's work ethic and spoke about the camaraderie they had as colleagues, then urged Jim that if he was listening, it was time to come home.

Stacey too found the courage from somewhere to stand up in front of the crowd and plead for her husband's safe return.

"If anyone knows anything about his whereabouts, please let us know," she pleaded. "Not knowing is almost the hardest. If anyone has done anything to harm him, we will forgive you. All we ask is that you tell us the truth because we can't survive in this nightmare much longer." Finally, she spoke directly to her husband, in the hope that he was listening, in the hope that he would come home of his own accord. Standing at the rear of St Mary's Cathedral, Britney very much doubted it. "Jim, if you're listening, I just want to let you know that no matter what, I love you. Zac and Cathy love you. And they miss you." On mentioning her children's names, she glanced down to the pew in which they were sitting, either side of Vera. As her eyes met Cathy's, her voice came close to breaking, forcing her to pause to gather herself. "Alan and Vera love you and they both miss you too. We all miss you. Please come home."

Through it all, Alan stood by her side and gripped her hand, hoping the physical contact would somehow bolster and combine their strengths. She would need strength over the coming weeks. They all would.

Where, he wondered, would he find his?

When Stacey finished, Alan took her place at the lectern. He hadn't intended to speak but with the cameras there, he felt it would be remiss not to take the opportunity to influence the thinking of the Gardaí. He wasn't surprised that his son's disappearance was fobbed off. Jim had been fobbed off all his life. Just as he had. That's the way it was for working-class people. But now it was almost two weeks, and two weeks was far too long to be ignored. And that's exactly what he told them when he stood up in front of the crowd.

"None so blind as those who will not see," he said stonily. "Two weeks my boy is gone, and the Gardaí have done nothing. They refuse to acknowledge he is even missing. When will my son be seen as more than just a nobody?"

Despite the questions hanging over his son disappearance, Britney couldn't help but be moved by Alan

Rourke's anguish. And that of the family. She really felt for them. Would feel even more for them once the truth as she saw it came out. Perhaps now that Alan Rourke had spoken out to the media, Flynn and the rest would listen. Nothing like media attention to get the wheels of justice turning.

With the vigil over, she got up from her seat and nodded at a stoic looking Timmy Dunne who occupied the pew in front of her, then waited for the crowd to clear away before approaching Alan Rourke. She knew it wasn't a good time, probably the worst time in fact but then what choice did she have? Three people were dead and the Gardaí, herself included, were jumping from Billy to Jack with theories. They needed a solid lead and despite all the information they'd uncovered regarding Flynn, her gut feeling was still the same. Jim Rourke was the key. Find him and you solve the case.

As she approached Alan Rourke, she saw his brown eyes narrow. She couldn't blame him for being wary. Their previous meeting hadn't gone all that well and right now, after all that had been said from the altar, his emotions would be red raw. Still, it was exactly because of that she was determined to forge ahead. His guard would be down, and his reaction would be instinctive. Unmasked. She could have approached Stacey with the incendiary question she had in mind, but the poor woman seemed way too fragile at that moment leaving Britney to decide it would be best not to bother her. Besides, Alan had clearly put himself forward as the family spokesperson.

She was working on how best to broach the subject of his son having a possible paramilitary connection when Ade Fagan cut in front of her. Though Alan had not proffered his hand, Fagan grabbed it and shook it firmly while at the same time glancing around as if to ensure he was spotted by the cameras.

"So sorry about the situation you're in, Alan," he declared loud enough for anyone close by to hear. "You've always been such a good servant to the organisation. If there's anything we can do for you, if you need any help at all, be sure to let me know." It was plain to see why Flynn would be keen to hang out with the likes of Fagan. The level of bullshit was right up Flynn's alley.

Alan stared at him coldly, obvious contempt in his eyes. "I need my son back. Can you do that?"

Ade Fagan's sympathetic smile was clearly forced as he eyed the cameras. "If I could, I certainly would, Alan. But I will pray for his safe return." With that, Ade Fagan moved along, his handshaking duty done, only for his son to take his place. Briefly. More meaningless words and a practiced pose before stepping after his father.

Britney noted that Alan Rourke had daggers in his eyes as he watched the Fagans depart. She could appreciate how he felt. Clearly, the Fagans were there for their own selfish interests and not in genuine support of Alan or the family. Alan kept his eyes on him until he had left the church then finally turned to face Britney.

"What do you want now?" he growled through gritted teeth.

"Sorry to bother you, Alan," apologised Britney, "but I have one more question about Jim."

"You can have all the questions you want," Alan Rourke replied while turning to walk away. "Doesn't mean I have to answer them."

"Your son used to drink in Bernie's a lot?" Britney said quickly.

"He might have. Drank in a lot of places, I'd say," he took a few paces away from her.

"Yes, but Bernie's is known as a republican bar. Biggest republican bar in town. Some say it doubles up as a recruitment office."

Alan Rourke stopped in his tracks. "What are you trying to say?" he asked without turning around.

"I'm asking if Jim was ever involved with the IRA?" Britney decided there was no point beating around the bush.

Now, Alan slowly turned to face her. As he did so his expression was like thunder. "How dare you?" he growled. "How dare you come here and ask me that?"

Britney held her ground. "I dare because people are dying. And they are being tortured beforehand. Kneecapped to be precise."

"Well, it's not my boy doing it," Alan Rourke replied through gritted teeth. "Jim could never kill anyone." With that, he turned again and this time he did walk away. However, the fact that he couldn't look her in the eye when he proclaimed his son's innocence convinced Britney that he was lying. Deep down, Alan Rourke believed his son could kill.

With that in mind, she decided getting to the truth trumped any sympathy she had for Stacey's obvious distress. She waited until the crowd dissipated, leaving Stacey standing alone with the kids. Three sets of wide, lost eyes watched her as she approached.

"Sergeant," Stacey acknowledged meekly.

Britney offered a sympathetic smile. "How are you, Stacey?"

Stacey shrugged in reply. "I just hope Jim was watching."

"I'm sure he was." Unable to think of anything else to add, Britney got straight to what was bothering her. "You told me during our initial meeting that Jim use to get into trouble from time to time. Silly stuff you said."

"Yes." Stacey's tone took on an edge of wariness.

"Did it ever become more than that?"

Stacey looked at her blankly.

"I mean did it ever escalate into fights?"

"Once or twice," she sniffed, "but I didn't want Jim fighting. Anyway, Jim never started anything, if that's what you mean. He just reacted." Her shrug was almost apologetic. "Maybe he shouldn't have but some of those people can be horrible. Really horrible."

"In what way, exactly?"

"Well…we were out one night and one of them assaulted me. Forcibly kissed me just to humiliate him. It was disgusting."

"Can you remember who it was?"

"Ahm, I think it was Toby something or other… Just some drunken clown Jim used to hurl with."

"Toby Cullen?"

Stacey gave a half-hearted shrug. "Possibly."

"That's sexual assault. Did you report it?"

"No. Jim said it would only make things worse. He said he'd deal with it."

"I see," Britney replied, then thanked her and left her to her hopeless thoughts. As she exited the church, Britney couldn't help but wonder how exactly Jim did deal with it. Is that what he is doing now? Dealing with it?

****

Believing she had enough to influence the investigation, and having spotted his car in the carpark, Britney knocked on the door of Superintendent Halley's office the very next morning. Halley's office was the last one at the end of a long hall in the station and was a sight more lavish than any of the others, with a large oak desk and a pair of leather swivel chairs taking centre stage. On entering, Britney was forced to wait for the Super to dispense with a document he was reading, so she took the time to glance around. The room was personalised as one would expect with photos of his stunning wife and beautiful young family plus several framed certificates and diplomas detailing the Super's achievements within the force. There was one photo in particular of Halley posing with Ade Fagan after the renovation of Fenian Park that caught Britney's eye. The HAI president certainly liked to press the flesh.

Once the Super had finished signing off on the document, he indicated for her to take the chair directly across the desk from his. The leather squeaked when she sat and seemed to mould itself to her shape. It was so comfortable she felt she could sleep in it. 'So, this is what life is like at the top,' she thought, 'and the likes of us minions have to beg for our overtime.'

"How can I help you, Sergeant?" Despite the pressure he must have been under with one of the biggest murder investigations in the country's history on his patch, the Super's voice was even. He seemed relaxed and willing to listen to whatever she had to say.

Forcing her expression to portray an air of confidence she just wasn't feeling, she filled him in on everything she had learnt over the past week, including the existence of the brothels and their possible link to the IRA. However, concerned that blood was thicker than water, she was careful not to mention Flynn's name or allude to his corrupt activities. Not yet.

"Remember when I was out of the station on Saturday?"

"Yes. We still have to get to that," he reminded her sternly. "Once all this settles down. And while we're on that note, did I spot you out of the office the other day? And out of uniform?"

"Yes, well…" Britney began while frantically scouring her memory for where he could possibly have seen her. She drew a blank. "I was following up a lead, sir."

"Were you now?" His fine eyebrows furrowed over arctic blue eyes that glinted momentarily. "After all we discussed?"

"It was regarding that missing person if you remember?'

Expecting him to explode, Britney braced herself but was surprised to see him simply nod, if a tad warily. "Yes, Jim Rourke. I hear they had a vigil for him last night. Media and all were invited. A bit of a circus by all accounts." He shook his head. "Still, it's the last thing we needed with all that's going on."

"I was there, sir, and it was actually quite moving."

"You were there?" Halley sat forward in his chair as he spoke. A single vein throbbed in his neck.

"Yes, sir. You see, sir, while I was working on The Courier case, I found a direct link connecting Rourke to the murders."

"A link? What link?"

After a calming breath, Britney outlined everything she'd learnt about Jim Rourke. The sighting of his van. His hatred of the Cullens. His father finding Cullen's body.

"You really think Jim Rourke is involved in all this?" On having the evidence presented to him, circumstantial though it may have been, Halley's opinion that the missing man was just a soak on a bender seemed to have softened. In fact, he seemed ready to accept her theories. Britney wondered how much the level of media attention attracted by the previous evening's vigil now swayed him.

"Yes, sir. I think he either saw something which has terrified him or…"

"Or?"

"Or, he could very well be The Courier, sir."

"I see." Halley's expression was unreadable. "Now, that would be a turn up for the books."

Chapter 13

With all the fuss, the doctor's present had been all but forgotten. After leaving work that fateful day, the secretary had picked up her three kids from the child-care establishment that was costing her an arm and a leg, a fact that begged the question whether there was any point in her working at all. Especially for a pompous ass like Doctor Carmody. Working for the doctor was really starting to get to her. Choosing a career in medicine was supposed to be a calling. A vocation. In her opinion, the only entity her boss felt a vocation to was himself. Not for the first time, she wished she'd had the courage to call him up and tell him where to stuff his job. The only thing was, it paid well, and the crèche fees weren't always going to be hanging over her. She dreamt that someday she might get a chance to actually enjoy the money.

There were also the other little perks, of course. The gifts were mere trinkets most of the time but every now and then she hit the jackpot with a box of expensive chocolates or a bottle of a decent chardonnay. Perhaps she would be lucky, and it would be something nice this time too. She needed cheering up. Although judging by the shoddy newspaper wrapping, she doubted it.

On her arrival home, she had taken the gift out of her bag to casually examine it. It didn't contain wine, that's for sure, not if the size of the box was anything to go by, but it could be a box of gourmet chocolates, she mused, or perhaps it could be something she'd pass on to her husband such as cufflinks or better still, a watch. Whatever it was, it would have to wait because the children were screaming for attention and her husband would be expecting his dinner once he got home. With so much to do, she decided to place the gift in a kitchen unit drawer to open it later in peace. However, unable to resist having one quick peek before securing it away, she tore free a corner of the clumsily folded newspaper that enfolded the gift. Her spirits dropped when she saw what appeared to be an old matchbox. Yet, she told herself optimistically, the most beautiful of pearls can be found in the unsightliest of shells. On that positive note, she closed the drawer and went off about her chores, first helping the kids with homework, then making a start on the dinner. Once her husband arrived home, they all sat down to eat their evening meal. Following this, was the washing up, tidying, and getting the children off to bed.

By the time she got a moment to herself later that evening, she was too exhausted to even contemplate opening second-hand presents. It, therefore, proved the destiny of the stuffed matchbox to remain forgotten in the drawer, at least until a Garda Sergeant called to Madeleine's house, asking if she'd ever received such a thing. By then, its contents had decomposed to such a degree it had started to emit an unpleasant odour and would soon have been rediscovered anyhow.

When the sergeant, a female Garda that introduced herself as Britney Kent eventually ripped off the tattered newspaper wrapping and opened the box, Madeleine could tell she didn't find what she expected. In fact, her pretty face turned white with shock and she at once dropped the box onto the kitchen table, the impact causing the contents to hop out and land next to the table's centrepiece – a pillar candle holder which the ungrateful doctor had previously received from a patient. Then it was Madeleine's turn to blanch at the sight in front of her. Not cufflinks or a watch as she had earlier anticipated but a pair of semi-decomposed human eyes.

"Jesus Christ!" Sergeant Kent cursed as she rooted her phone out of her pocket. Her hands were trembling as she thumbed the number of the Dublin detective. "We're missing a victim," she said the moment the call was answered.

"I'm guessing you've found the doctor's missing present?" Lyons replied, "And it wasn't Miss Cox's ears." If he was surprised by this unexpected turn of events, Britney couldn't tell. However, after she filled him in on what exactly she had found she could almost hear his mind working overtime on the other end of the line.

"As it happens, I've got some news for you too," he said eventually. "A possible location on Jim Rourke." Britney was gobsmacked as he expanded on this second bombshell. If what he said was true, then she was a step closer to finding her missing man. Something which would surely validate the theory she'd presented to Halley the previous morning.

"I also have something on the doctor. I knew he sounded familiar so after talking to you, I checked up on him. And guess what?"

"Just tell me," Britney replied impatiently, sensing that, at last, there was an end in sight.

"He was the team doctor for the Oldcastle hurling squad back in the early 2000s."

"So, we're back to the HAI again?" she remarked.

"I know what you're thinking, but the papers found at each scene do reinforce that connection. At first, I thought the killer was using them to point us towards Independent News itself but now I'm not so sure. I think it's more nuanced than that."

"Go on."

"The HAI is mentioned in all the papers. And it ties all the pieces – Rourke, Cullen, Cox. The scene of the first murder. I really think that's telling. And the HAI is far more corrupt than you think. In fact, it's real Animal Farm stuff. George Orwell could have been writing about the HAI when he penned that little gem. The pigs getting fatter while the workhorses suffer. Just look at the District Boards. Almost every leading member is on the verge of morbid obesity. Even the president himself, Mr Ade Fagan, is a walking heart attack. They don't get that way on bread and water, Sergeant Kent. The HAI is huge business. Big business is always worth killing over."

"Possibly. But it could also be coincidence. Almost everyone in this country has a HAI connection, especially in counties like Oldcastle. Hurling is the main sport. The only sport. But no one gets killed over sport, surely."

"Tell that to Andres Escobar."

Now she was lost completely.

****

Though Lyons cautioned her not to dare enter the property without backup she couldn't help herself. With the house just a ten-minute drive from the secretary's home, validation of her theory was within touching distance. But having just learned of the existence of another victim, validation seemed a petty concern in the greater scheme of things. She had to stop this maniac. And stop him now.

The house in question was a terraced property located on the Old Dublin Road which was considered a nice safe area occupied by mostly elderly residents. How would those residents feel, Britney wondered, if they thought they were sharing their street with a fugitive? Just in case she might alert any occupant to her presence, she parked her patrol car down a side street and walked the remaining hundred yards. When she reached the house, all was quiet and a quick peep in through the windows revealed no sign of life. Even though the evening was settling in, lights were off, meaning the interior was gloomy with shadows lurking in every corner. She cursed. She would have to be extra careful if she entered. There were so many places for concealment and with no one to watch her back she could be a sitting duck. If Rourke was in there, as Lyons suggested, he would certainly have the advantage. Ruminating on this, she momentarily rued the fact that she hadn't taken Lyons' advice and requested backup, but that would have meant returning to the station, something which she was loathe to do. The last thing she wanted was for Flynn to get wind of 'Operation Downfall.' His downfall.

On reaching the house she discreetly peered through the ground floor windows either side of the entrance. First the right, then the left. Bedrooms both, she noted, which tallied with what Lyons had told her. Both empty. A cautious twist of the doorknob told her the front door was locked which didn't surprise her. After all, if she was hiding out, she'd want to stay away from the street where anyone passing in a car could easily see her. If she needed to come and go, she'd choose to use the back entrance.

After one final glance through the windows, she edged her way down a side alley which led onto a narrow rat run that ran parallel to the street, along the rear of the houses. At one end of the rat run, she noticed a white van parked close to the boundary hedge. For some reason, it looked familiar. She debated whether she should go take the number plate, but it seemed too far away to be of significance – a getaway vehicle would surely be parked within striking distance of the house, not a hundred yards away. And there was also the risk of her being spotted from one of the upper windows if she ventured that far down the path.

Dismissing the van, she continued along toward the back of the property. This rear pathway was far more secluded than the front with large trees and thick hedgerows separating the gardens of each house, therefore offering any occupant cover for a quick and easy escape free from the attention of prying eyes. Halfway down the rat run, Britney located a small, iron gate which opened onto a narrow flagstone pathway. This, in turn, led to the rear door of the house that Lyons said was registered in Marie Cox's name. On reaching the end of the path, Britney spotted some cigarette butts discarded in the overgrown grass to her right, and more telling still, she noted muddy scuffmarks on the doorstep. These seemed relatively fresh.

When she reached the door, she found it unlocked and was tempted to burst in and try and catch Jim Rourke by surprise. However, she controlled that reckless urge and instead checked the rear windows for any signs of life. Again, she found herself peering into bedrooms, one as gloomy as the other, with no hint of anyone present. Yet, he was in there. She could sense it. Taking a deep breath to settle the fear rising in her stomach she slipped her telescopic baton from her belt, extending it to full length with a quick flick of her wrist, then slowly pushed open the door and took a tentative step inside.

All was quiet. 'Too quiet,' she thought, and she had to resist the urge to call out and declare the presence of a police officer. The last thing she wanted to do was give Rourke a chance to make a break for it. If he got away now, she might never catch him.

Taking one step at a time, she moved into the tiled hallway then paused for a moment to allow her eyes to adjust to the gloom. She was in a small utility, with two washing machines, one piled on top of the other, and a pair of dryers standing in the same order beside them. Someone has lots of clothes to wash she noted. Or linen?

Quickly making her way from the utility she entered another room that she presumed would be the kitchen. It wasn't, or at least it wasn't now. To gain space, the kitchen units had obviously been ripped out and now it was laid out as a bedroom. A rather luxurious bedroom with a large double bed covered in red satin sheets and heart-shaped pillows. A boudoir, if ever there was one. She did a quick search of the room then checked under the bed. The room was empty. From there she moved out into a wide hall which was finished with porcelain tiles, oak wainscoting, and had an expensive-looking chandelier hanging from the ceiling. Two rooms ran off the hall. She checked the one to her right. It was another bedroom, set out similarly as the first. It was also empty. A quick peek into the room on the left told her it was a third bedroom, one of the pair she had seen from the front window. Lyons' intel had been right. This was indeed a brothel. It wasn't lost on her that the Gardaí in Dublin knew more about the goings on in Oldcastle than the local plods themselves. Yet, she hadn't time to ponder on the significance of this with regards to The Courier investigation and Flynn's place in it. There was still the small matter of sweeping the rest of the house.

She cleared the remaining room then made her way towards the stairs and started to climb. One step at a time with the baton held in front of her, ready to swing it at the first sign of movement. The stress of remaining alert was so intense that her heart was pounding by the time she reached the top. She was about to climb off the last step when she heard a sound. It came from the room directly in front of her. Holding her breath, she paused to listen but heard nothing more. Silence. Moving on tiptoe, she noiselessly covered the three paces which brought her to the door of the room, then she quickly stepped to one side and placed her back to the wall. If there was someone inside, she was well out of their firing line.

Drawing a deep breath through her nose, she reached out a shaking hand, grasped the handle, and pushed. The door swung slowly inward with a squeak. Nothing. No movement. She allowed herself to relax a little. Perhaps the sound had come from outside. She pushed herself from the wall then moved into the opening and cautiously stepped inside. Suddenly the door swung violently closed catching her off guard, its momentum sending her crashing against the door jamb. She hit this hard and felt her shoulder wrench but managed to stay on her feet. Next, she sensed someone rush at her, so she swung blind with the baton, but her attacker was already too close. Panicking now, she tried to grab a piece of clothing, an arm, some hair, anything that would give her leverage and prevent her from flying over the wooden balustrade. She was in luck. Her fingers closed on the collar of her attacker's jacket, so she held on for dear life, detecting a tearing sound as she almost ripped the material from its seam. The attacker was on her now, his hands around her neck so she lashed out with her boot, her vicious kick connecting with his shin. In response, he swung a backhand catching her just above the ear. She screamed and went down but not before she shot a quick look at his face. And met with instant disappointed. She couldn't tell if it was

Jim Rourke or not. The man, she was certain it was a man – a strong man at that – was wearing a balaclava. With renewed frustration, she swung the baton and caught her attacker with a solid blow. She wasn't sure where – the hand or arm she thought – but wherever the blow landed it caused him to grunt with pain. Still, he managed to kick out at her again, catching her in the ribs this time. She heard a crack and felt the wind flying out of her, but she rolled with the blow then sprung to her feet, still holding the baton. Waving it in front of her like a vicious wand, ready for the next onslaught, steely determination in her brown eyes.

Sensing he'd bitten off more than he could chew, the man glanced around and realizing he was now closest to the stairs he made his decision. Without a moment's hesitation he dashed for the steps, taking them three at a time. He was almost to the end when he slipped and crashed to the floor, his momentum taking him sliding along the white porcelain for another foot or two. But within a moment he had regained control and was down the hall and gone. Desperate not to lose him after getting so close Britney tried to give chase but found the pain in her ribs slowed her to little more than a lumbering jog. In the time she got down the steps and had made her way to the back door, she estimated a one-legged man would have run a marathon. She hobbled down the path and had just about reached the gate when she heard an engine starting. Her instinct told her it was the white van and she cursed herself for not taking down the number plate when she had the chance. By the time she peered out, the van had pulled clear of the hedge and was speeding away. It was too far away for her to pick out anything more than the colour.

She swore loudly and kicked the ground, driving searing pain through her ribcage and into her chest. As she doubled over in agony, she couldn't help but wonder if she had just let her last chance of redemption slip through her fingers. And afforded Jim Rourke the chance to kill again.

She may have been empty handed as she headed for home, but her ribs ached like hell and her conscience was in overdrive. She knew she should call Lyons and fill him in on what happened, but her pride held her back. That and a niggling doubt in her head. Instead, she called Bob, but when he didn't answer, she was forced to leave a message. Which is just never the same when you are desperate to hear a friendly voice. See a friendly face. With the adrenaline from her ill-fated encounter wearing off, her spirits dropped to sub-zero. But shot right back up again when she found Bob waiting by her door. Hit triple digits when he wrapped her in his big, strong arms. A feeling that even the throbbing in her ribs couldn't override.

****

Detective Flynn calling a press conference wasn't much of a surprise. However, with it being just days after she had met with Superintendent Halley, Britney greeted the announcement with a sense of satisfaction. Was she getting somewhere at last?

Perhaps they had discovered the missing victim and had no choice now but to take her theories seriously. Having laughed in the face of all good policing protocol by going there alone, she was reluctant to inform anyone of the incident with balaclava man in the house on the Dublin Road but felt certain it had been Rourke who had left her with the heavily bruised ribs. A man of approximately the same build and height as the description Stacey had given them. Who else could it be? She had, however, informed Flynn of what she discovered at the secretary's house. The detective's reaction had been one of genuine surprise.

"That means…" he had mumbled inanely.

"There's another one," Joe Murray had finished for him. Britney had watched their faces closely. Both men's reactions appeared sincere. They seemed to know nothing about a fourth victim which suggested that despite Flynn's corruption and his possible connection to Jim Rourke, the latter was acting alone in this. Flynn may have created him but now Frankenstein's monster was off the leash.

There was also another possibility that had crossed Britney's mind. The eyes belonged to Jim Rourke, and he was the fourth victim. However, with eye colour clearly a different tone, she was confident DNA testing would quickly discount that possibility. Anyway, apart from Flynn, who seemed totally thrown by the discovery, would anyone really want to kill Jim Rourke? Those hurling people he had argued with? She very much doubted it. But it wasn't implausible. People were killed over the silliest of things. And HAI involvement was certainly a theory Lyons was considering. Before dismissing the idea, she made her away across to Ben's desk, stepping gingerly so as not to aggravate the pain in her ribs. Two days in and still they were sore as a boil. She was pretty sure something was broken, and by right she should get medical attention, but after her unauthorised visit to the house she was in no position to take medical leave. Halley would have her guts for garters if he got wind of it.

"You're into the HAI, Ben, right?"

"Yeah, I go to matches. Why?"

"Is it really as wonderful it's made out to be?"

"Well, it does do a lot of good work in the community but…."

"Go on…"

"Well, in an organisation like that there are always rumours about money grabbers. I mean, take the president. It's meant to be an amateur organisation, yet he pays himself a substantial salary. As much as any company exec. I mean we're talking about upwards of €150,000 a year from what I hear."

"Wow."

"Yeah, plus expenses. And we all know how they can add up."

"But if it's officially sanctioned, it couldn't be something worth killing over, surely?"

"Not a chance. Everybody loves the way the HAI is run. It's the heartbeat of communities."

"Any bullying within the HAI?"

"Bullying, nah… The worst that ever happens are a few irate supporters on a side-line giving it handbags at fifty paces. That and some sledging amongst players, of course."

"Sledging?"

"Yeah, players throwing insults at each other and stuff. To gain an edge, a psychological advantage. All usually left on the field though. And all pretty harmless."

'Sexual assault is not harmless,' Britney said to herself silently. "One more thing."

"Yeah?"

"If you were called to, ahm, say a disturbance at a house and someone was already there wearing a balaclava, what would you think?"

"I'd think he knew I was coming. And didn't want to be recognised. Why?"

"Oh, no reason. By the way who is Andres Escobar?"

Ben gave her a quizzical look. "A dead Colombian."

"That hardly narrows it down," she replied, but with her mind working overtime, she left it at that. On returning to her desk, she pushed thoughts of Lyons aside and focused her mind on the press conference which was due to start at noon. Having once again been kept out of the loop, Britney wondered what exactly was on the agenda. Would Flynn admit that overlooking the missing person that was Jim Rourke was a serious mistake or would he try and pass the blame to someone else? Would they acknowledge the existence of a fourth victim which was undoubtedly the case seeing as the eyes didn't belong to any of the others? And would they finally admit that the investigation was floundering and that the public had a right to be as scared as they were?

Basically, she wondered if Flynn would stand up and acknowledge that he was out of his depth. Then do the honourable thing and resign his position on the case. She doubted it. Flynn was all about self-preservation.

The question was where did Superintendent Halley's loyalties lie?

She knew that whatever was revealed in the press conference, would also reveal whether Halley was a man of honour or if he was willing to continue covering for his nephew's obvious incompetence and corruption. With public pressure having reached an incendiary level, she didn't think the Super could afford to do the latter, but nothing would surprise her. An ignorant pig like Flynn hadn't gotten this far in his career without someone holding his hand every step of the way.

As it turned out she was taken by surprise, and in a way she couldn't possibly have predicted. Just before the press conference was due to start, Detective Flynn approached her and rather contritely asked her to sit in.

"This missing person, Jim Rourke, is your lead. You're the one who sniffed it out, so you're the one who should get the credit. Especially if he turns out to be the one we're after."

Britney studied him warily. This wasn't like Flynn. Not one bit. Too accommodating by far. And there was no way he'd give over the limelight. Especially not to a nosy biddy like her. This came right from the Super, she decided. Right from the top. Perhaps Halley was prepared to throw his nephew under the bus after all.

"Ok," she nodded. "I'm grateful for the opportunity. Should I thank you or Superintendent Halley?" She couldn't help the satisfied smirk that tugged at her lips and was pleased to see how even this small defeat twisted in Flynnstones' gut. Still, she wasn't about to let him off the hook that easily. "Also, I was wondering if there is anything particular you want me to say, or should I just sit there and flutter my eyelashes?"

His reaction was a derisive snort. "Don't push it, Spears," he warned. "And don't get too sunburned. You know what they say – nights can seem very cold after a day in the sun."

****

When Stacey Rourke called her father-in-law, he was on the way out of mass. Every day he prayed for his son. For the kids. For Vera. And for Stacey. He hated seeing her so terribly upset. Or hearing the kind of anguish in her voice that he was hearing now.

"There's going to be a press conference," she sobbed. "It's going to be about Jim, I know it. People are saying that he's this killer, Alan. This Courier. Ever since the vigil, that's all I've heard."

"No, he's not, Stacey. Don't think that way." All Alan seemed to be doing these days was reassuring people but with each passing day it felt more and more like he was peddling lies. "They're just afraid. Desperate. They'll think anything to make themselves feel safer. But I know Jim couldn't do these things. And so do you. That's all that matters."

"But where is he, Alan? Where is my Jim?"

"Look, Stacey, I'm coming over. We'll watch the press conference together, ok? I'll bring some treats for the kids. Vera was baking this morning. Cake and buns. They like cake and buns." Even as he said it, he knew how hollow it sounded. No amount of cake and buns could replace their father. Nothing would. "I'll be over in twenty minutes so don't fret."

"I'll try not to," she replied in a tone that suggested she was already failing. Miserably.

Alan had earlier heard about the press conference. Reporters had been speaking about it all morning on the news as part of their update on the murders.

"A serial killer labelled 'The Courier' is active in the Leinster area. Three victims so far but the experts don't think it will stop there." It seemed to Alan that the announcer had said the latter with zest, as if she enjoyed the idea of a killer on the loose.

He silently cursed the vigil. He should have listened to his instincts telling him it was a bad idea. Drawing the media attention on them. All he had received out of it were crank calls from gobshites desperate for the limelight. One fool had even claimed to have seen Jim in a dream. A clairvoyant he'd said he was. Alan told him to fuck off or a fist would be the next thing he'd be seeing. If he was even capable of seeing it coming, that was.

But the calls weren't the worst part. Since the vigil, everyone was a detective. Idle tittle-tattlers forming amateur deductions and half-assed theories that invariably blamed the killings on his innocent son. Just because he wasn't there to defend himself. As if Jim hadn't had enough ridicule to deal with already in his life. As if Stacey and the kids hadn't enough to deal with. But Alan knew it wasn't his son. He knew that for certain. Jim would hurt himself before he'd hurt anyone else.

Fighting his anger, he collected some cakes and buns and said goodbye to Vera. Kissed her on the cheek. Vera too had seen enough. The worry about her son was etched all over her face like grey chalk marks. Greyer still, under her eyes.

"But I need you here too," Vera had argued when he told her where he was going. "He's my son. I bore him, and now they are trying to say he's a monster." She shook her head and started to cry in that quiet, broken way that he had become used to. "I didn't bear a monster."

"No, you didn't, Vera. Nor did we rear one. No matter what they try and say. But it will all be over soon. One way or another." He knew it didn't sound reassuring but if the past weeks had taught him anything, it was that there was very little reassurance to be found in words. Action was the only way forward.

"You're always gone these days," Vera cried. "Always. And I'm here on my own trying to cope." She looked at him with red, pleading eyes. "I can't, Alan. I can't cope."

"And you think I can cope?" he replied angrily. "This has driven me cracked. Night and day, I think of him," he said, his voice almost breaking. "I've been going around looking for him everywhere. Everywhere I can think of." He could hardly look at her when he offered the latter. He felt so false. So disingenuous. Like he was peddling lies again. He had to stop himself from screaming in frustration. *Jim is dead. Jim is fucking dead and no matter what we do, we can't bring him back.* But he didn't. He couldn't. Partly because by saying it out loud, he would be admitting it was true and he couldn't do that. Not yet. It would break his heart. It would break Vera's heart. Instead, he just left, like he had been doing so often lately. It was easier that way.

Alan drove the twenty-minute journey to Emmet's Hill in a daze. The press conference worried him. Had they found something? Something linking Jim to these people? Is that why they had asked for a sample of his DNA? He shook his head. It couldn't be the case. They could only be guessing. Grasping at straws. Trying to take the pressure off themselves by convincing the public they were making progress and using Jim as the scapegoat. It wasn't going to wash. Not if he could help it. But it wouldn't be easy, he knew. Clearing Jim's name could well drive him to breaking point. Had driven him halfway there already. Gritting his teeth, he rooted in the glove compartment of his car and took out his stash of cigarettes. Lit one and took a long draw. Then he located the naggin of whiskey he had stashed under the seat and took a bolstering swig of that. He had to be strong, he told himself. Now, he had to be stronger than ever.

A few moments later, he pulled into Emmet's Hill estate and parked up outside Stacey's house. She was at the door waiting for him, looking more tired than he'd ever seen her. She was in her bathrobe and Alan could see she still wore her pyjamas underneath. It was obvious she had given up on herself. No longer bothering to get dressed or fix her hair, while the idea of wearing makeup seemed a concept that may never cross her mind again.

"Thank God you came, Alan," she gushed. "I couldn't stand to watch it on my own. Not if they're going to try and hang all this on Jim."

"Of course, I came Stacey. You're family. We Rourke's stick together," he forced a smile that felt more like a grimace on his face. "Go on inside," he instructed, "and I'll make a fresh pot of tea."

She nodded. "Maybe it won't be about Jim at all," she said but Alan could tell by the tone of her voice she didn't believe a word of it. Her movements only served to reinforce his opinion. They were every bit as robotic as her tone when she turned and headed inside the house. As Alan followed, he braced himself for the worst.

****

It was hot in the crowded room. Dozens of media crews had arrived for the press conference. The bigger broadcasters were vying with smaller outfits from all over the country for the latest twist in what had developed into the biggest news story in decades. Between reporters and cameramen, there must have been over a hundred people in an incident room that wasn't designed to hold a quarter of that crowd. Once all the chairs inside were occupied, latecomers vied for position at the end of the room or were left stranded outside the door where they had to be content with sound only because they couldn't get a view inside.

At a desk set up at the top of the room, Britney sat to the right of Detective Flynn with Detective Joe Murray sitting to his left. Three local plods facing the world. Halley stood to the right of the desk, arms folded, like a school principal waiting to pounce on the slightest mistake. Britney didn't feel one bit comfortable. With either the crowd or the company.

Once the crowd settled down, Detective Flynn opened proceedings with a statement outlining the general points of the investigation, the Gardaí involved, and the progress made thus far in confirming the links between the victims both in Oldcastle and Dublin.

Though he made it sound impressive, he was intentionally going over old ground, therefore giving away as little as possible, something which even the most junior Gardaí involved in an investigation knew how to be adept at. Britney was well aware that what he didn't say was far more significant than what he did. For instance, there was no mention of the mutilations, no mention of the body parts being hand-delivered, and certainly no mention of a possible fourth victim. Though the first two facts were already public knowledge, he wasn't about to add fuel to the fire with an official statement.

What Flynn did officially confirm was that they were indeed dealing with a serial killer.

"Most likely a psychopath," he explained with what bordered on enthusiasm.

At that, the room exploded with a hundred and one questions but by far the most common theme was concerning a possible person of interest.

"You have a suspect, right?" one reporter insisted.

"What's your suspect's name?" another asked.

Yet another shouted, "Is it the missing man, Jim Rourke?"

Detective Flynn allowed the questions to fill the room for some long moments before holding up his hand for silence. An unnecessarily dramatic gesture from a man who was clearly enjoying his fifteen minutes of fame. Still, it took some time for the reporters to settle down to a point where Flynn could actually be heard.

"We have a suspect," he acknowledged, "thanks in the main to the diligence of our colleague, Sergeant Britney Kent." He nodded in her direction. "Seeing as it was Sergeant Kent who made the connection, I think it would be appropriate that she also get the opportunity to reveal the suspect's identity." He smiled unctuously for the cameras, then tailored his look into a more sincere expression. "Credit where credit is due."

Britney knew it was all PR. If the release of Jim Rourke's identity led to his discovery and in turn saved lives, then they all came out smelling of roses. However, if it all blew up in their collective faces, she was the one left holding the baby.

With the cameras now focusing on her, she gave the blemish on her face a nervous rub while sincerely hoping she hadn't put two and two together and come up with five.

"Sergeant," a reporter to the right of the room called out, "can you confirm for us the name of the suspect? Is it Jim Rourke? Is he The Courier?"

Britney sat forward and clasped her hands in front of her on the desk, hoping to display a level of confidence she wasn't experiencing, while at the same time wondering if the sinking feeling in her stomach was just old-fashioned nerves, and not her instincts warning that she had just been thrown to the wolves.

"I believe so, yes," she replied eventually.

"It's rumoured he has connections to the IRA, is that true?"

At this, Britney shook her head. "I can't confirm that," she replied while at the same time wondering who had leaked that little morsel. And also wondering how much more she should tell them. If Jim Rourke was in hiding as she believed him to be, this was her chance to flush him out, and perhaps light a fire under Flynn's ass too. She took a breath, and meeting the reporters demanding stares, she tried to be careful with her words.

"But what I can confirm is that working in tandem with Detective Lyons from Dublin we've uncovered a link between Jim Rourke and Marie Cox. It seems Marie Cox owned a number of properties around the Leinster area and in the past year had hired Jim Rourke to renovate them." Even from her seated position she could see she had the avid attention of the entire room. It was time for her next big reveal.

"We also believe those properties were part of a highly organised prostitution ring." She paused, then fired a contrite glance in Halley's direction before continuing. "In fact, I visited one of those properties recently and found it occupied. The man fled before I got a chance to identify him, but I firmly believe it was Jim Rourke. And that he was using the property to hide out."

The words had barely escaped her lips when the room erupted into a frenzy. Flynn sat calmly beside her. Far too calmly for Britney's liking.

She waited for the storm to subside before expanding on everything Lyons had told her. She avoided any mention of the HAI. She didn't want to embarrass herself.

****

"The bastards," Alan Rourke growled not five minutes later as he punched the off button on the remote and sat forward onto the edge of the couch. "The dirty bastards. They more or less said Jim is the killer." He flung the remote across the room where it bounced off a chair before crashing to the floor. "And that bitch of a sergeant is the worst, pardon my language. She came right out and said they were looking for him like it was some sort of a manhunt. And even made it look like he was involved with the IRA. And prostitution as well. Our Jim involved with that kind of thing!" He punched the seat in frustration. "They won't get away with this." Shaking his head vehemently, he turned to Stacey who shared the couch with him. "You should sue them. You should sue them when this is all over. Sue them for defamation."

Stacey shook her head sadly. "I don't want to sue anyone, Alan," she replied emotionally. "I just want my husband back. And the kids want their father." Her eyes started to well up. "When he comes back, he'll clear all this up, you'll see." Then the tears began to roll down her cheeks, confirming the fact that, once again, she didn't believe a word of what she'd said. "I don't understand it," she started to sob. "Why doesn't he come back? Or even call?" She wrung her hands together then started to nervously play with the wedding ring on her bony finger. "Unless…"

Seeing how upset she was getting, Alan moved closer to where she sat and put a comforting arm around her. "Don't even think it, Stacey," he said. "You know he couldn't do what they are saying. It's just not possible," he sighed. "I know my son."

"I know you do, Alan. I thought I did too…but…"

Just then she looked at Alan, her tearful eyes wide and staring, flooded corridors to her soul. He couldn't help but be torn by the level of anguish he detected in their emerald depths. Not depths, he corrected. Abyss. Each one a churning abyss. He was responsible. He was to blame for all the pain. Jim was his creation, after all.

"He's dead, Stacey," he whispered. "Deep down you know it and you need to accept it." His voice wavered. "Jim's dead and he's not coming back. And it's all on me.

His depression, his acting out, his drinking. I blame myself for all of it. For what he drove you to.

Now this. It's all on me."

"Whatever Jim has done, Jim has done," she gave a quick shake of her head then paused as she wiped the tears from her cheeks. "And whatever I have done, I have done."

Now Alan studied Stacey closely, noting the troubled look was back in her eyes. "You haven't done anything Stacey," he said, struggling to find the right level of conviction. "You are innocent in all of this."

"Am I, Alan? Am I really?"

Alan eyes narrowed, as if to figure out what exactly was in her head. Was she finally ready to admit the truth? To accept the hurt she had caused. He desperately wished it so, but her expression was impossible to read.

"Of course, you are," he replied, his tone hardening. "When all this is over, people will see the truth. I promise you that." With that, he reached forward and lifted the mug of tea off the coffee table where it had sat untouched for the past hour or more. It had grown cold while the rest of the country got all hot and bothered about the threat a mild-mannered boy like Jim posed to their safety. Just like the time that psychologist claimed he had anger issues. But who had been wrong there? Who had chosen to air the family's dirty laundry in public?

This time, though, Jim's disparagement was all down to that Sergeant Britney Kent. Oh, the rest may have been thinking it, but she was the one who had aired the theory, even going as far as alerting the country about the danger that Jim may pose if confronted, something she claimed to have first-hand experience of. If anyone spotted him, she had warned, they were to call the station immediately. Then to make it worse, the sergeant had held up for the camera a blown-up copy of the photo she had taken from Stacey's house the previous week – with Stacey cut out of course. To help individuals identify him, she had said. Stacey had been shocked. Not just to see her husband's image on national television but that the sergeant should betray the confidence Stacey had placed in her without so much as a heads up, as Kent had promised she would give. Stacey had told him that herself. Even showed him the card the sergeant had given her. Had held it up like it was a candle in the dark. Though he had acknowledged it with a nod, Alan had known better. Now, it was clear that Stacey felt like she had publicly betrayed Jim herself. Stabbed her husband in the back. But she hadn't. Not this time. Unless… Alan shook his head to clear it. He was getting paranoid. Seeing shadows where there were none. And it was all their fault. He made a mental note to set the sergeant straight before this was all over.

"I'll make a fresh pot," he offered as he stood with the mug of cold tea in his hand.

Stacey nodded and smiled gratefully through the tears. 'At least I have Alan,' she thought as he headed for the kitchen. 'Alan and the kids.'

Thinking of the little pets now, she thanked God that she had sent them to their room before the press conference had started, and they hadn't seen their father's picture on TV. Hadn't got to see the type of crazy person

Sergeant Kent was making him out to be. God knows they were worried enough without that. To help ease that worry Stacey had been telling them that their father was away working but she could tell by the look in their eyes they no longer believed her.

"Why are you crying all the time then?" Cathy had asked, leaving Stacey struggling for an answer. Then later had whispered to Zac that Mammy and Daddy were getting divorced like her friend Amy's parents.

"They're going to live in different houses," she explained when Zac asked what divorced meant. "And Mammy's going to have a baby with another man."

"You mean with Grandad?" Zac asked, looking confused.

"No, silly. A stranger. But I'd prefer if it was Grandad."

"So would I."

The poor little mites, Stacey thought as she worried about them now. What in heaven's name am I going to tell them if the truth finally comes out? As if summoned by her mother's desperate thoughts, a little voice called out from the hall door, startling her.

"Mammy?"

It was Cathy. She had disobeyed her mother's instruction and crept downstairs unbeknownst to her.

"Yes, darling," Stacey replied, perking up a little at the sound of her daughter's voice – not a cure but a temporary anaesthetic to the pain. "What are you doing down here, sweetheart?" Though Cathy had defied her, Stacey kept her anger in check. She didn't want her daughter to see her vexed, especially not now. She needed her more than ever. They needed each other more than ever.

"I heard a noise. So, I went outside to look."

Stacey sat up straight, the protective mother in her, already unsettled by recent events, now stiffening with alarm. "What noise? And what were you doing outside on your own?" she barked, no longer able to keep a reign on her anger. "I told you never to do that."

"I thought I heard Amy and Paul playing," Cathy explained, as she fought the tears in her eyes, "but when I looked outside, they were gone."

"But you know you're not meant to go outside on your own," Stacey reiterated.

"I just went to say hello, Mammy," Cathy pouted. "Maybe play with them a little. Good that I did though," Cathy continued more brightly, "'cause I wouldn't have found this. I think it's more biscuits." Her eyes twinkled hopefully as she produced a rectangular box from behind her back. "Or buns."

Zac liked biscuits but she preferred buns, especially when they were smothered in homemade icing.

Stacey's eyes narrowed as she reached for the box. It was certainly the shape of a biscuit tin, but unlike other presents she'd received this was crudely wrapped. And, strangely, in newspaper. Considering the lack of embellishment, one could reasonably assume it was sent by one of her male neighbours. A woman would never wrap a present in such a way, would she?

Just then Alan returned from the kitchen with the fresh pot of tea in his hand. On seeing what Cathy was holding, his eyes widened in alarm, and he quickly set the teapot down on the coffee table, spilling half of its contents in the process.

"What's that you've got there?" he asked with an edge to his voice. He had heard the stories. Read about them. By now, everyone had.

Cathy looked at him as if he was stupid. "It's a present, silly." Her tone implied she was put out having to state the obvious to an adult who should know better. She punctuated her displeasure with a tut then started to rip at the paper.

"Give it to me," Alan suddenly ordered. He shot a warning glance at Stacey before moving forward.

"It's for Mammy," Cathy objected, and boldly held her ground. "To help her stop crying."

"Give it to me, I said." With three quick steps, Alan covered the ground between them and grabbed the box out of the girl's possessive clutch.

Cathy stood stunned for a moment, staring up at him in shock. Then as her face began to scrunch with emotion, she turned and ran back upstairs, her little feet beating an indignant rhythm on the steps.

Stacey said nothing. Just stared from the box to Alan and back again, as if wondering what he suddenly found so alarming. Then her bleary eyes widened.

"It can't be," she whispered, now staring at the gift as if it was about to explode in Alan's hands. That was why they called him The Courier, wasn't it? He always sent a gift. A portent. Its appearance meant someone was going to die.

As she processed this certainty, Stacey stood frozen in place before visibly breaking. First a mere whimper escaped but within moments her terrified cries reached such a crescendo they were heard by the children playing on the green. As if commanded by a whistle the daily soccer game came to an abrupt halt, the ball once again forgotten. Joy too, as fear rippled like a breeze across the grass.

****

No sooner had the press conference ended than Oldcastle Garda Station became inundated with callers claiming sightings of Jim Rourke. One minute he was in Dublin, the next in Cork. They even got a call from New York saying someone had seen him in a bar on McClean Avenue, drunk as a lord but as harmless as a pet pig.

When the calls began flooding in, Flynn decided to show a bit of leadership for once and delegate the task of weeding out the definite cranks from the possible leads.

"Seeing as you were the one to finger him on live TV, Sergeant Kent," his expression unreadable, "I think it only right that you be the one to run him to ground. Someone out there knows where he is. We just need a Garda of outstanding ability to sift through all the shit." His cigarette-stained smile was of mock self-deprecation. "An important task like this is not something us ordinary plodders could manage." He turned to go back to his office but paused and leaned close to her so that he wouldn't be overheard. The stink of his cheap aftershave almost overwhelmed her. "If I were you, I'd knuckle down because this just might be your last chance to finish what you started."

Britney recognised the underlying threat in his words, but she refused to give him the satisfaction of seeing her react. She simply nodded and got to work with her pen and paper, determined to make the most of the opportunity the press conference had given her and uncover Jim Rourke's whereabouts once and for all. And in doing so, shut Flynn up. Permanently. She'd stay there all night if she had to. The volume of calls suggested she could well be doing that, the flip side being she wasn't alone in the task. Many of her junior colleagues were on phone duty as well, Ben Youngs being one of them. He had his jacket off and was starting to sweat beneath the shirt that clung to his muscular frame. Any other time she would have gotten a nudge and wink from Fiona, but with Fiona swamped with calls of her own, she hardly seemed to notice. Neither of them appeared happy at their work.

Answering calls and taking notes were only the first steps, eliminations and follow-ups were where the real work began. All in all, it was a laborious, painstaking job. Made no easier by the blasé look she spotted on Flynn's face every time she looked in the direction of his office. He simply sat in there behind the glass, drinking coffee and reading over the case file. As if.

'We all know what's in the damn case file,' Britney thought to herself at one stage. 'What's not in it is the problem. Detail, Flynn. Fucking detail. But soon everyone will know why that's missing, Flynn, won't they?'

Just then she heard a commotion erupt at the service counter – loud voices followed by irate banging.

"I want to speak to Sergeant Kent," a man shouted. The voice was worryingly familiar and soon she recognised it as that of Alan Rourke. But fraught now. Apoplectic.

"Sergeant Kent, if you're in there, come out and show yourself… I have proof that our Jim is innocent. Sergeant Kent, I have proof."

Britney's heart sank. She didn't need to see the proof to judge she had made a major error of judgement. She could tell by the certainty in Alan Rourke's voice. She pushed herself away from her desk and rose. Took a deep breath to compose herself. As she turned toward reception, she had a sense of foreboding.

That all her chickens were about to come home to roost.

****

There was no way Britney would have recognised what was in the box if she hadn't already known about the mutilation of Doctor Carmody. When she ripped off the partly torn newspaper wrapping and opened the lid of the biscuit tin, she was left staring at a mutilated mess of flesh and blood which could easily have been the liver of a cow or sheep or even the stomach of a pig, but she immediately knew it wasn't. It was the doctor's missing heart.

"Now," Alan said between gritted teeth. "While you were on television telling the entire country how dangerous our son could be, this arrived at Stacey's door. Her daughter Cathy found it. Carried it around like a Christmas present." He angrily banged his fist on the counter. "Our Jim can't be the damn maniac you made him out to be, can he?" he shouted. "Not if he's receiving a box just like the papers say the others did."

Britney was gobsmacked. The contents of the box changed everything. Blew her nationally televised theory out of the water and left her facing a shitload of egg on her face.

"Did she see who delivered it?" she asked after a moment. Despite her best efforts to sound unruffled her tone reflected the anxiety she was feeling.

"No. I was there at the time, and we saw no one. As I said, Jim's little girl found it at the door. Carried it into the house, for God's sake, thinking it was a present for her mother."

"Then it could have arrived earlier?" Britney asked, her mouth dry. "Even the day before?" It just seemed too much of a coincidence that it would arrive as she was declaring Jim Rourke a suspect on live TV.

"Yeah, possibly, but what difference does it make?" Rourke retorted. "It's obviously from that Courier that all the papers are talking about." He held his clenched fist in front of her. "Now, you just get back on that television and tell everyone the truth. Tell them that our Jim is innocent and that he's the one in danger. Or by God, when this is over, I'll make sure you publicly apologise for painting him as a madman."

All Britney could do was offer a barely perceptible nod. Alan Rourke was right. She would have no choice but to make a public apology. Add in her unsanctioned search of Marie Cox's house and Halley would more than likely request her dismissal once the case was closed. It was her own fault. She should never have opened her mouth. But she had been so sure. And oh, so wrong. Belated as it was, the delivery of The Courier's death-gift to Jim Rourke proved that. At least she hoped it was for him, and not Stacey or the kids. Christ, that wasn't even worth thinking about.

Just then, Detective Flynn came out of his office and made his way to the counter. For once she was happy to see him.

"I'll take it from here," he said as he approached. All Britney could do was nod dumbly and stare from Alan Rourke to the gruesome delivery and back again. On reaching her, Flynn gave her a suspiciously well-placed dig in the ribs, causing her to wince.

"You're dismissed, Sergeant," he said, a loaded statement delivered with a tone of supreme arrogance – the kind of arrogance that she knew would grate on her for years to come. As would the smug look that spread across his face as he watched her sleepwalk back to her desk.

"That's it, Sergeant. Slink away," Rourke called after her. "If I have my way, your career is over."

"No need for that, Mr Rourke," Flynn interjected. With the sincerity of a slithering snake, Britney thought bitterly and collapsed dejectedly into her chair. "The sergeant was only trying to do her job. Once I've this bagged as evidence I'll take you through to my office and take your statement."

Rourke spent over an hour conversing with the detective behind the glass divider. When he finally reappeared, he seemed resolute but somewhat pacified. On his way out he glowered at Britney but said no more.

Flynn followed him to the door, the smug look lingering on his face as he passed Britney's desk. Once Alan Rourke had gone, Flynn took a cigarette from his pocket and motioned for Joe to join him outside.

"All clear for landing by the looks of it," Joe stated as he approached the door. "I'd say she's one less headache to worry about." The man hadn't even the decency to wait until he was out of Britney's earshot.

"Yeah, I couldn't have timed it better if I had planned it myself." Flynn replied, his voice loud enough to carry. "You see, that's what happens when you save your legs and let the ball do the work." With that, they disappeared outside and closed the door with a thud.

The finality of the sound seemed to spur something in Britney. She got up from her desk and approached Triona Maguire who was obliviously typing away at her desk in the corner.

"Anything on a possible warehouse, Triona?"

"Nothing to fit our specific criteria," Triona replied without taking her eyes off the screen in front of her, "but I have narrowed the search. Could have something definite in the next day or two."

"Good. As soon as you've got something let me know, will you? And while you're at it, have a look at the newspaper found at the Cullen scene for me. Compare it with the one on that box Rourke just brought in. And the others."

"Ok. But what am I looking for?"

"Not sure. But you'll know when you see it. You always do."

Britney moved away from the desk and rooted her phone out of her pocket. On locating the desired number, she quickly thumbed a message. If Flynn thought she was about to roll over, he was wrong.

Chapter 14

When Detective Richie Lyons awoke that same day, he felt like he'd just gone a whole eighty minutes against the All Blacks. His head was spinning, his mouth was stuck together, and he felt bruised from head to toe. Every time he moved, his knees ached like hell and his hips were no better. He couldn't remember where he'd been, what day it was, or what time he got in at. He certainly couldn't remember if he'd paid his guest in the spare room a visit. He hoped not. Calling in pissed in the middle of the night would do neither of them any good. On the contrary, it could well destroy everything he was working towards.

He was way past late. He didn't have to check the clock to know that. He was invariably late these days. It had all become so difficult since Molly died. Getting out of bed, going to work, staying sober. But he had to. He had to be strong. She had asked that of him with her last breath, and he'd readily agreed, with all his heart. But as always, that memory brought a pang of guilt. He was failing her, he knew. Failing her in every possible way, just as he had done when she was alive. For a long while, he lay in the bed with his eyes closed and wished he could just stay there and let the world carry on without him. With any luck, he'd never have to open them again. Not in this world anyway. Not without Molly.

But he couldn't do that. Not yet. People were depending on him. She was depending on him. With a loud, weary groan, he pushed himself out of the bed and slipped back into the clothes he had worn the day before. He needed a shower badly but that just seemed like too much effort. Instead, he sprayed copious amounts of deodorant under his arms and over his clothes. His shirt had a line of Guinness stains down the front, but he couldn't be arsed to change that either. Instead, he slipped on his waterproof mac and zipped it closed to disguise the grubbiness beneath. With the weather deteriorating as it was, he'd get away with that, especially if he stayed clear of the station which he intended to do.

Clothed now, rather than dressed, he went to the bathroom to rinse his face and wash the drink out of his eyes. He looked every bit the mess he felt. His eyes were bloodshot, and his face was no longer the colour of a dead mouse, but a semi-decomposed one. Despite his hopes, the beard he had taken to growing did little to disguise the fact that he was living on the edge, and it didn't take a genius to understand that if he could see it, so could everyone else.

Top brass had given him leeway up to now, mainly because of his excellent record at closing cases. They allowed him to jump on The Courier case and take the young Garda with him as long as he reported back to the lead detective, a clean-cut asshole by the name of Sharp. But he knew their patience was wearing thin, both with his lack of reports and his continuous absence from the office. And the obvious effects of his drinking, of course.

Eventually they would stop making allowances for Molly's death and his apparent inability to cope. Molly's death couldn't be blamed for everything, they'd reason. Some things were of his own doing. Derived from his personal failings. Failings that surely would have surfaced eventually with or without her. Perhaps had been there all along, they'd whisper, only cleverly hidden. Once they started down that road, they wouldn't be long about cutting him loose. Better, they'd say, to close the book on him while they could still control the ending. Which meant time was running out.

Now, as he looked in the mirror, all he saw was the stark reflection of that reality. He was a dead man walking. A dead man with far too much to do.

After he freshened up, he left the room and wandered across the hall to the second door down, not the first like normal. Between transferring the chains and the reinforced see-through polycarbonate barrier inside the window, it had been quite a job moving her, but he felt it was a necessity. Young Danny had spotted her, he was sure of that. It had been his own fault. His own compassion had very nearly been his ruin. With her behaviour being more agreeable of late, he had not only reduced her daily dose but had also lengthened the chain to give her more freedom and therefore more scope to explore the empty room. Empty except for the stiffened cardboard containers he used for her food, and the bed, of course. He called it a bed, but in reality, it was just a mattress on the floor. No hard edges. Benign. Like the cardboard.

Yes, his soft heart had nearly undone him. He could consider himself lucky that the young lad couldn't hold his drink.

Lyons was also aware that the neighbours may have noticed her once or twice, but it was an easy out to tell them that sometimes his daughter came to stay with him. And that being severely autistic, she ventured out little. How could they know any different? Lyons was relatively new to the area, and he knew he could use that. His work colleagues, however, might make a point of checking him out, if given reason to. It happened all the time at the station. One colleague using the data systems to check up on another. He would never again make the mistake of bringing a colleague close to his house. Not until this was over.

With these thoughts running around in his head, he stood outside the door, debating whether to go in. Finally, he decided it would be better not to. Not in the state he was in. He would have to satisfy himself with listening. Listening for any sign of her. A movement, a word, the soft inhalation of her breathing. He could hear nothing. Silence. If he was lucky, she was asleep and might even sleep all day. If she did awaken, she had enough food in the room to stave off that unnatural hunger, he'd made certain of that, and bottled water, of course. Satisfied, she'd be ok, he decided to leave her for the time being and check on her later. Perhaps she might be pleased to see him then. Though he didn't think so.

He left the hall and headed for the kitchen where he brewed a strong coffee. While he was waiting for the machine to beep, he washed the fuzz off his teeth with his finger and spat his alcohol thickened saliva into the sink. He felt like retching but forced himself to take a few deep breaths and wait out the feeling. Out of habit, he flicked on the small TV that stood on the worktop next to the coffee machine and began to flick through the channels. Suddenly he leaned forward, doubting the reliability of his beer-fogged eyes. There she was – the bold Sergeant Kent staring right back at him, looking like a cross between the cat who got the cream and a rabbit caught in headlights. It was a rerun, the caption said, but rerun or not he couldn't take his eyes off it. For the next ten minutes he listened in dismay as the sergeant delivered an update on the case. As she saw it.

When the sergeant's cameo finally came to an end, he silenced the TV, filled a battered travel mug with hot coffee and took a long draw. As it turned out, he wasn't the only one whose career was as good as over.

Outside, the air was fresh with a promise of winter coming and the minute he opened the door, it hit him like a hammer. Suddenly a chill ran through him, deep into his core, and the onslaught of uncontrolled shivering underlined how truly shitty he felt. It would be a long day he knew. Longer than most. But on this day, the memories tormented like on no other.

"Soon," he told himself for what must have been the thousandth time. "Soon, this will end." It was a prayer as much as a statement. He couldn't possibly continue like this.

When he finally stopped shivering, he spotted a squad car parked outside his drive. He glanced up and down the street, his eyes narrowing, but there was just the one.

"Surprised to see me, sir?" Danny called from the driver's window of the car. "Or just surprised that it's morning already? Or should I say afternoon." He knew his tone was far less deferential than it should be, but he didn't care. He hadn't heard from Lyons in more than forty-eight hours and was sick of making excuses for him at the station.

'He's working the streets, sir. He's following a lead, sir. He's…'

As a result, Danny feared that being associated with Lyons was poisoning his career. He had attempted to broach the subject with the Super, but the station head wasn't impressed by his concerns, having heard them a thousand times before. As a result, here he was, at the detective's door, 'getting on with it' as the Super had suggested, but not exactly feeling the love.

Having intentionally parked down the street from the house, he could keep an eye on the room at the gable end, but he detected no movement. With the lace curtains drawn, what he could see of the inside of the room was dark. Empty. Perhaps he had been mistaken that night. One thing was for sure – he would never drink like that again. The pounding in his head the following day had very nearly finished him.

"And what a lovely afternoon it is," Lyons replied without a hint of enthusiasm. In fact, to Danny, he looked the opposite of pleased. He looked as if his colleague's un-announced presence concerned him.

"Thought for a minute they had sent the cavalry to take me away at last," Lyons said, "but then it occurred to me that if they did come for me, they'd send more than one squad car and a pup barely out of nappies."

Danny wondered if the forced humour was designed to disguise his initial unguarded expression. If so, too late.

"Good to see you too, sir," Danny replied amicably. "I see you had another good night."

Lyons hobbled across the street, looking like a tired old man riddled with arthritis, then slowly folded himself into the car, the pains clearly antagonising his joints. He took a long draw of the coffee before placing the travel mug into the holder on the dash.

"The best. Didn't have to worry about a novice puking his ring up all over my local this time. I do have a reputation to keep, after all."

Despite the look of him, he seemed to be in good spirits. Danny gave a shake of his head. Jekyll and Hyde once again.

"Did I really do that, sir? Get sick in the pub, I mean?" Danny sighed. It was bad enough that he couldn't remember.

"No," Lyons replied as he settled into the seat, "you didn't. You had the good manners to wait until you were outside. Then you spewed like a kid who had just stuffed his face with way too much chocolate."

Danny sighed ruefully. He knew if that little gem got around the station, he wouldn't live it down for a long while.

"The Super sent me over, sir," he said, quickly changing the subject.

"To check up on me?"

"To make sure you find your way back into the office, sir."

"Sounds about right."

As Lyons yanked at his seatbelt, Danny glanced past him at the car parked in the drive. "Nice wheels," he observed. Now sober, he could see it was a Mercedes. "That must have cost two years wages. What is it, an E-Class Coupé?"

"S-class," Lyons replied indifferently. "And it cost far more than two years wages." He shook his head. "Don't drive it much though." He forced a tired smile. "It tends to interfere with my drinking."

"If I had a car like that, I'd drink less and drive more, sir," Danny advised.

"That's rich coming from someone who drives like…"

"Like Miss Daisy," Danny cut him off with a rueful shake of his head. Sometimes Lyons could actually be fun to be around. After a moment of reflection, his expression grew serious. "You look like you could do with a good breakfast, sir." And a good shower, Danny added in his head.

"First intelligent thing you said since you arrived, Daniel," replied Lyons, before quickly correcting himself when he saw the look of irritation cross Danny's face. "I mean Danny." He might have added a sardonic smile only his earlier effort made his head hurt. "And speaking of intelligent things, did you see that car crash of a press conference?" The bear gave a disagreeable shake of his head. "There's a golden rule, my boy. If you have nothing constructive to say to those bastards, you say nothing. Otherwise, you are taking a big chance with public opinion. And in an investigation like this, you need public opinion on your side." He puffed his pasty cheeks. "She mightn't realise it, but they hung our sergeant out to dry."

"In that case, Sergeant Kent will need our support more than ever," Danny observed. "And, perhaps, even our protection."

"Possibly. But it's not our job to protect Sergeant Kent," Lyons reminded him. "We've warned her and that's all we can do. It's our job to figure out who killed Miss Cox. And in doing so, figure out who this rampaging madman is. If we happen to support Sergeant Kent in the process, then well and good. Speaking of which, any luck with the street cameras near Miss Cox's apartment. We know that hand didn't just arrive there by itself. The body either, if our theory of a separate murder site is correct."

Danny shook his head. "Plenty of couriers coming and going in vans, trucks, motorbikes. But none we could ID. He'd probably avoid the main roads anyway. And, of course, there were no working cameras near her building."

"Any sign of the elusive Jim Rourke then? Surely someone's talking now that Sergeant Kent has sparked a nationwide manhunt."

"Not yet, sir," Danny replied, sounding a little deflated. "Looks like he disappeared completely since our Sergeant Kent's run in with him. No activity on his bank cards or his phone. We've raided all of the properties we found in Marie Cox's name but so far, no sign of him there either. In fact, all the properties were empty which makes you wonder when you think about it."

"A tip off?"

Danny shrugged. "They were all set up as brothels but not a sinner in sight. Seems to me the chickens knew the fox was coming."

Lyons reached for his coffee and took a sip, his expression dubious.

"It ties in with something interesting I've learned about Marie Cox," Danny added quickly.

"Miss Cox?" Lyons asked with distinct annoyance in his tone. "I thought I told you to leave Miss Cox and the others to me."

"Yes. But I was getting nowhere with Jim Rourke, so I thought I'd…"

"You thought you'd act like Sergeant Kent and head off on your own little tangent," Lyons shot back.

"Just using my initiative, sir." Danny held his ground along with the detective's irate gaze.

Lyons sighed then glancing away, he rubbed his bearded face with his hands. When he looked back, he seemed more composed, if only a tad. "Ok, what did you find out about Miss Cox?"

"Well, sir," Danny began, while carefully studying his superior. "According to one of her colleagues, she was seeing a cop."

Lyons sat back in his seat, but his dark brown eyes suddenly seemed to focus.

"Now, that is interesting," he admitted slowly. "Very interesting. Did this colleague mention any names?"

Danny shook his head, still watching Lyons closely. "No. She said she never met him. But…"

"But what?"

"Judging by the way Marie Cox's spoke about him, her colleague did suspect he was married."

Lyons nodded slowly as if mulling the significance of this new information over in his head. His face remained impassive forcing Danny to admit he was either completely innocent or he was a born poker player. Danny found himself leaning toward the latter. Just then his phone vibrated in its cradle on the dash as a message came through. He thumbed the screen and found his thoughts reflected in the lines of text.

Hi, there's been a development so need to talk. Call me when you get this! Sergeant Kent. Ps…best not tell Lyons.

"Something you need to share?" Lyons asked, his bloodshot eyes fixed on the phone. Now it was Danny's turn to bluff. "Just personal stuff," he replied, glad that Lyons wasn't wearing his glasses.

"In that case it can wait because right now there's some place I need you to take me."

Danny groaned silently. It couldn't be the damn pub at this hour?

"I need to visit St Monica's," Lyons replied to the look.

"St Monica's?"

"Yes. The graveyard. There's someone I need to talk to."

The sudden solemnity to his tone reminded Danny of their little chat in the Sheep's head. No matter how exasperated he felt, he couldn't deny Lyons' request.

Not on his wife's anniversary.

****

A watched kettle never boils, Britney kept reminding herself as she waited for Danny's call. With the sudden turn of events, locating Jim Rourke became an even bigger priority while news of another attack by a group of heavies in vans concerned her – the target being the car company that Fiona and herself had previously visited. Seemingly, the staff had given as good as they got but still the objective was clear. Flynn was trying to shut witnesses up. If he managed that, Britney had nowhere left to turn. Never before in a case had she found herself so conscious of time being of the essence.

Especially now with Flynn' eyes watching her every move from behind his glass divider. Since returning from his cigarette break, his interest in her seemed to have renewed. She caught Joe Murray watching her several times as well, his expression neutral but his eyes taking it all in as usual. It was if they knew she wasn't about to roll over. If Britney didn't know better, she'd think they'd somehow hacked her phone. She wouldn't put it past them.

From her desk across the aisle, Fiona had witnessed the entire exchange, from the calamitous appearance of Alan Rourke to the powwow Flynn and Murray now seemed to be having in the office. "That smug look on

Flynn's face would make you sick," she said in a low voice. "I'm so sorry, Brit. I really thought you were on the right track with Rourke."

Britney gave a despondent shake of her head. "Flynn didn't. He knew I was wrong from the start. And I'm the one who should be sorry, Fi. My big mouth means any case we had against him loses all credibility. Because I've lost all credibility." She ran her hand through her hair in frustration. "But I know we're on the right track with Flynn and that lapdog of his. Something big is going down. I can feel it."

Fiona nodded in agreement. "I know what you mean. Those two are huddled together like a pair of old women since this whole thing started." She cast a furtive glance in the direction of Flynn's office. "I'll keep my ear to the ground, Brit. And I'll get Ben to do the same. Someone around here must know what they're up to." Sensing Flynn was watching them again she busied herself at her desk. Not wanting to draw undue attention to her colleague, Britney did the same. Since discovering the true nature of Flynn's activities, Fiona's attitude toward her superior had clearly evolved from dislike to genuine fear and having been the one to stir the hornet's nest, Britney felt somewhat responsible. 'Will I ever set things right,' she wondered, 'and break his power over us?' As if in answer to her thoughts the phone rang.

"Bob the builder," Fiona asked in an attempt to lighten the mood.

Britney shook her head reproachfully. "Reinforcements!" Her expression was one of relief as she pushed herself up from her desk and made for the exit. It wasn't a call to be taken under the gaze of all-seeing eyes.

Outside, the evening was drawing in. Dark clouds hung ominously low on the Oldcastle skyline and the high walls of the carpark made it a haven for menacing shadows. Britney made for the relative comfort of the Ford Fiesta that acted as her service vehicle and leaned against it as she took the call. It didn't take long to outline her situation to Danny. To her surprise, the young Garda seemed open to her line of thinking.

"But what makes you think he's involved?" he asked finally.

"Just something he said." Britney explained as she finished up her call. "And something he didn't say. I'll explain more when we meet."

She had barely hung up the phone when she heard a soft rustling noise coming from the shadows cast by the building directly behind her. Then a sickly, sweet odour wafted on the night air. Cheap cologne.

"How many times do I need to warn you, Spears?" Detective Flynn's voice growled menacingly, causing her to jump. As she did, she felt the phone slip from her grasp and crash to the tarmac, a clattering admission of the level of power he held over her. If he didn't know already, he knew now. Silently, she cursed to herself. "Trouble with you is you don't listen." He stepped toward her, his stride controlled, deliberate. Menacing. A cigarette causally dangling between two crooked fingers. "Like going to that house alone. Seriously, how many warnings do you need?"

Britney slowly turned around, her heart racing. 'Be strong,' she told herself. 'Be strong. He's only the bully in the schoolyard. Behind the façade, he's nothing but a coward.' "Tell me something, Flynn. How were you so certain about Rourke?" she asked in the most assured voice she could muster. "I mean you were certain from the very start." Although with the onset of dusk she couldn't clearly see his expression, she could sense that arrogant smile tugging at his lips.

"A man can't do that kind of wrong if it isn't in him to do it." He shrugged. "And I've known Jim Rourke for years. A weak man like that just hasn't got it in him."

"But you do," Britney pointed out.

He nodded. "Off the record?"

Britney snorted. "What else is there out here?"

"Ok, off the record…yes, I've got it in me. More than you know." He stepped closer and fixed her with a cold stare. "So, be careful, Spears. You think you've lost everything now, but you haven't. You have far more to lose."

"Are you threatening me?"

He shrugged casually once more. "You know I've witnessed many women lose their dignity. Lose it to such an extent that they can never get it back. It's not a pretty sight. Many think that death is worse. In fact, they often beg for it, Spears." He took a drag from the cigarette now held between his thumb and forefinger then casually puffed smoke from his nostrils. The glowing ember bathed his face in an eerie half-light, giving it the freaky appearance of a Halloween mask. And adding further malevolence to his already wicked grin. "I'd like to hear you beg for it."

Britney shook her head. "I won't be begging for anything off you, Flynn," she replied, struggling to keep herself from shaking. She knew he wouldn't be stupid enough to try something right then and there at the back of the station, but the vile intentions his warning carried were unmistakable. Still, unwilling to give him the satisfaction of knowing she was rattled, she forced herself to keep her voice steady as she spoke. "And if you threaten me again, you'd better be prepared to back it up. Because if you don't, I'll finish you."

Flynn pursed his lips and nodded thoughtfully to himself as if weighing Britney's words. "Strong words from someone whose neck is in the noose." Then he smiled coldly. "When it comes to it, I'm going to enjoy every last minute, Spears." He paused for effect. "Might even put that scar on the other side of your face." With that, he tossed the cigarette at her feet then turned and went back inside the station.

The moment he disappeared, Britney's legs almost gave out. Her entire body was shaking as she fell back against the car, like a drug addict experiencing a withdrawal. Her heart pounded against her damaged ribs. It wasn't just what he had said that had got to her. It was the cold look in his eyes. Even in the dark, she could tell that he wouldn't hesitate to kill her if it came to it. With that certainty in her mind, she stooped down to retrieve her phone and forced her palsied fingers to send another text. She needed to see a friendly face. To be held by strong arms. The speed of the reply bolstered her flagging resolve. There were still some good people out there. And on her side.

As she drove away from the station, she swore to herself that her earlier threat would be far more than just bluster. By the time this was all over she would indeed finish Flynn. Or die trying. It had come to that. Him or her.

****

Little over a half-hour later, Britney heard the comforting roar of a motorbike pull into her drive then park outside her house. This time she welcomed the nervous energy that coursed through her. Ignoring the pain that flared in her ribs, she hopped off the couch and made her way to the hall, forcing herself to walk instead of run. Still, Bob had barely pressed his finger to the bell when she opened the door and welcomed him in.

"It's so good to see you," she beamed but her relieved smile soon faded when she saw that he was hurt. "My God! Bob, what happened?"

He had a thick bandage wrapped around his head, and an apple of a bruise under his left eye. A raw looking graze sat below it, running down to his neck.

"An accident in work," he explained, almost apologetically. "I was unloading some scaffold when some of the bars came rolling off the truck. Gave me a gash on the head and nearly broke my arm. Left a nasty bruise on my foot too." Seeing the concerned look on her face he quickly reassured her. "It could have been much worse."

"My God! You could have been killed." She took his hand and standing on tiptoe, kissed him tenderly on the cheek then led him into the hall and on into the sitting room.

"I was just leaving hospital when I got your text." He smiled. "It was better than any painkiller."

"I'm glad. Because I really needed to see you too."

"Flynn again?"

"Who else?" She had so much more she wanted to add but she shelved her concerns, the sight of her man in distress being far more pressing.

As they entered the sitting room, Salem who was curled up on the end of the couch quickly hopped up on catching sight of their visitor and ran away into the kitchen.

"He's shy, like me," Britney explained.

"Not so shy is how I remember it," Bob replied playfully.

Britney initially blushed, then smiled. Even the sound of his voice made her weak. Made her want him more.

"You weren't so shy yourself," she recalled coyly.

Before she said another word, he leaned in and kissed her. Tenderly at first, then passionately. Intensely. Every bit as hungrily as the first time. The last time. As he pulled her close, a gentle sigh escaped her lips. Wrapped tightly, even in his one good arm, she felt safe again, her pent-up anxiety abating with each probing kiss. Allowing herself melt into the moment she wished she could feel like that forever.

Salem looked on from his bolt hole in the kitchen. He knew when he wasn't wanted.

****

The hooded man worked with a wry smile on his face. They still hadn't a clue, none of them. All they could come up with was a silly nickname. As if the delivery of the little mementos was the most significant part of his undertaking. Far from it. It was just an extra. An afterthought. Yes, it did bring added value to his endeavours – the fear his little deliveries instilled in his victims was worth every bit of the undoubted risk involved – but they had yet to understand. And their understanding was his goal. His objective. 'The Courier' they were calling him, but they really should be calling him 'The Prophet,' or better still, 'The Enlightener.' Because that's what he was in a way. Not just a carrier of God's word but a liberator of people's thinking. All men were created equal, God said. Therefore, they should be treated that way. It was that simple. But simple seemed to have been buried beneath the weight of modern day lies and manipulation. However, his little trinkets would help to expose that simple truth and lead them along the path of enlightenment. They would soon see it his way. And God's way too. If there really was a God.

He studied the contents of the letter, the blood hardly dry on the names of his latest achievements. The bureaucrat and the doctor. As far as he knew, they had yet to discover the unexpected demise of the former and even if they did, he knew that with all the international red tape involved, it could be quite a while before the force made the connection. He'd travelled quite a distance for that one but that couldn't be helped. It was a necessary risk. His only regret was that the death wasn't witnessed. This time his word would have to be enough. And the blood on the letter, of course. Another name erased. He was down to one now. One more and his work was done. It would all be over then.

He was amazed at how easy it had all proved to be. The planning, the deliveries, the killings. He was a nobody in the grand scheme of things and always had been, despite being a conscientious member of the community. A husband, a father, a provider. An honest taxpayer. Years of service, yet no one paid him any heed. He could come and go, and it would be like he was never there except for the deliveries he left behind. And later the bodies. People would see him, nod to him, perhaps say hello but out of uniform, they had nothing to remember him by. Nothing but that silly disguise. Days would pass and by the time the Gardaí would start asking their questions, any resemblance to the real him would be all but forgotten. Just like his life. And not just his life. The life of the one that mattered.

And now with only one more, he was confident he would get it done without a hitch because no one would put two and two together. Yes, there was a direct link to two of his victims, but the rest were all but strangers to him. All corrupt, all users, all deserving of his attention but unconnected to him as far as anyone looking in from the outside could see. Unless they did some serious digging. Even then, any link would be tenuous at best. Dated. Past tense. Nothing that would stand out to an investigator as noteworthy. Except maybe to that young sergeant, Britney Kent.

He never thought he'd see the day that he was wary of someone called Britney. But she was worth being wary of. Even after all that had happened, he knew she wouldn't let it go. She was that kind of person. A dog with a bone. 'A bit like myself,' he thought. A real bloodhound. Once bloodhounds fixed their minds on something, they never gave up, no matter what was strewn in their path. So, it would be Bloodhound Britney from now on, he decided, somewhat amused because it had such a nice ring to it. Miss Cox would have called that alliteration, he was sure, but they were just two words with a nice sound to a literary plodder like him. At least that's the way people saw him. Had done before this even started. A plodder. A man washed-up. Passed his best. He didn't mind. Their perception of him served his purpose. Still, he had to be careful. The sergeant could see things others could not.

"Beware of Bloodhound Britney," he mumbled to himself as he prepared for the next stage of his work. This was the part that had him torn. The part that he dreaded.

He wondered would he be able to go through with it when it came to the crunch. But he only wondered for a moment. He had to. He had no choice. If he faltered now, it was all for nothing.

Chapter 15

This time around, the meeting place wasn't quite as elegant as the coffee shop in Oldcastle nor was it quite as prominent. Sergeant Kent, who seemed to have grown worryingly paranoid since their last meeting, insisted they meet in the carpark of a derelict hotel on the outskirts of the small town of Athy, which was located approximately halfway between Oldcastle and Dublin. The obsolete hotel was a remnant of the Celtic Tiger and the then-government's erroneous policy of offering substantial tax breaks to anyone who could find a plot of land to plant a few bedrooms on. Location was irrelevant. Circulating money was all that mattered. The result was planners and builders treating the Irish landscape like a monopoly board.

The hotel car park was both empty and dark when Danny arrived, so he turned the car around and faced it to the road before killing the engine. Perhaps it was Kent's paranoia rubbing off on him, but he felt far more comfortable with an eye on the entrance. Then, satisfied that he could see anyone coming and going, he sat back and waited. As the minutes dragged on, the silence became oppressive, and he began to wonder if she was going to show at all. Perhaps she had changed her mind or perhaps he had misheard her. Whatever the case, he decided to give her one more minute after which he would head back to Dublin and that overpriced flat, which was about as spacious and comfortable as the Corolla he was sitting in. Still, it was better than freezing in an empty car park on a Saturday night. He was just about to start the engine when he was startled by a click as the passenger door of his car swung open. Before he could react, a dark-clad figure sat in beside him and the door clicked closed again, causing him to recoil.

"No need to be so jumpy," the out-of-breath female voice assured. Reluctant to leave the safety of Bob's embrace, Britney had dallied after kissing him goodbye outside her house. He had been keen to stay, and she had been just as keen to stay with him, to mind him, to heal him, to heal with him. He had a way of probing her innermost secrets that was better than any therapy money could buy. So much so that she found herself recalling words her mother told her the day she left them for good. 'I've found the one, Britney. Someday you'll understand. And someday you'll forgive me.'

Watching from her door as Bob disappeared into the city on his bike, she thought she did understand. But forgive? She traced the line on her blemished cheek. That was another story. A story that, in its own way was every bit as distracting. As a result of the long goodbye, she found herself more than a half-hour late for the rendezvous but more resolute than ever as she declared, "It's just me."

Danny exhaled slowly. The declaration had been unnecessary. He could recall the soft, sensual whiff of Sergeant Kent's perfume from their meeting in the coffee shop.

"Jesus, Sergeant, you took a decade and a half off my life. Why all the James Bond stuff?"

"Because I don't know who to trust anymore," Britney replied. "Every move I make feels like it's being watched, and this evening Detective Flynn threatened my life. Amongst other things."

Danny pushed himself up in the car. There had been undoubted menace in Murray's threat but for one Garda to openly threaten the life of another was taking it to a whole new level.

"Threatened…how?"

Britney took a breath to calm herself then launched into a recount of events, beginning with her altercation with balaclava man, continuing with her calamitous revelations at the press conference and finishing with her latest run-in with Flynn. All the while, Danny listened attentively, becoming more and more aghast as the tale unfolded.

"What were you thinking?" he asked incredulously when she had finished. "You practically declared a man guilty on live TV. With what? Little more than circumstantial evidence. Talk about counting your chickens." He had watched live coverage and several reruns of the conference. It was compulsive viewing simply because it was such a train wreck from an investigative point of view. Danny wouldn't be surprised if, in the future, recruitment used it as a training video on how not to deal with the press.

"I know," Britney replied with a rueful shake of her head. Danny heard the gritting of teeth as she spoke.

"Flynn just dumped me in it. He came to me just before it started and asked me to sit in. Before I knew it, he had the cameras focused on me and I got brain-freeze. I realise now I walked right into his trap."

"Pride comes before a fall," Danny observed, thinking mouth-freeze would have been by far the better option. "And if you rise too high, the fall can be great indeed."

"What are you – some sort of preacher?" Britney barked then sighed apologetically. "I know, I was getting too big for my boots." She forced a wry smile. "Be lucky to afford a pair of boots once this is all over."

"Detective Lyons did think it was a mistake," Danny told her. "He could see it was a setup."

"Yeah, well I'm starting to think that he and Flynn may be cut from the same cloth. He was holding something back at our meeting, wasn't he?"

Danny hesitated, his own doubts regarding Lyons, resurfacing. Could he really be part of all this?

"And he gave me that tipoff," Britney continued anxiously, "with that link between Cox and Rourke. And when I went to that house in Oldtown balaclava man was expecting me. I'm convinced of it. What's more, Flynn already knew about it. I could see it in his face. As I said on the phone, himself and Flynn have history, don't they?"

"They know each other," Danny agreed. "They hurled together years ago."

"I thought so." Recalling Flynn unwittingly reiterate Lyons' comment about letting the ball do the work and doing so verbatim. "But he told me he didn't know Flynn at all. Why do that, unless…" She sighed in frustration.

"And then there was those failed raids you guys carried out on Cox's Dublin properties."

"You think it was Lyons who tipped them off?" Danny asked, careful to hide his own suspicions. "That he's involved in those brothels?" Now, he was hit by the image of the ghost he'd seen at Lyons window. The trapped girl.

Britney shrugged, a barely perceptible movement in the semi-darkness. "I don't know. Feels like I don't know anything anymore. Except that I'm up shit creek and you're my only paddle." And Fiona, she reminded herself. The three musketeers. Or the three stooges.

"Glad to be of service," Danny replied dryly. "Don't know which is worse – being chauffeur for Lyons or a shit paddle for you." He paused, silently debating how much he should reveal. "He did hold something else back. Something quite serious," he finally admitted, glancing out the window pensively. Just then something caught his eye. A change of the light or movement in the shadows. He couldn't be sure. Perhaps it was just the wind blowing some debris across the open space of the yard.

"Well?" Britney urged. "Are you waiting for me to guess?"

"We saw the killer," Danny confessed after a moment. "We saw The Courier."

"You what?"

"Don't get your knickers in a twist, Sergeant," Danny admonished with a shake of his head. "We only saw him briefly. Not long enough to get a proper look at him. Anyway, I'm pretty sure he was wearing a disguise."

"What exactly did you see?" Britney enquired, her nostrils flaring. "Was he young or old? Tall or short. Was it even a man, for God's sake?"

"Yes, it was a man. Tall. I'd say well over six feet. Relatively slim but not that agile. I chased him and very nearly caught him, even though he had a good head start."

"Could you ID him?" she asked anxiously. "Was it Jim Rourke?"

"Can't say for sure. As I said, he wore a disguise. That long coat with the hood that fell low over his eyes. And he had something covering his face. At first, I thought it was a beard but now I think it was more like one of those snoods that you pull up from around your neck. Anyway, even if I could ID him, it's not going to be Jim Rourke now, is it? Not after what you told me."

"I guess not. Unless…"

"Unless he delivered that heart to his own house?"

Britney shook her head. "That's not what I was thinking. Crazed or not, I don't think he would target his own family. If that's what was driving him, they would be already dead." Her expression was grave as she looked at Danny. "But after all I've learned about Flynn, I really think there's more to all of this than a crazed killer acting alone. And with him threatening me like he did, only reinforces my opinion that he's knee-deep in shit and now scrambling to get out of it. Apart from the protection racket, I'm certain he is involved in the brothels. Perhaps not the high-ranking Garda running them, 'cause I don't think he has the brains for that level of organisation, but he's certainly earning a cut."

"You think Flynn is working for some sort of master-mind? And that mastermind could be Lyons?"

"It's possible, isn't it? And all his talk about the HAI is just a red herring."

Danny nodded. "And now the wheels are starting to come off? People are starting to talk, or to look for a bigger piece of the pie and they need to be silenced?"

Britney shrugged. "What better way to cover their tracks than have us all running around after a psycho that doesn't really exist? It would explain how he was so sure that Jim Rourke was innocent. The heart just served to confuse us even further."

"Ok," Danny replied, wondering if he really wanted to go down the road this was leading. "Let's say we run with that. We're then accusing senior Gardaí of not only extortion and running an illicit sex ring, but of multiple murders."

"I know. That's what has me scared shitless. Flynn's threats aren't idle. I'm certain he'll kill me if he thinks I'm getting in his way. Perhaps anyone associated with me too."

Danny wasn't sure what to believe. His instinct told him that Britney was genuinely scared and that all she had told him was true but then again, she had already cried wolf and on live TV, no less. Was she prone to exaggeration or worse, was she a melodramatic with a major chip on her shoulder?

"If what we're thinking is true," he hedged, "then this is too big for us. We've got to take it to top brass."

"We can't. As yet, all I have is unverified statements from flaky witnesses – witnesses that Flynn can get at, so technically they're little more than hearsay. I haven't a shred of proof. Not something that would stand up in court anyway. Especially now that my credibility is shot."

"And," Danny added, with an exasperated sigh, "even to me, it's starting to sound like the claims of a conspiracy nut."

"Don't tell me how it sounds," Britney replied in frustration. "I know exactly how it sounds. I just don't know who to trust."

"You can trust me," Danny replied readily, keenly aware of how it came across. Though he'd only met her twice, deep down he knew he was developing feelings for the sergeant. Right then, sitting next to her in the dark, he would do anything to protect her.

"I know," Britney replied sincerely. "And it means a lot." She glanced across at him and even in the gloom, Danny could detect the strain on her face. It was clear that the events of the last few days were taking their toll. "That's why I'm sitting here with you and not with Detective Lyons. Or any other high-ranking Garda for that matter. I'm seeing dirty cops in my bloody sleep."

Danny was starting to understand how she felt. "Ok, if we're to drag this out of the realms of conspiracy theory, we need real proof. Any suggestions about where to start?"

"We start by connecting the victims to the sex ring. And in doing so, connect them to Flynn. And to your buddy Lyons as well if he's the one running it. Think about it," Britney continued, "anyone of them could have been using the brothels and any one of them might have spotted Flynn there. They might even be his partners. Who knows?" She shrugged. "If we find a definite link between the victims and our crooked cops, the whole thing will fall like a house of cards."

"And Jim Rourke?"

"I bet if we nail Flynn, he wouldn't be long about coming out of the woodwork."

Danny knew she was right, of course. A link to the victims would open up the entire case. One link is all it would take. Danny was fairly sure he had two.

"I think I might just have the connections you need," Danny replied hesitantly. "But I need to get my ducks in a row first." He glanced out the window, glad to be sitting in the cover of darkness. He felt guilty for not confiding everything right then and there and he knew the guilt would be written all over his face. "When I do, I'll call you," he said with a note of finality.

Britney nodded sensing not to push. It was understandable if he harboured a certain loyalty to his colleague. She just hoped it wasn't misplaced. And that in the end he'd make the right decision. Lives depended on it. Not least hers.

"I'll be waiting," she said before getting out of the car. Danny watched her go then recited a silent prayer that his hesitancy wasn't putting her in further danger. As she melted back into the shadows, Danny thought he saw movement near the door of the abandoned hotel. He kept his eyes focused on that direction. Nothing stirred for long moments until suddenly a plastic bag went flying by in a gust of wind. He cursed silently. He was worse than Sergeant Kent now. Seeing things that weren't there. This whole thing had him jumpier than a naked arse in a field full of thistles.

He waited a few moments longer, watching for the lights of Britney's car to illuminate. Finally, he spotted them a few hundred yards from the car park and then they begin to move further away. She must have parked on a side road, he judged, then covered the remaining distance on foot. No wonder he hadn't seen her arrive. Christ, she had really feared she'd be followed to their meeting. With a growing sense of foreboding, he drove out of the car park and headed for home.

As he drove, his mind was so focused on everything Sergeant Kent had told him that he failed to notice another car pull out of a nearby laneway and follow him. The car kept its distance at first but then began to move closer until soon it was hovering only yards behind him, its powerful lights reflecting in the rear-view mirror, and nearly blinding him.

"If you want to pass," Danny cursed, "then fucking pass." He slowed and pulled closer to the verge, inviting the trailing car to overtake him. It didn't. Instead, it remained in his slipstream, only feet from his bumper, close enough to read the serial number of his damn exhaust. Suddenly he felt a shunt as the car bumpers collided. Feeling panic rising, Danny sped up, hoping to gain some distance from his pursuer, but the car kept pace, its lights still blinding. All Danny could make out was a blue tint outlined in the mirror. Possibly a sports car. Shit, he cursed in recognition. With one hand on the steering wheel, he fumbled in his pocket for his phone and thumbed Sergeant Kent's number. She answered on the first ring.

"That was a quick change of heart," she said. "You confirm what you needed to?"

"It was confirmed for me," he replied quickly. "There's a car right up my ass and I can't shake it. I think it's trying to run me off the road. I'm nearly sure its Detective Lyons' car."

"He must have followed you," Britney responded, her tone becoming alarmed. "Where are you now?"

"I'm not sure. A few miles outside of Athy."

Then he felt another bump to the rear and when he glanced in the mirror, he could see the car moving right up close again, ready to give him a third shunt for good measure.

"Fuck," he exclaimed, "he's not just trying to run me off the road. He's trying to kill me!"

Panicking now, Danny dropped the phone on the seat beside him and hit the accelerator hard. He felt the car leap forward eating up ground but within moments the trailing car was on top of him again, ramming the right-hand corner of his vehicle. Danny recognised it as a police manoeuvre, designed to make a fugitive's car spin. It would have worked too, but Danny had learned the move in training college and was braced for it. He let the car slip left, like a boxer rolling with the punches, then gripped the steering wheel hard as he shot onto the muddy grass verge. With two wheels on the road and two off, the car was pulling toward the hedge, but he battled against the drag, keenly aware that the last thing he wanted to do was oversteer. Do that and the car would certainly spin. And his pursuer would have him where he wanted. For what seemed like an age, he wrestled with the steering wheel, as the car ploughed along by the ditch, low lying branches whipping off the windscreen and battering the side panels.

Finally, he regained control and managed to ease himself back into the centre of the road. A glance in the mirror told him he wasn't alone. With the car steady once more, he hit the gas in the hope of putting some distance between himself and whoever was trailing him. This time he gained some breathing space. As he sped forward, he spotted a laneway to the right so, with a quick change of gear he spun the steering wheel fast, barely holding the tail of the car as it skidded on the loose gravel that covered the junction.

Once he'd regained control he sped forward, eating up the short distance to the end of the narrow road. Then he took a quick left, hoping the sudden changes in direction would shake whoever was following. A few yards further on he spotted a farmyard with the gate hanging open. He sped through the gap and swung a handbrake turn to land in behind the thick roadside hedge that bounded the yard. Then he at once cut the lights and killed the engine. For a moment all was dark with no sign of lights following so he allowed himself to relax a little. Only seconds later the angry headlights appeared, hurtling down the narrow track. The car took the same left that he had just taken and for a terrifying moment Danny thought it had found him, but it passed off by the gate, at terrific speed. Danny cracked the window of his car and held the phone out the gap, hoping to pick up the distinct sound of the sports engine.

Soon the night grew quiet, and the lights began to fade into the distance. At last, Danny could breathe a sigh of relief. Once he had calmed enough, he held the phone to his ear with a hand that refused to stop shaking.

"I think I've lost him," he informed Britney.

She could hear the relief in his voice. "Are you ok?" She asked.

To Danny, she sounded every bit as terrified as he felt. "I'm fine, considering I'm trembling like a newborn calf," Danny replied, while keeping one eye on the gateway and the other on what bit of the road he could make out through the hedge. "I'm going to tell you everything so just listen," he instructed sharply but with a voice pitched low. "While I was researching Marie Cox, I discovered she was seeing a married Garda. I got no name, but my informant did tell me he drove a fancy sports car. Detective Lyons was married and has a sports car. And when I told him what I'd heard, he got all funny. Defensive, kind of. Almost as if he was put out by what I'd uncovered."

"So, you think he was the one she was having the affair with?" Britney wondered. "That he knew her beforehand and that it was more than just a coincidence the case landed on his desk. That's what he said, wasn't it? It was all a coincidence."

"But it wasn't. She asked for him specifically. And it was plain as day they knew each other from before. I remember they didn't seem to like each other. At least Lyons let on he didn't like Marie Cox. It was clear she had some sort of history with him though. I'm thinking it's like you said. She was involved with him and Flynn in the brothels and for some reason it turned sour. When it did, she threatened to expose him. Perhaps through her paper."

"So, they sent her Cullen's severed hand as a warning," Britney mused on the other end of the line. "Maybe he was threatening to expose them too. Being a notorious womaniser, it wouldn't be a stretch for Cullen to be visiting the kind of establishment they were running."

"Or maybe he was involved and was looking for a bigger cut. Either way, it makes sense. I think they knew Marie Cox considered herself untouchable and that her overbearing personality would ensure she'd confront Lyons with the severed hand before approaching anyone else, thus ensuring he was on the case," Danny explained. "And therefore, he'd be in a position to direct it or at least have the inside track. Between himself and Flynn they could kill off any headaches that had developed in their little venture, including the unsuspecting Miss Cox, and blame those deaths on Jim Rourke."

"The devious bastards," she exclaimed. "That's our link. Detective Lyons to Marie Cox. And Marie Cox to Jim Rourke by virtue of those properties he renovated." She paused. "I bet it wasn't Lyons who first included those houses in the investigation."

"No, it was me," Danny replied quickly. "Which brings me to something else I've been wondering about. You said that initially no one paid any heed to the fact that Rourke was missing. What if that was intentional? What if Flynn got you assigned to desk duty hoping that when the call came through, you would be the one to investigate? Then they guided you in the direction they wanted you to go."

"But I took their bait, so why not back me when I declared Rourke the killer?" she asked, then immediately answered the question herself. "Because Rourke wasn't enough. They wanted to discredit me as well. I'd been suspicious of Flynn all along, and it was only a matter of time before I found something on him, so they planned to kill two birds with one stone. Lead the investigation down a garden path with a view to taking any possible suspicion away from them and at the same time, make me out to be a loose cannon. That's why the heart was delivered to Stacey Rourke's house. It was the final nail in my coffin. I wouldn't be surprised if the next body we find is Jim Rourke's."

"Very likely," Danny agreed. "And that's another thing, Lyons knew Jim Rourke's father. He hurled with him. I saw their names on a team photo in Flynn's office."

"That means Flynn would have known him too. Christ!" Britney exclaimed. "What if I've been looking at this wrong from the start. What if Jim Rourke is not in hiding for something he's done? What if he was the first victim? What if he was roped in to using his van to traffic girls but his conscience played up, so they killed him as a warning to the others?" She paused. 'But then who was the balaclava man?' she asked herself.

"Could be. But that's not all," Danny continued urgently. "I dropped Lyons home one night. Now I was pretty pissed, but I saw someone in a room upstairs. A girl or young woman, I think. I got the feeling something wasn't right though. She was walking back and forth in front of the window as if she was trapped."

"Could it have been a family member?" Britney wondered. She couldn't think of any other legitimate reasons why a man of his age would have a young girl upstairs in his house.

She imagined Danny shaking his head even though she couldn't see him. "Could have been but I don't think so. He's has no family and as far as I'm aware, he's living alone. Has been since his wife died."

"Did you ever ask him about it?" Britney asked, as the obvious conclusion started to form in her head. "Or look up his record?"

"No. I'd no valid reason up to now. Anyway, I didn't like the idea of going behind his back." He paused, glancing around nervously. He'd thought he heard a sound behind the car but could detect no movement. Only the shadowy darkness of the farmyard. "But after tonight, I will do. Look, this place is giving me the creeps, so shut up and listen." He filled her in on the rest as quickly as he could, before informing her he was getting out of there.

Just then he saw a shadow shift a few feet from the car followed by what looked like a glint of light or flash of steel.

"Shit," he said, his voice dropping to a whisper. "I think he's found me, Britney. I think he's got a…"

Suddenly there was an unmerciful bang and the window next to him shattered. He instinctively leapt back and sideways toward the safety of the passenger seat, dropping the phone as he scrambled for safety. In his heart, he knew he was too late. Too slow. He could sense the man in the dark, reaching for him. He could even hear him breathing. Then the light shifted, and he got a glimpse of the man's face. Just enough to see it wasn't Richie Lyons, after all.

He clambered backward, trying to push further away from the man, but he only gained a few inches before he was trapped. Pinned between the passenger door and his assailant. The man moved closer and now he could see him clearly. See the white of his cold eyes and the arrogant smirk on his face.

"You," he accused, staring in shock. Just then Danny remembered the phone. He might have dropped it, but it was still operating. At least he hoped it was. "I was wrong Britney…" he shouted, hoping the sergeant could hear him clear enough to make out what he was about to say. "It's not Richie Lyons… It's your bo–"

The last words got caught on his lips because when the knife slashed across his neck all he could do was scream. Soon, he couldn't even do that.

On the other end of the phone, Britney echoed his screams, but Danny couldn't hear her. Not above the sound of his own blood gurgling.

****

As Britney screamed into the handsfree, she spun a one-eighty on the road.

"Danny!" she cried. "Danny!" but there was no answer. It was as if the phone had suddenly gone dead. Or been switched off.

"Danny," she cried again as she fumbled for her radio.

"Garda in distress," she reported, "Athy area. Needs immediate assistance." She waited for a response then supplied the male voice on dispatch with as much detail as she had – Garda ID, location, level of danger. Mobile number for tracking. Seeing as he was driving his own car, they would have no other way of locating his exact position. A squad car would have built-in GPS.

"Just get someone there," she ordered sharply when more questions were fired at her.

With that, she floored the accelerator. She flew past the few cars that were on the road at that time of the night, then screamed at a truck hogging the road to get the hell out of her way. When it finally gave way, she flew past it and honked the horn with such anger and frustration that the driver gave her the finger in response. Another day she might have pulled him over but now his gesture hardly registered. She had to get to Danny fast. Yet at the same time, she knew her speeding was in vain. Deep down she knew it. No man screamed like that unless… She left the thought hanging, unwilling to go there yet.

She ate up the miles and was soon back in Athy and heading out the Dublin road but after that, she had no idea how to get to the farmyard. She called dispatch.

"Did you get a track on his location?"

"Yes," a female Garda replied with urgency. Britney recognised the voice as that of Triona Maguire. "He's at what looks like an abandoned farmyard just three miles from your current location. His phone is static. You drive, Britney, I'll give directions."

"Make it the shortest route," Britney instructed. "I need to get there!"

A few minutes later, Britney took the left that Danny had earlier taken and spun in through the gate of the farmyard. The first thing she spotted was the grey Corolla Danny had been driving earlier. It was parked close to a thick roadside hedge and seemed to be abandoned. She rooted a torch out of her glove compartment then hopped out of her car and rushed over. As she drew close, she saw that the driver's door was wide open with the window smashed. After a brief search, she located Danny's phone discarded on the floor of the passenger side of the car. The screen was shattered. Otherwise, the car was empty. As she withdrew from the car, she noticed dark stains on the edge of the driver's seat. When she tested them with the tip of her finger, she found they were warm and sticky. Her heart sank. The evidence was piling up, screaming at her that her instincts were right. She was too late.

Desperate now, she spun and splayed the light of her torch around the farmyard. In front of her she saw nothing only piles of dung, a few rotting bales of hay, and some rusted machinery. Peering further through the gloom, she spotted several rundown sheds located to the rear of the yard. Seeing no other viable option, she slowly edged her way in that direction while continuously glancing left and right, prepared for a possible attacker. As she crossed the yard her whole body was shaking with fear and, for a moment, she debated whether she should return to her car and wait for backup. But she knew she couldn't. What if Danny was still alive? Hurt, but still alive? She had to keep going.

Having foolishly left her baton in the car, she was unarmed apart from the torch. Seeing a discarded rust iron bar in her path, she picked it up and continued. One terrified step at a time. It seemed like an age before she reached the entrance to the first barn but when she eventually got there, she noted the door swinging open. Someone had been inside.

Peering in past the door, she saw that it was even darker inside than out. Before taking another step, she shone the torch through the entrance, illuminating the area directly in front of her. The beam cut through the gloom, revealing mites of floating dust, the light seemingly drawn to a spot near the middle of the shed. She took a step inside, following the light as it led her forward. Its beam an inversely tapered finger pointing out the anomaly in the shadowy scene ahead. It took a moment for what Britney was seeing to register. But when it did, she dropped the torch and fell to her knees, completely unaware of the shuddering impact they made on the cold concrete floor. Then she screamed for the second time that night. A raw, heartrending scream that bounced off the walls of the barn. But once again, it fell on deaf ears. Danny, hanging there like a gutted pig, could hear nothing. Would never hear anything again.

****

Britney couldn't get the image out of her head.

Danny had been butchered, there was no other word for it. His neck had been slashed, and his gut slit open so that he bled out on the barn floor. Britney suspected some of his organs could have been missing but she couldn't be sure. Anatomy was never her strong point. Anyway, he was in such a mess that even an expert would struggle to make sense of the ball of guts hanging from the gaping hole in his abdomen. Whoever did it, hadn't even bothered to open his shirt but cut right through the thin fabric. Whoever did it was an animal. In her head she used the word whoever, but she knew who did it. Danny had all but told her with his last words. Not Lyons, he had shouted, but her boss. At least that's what he would have said if he'd had a chance to finish.

Her boss meant Flynn. And it was her fault because she had led Flynn to Danny. If she hadn't called him, Danny would still be alive. It was a mistake she would never forgive herself for. And neither, it seemed would Internal Affairs. She seemed to be drawing them like shit draws flies. She'd spent the best part of the night explaining herself to one IA detective after another. One of the Gardaí's own being killed had taken an already horrific case to a new level. The fact that the Garda was butchered meant, officially or otherwise, the entire force was now focused on finding that butcher. And whether she liked it or not, Britney was now the focus of IA's attention.

Involved in everything from the start and being the first to arrive at the scene of the young Garda's gruesome murder, they were keen to uncover what role she could possibly have in the killings. They were convinced she must have some. But IA were fools. Danny's murder wasn't the work of the previous killer. It was clearly a spontaneous act made to look like it was perpetrated by The Courier, but in reality, carried out by a copycat. A copycat with inside information. The level of detail pointed to someone inside The Courier investigation, someone who understood his MO, someone who had access to all the evidence. Or perhaps someone who was behind it all in the first place. Like Detective Flynn, Sergeant Kent argued. Or some henchman working for himself or Lyons. However, the detectives from IA refused to listen. In fact, they just stopped short of laughing in her face. They made it clear that as a member of the force, her integrity was shot and therefore why should they listen to her? As if to reinforce their attitude, they asked her all sorts of indicative questions.

For what reason did Danny meet you in Athy?

Why did you need to meet him after dark?

What was discussed?

Did you head straight back to Oldcastle? And if so, did anyone see you?

They just stopped short of accusing her of being directly involved in Danny's death. It was ridiculous, of course, but she also knew it wouldn't take much to twist the facts against her. After all, that's what corrupt people did best. Twist everything in their favour. And with Danny gone, she was now alone in all of this, with no one to turn to for help except Fiona. She hoped Fiona would have something for her soon because if she didn't, Britney Kent was finished. And not just as a Garda.

She answered the questions as best she could, trying to keep her cool despite the unveiled hostility from the detectives, and the lingering images of the horrific scene. When IA finally finished with her, she was both physically exhausted and emotionally drained, little more than a zombie as she trudged out of the farmyard. There she spotted Detective Lyons hanging back near the gate. He was alone and looking suitably distraught, but she knew it was just an act.

As she neared him, she had so much she wanted to say, so much to accuse him of, but when she got face to face with him, the pungent smell of alcohol and the intoxicated look in his eyes threw her. The grubby clothes, the brown stains on his shirt, he was starting to look like a down and out. And smell like one too. He certainly didn't have the air of triumph, she expected. Yet, despite her addled brain, she knew he must be feeling it. Another thorn had been plucked. A potential problem eradicated. Further clearing the way for them to move forward without contention.

She shook her head wearily. "How could you?" was all she could manage to utter before walking on. Then she stopped, the anger, fear, and frustration boiling over. Directed as much at herself as Lyons. An innocent, decent, young man with his entire life ahead of him was dead because of her and all she could muster were a few meaningless words and a shake of her head. A parent dealing with an errant child would do better. Yet it was enough to earn a guilty look from the detective. "You killed him," her tone was far more forceful now. Aggressive. "You fucking killed him."

"I know," he replied eventually, staring down at his shoes, and ruefully shaking his head. He toed some of the gravel that lay strewn across the yard. "It's my fault. I should never have gotten him involved in this."

"You did more than that and you know it," Britney replied as she moved toward him until they were face to face, as they had previously been in the coffee shop. Only this time she didn't doubt. She knew.

"You and your damn cronies. You were pulling the strings from the start. That's why you did this. That's why you butchered that poor..." The enormity of it all suddenly got the better of her, prompting her to turn away from Lyons. She held her hand to her eyes to disguise her tears. Her weakness. She was too tired to stand there, toe to toe with the detective. Far too emotional. Their time would come. She promised herself that. Promised Danny that.

She moved to walk away but before she could take a step, Lyons grabbed her arm and drew her back toward him.

"What are you trying to say?" he asked through gritted teeth. The despair she'd earlier detected in his voice and believed to be feigned, had sharply turned to anger. This was clearly real. Visceral.

"Not trying. I'm saying it. I'm saying you killed him. You killed him to protect that sex racket you and Flynn are running. Oh, it all works so perfectly, doesn't it? One of you running Dublin, the other running the rest of the country. Then when it starts to unravel, you kill off the loose ends and make it look like some psycho is on the loose. But you made a mistake, Detective Lyons. Danny recognised your car."

"My car?" Lyons thick eyebrows furrowed in what appeared to be confusion. Britney reckoned he wouldn't have been lost on stage.

"Yes, your car. He recognised the car that was following him. You own a blue sports car, right?"

Lyons shook his head despondently then glanced at the group of onlookers that had started to shift closer and now form a loose ring around them. To Britney's eyes, he looked intensely uncomfortable, uncertain. This unease only served to underpin her beliefs.

"First of all, that's not my car," he stated, loud enough for everyone to hear. "It was my wife's car. Second of all, I've haven't driven it once since she died. Not once. And thirdly, I certainly didn't drive it tonight. I was in a pub called The Sheep's Head Tavern all evening, if you must know. And I have witnesses, not that I need them."

"You mightn't have been driving it, detective. You're too smart for that. But you were the one behind the wheel. Right from the start."

Lyons fixed Britney with a cold stare as if trying to ensure that what he was about to say hit home. When he spoke his voice was firm, but Britney also detected an air of frustration. Was it real?

"Look Sergeant Kent, I'm not really sure where you get your crazy ideas from but if I'm guilty of anything it's of getting pissed while that innocent young man was being cut to pieces. And for that, I'll never forgive myself. Never."

As he spoke, tears formed in the detective's worn-out eyes and Britney began to doubt her own mind. She found it hard to believe his shame wasn't genuine. Yet Danny had been so sure of the car, and of his suspicions. So sure, in fact, that if he had lived, he was going to follow up on those suspicions first thing. She sensed Danny wasn't a man for loose talk, therefore she wasn't about to dismiss that lightly. Feeling less certain now, she moved to walk away once more but Detective Lyons wasn't ready to let her arm go just yet.

"We should talk," he insisted in a more even voice. "For Danny's sake."

"For Danny's sake?" Britney erupted completely, spittle flying from her mouth, like a volcano spitfire. "For Danny's sake?" She pointed a shaking finger toward the barn. "He's in there butchered and hanging like a side of meat, so it's far too late to talk for Danny's sake. You want to talk for your own sake. Just to make yourself feel better."

"Maybe," Lyons conceded. "Maybe you're right. But I also want to talk for yours. You're barking up the wrong tree with this."

"I suppose you're going to tell me that this is HAI related too. That Ade Fagan killed Danny Owens because he accused him of eating one too many free dinners," she scoffed.

"No. Just that you're in over your head and if you're not careful, you're going to end up like Danny."

On hearing this, Britney bristled. "Is that a threat?" she asked loud enough for all around her to hear. The crowd had moved closer now, their faces gobsmacked at what they were witnessing.

Lyons shook his head coolly. "I'm not threatening you, Sergeant." He deliberately kept his tone even. "I'm trying to assist you. You're on your own, so you've got to trust someone. Five minutes is all I ask. Five minutes that could very well save your life."

"You can shove your five minutes, Detective Lyons," she fumed. "Better still, you can go give your five minutes to Flynn and the rest of your cronies. I'm not interested." Her gander up now, and even though she had already learnt the hard way that suspicions alone weren't a basis for guilt, she couldn't help herself. She turned around slowly, arms out, playing to the gathering of Gardaí and forensic staff that stood transfixed by the confrontation.

"Do you know about Detective Lyons?" she asked, dramatically. "Oh, you might know he's a useless drunk, everyone knows that. But did you know about his affair with Marie Cox?" She nodded enthusiastically when she was met by looks of disbelief from those staring back at her. "Oh, yes. Detective Richie Lyons had an affair with the second Courier victim which links him directly to this case. Something which he deliberately kept concealed. Oh, and do you know about the trafficked girl that he keeps locked up in his bedroom. The poor innocent little girl that he does God knows what to when he goes home from the pub. No? None of you knew? Well, you know now," she continued unabashed, even though without evidence it was all just pie in the sky. "So, what are you going to do about it?" she demanded between gritted teeth, then angrily pointed in the direction of the barn. "What are you going to do about the fate of that innocent, young man in there?" Her voice had risen several octaves so that it was now close to a scream. In the surrounding darkness, the scar on her face seemed to glow.

Those staring back at her did so goggle-eyed, as if they thought she had completely lost the plot. Perhaps she had. Perhaps the sight of Danny murdered had driven her over the edge. For a long moment, no one spoke a word.

Finally, Detective Lyons turned to walk away. "You stupid girl!" he grumbled with a disgruntled shake of his head. "You, stupid, stupid girl." Then he paused as if thinking better than to leave it at that. Searching for words, he stared at the ground and kicked the loose gravel out of his way. When he had gathered himself, he turned back to face her once more. "Yes, you're right," he declared. "I did know Marie Cox. I was introduced to her once at a staff party. By my wife who worked as admin briefly for the same paper. That was it. No sordid affair." The latter was said without conviction and Britney thought she detected a hint of shame cross Lyons' face, leading her to believe it was all a lie. "And in case Danny didn't tell you, I was there with him when we spotted her killer running away from her apartment. Danny even chased him, for God's sake. Would have caught him too only he hopped on a damn bus at the last moment."

Britney shook her head. She wasn't having that. "Oh, he told me alright. He told me you tried to convince him not to give chase and that's what delayed him. He said he might have caught him only for that delay. He also wondered about the convenience of it all. How the man appeared right in front of your car when he did?" 'Not to mention balaclava man waiting for me,' she added silently.

"Are you suggesting I set that little scene up to give myself an alibi? That's ridiculous."

"I'm not suggesting it. Danny did. He was pretty certain about your accomplice too. Some druggie informer who'd do anything for a few bucks. Oh, he had you figured out, Detective Lyons. He didn't trust you one bit in the end, and you knew it."

"That's because you put all that nonsense in his head," the detective argued. "You and all your silly speculation. A damn girl not long out of a frilly frock and long stockings, playing at Miss Marple. And if you think I had anything to do with his death, then you are even more deluded than I thought. Check with the staff in The Sheep's Head. I could barely stand up to piss, let alone drive halfway across the country to commit murder. Or order it done for that matter. Oh yeah, and I suppose I fell home again in time to be there when the call came through. Go on, check it out," Detective Lyons insisted. "Me, I'm going for a drink. After all, isn't that what pissheads like me do?"

This time when he turned, he gave no pause. Disappeared in the passenger door of a service vehicle which slowly pulled away from the scene. Britney couldn't see the driver but presumed it was another poor innocent taking his life in his hands, simply by associating himself with Lyons – the loose cannon, the drunk. The kingpin?

****

It was almost bright by the time Detective Richie Lyons made it back to his house. He had been tempted to return to The Sheep's Head and knock them up for a few early ones, but he knew Benny wouldn't be pleased. He'd serve him ok, but it would be a black mark against any future liberties. On that score, he was fairly sure he'd taken too many already, not that Benny would tell him in so many words. Benny was more subtle than that. He'd just cut him off the next time he was within a beer or two of blissful oblivion and do it close enough to closing time that he had nowhere else to go, only home. Or kick him out some night into the pissing's of rain when he was three sheets to the wind and with nothing only a shirt on his back. Yes,

Benny could make himself heard loud and clear without so much as opening his mouth. Despite their little deal.

Upon entering his house, he went directly to the sitting room where ignoring the discarded newspaper and accumulating rubbish, he opened a bottle of whiskey and poured himself a large tumbler.

He was desperate to get sozzled again. Just top up on what Benny had served him earlier that night and let the warm feeling of nothingness take him away once more. His confrontation with Sergeant Kent had been enlightening. He had called her a silly girl, but she was far from that. In fact, she was even smarter than he had initially given her credit for. Others may have been fooled but she knew Danny's death wasn't a match to all the others. Not that every effort hadn't been made to make it look that way. The body hanging by the neck, the knife wounds, the suggestion of an appropriated organ, all tallied with the previous crimes. However, there were also striking differences. Danny's killing had been rushed, sloppy as if the killer struck on impulse and not as the result of meticulous planning. The blood found in his car suggested this was not the act of an organised psychopath but a spontaneous killer, as did the slashing of the shirt. There were no traces of fibres found in any of the other victim's knife wounds, meaning clothes had been removed or pulled back from the areas of the body where they were mutilated. Even Marie Cox's hair had been tied back out of the way to allow the killer to cleanly slice her ears.

Of course, it was still possible that the killer was the same, but Sergeant Kent clearly didn't think so. Worse, she had made her assumptions public, assumptions which included him.

As he stood with the glass of whiskey in his hand, he wondered if there was any point trying to convince her otherwise. No, he decided. She knew too much and too little. And that's what made her dangerous. He rooted his mobile out of his pocket and made a call. The receiver answered on the second ring.

"Yes." The male voice on the other end of the line sounded subdued as if worried about being overheard.

"You have a problem," Lyons stated directly. There was no need for introductions. The two men went way back.

"Sergeant Kent?"

"Yes. She's like a bull in a china shop. She needs to be controlled. Otherwise, she could ruin everything. Years of work," Lyons paused as he pondered the best way forward. "Is the consignment still on schedule?" he asked.

"Yes."

"Well, then I think we need to orchestrate it that she be there. I know it's dangerous but it's the only way for you to finish it cleanly."

"Eradicate any doubts, you mean. Ok, I'll try and arrange it. I presume you'll be attending in person?"

"Of course," Lyons replied. "As agreed. There's too much at stake not to."

After he hung up, his thoughts remained with Sergeant Kent. Clever and all as she was, she still hadn't discovered the real significance of the newspapers, even though he had alluded to them. On the face of it, the papers contained nothing but a jumble of sports stories, but it should be clear to her by now why they had been placed at the scene. There's a reason for every move in a game like this.

If she'd only stop running headlong into everything and learn to look. Really look. Detecting was done with the head, not the heart. Yes, she was young yet and had a lot to learn but if she wasn't careful, she wouldn't get the chance. And that would be a pity because he had come to like Sergeant Britney. Still there was nothing he could do. Survival was a huge part of the path she had chosen.

With a sigh, he pushed the sergeant from his thoughts then swirled the whiskey in the glass and took a deep breath of its sweet aroma. Molly had always hated whiskey. She was of the opinion it was conceived by a demon and distilled by the devil himself. Perhaps she was right. Perhaps it was the devil that had taken hold of him. Whatever it was, it had extracted a terrible price. The look of horror he had seen frozen on Danny's face would never leave him. It shouldn't have come to that. If he had been sober last night and the nights before, then maybe Danny wouldn't have died doubting him. Hating him. Maybe he would have spotted the reservations Danny harboured and convinced him otherwise. At worst, he might have explained to him the terrible things he had to do and why he had to do them. Then Danny mightn't have felt the need to go behind his back and might still be alive.

It had been the same with Molly herself. The devil inside him had let her down too. If he'd been sober in the weeks and months leading up to her illness, maybe he would have seen her death coming. Prevented it somehow. Realised how that damn doctor was more interested in playing golf and fraternizing with his buddies than actually doing his job. If he'd been sober, maybe everything would be different, and he wouldn't be in the position he was in now. Doing the things, he had to do. Trying to save the unsavable.

He raised the glass of fiery liquid to his lips and held it there, teasing himself with the sweet nectar. Playing chicken with the unrelenting devil. But this time he forced the devil to relent. Stared it in the eye and waited for it to blink. Finally, with a sigh of deep regret for all the devil had cost him, he entered the kitchen and upon clearing piles of grubby dishes out of the way he dumped the fiery liquid down the sink. As he watched it swirl beguilingly down the plughole, he was reminded of what he still had. The unsavable. Muttering in self-reproach, he left the kitchen and went upstairs, stopping at the room across the hall. Knocked on the door and waited.

As usual, there was no answer. No enthusiastic 'come in.' Still, he opened the door, and though it squeaked slightly on its hinges, he entered with the usual degree of hope in his heart. Fragile hope but hope still. It blossomed when he saw her lying there waiting for him, her doe eyes watching him as he slowly made his way to her bed. The drug was clearly wearing off and he was glad. For he preferred it that way. If she behaved, of course, he reminded himself, as he studied her. Curled up under the blankets in her usual protective pose, she had her knees pulled up so high that they very nearly touched her chin.

Still, she seemed calm tonight, and open to his advances. Heartened, he took off his shoes and jacket and climbed into the bed beside her. Slowly, he put his arms around her, his movements careful and practiced. In the silence, he heard her groan softly as if she was dreaming but otherwise, she gave no reaction to his presence. At least she didn't try and push him away this time. Or worse, turn around and rip his face off. She might still do so if she became aware of the stink of him. The giveaway Guinness stains on his shirt. She would rip and claw and accuse him of hypocrisy. It was a chance he was willing to take. He moved closer until he could feel the warmth radiate from her, the warmth and vitality of youth, but also the heat of the poison inside her. The necessary poison. Then he felt her failing body unfurl, little more than skin and bone as it moulded itself into his. He breathed a sigh of relief.

He needed her tonight. Every bit as much as she needed him.

Chapter 16

"You bastard," Sergeant Britney Kent bellowed as she stormed into Oldcastle Garda Station and made a beeline for Detective Flynn. It was mid-morning on Sunday, the day after Danny's murder and Britney had hardly slept a wink. Flynn was standing at the head of the office cum operations room analysing this latest development in The Courier case.

"You murdering bastard," she continued, pointing a tremulous finger at her adversary before directing it toward the whiteboard next to which Flynn stood. "You did this."

On the whiteboard he had written up details of the murders. Four murders so far, at least four they were certain of. The fifth body had yet to be uncovered. In the centre of the board was a picture of Danny with a circle drawn around his far too youthful face.

"You killed him," she stated unflinchingly. Though her voice had reduced in volume, it lost none of its potency. "You killed Danny Owens. And you killed the rest of them. All to cover up your illegal activities." She turned to face her colleagues, all of whom had stopped what they were doing and were now watching her closely, displaying both traces of surprise and concern on their faces. Joe Murray bore a disgruntled frown while Ben and Fiona had traces of sympathy in their eyes. Triona Maguire's eyes were hard to read behind her thick glasses but seeing as she had yet to provide the requested list of abandoned buildings, Britney could guess where her loyalties lay.

To hell with her. And the rest of Flynn's cronies. She had their attention, that's all that mattered. She had their attention just like she'd had the attention of the officers at the crime scene when she'd similarly accused Detective Lyons. With a dearth of evidence, shaking a few trees was the only way she could think of to force their hand, and perhaps provoke a mistake.

"Did you know about his illicit sex ring?" she asked boldly. "That string of disgusting brothels he runs."

Flynn shook his head as if saddened by her hysterical outburst. He calmly placed the marker he was using onto the ledge of the whiteboard and turned to face her. "Sergeant Kent," he acknowledged in his most patronising tone, cleverly utilised to rile her even more. "I believe you have been instructed to remain on enforced leave until last night's disastrous fiasco is thoroughly investigated. In other words, if you have any interest in saving what's left of your career, you shouldn't so much as set foot in here, let alone mouth off at your superiors like some demented fishwife." He underscored the word superior with a brief but condescending smirk. Britney knew he had her where he wanted her, but she wasn't going to roll over.

"To hell with my career," Britney retorted, "if it means having to serve with the likes of you, I'd rather be a bag lady."

"That's exactly what you're going to be…if you're lucky, that is." The underlying threat may not have been obvious to the onlookers, but it was unmistakable to her.

"What? Are you going to kill me too?" she asked provocatively, leaning forward and sticking out a bold chin. "Pose me as the next victim of The Courier?"

Flynn refused to take the bait. Instead, he glanced around at the Gardaí who had gathered closest and threw his eyes up to heaven in a dramatic fashion. "There she goes again," he said in that smug, condescending tone. "Throwing accusations around like confetti. Next, she'll be accusing the Pope of being the gunman on the grassy knoll."

At that, many of the onlookers laughed openly while others smirked, obviously amused by the play on the historical reference. It was clear to Britney what side the majority of her colleagues were taking. She couldn't blame them. It was the weakness of human nature to jump on a bandwagon. Still, the humiliation hurt. Hurt so much that she felt herself losing control. Sometimes one had to lose the battle to win the war, she reminded herself, in an effort to keep her temper under wraps. It didn't work. She hated the man in front of her with such passion that all she wanted to do right then was tear his eyes out.

"You bastard," she screamed and made a go for Flynn. If she could only get close enough to him, she'd mark him for life, as she herself had been marked. Ben, who was closest to her, jumped to bar her path and a moment later, Joe Murray was there too. Together they pulled her back before she got hold of Flynn. Still, she managed to stretch out between the two men and catch Flynn with a vicious swipe, scratching him with her nails and drawing blood in four parallel red lines across his cheek.

"That's just the first blow," she snarled. "The next time, I'll rip you asunder, so help me God."

Flynn dabbed his cheek then made a show of studying the blood on his fingertips. "Assault of a senior Garda, Sergeant Kent. And in front of witnesses. You are finished here. For good." Then he offered an unctuous smile. "Thought you might like to know that we've located your mother." He glanced at his colleagues, his expression one of concern but again the disguised threat was evident to Britney. "We thought she might be a support to you right now…considering what you're going through," he finished condescendingly.

"Leave my mother out of this," Britney growled then made another leap towards him. This time Fiona caught her arm in time to stop her just short of his face.

"Leave it, Brit," Fiona warned as she threw a disgusted glance at Flynn. "He's not worth it."

Flynn stared at Fiona, then nodded coldly as if he was accepting the fact that she had taken Britney's side but was warning her of the inevitable consequences. To her credit, Fiona seemed unruffled. She continued to pull Britney away.

"He's just scum," she said for all to hear. "The lowest form of scum."

"I know that, Fiona," Britney agreed loudly, as she allowed herself to be drawn toward the exit, "and you know that. In fact, the entire fucking force knows it as far as I can see." She emphasised the latter and cast a withering look at those nearest to her. "Trouble is, in the world we live, scum always seems to come to the top."

"I know," Fiona agreed sympathetically, "and it's the innocent ones that always get hurt." However, once she got out of earshot, she changed her tone. "But maybe scum won't win out this time."

"What do you mean?"

"You were right. There is something big going down," Fiona whispered as they stepped outside the station. "I overheard Flynn and Joe talking and they weren't talking about the case. Something about a consignment coming into a warehouse tonight. At 11pm, they said."

"A consignment?" Britney wondered. "Girls? Drugs? What?"

Fiona shrugged as she glanced nervously over her shoulder.

"I don't know but I'll try and find out more. Once I do, I'll let you know. In the meantime, go home and get some rest. You look like something my dog would puke up."

"Thanks, Fi." Britney forced a smile. "I'll take that as a compliment because the way I was feeling, I didn't think I looked good enough for a dog to contemplate eating in the first place."

After that weary admittance, Britney took Fiona's advice and headed for home. She desperately needed a shower and a change of clothes. And spending some time with Salem didn't sound bad either. Cats were far more affable than humans. Most humans. She called Bob, just to hear his voice but the phone rang out, and desperate as she was for some comforting, she decided a bit of Kris Kristofferson was called for before going upstairs to change. This definitely felt like a *Sunday Morning Coming Down* moment. Topped off with chocolate chip ice-cream.

Stirred by the music, Salem appeared from the kitchen purring for attention, his pleading eyes impossible to ignore. Scooping him up she sat back on the couch and cuddled him. Tickled him under the chin. He purred contently in response. Feeling herself relax a little, she let the music draw her mind back to days spent with her father. Simple days. Summer days. Days when she had felt safe. Protected. Secure. She didn't feel secure now. As Kris sang about *the kid cussin* at the can he was kicking, Britney curled up on the couch with Salem, pulling her knees up to her chest like she had when she was a girl and let the notes of the song wash over her. Her father had loved that song. He used to play it every Sunday morning as he made her breakfast. He'd spend long minutes fiddling with the old cassette player, fast-forwarding and rewinding until he located the very beginning of the tune. He didn't like to miss a note.

Back then, Britney hadn't been sure if the song made him happy or sad but listening to it now, she realised it probably did both. That was the beauty of Kris Kristofferson's masterpiece, she reckoned. It at once made you feel alive in the now but nostalgic for the innocence of the past as well. Had her father felt the same? Had he pined for what he'd lost? Of course, he had. Her father's grey eyes told her so, always weary was how she remembered them. As did the lines that had burrowed into his forehead and gathered around his mouth. His thick brown hair, much like her own, which seemed to turn grey almost overnight. Britney knew her mother's affair had broken her father. Had ripped the heart out of him. Had killed him in the end.

Feeling old tears come, she released Salem then sat up and dipped her hand into her pocket for a tissue. It was then she discovered the errant piece of paper. It crumpled against the lining of her trousers as she rooted around for the hankie. Thinking it was some cash that had gone astray, she pulled it out intending to slip it into her purse. As she unfurled it, she saw that it wasn't cash at all. It was a note, hastily scrawled on a piece of paper that had clearly been ripped from one of the station's memo pads. She read it once, stared at it incredulously, read it again. In the background, Kris' weathered voice sang about the lonesome sound of Sunday morning coming down.

'You're not alone,' the note read as if to challenge the sentiment of the song. Challenge the way she was feeling. She looked at Salem who was staring back at her wide-eyed.

"Did you write this?" she asked, her mind once again in overdrive.

****

The hooded man waited until well after dark before driving to his destination. He couldn't imagine anyone being there at that hour to hinder him in his task and that was how he needed it to be. He needed time. He needed privacy. He needed strength. This next stage was going to test him the most. Test him to the point of breaking. But he had to be strong. Things were coming to a close but lately, they hadn't exactly gone according to plan. He had seen the papers. The young Garda was all over the front pages. With his innocent young face, he would posthumously become the poster boy of the investigation. The latest and the youngest victim of The Courier. They would use the boy now. Use him to highlight the terrible battle they were fighting. The battle between light and dark, good and evil, upright guardians and immoral psychopath. They would use him just as others were used. Even in death.

Already they had treated the young Garda's murder as an opportunity to label him again, referring to him now as a cop killer. Brandishing the term in headlines like a call to arms. As if killing a cop was worse than killing that tramp of a reporter or the doctor, or that thief of a HAI official or…he shook his head. They hadn't a clue. But soon, soon they would. As long as there were no more unexpected twists like the killing of the young cop. It was a totally unplanned occurrence, and he couldn't afford such unforeseen events. But some things couldn't be accounted for. Some things just happened outside of a person's control. No matter what level of planning or attention to detail.

And boy, had he planned. He had planned everything down to the last. Even his own demise.

Chapter 17

Adolf was a family name, derived from his Austrian heritage and passed down through the generations. Over time it had been pruned back to Ade because of what some saw as sinister connotations. The irony was Ade secretly welcomed the implications the name aroused. The concept of absolute power was something to be appreciated, not balked at. For that reason, he readily accepted his nickname. In fact, he revelled in it.

Sitting at his preferred table to the rear of the elegant dining room he leaned back in the leather-bound chair and dabbed his lips with a napkin. The meal had been sumptuous, while the sparkling water had been exactly as he requested it – ice cold and refreshing. Then again, that was always the case in Jude's.

When an establishment so close to his heart had been chosen to host the Mayor's annual function, he had been pleased on two fronts. One, it guaranteed the food would be to his liking and two, his connections ensured he could secure a table away from the main gathering, and therefore be in a position to conduct his business undisturbed but still be present to press the flesh afterwards.

"As you were saying, you are a man of principle," District Board Secretary, Shane Fitzpatrick suggested a tad wearily from his seat across the table. The inevitably drawn-out speeches were concluding, and Fagan had yet to explain why he requested this private meeting.

"Yes," Ade smiled confidently, "principle and self-discipline. Those are the virtues that have gotten me to where I am today."

'Apart from your penchant for fine living,' Shane corrected in his own mind. Otherwise, he had to admit, the statement was relatively true. It was well known that Fagan didn't drink or smoke – he had never done so, and this was something he prided himself on. As was the strength of his marriage in a time when marriage had become transient for many.

"Vices are merely a crutch for the weak," he was often heard say. "And weakness is a vice in itself." However, Shane Fitzpatrick couldn't help but wonder about the marriage thing. It was true Fagan had been married for over thirty years, but in that time, he had seldom seen Fagan socialise with his wife outside of official functions. Even then, Shane always got the impression of a couple trying to portray a united front rather than being one of real unity. In fact, he was pretty certain Fagan lusted after other women. He was doing so now. His beady eyes following their young waitress around the dining room, just stopping short of stripping her bare. And, of course, there were the rumours about that reporter lady. The one who was recently murdered. He found those rumours hard to believe though. She was a stunner, after all. And even on his very best days, Ade was far from that. But then for some women, power was quite the aphrodisiac, he knew.

"If you adopt those principles," Fagan continued, "I can see no reason why you shouldn't fill my shoes, Shane. Having you as District Director here in Oldcastle would certainly be welcome. And of great value."

'Yes, great value to you. And to your prick of a son,' Shane agreed in his head. 'We're getting to the crux of it at last!'

"In fact, that's the reason I asked you to meet me here," Fagan continued with an unctuous smile.

"Oh?"

"As we previously discussed, I am stepping down as president at the end of this year... Oh, by the way, are the preparations being made for that little event? My commemoration. As I said, I want it to be special. The terrific work I've done deserves to be honoured. After all, I practically built that stadium."

"Yes of course, Ade. It will be a memorable occasion," Shane assured him. "The District Board has ratified your request to rename Fenian Park. We are already preparing the appropriate decorations for the unveiling."

"Good, good..." Ade Fagan sipped some water then smacked his bloated lips. "Important people should be treated with importance, don't you agree?" He didn't give Shane a chance to agree or not. "Now, as I was saying, my tenure as president is up at the end of the year. However, that does not mean I am stepping away from the organisation. I intend to retain a certain, ahem, involvement, if you know what I mean?"

Shane nodded. "I understand." 'Keep your hands on the money, you mean,' he thought to himself.

"With that in mind, I want to offer my support in your bid to become District Director. I know you've sought that position before and failed – what is it, three times?"

"Twice," Shane corrected.

"Well, third time lucky then, because with my backing, I can guarantee you will be elected this time around."

"And in return?" Shane asked somewhat warily.

"In return," Ade repeated contemplatively, "in return…" He sighed as he made himself even more comfortable in the chair, reclining his great bulk like a king on a throne. "As you are well aware, the HAI prides itself on being an amateur association which means all its players and members are expected to offer their services gratis, yet here we are, you and me – the head of this amateur association, and the future District Board Director – dining in the lap of luxury. We're not the only ones, of course. All of us at the top – and by that, I mean those who have their hands closest to the money – reward themselves generously for their efforts." He shrugged casually. "Why shouldn't we?"

"As for me, well, having risen to the highest position of all, I just reward myself a little bit more. It's only right don't you think?" It was a question that Shane didn't get time to answer. "People like you and me who have the willingness, discipline and talent to shoulder the weight of real responsibility deserve to be rewarded, do they not? The rest are just minions. Ants in a heap. It's simply the way of the world. And that's the way it should be. After all, we have turned this organisation into a monster. A business behemoth while all those muppets still volunteer for nothing. Players, youth coaches, groundskeepers – all necessary parts of the wheel, I'll admit, but they have no vision. They still see this as being about our national game. It's not. It's about product. It's about marketing. It's about money. We see that, and because of us, the HAI has turned over €65 million nationally this year. €70 million at local level. We're right up there with the GAA itself, something no one thought possible only a few years ago. Soon we will pass them out on our way to becoming the biggest sporting organisation in the country. And those are only the official figures, of course. But people are starting to wise up. When those kinds of figures are rolled out, more and more want a piece of the pie. But that's why we have to work together. We've got to be ruthless. We have to stamp them down before they get a chance to lift their boots out of the mud."

"I suppose so," Shane agreed, once again reminded why people called his colleague Hitler behind his back. It wasn't just because of his name.

"Of course, we have to," Fagan continued. "It's a philosophy I've believed in all my life. Because of this philosophy, I've made it to where I am now. That philosophy and discipline. Always discipline."

Shane nodded. He understood where this was heading. Had known from a long way off.

"Because of my philosophy and drive, I've become the first President of the HAI to be suitably remunerated for his work. I make more in a year than some men make in a lifetime. What do you think of that?"

"Impressive," Shane agreed, very much aware that Fagan was costing the HAI far more than his excessive salary. Unvouched expenses quickly piled up. Shane had a philosophy of his own which was to never wrestle a crocodile unless he had first measured its teeth. With that in mind, he had prepared himself for this little meeting. Had been preparing himself for many months now. Ever since he'd failed in his previous bid to become District Director. Having expected a landslide, he had been beaten by a single vote. He had suspected Fagan had a hand in that failure and now he was certain of it. Clearly to become Director, Shane would have to go through the president. For a price, of course.

But two could play that game. Shane had done his homework and therefore knew all about Fagan's expenses. He knew Fagan stayed in the most expensive hotels, even if on those occasions his job didn't require an overnight stay and he dined at the most expensive restaurants, at least once a day, if not twice. He knew he had a chauffeured car at his disposal 24/7 and he booked holidays and flights on the association's credit card anytime himself or his wife needed to getaway. He knew he frequented the theatre and concerts and never once put his hand in his pocket, and he went to as many of the association's games as his other interests would allow. All for free. He even had an apartment in Dublin that was paid for by his position, and a couple overseas which he thought no one knew about but him. Certainly not his wife, Shane suspected. Shane knew all this and more. For the sake of the organisation, he had taken the prudent step of anonymously sharing it with a tabloid. If those hacks did their job properly soon everyone would know.

"So, to answer your question," Ade Fagan smiled that unctuous, fat-lipped smile once more. "In return for you getting a bigger piece of the pie, and it's a very big pie I needn't remind you, I get contracts."

"Contracts?" Shane asked, a little thrown. Not some sort of agreement to expedite his son's rise up the ladder!

"Yes. I intend to become a consultant. A consultant to the HAI. And if I can trust like-minded individuals like you to sign off on my contracts, I expect it to be a nice little earner for all of us."

It was Shane's turn to smile. For some more than others, I'm sure. "You can guarantee my position?"

"Consider yourself elected, Mr Director," Fagan replied evenly.

Shane nodded slowly then stood, not bothering to wait for dessert. He'd gotten what he came for, and without having to wrestle too much. Any costs incurred would be to the organisation and not to him. He could live with that. After all, as Fagan had just stated, the HAI could certainly afford it.

"And consider yourself a consultant, Mr President." He held out his hand.

Ade Fagan didn't stand. He did, however, accept Shane's handshake. Loosely.

"Nice doing business with you, Shane," he said, somewhat dismissively.

Shane turned to leave.

"There was one other thing," Ade Fagan said before he had taken a step.

"Yes?"

"My son. Once you become District Director, I want him to be appointed Treasurer. Is that clear?"

Shane nodded curtly, then turned and left. The meeting had gone well, all things considered. Better than expected. Still, he wasn't about to count his chickens. He knew what Fagan was capable of. Had seen his cruelty first-hand. He still remembered the day that promising young hurler had shattered his leg while playing for the district. Would never forget the poor chap's screams and roars. Still, Fagan had refused him an ambulance, citing lack of funds. Sent him home in the back of a car, his leg flopping around like a dead fish. As cold a stunt as Shane had ever witnessed. And a perpetual reminder of the kind of ruthless individual he was dealing with.

As Fitzpatrick exited the restaurant, Ade Fagan watched him go. He knew it had been a risk bringing him onboard, but he had judged it a risk worth taking. Keep your friends close but keep your enemies closer was another philosophy he adhered to. He was well aware that Fitzpatrick had been keeping tabs on his not so little expense account. But of course, he had a guarantee of his own. Like he had guarantees on everyone he dealt with. Generally, the sordid type and only to be revealed when needed most.

'Amateur association,' he scoffed to himself. They might be amateurs. He certainly wasn't.

Purring like the cat who got the cream, he called over the waitress. He was ready to order dessert. He had decided on chocolate roulade and a coffee. Oh, and a box of after-dinner mints. He liked the mints. The waitress took his order then hesitating, she checked her watch. The man had told her to wait until 10:45 p.m. exactly. It was that now. If the waitress thought it a strange request, she didn't dwell on it because the man had given her a substantial tip. Far more than any tip she'd ever received from the leer sitting at the table, that's for sure. So, before she left his side, she leaned closer to Ade.

"A package has arrived for you, sir. By courier," she smiled routinely then added just for her own amusement. "From an admirer perhaps." The waitress knew only too well that the man she was speaking to had very few of those.

****

The dying had occurred earlier, far too soon, but there was nothing he could do about that now. No matter how difficult it was, he just had to accept it. Accept it and move on with his task. Searching deep inside himself, he would find the strength to remain detached, but focused, because what he was about to do next was crucial. Crucial to him. Crucial to this journey he was on.

The place was abandoned, just as he expected, the entrance accessible to him as he knew it would be. He parked in the shadows and killed the lights of his vehicle then said a prayer of forgiveness to the only one that mattered.

"If you are listening," he said, "please understand I am doing this for you. I'm doing this for you and for me, and I do it for those left behind. Once it is done, I will join you in death, if not in the everlasting life you deserve."

Once his prayer was complete, the hooded man stepped from the vehicle to remove the body from the rear, where it had been stored. Even in death, it looked so innocent – the only innocent in a festering pit of snakes. The only blood on his hands he wished he could erase. 'But if wishes were fishes,' he thought bitterly.

Just then his phone rang and pierced the silence of the night, sounding so loud that his heart nearly stopped. Puffing out his cheeks in frustration, he fumbled in his pocket and killed the call. He glanced around anxiously, hoping no one had been close enough to hear it. A moment later a message pinged through, sounding every bit as loud as the call but thankfully brief. Still, it was enough to set his nerves on edge. The vibration in his pocket was matched in tempo by the sudden and debilitating shake in his limbs. For a long moment, he stood there like that, shaking, and barely allowing himself to breathe, as his eyes and ears scanned the grounds. Finally, satisfied that the damn phone hadn't garnered any unwanted interest, he relaxed and returned his attention to the job at hand.

The body was lighter than he remembered, and as he hefted it, he wondered if perhaps conventional thinking was erroneous and the passing of one's soul released more than a spiritual burden. Perhaps there was a physical element to the mystical core of a person's being. Perhaps the soul was a living organ, just like a heart or a liver or a kidney. An organ that could contract a disease like any other, be devoured by consumption, or riddled with cancer. If that was the case, his own soul had become host to a plague. Host to a thousand plagues – guilt, anger, hate – the list went on. But if so, it was them that had made it that way. Them with their greed and their lust for power. Them with their cruelty. But it was his own fault too. Caused by his own desperation to be part of the crowd. His own willingness to turn a blind eye even though deep down in his heart he knew what they were. He had learnt, though. Or rather he had been taught. To turn a blind eye is to court the beguiles of corruption. He would turn a blind eye no more. By the time he was finished, neither would they.

Feeling bolstered, he turned away from the vehicle and began to move through the shadows with the confidence of familiarity. Shadows were his playground now. Taking care with each step, he clutched the dead weight, carrying it in his arms like a mother carrying a babe. He knew exactly what he wanted to do and how he should do it, for he had seen it done already. He set the body in place then once the rope was positioned and the noose tightened there was little left to complete. He had already taken his token. His memento. A lock of hair that would serve as both a reminder and a warning. The final warning. Already served.

With his work done, it was time to leave but leaving like this was the hardest part. Yet leave he must. He sighed heavily then bowed his head and offered one more prayer to the only soul that mattered. Finally, he blessed himself then turned from his altar and returned to his vehicle.

One more lesson, he thought bitterly, wiping the tears that had gathered in his eyes.

One more lesson and then he would be done.

He checked his watch. He was on schedule. Fagan's blood would be starting to run cold by now. And colder it would get.

****

The lights broke into the alley at exactly eleven p.m. They swung past where Britney was hiding, forcing her to duck in case she would be spotted, then settled on the warehouse opposite, illuminating the entire building and chasing the shadows into the corners where they cowered like vampires surprised by an early dawn. So much for the cover of darkness, Britney thought. The arrogant bastard isn't even concerned about being seen. He acts like he owns the damn town. He does own the damn town, she corrected herself. And many others with it from what she was hearing. If you own the women, you own the men. And if you own the men, you own the town. Simple as that. She bet he had dirt on more politicians, government officials, cops, priests, businessmen and ordinary Joe Soaps than both the KGB and the CIA put together. She bet he used all that information to keep ahead of the posse and ward off any potential trouble. But, she wondered, what would happen if someone managed to open the can of worms? Hopefully, she would see before the night was out.

After finishing her shift, Fiona had sent a message to Britney's phone to tell her that Triona had drawn a blank with the street cameras but had some success with the list of abandoned properties. Having cross referenced these with what Fiona overheard, Triona believed one of those properties seemed the likely location for the expected delivery – an abandoned warehouse on the Dublin Road. Triona also considered the building a suitable location for The Courier to do his work as it had previously been an engineering works and therefore had been insulated to deaden the sound of the heavy machinery.

'So, our IT marvel came through after all,' Britney said to herself, making a mental note to thank her the next day at work. If there was to be a next day.

Arriving at the industrial estate early, Britney concealed herself and some newly acquired camera equipment next to a large window in the building directly opposite the warehouse in question. The window offered a full view of the entrance to the building opposite, including the four large, but dirty windows set into its facade. Perfect.

As she sat and waited, she contemplated what the consignment would be. Young girls, she presumed, probably from Eastern Europe or Asia. Kidnapped, trafficked. Terrified. Perhaps drugs as well but thought that unlikely. Women were Flynn's thing. Vulnerable women. Whether trafficked and paid for or just preyed upon like herself and Fiona. And if Danny was right in what he saw, then they were Lyons' thing too, meaning the odds wouldn't be in her favour. Considering this, she wished she had backup. But there was no one left to turn to? No one she could trust. Apart from Fiona and possibly Ben. But she wasn't willing to place either of them in the same position as she had put Danny. If anyone was going to die tonight, it would be Britney herself.

The first thing she noted was the colour and type of car. The power of its lights reflecting off the building told her it was a metallic blue coupé. She couldn't be sure of the make, but it certainly fitted the category of sports car. And the roar of its oversized engine certainly sounded familiar. Danny's quick thinking with his phone had made sure of that. Clicking record on her camera she let its night vision setting go to work. Envisaging what was ahead of her she had bought the camera earlier that evening for that very feature. That and its ability to pick up sound at long distances. The camera had been expensive, almost a thousand euros that she paid out of her own pocket, but if it did what it said on the tin, it would be worth every penny and more. The last thing she wanted was the camera to fail her. Grainy footage or poor sound quality just wouldn't cut it. She would need her evidence to be indisputable. Otherwise, she was just pissing in a storm.

The blue sports car was a start. She swept the camera across the body of the vehicle, picking up as much detail as possible before focusing the lens to see directly into the car's interior. Flynn was in the driver's seat, a cigarette hanging nonchalantly from his lips. Detective Joe Murray was sitting next to him. Two peas in a pod. They looked like they were settling in to wait for someone. So far so good.

The wait didn't take long. A few moments later a second vehicle arrived. A large white van, similar in size and shape to those used by construction companies to carry their equipment. It came from the other end of the alley, and when it reached the warehouse, it was facing the blue coupé, one set of lights battling to outshine the other. Then suddenly both the driver's killed their engines and all was darkness.

Britney focused the camera on the van. She had a feeling she had seen it before, but she couldn't remember exactly where? Was it near Stacey Rourke's house? She wondered. It was a builder's van, after all. Her heart raced at the possibility that she had tracked the missing husband down at last. Could she really be that lucky? She doubted it. It seemed to her that Lady Luck had left her particular building a long time ago. Her hands shaking with tension, she adjusted the lens in the hope she could pick out the driver. The infrared light of the camera was immune to the gloom and when she focused it right the man's face appeared in front of her as if on HDTV. She was surprised to discover she had a vague recollection of him but for the life of her couldn't recall from where? One thing was for sure, it wasn't Jim Rourke.

A second man was sitting next to the driver. At first, she couldn't see him clearly but then he turned to talk to his colleague and in doing so faced right in her direction. Britney's heart nearly stopped. If the appearance of the first man was a surprise, then the presence of this man left her reeling. She had been so wrong. So wrong about everything.

Now, it clicked.

She had seen the van before. She had seen it on the building site in Emmet's Hill, parked up near the entrance. Worse still she didn't only recognise the man sitting in it. She knew him. Knew him too well. Let him know her too well. She felt sick as she recalled his hands all over her, his lips tasting her, his pulse inside her. She had opened up to him, smiled, and laughed with him. Had even gone as far as falling in love with him. The man staring at her was the person she really believed was 'the one.' It was Bob.

It took Britney a long moment to gather herself and refocus on what she was trying to do. She would never have imagined Bob Harris was involved, not in her wildest dreams. Yes, he'd asked a few too many questions on their first date and seemed to know a tad too much but at the time she thought he was only trying to initiate conversation. She'd put it down to first date jitters which, despite her initial suspicions, later found cute and endearing. Even when she had gotten a little uncomfortable with their discussion, he had managed to make her feel like it was her own insecurity that had the alarm bells ringing and not anything he had said. Looking back on it, he had been the one who broached the subject of the brothels in the first place, no doubt in an attempt to figure out exactly what, if anything, she knew.

Then, of course, there was that injury he'd supposedly received at work, coincidentally on the same day as the car company was raided. Even though she knew some of the raiders had gotten a taste of their own medicine, she readily believed what he had told her. If it had been anyone else, she would have checked it out further but because it was him, she hadn't even followed up with the hospital. She had chosen to believe him. To believe in him. Now, here he was, brazen as brass.

While cursing her blind stupidity, she watched the four men get out of their respective vehicles and move toward the rear of the van. Harris carried a torch which he shone into the cargo hold once the rear doors had been opened. For a moment, the four men studied whatever was inside before Flynn tossed his smoke and gave an order while gesturing toward the warehouse. He then moved away from the van and towards the entrance of the building. Joe Murray dutifully followed. Harris and the other man waited by the van, gesturing angrily, and shouting at whoever or whatever was inside. Now Britney noted this man had a cast on his arm. And a rip across the collar of his jacket. Glancing back at the van, another piece clicked. Not only had she seen it in Emmet's Hill, but she had also seen it in the rat run outside the house on the Dublin Road. Jim Rourke wasn't balaclava man, after all.

With no one appearing, Harris soon lost his patience and reached inside the van to drag the occupant out into the open. To Britney, the cargo seemed to be exactly what she had anticipated. A young woman. A young woman in high heels and a skimpy dress with a coat pulled over her head. The only surprise being there was merely one.

She had expected several women. Six or seven at least. One woman to four men was surely a waste of resources. She must be very special, Britney decided. Very special, indeed. She made a mental note to check the database for any significant disappearances over the last few months. The daughter of a wealthy family, the sister of a sports star or perhaps even Middle Eastern royalty. A young girl like that would afford a hefty price and therefore, the extra attention.

While she was musing, Flynn and Detective Murray disappeared inside the warehouse and were soon followed by Harris and his driver. Harris dragged the woman by the hair, violently hauling her any time she tried to resist. When he reached the door, he aggressively shoved her inside. She immediately took her moment of freedom to fix her dress by shimmying her hips, a move that twigged with Britney for some reason, though she didn't immediately grasp why.

With the woman safely inside, Harris glanced around as if checking all was clear before entering himself. Once he had joined the others, he slammed the door closed behind him, effectively cutting off the camera's view. In response, Britney swung the camera left, focusing it on the first window, hoping that she could pick up their movements through its large pane of glass. The glass was thick with dirt, rendering the infrared practically useless and dashing any hopes she had of even a half-decent view. Still, she had to accept that half-decent was better than no view at all. She held the camera in that position and waited but no one appeared. They must have moved deeper into the warehouse.

Britney swore. So far, she had nothing only four men and a woman. A blue car and a white van. Yes, the men's actions did look suspicious and yes, the woman looked frightened and under duress but all of that could easily be explained away. They were just role-playing. An adult game that they all consented to. The woman was there of her own free will with no money or inducements changing hands. Yes, it might look sordid. It might even look illicit. But looking illicit wasn't a punishable crime.

No. She needed more. She needed to get inside.

She hefted the camera but kept it running as she moved away from the window toward the exit of the warehouse she occupied. On reaching the door, she took a moment to attune her senses to both sound and movement. Detecting nothing untoward, she quickly left the shadows of the building and crossed the alley to where the others had parked. She paused on reaching the vehicles, using them for cover as she scanned the area directly in front of the entrance. It was clear. Hefting the unwieldy camera once more, she prepared herself for the quick dash to the door.

However, with the vehicles so close and unmanned, an idea occurred to her – an opportunity she couldn't pass up to take out a little extra guarantee in case things went awry. Two little extra guarantees, in fact. With that little job done, she sprang from her cover, quickly covering the ground between the vehicles and the building, satisfied that the sneakers she was wearing lived up to their name. On reaching the warehouse, she flattened herself up against the front wall and listened. Nothing, only her own heart beating.

Reassured, she reached for the door and slowly pulled it open, her heart jumping at even the slightest squeak of the hinges. Once open wide enough for her to squeeze through, she entered, tiptoeing so that she was quiet as a mouse. It was dark inside, just as she expected. She held the camera at chest height, its lens focused in front of her, to allow it pick up any movement. She knew that in the heavy gloom, she'd spot any activity on the camera screen before her own eyes could detect it. Again, there was nothing. No flicker of light, no shadowy movements. Not even the sound of footsteps. Flynn and co must have taken the woman deep into the warehouse, perhaps into a separate room. A special room? She moved on, her blood pumping so fast that it pounded in her ears, her legs weak to the point of buckling.

Then she heard a sound. Soft movement directly behind her. She spun but with the sinking feeling in her heart that she was too slow. That she was trapped. In her terrified haste, she dropped the camera, the sound of it crashing to the concrete floor, heralding the beginning of the end.

"Welcome to the party, Britney," the woman's voice cut through the gloom. At the sound of it, Britney's breath caught. The memory that had twigged with her earlier came crashing back – the woman wiggling her hips as she adjusted her clothes. She had seen that same movement before. In the Castle Park. And now as she paired the memory with this woman's voice, she realised she had been duped. Duped from the very start. This was no wealthy family's daughter or Middle Eastern royalty. This was her friend. Her fellow comrade-in-arms. To confirm her deduction, a dull fluorescent light came on overhead, illuminating the perfect teeth that formed the treacherous smile of her last hope. Fiona.

****

The package – a small rectangular box rather crudely covered in newspaper sent shivers down Ade Fagan's spine. He didn't need to open it to understand its significance. Reports about The Courier littered the media, with many references made to the little gifts he sent his prospective victims. Little harbingers of death, one newspaper had called them. But it wasn't the stories in the media that made him uneasy. It was the fact that he knew. Had known for a long time. Ever since he'd listened to the panicked message left on his voicemail by that tease of a reporter. The Courier was coming for him.

The reason was simple. Revenge. Revenge for something that had happened a lifetime earlier. Something so insignificant in the grand scheme of things that he had forgotten all about it.

But then they had started dying. First Cullen and Cox, then the doctor. And now Peter Dunford was missing. He had tried to call him several times to no avail. Had left messages on his answering machine and even contacted his neighbour in Spain, where Peter liked to spend his time now. Just like Ade, Dunford had a number of overseas properties, with the Spanish villa where he passed the winter being his favourite by far. 'Was,' Fagan corrected himself, 'was his favourite.' For he was certain the former district board secretary was dead. 'If I was The Courier,' he thought to himself, 'that's exactly the way I would have done it. Kill the foot soldiers first. Then go after the general – the man who gave the orders. The man who stole your future. Cut the snake off at the head.'

The waitress had left the package on the table, directly in front of Ade, next to the roulade, the coffee, and the mints, all of which remained untouched. Ade, who normally considered dessert the crowning glory of any meal, now only had eyes for the box. He reached for it, then withdrew his hand, as if it were some venomous snake he daren't touch. Finally, he plucked up the courage to pick up the 'gift' but before attempting to open it, he glanced toward the main body of the restaurant. He was looking for anyone paying him undue attention. Perhaps The Courier was one of the mayor's lesser guests and was watching him right then. Studying his reaction to the news that he would be next. There were one or two sets of eyes casually cast in his direction, but he dismissed them as the usual pathetic glances of star-struck celebrity spotters, which he disdainfully considered bottom feeders while at the same time accepting them as standard fare for a man in his position. Normally, their attention would only serve to annoy him, or on a bad day – a very bad day, boost his flagging ego but this evening their glances made him distinctly uneasy. Any one of them could be the person who had sent him the gift. Any one of them could be the one planning to kill him. Possibly even the mayor himself? No, the likelihood was that it was none of them. From what he had read, The Courier delivered his gift then disappeared, to reappear at a later stage for the hunt. And that's exactly what it was. A hunt. With himself, Ade Fagan, President of the HAI, the final prey. The trophy.

He turned the package over in his hands one last time then began to rip at the newspaper with his chubby fingers. Even though it only took a moment, and he could only have expended the slightest bit of energy, he found he was sweating profusely – like a member of a bomb disposal unit would if forced to choose between the red and blue wire. He picked up the napkin and dabbed his forehead before continuing. Finally, with all the paper removed, he took a deep breath and opened the matchbox. What he discovered inside wasn't what he expected. He had expected blood and gore, a mutilated piece of another human being, perhaps a finger or toe or even a chunk of liver but all he got was a lock of hair. The narcissist in him actually felt disappointed. Thinking logically about it, he should have been sent a heart. Or better still, a decapitated head.

He set the box down on the table and sat back in the chair, forcing himself to relax. The box was only a warning. A warning that the hunt had begun. But unlike the previously hunted, Ade Fagan had an advantage. He was a top dog, which meant he too could hunt, and hunt with tremendous efficiency. Quickly switching from a fear-induced defensive mentality to attack mode, he dismissed the box as a distraction then dipped his hand into the jacket pocket of his handmade suit and pulled out his cell phone. If ever there was a time to call in a few favours it was now, although after hearing Flynn's little racket was under the microscope, he knew his options were more limited than before. Rumour had it, Superintendent Halley had enough of covering for his nephew and was ready to throw him to the wolves, something which Ade considered a shame. Flynn and his mercenaries had been his go-to guys. His fixers. One of the reasons he had gotten to where he was. They would be a loss, but it didn't mean he was out of options.

There were others, higher up the food chain. People with the power to protect, people with the power to eliminate. He flicked through his phone until he found the number he was looking for and was just about to dial when he noticed the small piece of paper in the box. In his bout of narcissistic disappointment, he hadn't noticed it at first, stuffed as it was into the bottom of the container, half-hidden beneath the lock of hair. He tentatively reached for it, using the tips of his stubby fingers to catch hold of one corner, then eased it out from its resting place, loathe to touch the hair that lay across it. Once it was completely free of the box, he noticed that the paper was folded in half and that inside the fold there seemed to be writing. On opening it, he found it contained a brief, scribbled note.

I have your son. Contact the police and he dies. I will be in touch.

He read the note a second time. Once the significance of what he was reading sank in, he immediately cancelled the call he was about to make and dialled a new number, one he had on speed dial. It was only a moment before the connection was made and he registered a dialling tone.

"Come on. Come on," he urged as he took the phone from his ear and stared at the screen. Still dialling. "Damn," he cursed, sounding so agitated that many of the other guests looked up from their desserts to throw curious glances in his direction. Something told him he could curse all he wanted. The phone wasn't going to be answered. Still, he stared at the screen.

The longer it rang the more his blood ran cold.

The Courier had his son.

****

Britney tried to run but strong hands snaked out from the gloom to restrain her then rotated her until she stood facing Fiona, whose hood was now pulled back and sitting on her shoulders. Even in the semi-darkness, Britney could see the look of satisfaction on her colleague's face. The look of triumph.

"Did you like our little performance?" Fiona asked with a mocking smirk. "I hope so. We put it on especially. Put a lot of thought into how best to engage the audience. To lure it in, you could say."

"You bitch!" Britney spat when she eventually found her voice. "You back-stabbing bitch."

"Now, now, Britney," Fiona mocked. "No need for the language. We're all friends here."

"No," Britney objected. "Not friends. You're no friend of mine and Flynn is certainly no friend to you. You're only his vassal, his dog's body, his whore."

"Oh, we all know who the whore is here, don't we, Bob?" she smiled and glanced beyond Britney at the person who had fixed his iron grip on her arms. When once she welcomed it, lusted for it, now Britney felt her skin crawl at the feel of Harris' touch. 'I should have known,' she said to herself. 'Even Salem didn't like you.'

"Yes. And what a practiced whore she is," Harris replied. Inside Britney winced. She could sense the sneer on his lips. "Very obliging. If she wasn't so headstrong, we might even find a nice little position for her."

"The doggy position," Fiona suggested with a titter. "Isn't that where you said her expertise lay? Pardon the pun."

Feeling blood burn like acid inside her face, Britney snarled and lunged for Fiona, but she only gained a couple of inches before Harris pulled her back. He was far too strong. The arms, once warm and comforting, were now shackles of hard, unrelenting steel, their grip carrying the cold promise of death.

"You set me up from the start," Britney growled. "Danny was right. When Stacey Rourke first made her report, you deliberately handed over that phone call. In fact, you were expecting it because you lot already knew he was missing. And then you cosied up to me. Confided in me to gain my sympathy. To draw us closer. Flynn wasn't hitting on you at all. And then, of course, you encouraged me to date this prick." She tossed her head back in the direction of Harris. "You made sure we'd meet at that party, and you suggested we go to the building site that day. All part of the plan to keep me close." She shook her head. "I sensed something was off with that lady in the electrical shop. She had seen you go into the brothel, hadn't she?"

"Yes, dear. She had. I was never in her store. I certainly never bought a kettle there. And just to fill you in, I was the young Garda Terry here had an affair with in Carlow. Been with him ever since." Fiona's manicured smile appeared ghoulish in the gloom.

"You tramp," Britney spat and threw a kick at Fiona, catching her in the shin. She felt a rush of satisfaction on hearing Fiona cry out. It didn't last long. Fiona reacted by slapping her in the face. Hard. So hard that her blemished cheek stung, and her ear rang like a bell tolling.

"That's enough," the authoritative voice cut through the gloom like a whip. Fiona's posture immediately stiffened, and Britney could feel Harris tense as if suddenly apprehensive. It wasn't the voice of Flynn or Joe Murray. It was the voice of a newcomer, lurking somewhere in the shadows to the rear of the warehouse.

"We're not here to play games." That all too familiar voice continued in a tone that brooked no-nonsense. Clearly the voice of the boss. But not the boss she expected. "We're here to swat a troublesome fly," the newcomer reminded them as he confidently strode out of the shadows to halt close to where she was being restrained.

Harris hardly loosened his grip as he spun her so that she was now facing the person she was certain was the mastermind. The darkness disguised much of his features, yet the outline of his pristine uniform and ever-present cap made him instantly recognisable to anyone who worked in Oldcastle Garda Station, for the man standing in front of her was Superintendent Halley. Flynn's uncle Harry. She shook her head in dismay. She had suspected him of covering up for his nephew's incompetence or at worst, turning a blind eye to his criminality but she had no idea that Halley himself was the orchestrator of it all. She glanced at the floor. The camera was concealed in the gloom, but she could just about make out its outline. It seemed intact. She hoped so. If it kept running it might still catch enough on tape. If not visual, then audio.

"So, it is you, after all," Britney observed as casually as possible. If she could keep them talking, she might have some hope of finding a way out of there alive. A slim hope. If the worst came to the worst, perhaps the camera would go unnoticed and be found at a later stage. And hopefully, fall into the hands of an honest cop. If one existed. "You see that was always what threw me," she remarked, thinking to at once encourage Halley to talk while at the same time taunt Flynn. She had a location on all other five but had no idea where Yabba Dabba Doo was hiding. Though she could smell his shitty cologne wafting from somewhere to her right.

"I knew Flynn was too much of a dumbass to run a raffle, let alone a highly organised crime cartel. It had to be someone else. Someone with brains. Brains and clout. Initially, I suspected it might be Joe over there in the shadows." She nodded in the direction of Detective Murray who she had spotted lurking at the edge of the gloom to her left, alongside the van driver whom Britney now recognised as Fiona's 'date' that night she'd seen her in Frampton's restaurant. "But I soon realised he was just a yes man. Another gofer. Then when Richie Lyons got involved, I was sure it must be him. He's certainly sharp enough. Far sharper than that oaf of a nephew of yours anyhow."

Flynn fell for the bait. "Lyons is just a has-been," he spat, from a position to her right.

Bingo. She had a location on all of them. It was a step in the right direction. A mini win. She'd take it.

"A drunken has-been who couldn't find his arse with a sheet of toilet roll," Flynn continued.

"Shut up, Flynn," Uncle Harry barked with contempt, his arctic eyes flashing dangerously. He didn't even bother to use Flynn's first name.

"I've had enough of her shit-talk. Just strap her to the chair and get this over with," he instructed. "I've got that mayor's function to go to."

"But Richie Lyons had nothing to do with it, had he?" Britney continued even as Harris dragged her toward a chair set in the centre of the warehouse a few yards away, over which the fluorescent light hung.

Halley didn't respond.

Was his silence an acknowledgement of Lyons guilt or innocence?

"He was just doing his job. The only honest one in the whole sordid affair. Him and poor Danny, of course." She grunted as Harris shoved her into the chair and pinned her there with his hands on her shoulders. His grip was like a vice. She couldn't move. All she could do was continue to talk. Talking was her only hope. The sound of her own voice reassured her that it wasn't over yet. As long as she could talk, life went on.

"So, the construction company is a front," she continued desperately. "Just a medium to launder your dirty money. And the vandalism attack on the site wasn't aimed at Jim Rourke. It was aimed at you. Revenge for the beatings they got off Flynn's goons."

"As you can imagine, I wasn't happy about that," Halley admitted. "If Flynn hadn't been so boneheaded, you wouldn't have sniffed a rat and we wouldn't be here having this conversation. Unfortunately, he takes after his father in that regard."

"And the brothels? They're yours too?"

Now, Halley sighed. "Don't you get it? The site, the businesses, the brothels, we own the damn town. And a few more along with it." She sensed him grinning smugly in the dark. "McBride is my mother's maiden name. I liked the idea of it – having the connection out front like that on the building site entrance for all to see. A clear link for anyone who was clever enough to spot it. I knew no one would be."

"If you're so damn powerful, why did you have to kill a harmless chap like Danny Owens?" she asked of no one in particular. As far as she was concerned, they were all guilty of his murder. Each one had a part to play.

"That's on you, Spears," Flynn piped up as he stepped closer into the light. Once again, he proved he just didn't know when to keep his mouth shut. She desperately hoped that it would stay that way. Noting the raw-looking scratch marks her nails had earlier left on his face, she felt a grim satisfaction. "You caused his death. By prying into affairs that were none of your business. He was just collateral damage. We were following you, you see. Watching you from the start."

That explained Fiona's presence in the restaurant when she was out with Harris. At the time, she had put it down as a coincidence and thought no more of it. But it was no coincidence. With that in mind, Britney decided to throw a little spanner into the works.

"You were watching Harris, you mean," she accused with more brazenness than she thought she could muster. "At the restaurant. If you really trusted Harris, why send Fiona to watch me too? But you don't trust Harris, do you? People like you trust no one. And that's why so many people had to die."

"Just to be clear," Uncle Harry interjected. "We had nothing to do with those other people's deaths. Not even Marie Cox."

"But she worked for you?"

"Yes. She used her connections and influence to direct the wealthier clients our way, not to mention her other assets. You could call her our honey trap. But we had no connection to the others. Whether you want to believe it or not, the serial killer is out there. Not in here. You just got the whole thing jumbled and you wouldn't let it go. I even put you on desk duty to keep you out of the way, but you had to keep meddling, didn't you? And once you shared your silly suspicions with that young Garda, a Garda outside of our control, we couldn't risk letting him go."

Britney nodded to herself. They were right. Her meddling had led Danny to his death. But she wasn't the one that plunged the knife into his neck. Which of them did, she wondered? Which of them had butchered him like a pig? Her money was on Flynn. Her boss.

"So yes," Halley declared with a twisted smile, "your boyfriend Harris here, killed him to protect our interests," he paused to let the enormity of that sink in. She had slept with more than a sex trafficker. She had slept with a bloodthirsty butcher. The thought of it made her retch.

"And now," Halley continued after a moment, "once you get over your little stomach upset, he's going to kill you too." Then he paused as if a thought suddenly struck him and instead of instructing Harris he calmly turned to his right. "Actually, I believe you're up Detective Murray. The time has come to cut your teeth." He smiled as he held out a long, evil-looking knife for Detective Murray to take. No serrated edge, Britney noted. Was that good or bad for her?

"Let's see how much of a 'yes man' you really are."

"Oh, and make it look good," he ordered. "So good that our cop-killing Courier will have one more Garda to answer for."

Detective Joe Murray silently nodded. He had remained still throughout all of this but now he stepped out of the gloom and took the knife from Halley's outstretched hand. He then moved forward until he was so close to Britney that she could smell his sweat. See the strain his bulging belly put on the buttons of his jacket. She looked up from her sitting position to see a cold determination in his eyes. She gulped. It was clear he was every bit the killer that Harris was.

"How does it feel to be alone?" he asked with a sneer that made her shiver with fear. She knew it was all over. As she stared pleadingly into his eyes she started to pray. Then he did something strange. Holding out three fingers on his free hand, he held it low in her eyeline and in front of his body where only she could see it. Then he subtly popped the buttons of his jacket to reveal the butt of a gun in his belt. A police issue, Sig Sauer. As he did, his cheeks played a game of ping pong.

"You should have backed off, Britney," he told her as he caressed her face with the edge of the knife. She automatically flinched but kept her eyes fixed on his left hand. His left hand and the gun that only she could see in the gloom.

Two fingers.

"You should always heed the warnings and understand that the real danger is never at your back," he continued cryptically but he wasn't looking at her. He was looking past her. Past Harris. As if there was something he alone could see in the shadows. Or someone.

One finger.

"It's the ones in front of you that you should aim for."

"Just hurry up and cut the bitch," Harris cut in, the killer in him sensing that something about Murray's tone was off. With that, Halley stepped closer and reached out to catch Murray by the shoulder and swing him around to face him.

No fingers. Suddenly the room erupted as Detective Murray lunged for Harris with the knife, holding it like a bayonet, causing him to release his grip on Britney's shoulders. At the very same moment, Britney grabbed the semi-automatic from Murray's belt and with all her strength, propelled herself sideways. Ignoring the flare in her ribs, she flew through the air, while pulling the trigger. Once, twice. Hitting Halley square in the chest and catching Flynn in the shoulder, sending him spinning to the floor. On landing, she felt another rib crack but ignoring the pain, she immediately jumped to her feet then spun and just as he was raising the gun, she emptied two rounds into the van driver's torso. The man fell with a dying groan, the weapon he was brandishing flying from his fingers to skitter across the concrete floor.

Feeling the adrenaline pump through her, she then darted towards the wounded Flynn who was now climbing to his feet. He watched her coming with a stunned look on his face. She didn't break stride as she reached him but leapt in Karate Kid style, landing a scissors kick square into his groin. With some satisfaction, she saw his eyes almost bulge out of his head. Then he groaned and fell backward.

"My name is Kent, you slimy piece of shit," she growled as she stood over him. "Not Spears or Cunt.

KENT! Remember that when you're bending over for the soap and some horny queen is eyeing up your hairy ass. And by the way. They don't supply KY jelly in the nick."

"Or in the grave either, you meddling bitch."

Even as she turned toward the voice, Britney knew she had made a big mistake. A life-ending mistake. Hoping the darkness would disguise her movements she began to raise her gun.

"I wouldn't do that, Sergeant."

The impact of the bullet had landed him on his back but now Halley had climbed to his feet and was holding a gun pointed directly at Britney's head. Far too close to miss. Britney froze.

"The good old vest," he explained with the same sickeningly smug grin his nephew often wore. He gestured toward Flynn. "Unlike that clown I always come prepared." The grin morphed into a cold smile. "It was nice knowing you, Sergeant. Maybe in the next life you'll learn to keep your nose out." With that he slowly squeezed the trigger. Britney shut her eyes, bracing herself for the descent into never-ending darkness. But it never came.

Suddenly Lyons exploded out of nowhere. Roaring like an angry bear, he dived out of the shadows to rugby tackle Britney to the ground, just a fraction before Halley's bullet hit. At the same time, he popped off a brace of shots from a gun of his own. Blood splattered her face and neck, but Britney hadn't time to wonder where she'd been struck. She rolled on landing, preparing to fire in Halley's direction, before he had the chance at a second shot. She needn't have worried. He lay on the floor, dead, one of Lyons' bullets having almost ripped his neck out.

Britney hadn't time to feel relief. Next to her Detective Lyons lay unmoving. One look told her the blood splatter she'd felt wasn't hers. He had taken a bullet for her. A bullet to the head. Acting on instinct she turned him over onto his side and taking off her hoodie she rolled it up then wrapped it around his head and tied it off with the sleeves. It was a crude tourniquet but if it stemmed the blood he might survive. And she might get some answers. As if reading her mind, his eyes fluttered open.

"Vanessa," he whispered, his voice faltering. "Save Vanessa."

"Vanessa?" Britney asked, leaning close. "Whose Vanessa, detective?"

"Vanessa…was an innocent," he replied, his words trickling out between breaths. "A saint…but not the others, except…except…" He took a rattling breath. "Don't you see. It's too late…for them now…but you can save her. You can save Vanessa."

"Is Vanessa the girl in your house, detective?"

Suddenly his eyes took on a wild, untethered look as if chasing a memory. His hand reached out to grab her arm and pulled her close. His grip was like iron when his eyes eventually focused on her. "Don't you see? It was his child…that's why I… The drugs… That's why they had to die… It was his child."

With that, his head lolled, and his hand fell away. Britney checked his pulse. He was still alive. Barely. Something she wouldn't be if she didn't move.

Pushing herself to her feet, she searched the gloom for Fiona, but found no sign of her. She'd obviously taken the opportunity offered by the sudden mayhem to make a run for it. Britney decided to let her go for now. She was a bottom feeder. A nobody with nowhere to go. Nowhere to hide. Right then, she had more immediate concerns. There had been no sign of Detective Murray since he leapt at Harris, so she peered through the gloom to see how he had fared. Not good by the looks of things. Whatever way they fell, Harris was now on top of Murray, pinning him to the ground. Britney's heart sank. It didn't look like Murray was moving. Then she saw Harris arm rise upwards and thinking he was about to lash out, she quickly stepped forward with the gun pointed downward and shouted, "FREEZE!"

"You're not in the fucking movies," came the sarcastic reply. "So, just get this sack of shit off me."

It was Joe Murray's voice. Obviously, the movement she had spotted was Murray struggling out from under Harris's dead weight. Britney smiled happily. Less than an hour earlier, she had hated Murray almost as much as she hated Flynn, but now she could kiss him. A big wet smack on the lips. She lowered the gun and with her free hand, helped flip over Harris' body allowing Joe Murray to slip out from under it and breathe freely again.

"Thanks," he said, an impish grin spreading across his face as he climbed to his feet. "Kinda creepy having that scumbag's hands all over me."

"Tell me about it," Britney replied as she glanced down at the body to confirm he was dead. He certainly seemed that way.

Detective Murray's lunge had caught Harris square in the chest resulting in the knife being buried to the hilt in his sternum. It had most likely killed him instantly. Britney cursed to herself. Far too quick for her liking, considering what he had done to Danny. 'So much for justice,' she thought bitterly. On impulse, she hawked deeply then spat out on Harris' face. She regretted lowering herself almost instantly. Anyway, a scumbag like that was a waste of good spit. Just then a gurgling sound escaped Harris' lips as his right hand shot out to catch Joe's ankle. His other hand reached for the knife in his chest as if to pull it clear. Britney stepped back then snapped up the gun and fired two rounds, one of them hitting her target in the chest, the second right between the eyes. There was no coming back from that one.

A few yards away, Flynn groaned as he rolled and pushed himself to his feet, his balls obviously having dropped back to somewhere close to their rightful position. He glanced in Britney's direction with a face like a bereaved frog, then took off lumbering toward the rear of the warehouse, leaving a bright red trail behind him. Britney reached for the gun in her belt, but Joe Murray stayed her hand.

"Flynnstones is mine," Joe said with a cool smirk. "That Fiona bitch is yours."

Britney nodded. "Yes, she is." Her smile was wicked. Having no idea where Fiona had disappeared to, Britney focused on an invisible spot in front of her in the hope her peripheral vision would detect any movement. Everything was still. Then she had a thought. The camera. If it was still running it might have picked up in what direction Fiona had fled. She glanced around and found it only a few feet away. She was in luck. The camera was solid and had landed with its lens facing in the general direction of the door – the red recording light still blinking. She stooped to pick it up then pressed the stop button and rewound the footage until she found what she was looking for. A terrified looking Fiona making a break for the exit and the getaway vehicles outside. Britney smiled to herself as she followed. Fiona would have a surprise in store.

Once she reached the door, she paused preparing to hold her breath and listen for even the slightest sound. She didn't have to. An engine desperately trying to turn over growled like a hungry dog and left no doubt as to Fiona's location. She was in the van. Must have tried the car first. Who wouldn't? The engine growled again, drawing a satisfied smile from Britney. Fiona was too thick to realise what she had done. The two little extra guarantees she had taken out were the vehicles' injector fuel lines. They now lay discarded beneath the car. Fiona was going nowhere.

When she spotted Britney emerge from the door, she panicked and jumped from the van, snapping one of her high heels in the process. She cursed angrily then she took off in a lumbering run down the alley, getting nowhere fast. Britney jogged after her, catching up with her before she'd managed twenty yards.

"Fiona," she said smugly, as she held the gun out in front of her, pointed right at Fiona's head, "Did no one ever tell you…you should never wear heels to a gunfight?"

Fiona stared at the gun, then at the road ahead. Finally, she collapsed to the ground with an anguished sob, the sudden onslaught of tears streaking the makeup on her all too-perfect face.

"He made me do it," she cried. "I was only following orders."

"Funny, that's exactly what the Nazis said," Britney replied. "But then they were cowardly sons of bitches too."

For the first time in weeks, Britney felt good to be a Garda.

Chapter 18

"It was you that stuffed that note in my pocket. You were undercover all along," Britney said, surprise still evident in her voice. Herself and Detective Murray were leaning against a Garda van outside the warehouse, their arms folded, and their legs crossed. To any onlookers unaware of recent events, they could easily appear like two friends shooting the breeze. But if there was any lesson to be learned from this night, it was that appearances could be deceptive. Troubled by what Detective Lyons had revealed before passing out, Britney had called Swords to arrange a squad to visit his house. She desperately hoped they would find this girl called Vanessa. And find her alive. She had yet to inform Joe about what Lyons had told her. Trust wasn't coming easy right then. He may have saved her life but so had Lyons. Concerning the latter, she couldn't help but wonder for what purpose. With Lyons clinging to life by a thread, she knew it would be a long wait for answers. He remained in the warehouse where he was receiving attention from a team of paramedics who daren't move him until they had him adequately stabilised. The looks on their faces said it would be touch and go.

Combing the crime scene, a team of investigators struggled to come to terms with what had occurred. Joe had given them a brief outline, but Britney knew from previous experience that they would be asked to go over it again and again. And that was before Internal Affairs got their teeth into it. All in all, she got the feeling it would be a very long night. The stars were out and there was a chill in the air, but Britney felt safe for the first time in weeks and that warmed her up no end. As did the sight of Flynn being carted off in handcuffs.

The nature of his capture had given her great satisfaction. And not just the fact that she got to kick him in the balls. Despite his discomfort, he had managed to reach the rear yard of the warehouse but found himself penned in by security fencing. With nowhere to run, he attempted to climb over the eight-foot barrier, but his injured shoulder curtailed his attempted escape. What happened next might never become clear but when Joe Murray eventually dragged him through the front door, he had far more scrapes and bruises than a bullet and kick in the groin could account for.

Registering the stares, Joe just shrugged, "Well someone like him should know better than resisting arrest, now, shouldn't he?" He directed his smirk at Flynn. "Capeesh!"

No one uttered a word of objection. Not even from Flynn himself. He was all too aware that it would get a whole lot worse from there on in. Both for him and his hairy ass.

The bodies of Superintendent Halley and Fiona's 'date' were still lying where they had fallen and were now the focus of a busy forensics team. As far as Fiona herself was concerned, Britney had taken great pleasure in cuffing her colleague and even more on seeing her carted off in the back of a van – as she had arrived. She hoped to never again set eyes on the backstabbing bitch.

Nodding sombrely, Joe responded to Britney's enquiry. "Yep. We have been investigating this cartel for more than two years. Found evidence of them operating in towns and cities across the country but could never quite pin them down. We knew it was run by Gardaí but even though we had our suspicions, we had no concrete evidence." He shrugged. "Then Flynn got careless. During his time in Carlow, he started flaunting his wealth. Flash cars, expensive restaurants, high end apartments. Stuff that a detective's salary just couldn't account for. That's when I was called in. My job was to buddy up to Flynn."

Britney smiled, the slight gap in her teeth giving her an innocent little girl look. "You certainly did a good job of that."

"Yes, sorry if I alienated you but I had to be convincing. And I had to be sure you weren't involved. Especially once I discovered you were seeing Harris."

"Big mistake!"

"Understatement of the year, I'd say."

"Of the century!" Britney replied but didn't want to dwell on it. "When did you suspect Halley?"

Joe shrugged. "I knew from early on that Flynn wasn't Mr Big. Like you said in there, he just hadn't the smarts to keep such an enterprise running smoothly and under the radar. They were running brothels, drugs, protection rackets – you name it. As Halley said, even the building site was theirs. They had a lot of similar interests around the country. As I'm sure you know, legitimate businesses are great for laundering money. When you began questioning things, they started to get nervous."

"So, they put Harris onto me. To get close to me, to see what I knew," she said shaking her head ruefully. "And I fell for it. Hook, line and sinker."

"Don't beat yourself up. He was a good-looking guy – for a sadist!"

Britney forced a wry smile. "Why couldn't he have been a nice fella like that poor Jim Rourke? The only mistake that poor chap made was lending them his van."

"Yep. A construction van is good cover. That's why they used them. Different vans all the time but kosher ones. Taxed and insured with valid owners and number plates. They roped in the likes of Jim Rourke who couldn't say no to the bit of extra cash."

"And the hold Flynn had over him because of that arrest," Britney added. "Where do you think Jim Rourke is now?"

"In hiding, like you presumed. Because if Halley is to be believed, the killer is still out there."

"I'm not so sure." Britney replied. "Regarding Jim Rourke being the killer, I mean."

"Oh?" Joe's eyes narrowed as if he was about to object to her unspoken thoughts, yet she held back on revealing Lyons' ramblings. Between the uncertainty of it all and the onset of fatigue, the killer could have been standing in front of her right then and she wouldn't have known it.

"Well, if he's not in hiding," Joe said, "he's probably buried in a ditch somewhere. Or under a foundation. Because if he started getting suspicious of what they were using his van for, he was a loose end. And Halley didn't like to leave loose ends," Joe sighed. "But only for him going missing, we might never have cracked this case."

"A lot of good that is to Stacey and the kids," Britney replied, critically assessing all the torment she must have caused that family with her unfounded accusations. She owed them an apology. Alan Rourke too.

"Collateral damage Flynn would call it. But then Flynn is such an asshole. And such a dumbass, as you put it. That's why I always knew there had to be someone else. Someone with influence. When Uncle Harry pulled some strings to get Flynn posted to Oldcastle, it was the link we were looking for. But they were so tight lipped, I only had my suspicions. Nothing we could close a case on until tonight. Still, I wasn't quite as surprised as you were when he walked in."

"To be honest, I had pegged Lyons as the mastermind."

"I guessed as much, and I can see you are still not convinced." Joe forced a tired smile. "Richie might be a lot of things but he's not crooked. I should know. We trained together and worked on some really tough cases over the years. But I haven't seen much of him since his wife died. So, you can imagine my surprise when I was informed that he was coming to Oldcastle Garda Station to discuss The Courier case."

"You played it well then. Both of you. I never would have guessed you knew each other at all."

Joe puffed out his cheeks and shrugged. "We couldn't risk Flynn finding out. It had been hard enough to break into their circle in the first place, so the last thing I wanted was to have them take another look at my background because they'd soon realise I've so much history with the redoubtable Richie Lyons. It would have been six months work down the drain. Or worse." He ran his fingers across his throat suggestively.

"Ok, I see that. But you involved him on the QT?"

Joe nodded. "After his visit to the station, I called him to fill him in on the case I was running. He'd known Flynn and Halley from before and always suspected they were dodgy, so he readily jumped on board. He could see I was in a bit of a pickle. You see, you didn't realise it, but you were on the verge of blowing my entire case, and probably getting yourself killed, perhaps me along with you. When Richie called me and suggested I should bring you in, I agreed it was the best way forward." He looked at her a little sheepishly. "Things were hotting up, so I needed back up anyway. Who better than someone already in the heart of the investigation? We also thought that by having you involved, we might keep you out of harm's way." He smiled wryly. "Keep us all out of harm's way."

"Hmmm," Britney replied dryly, "I wonder who kept who out of harm's way in the end."

"Anyway," Joe said, letting on not to hear the dig, "Flynn had arranged for 'a consignment' of girls to arrive this week. He had kept the exact date under wraps, so when I found out it was tomorrow night, I hadn't time to arrange an official raid. Plan B was to approach you and get you on board. I thought between me, you and Richie we'd finally get the evidence needed to break open their ring."

"So what happened? Where's consignment? And why bring it all forward to tonight?"

Joe pursed his lips and gave a quick shake of his head. "Perhaps they got jittery when Richie appeared at the station or, perhaps they were suspicious of me all along. Either way, they must have smelled a rat."

"Or there was a rat," Britney said quietly, thinking of the failed raid on the Marie Cox properties. And everything else she'd learnt. "I take it you filled Lyons in on the change?"

Joe nodded slowly. "I called him to tell him a few times, but he didn't answer, so I left a message with all the details. He didn't call back but that didn't surprise me. Richie understands better than anyone that when a cop is working undercover, every call is a risk." His voice trailed off as he shook his head. "I know what you're thinking but it's not him, Britney. He's a good cop."

"People change," Britney argued. "They act differently under stress. Think differently. Especially under long-term stress. And everyone knows he lost it after his wife died. Think about it," she continued ignoring the look on Joe's face, "wouldn't tonight have been a good way of getting rid of both of us. Flynn too. With a bit of luck, perhaps everyone involved in The Courier investigation."

"But he's the one with the bullet in his head, remember," Joe argued. "Why turn up at all?"

"Perhaps his conscience got to him. I don't know. If he delayed a fraction later to make his move, I was dead."

Joe chewed his lip. "To be honest, that delay bothered me too. I saw him in the shadows and thought he would intervene, but he just stood there. Watching. It was like he was waiting for something."

'For us to get popped,' Britney was about to reply, 'or maybe himself,' but just then Joe's phone rang. He answered it and listened attentively for a few moments.

"That was Commissioner Wilson," he said as he hung up.

"Congratulating us on a job well done, I'm sure."

The look of Joe's face said, 'as if.'

"Ade Fagan just informed Wilson his son is missing. Now this is strictly need-to-know, but Fagan is adamant The Courier has taken him."

"Lyons was adamant this was about the HAI," Britney pointed out. "He had a major grudge. And with Fagan being the HAI's headman…" She left it hanging.

"That's not all," Joe said, his expression grave. "They found Jim Rourke's body earlier. And not in any foundation."

"Oh God, no! Where?"

"Hanging from the gates of Ballyfeud hurling field. Murdered like all the rest."

"Shit," Britney cursed, thinking of the heartbreak it would cause his poor family. She gave a despairing shake of her head. "Like it or not, Joe, we're running out of options." She paused. Right then felt like a good time to fill him in on what Lyons had told her. Cryptic and all as it might have been, if Lyons died it could be taken as his deathbed confession.

As he listened, Joe played that silent game of ping pong.

****

A faint light shone from an upstairs bedroom of Detective Lyons's house but otherwise, the place was in total darkness. Outside, a rather dim-looking Garda who introduced himself as Tim was waiting for them when they parked next to the kerb.

"Well, did you find her?" Britney asked eagerly as she got out of the car.

"We've secured the house," he replied evasively, managing to sound bored despite the gravity of the situation. Britney wondered if it was the same apathetic person she'd spoke to on the phone when first she had contacted Swords' station.

"Just waiting on a search warrant."

"To hell with that," Joe said. "We've got permission from the owner. Isn't that right, Sergeant?" He didn't wait for an answer. He went straight for the door and knocked. "Vanessa, if you're in there, it's the Gardaí."

During the journey from Oldcastle, he'd fought the possibility that Lyons could be the man terrorising the nation but with Britney adding to the evidence with all she'd learnt from Danny, the stark reality seemed to sink in. Now his face bore the expression of someone who had been stabbed in the back. With no answer at the front, he made his way around to the rear of the house and knocked again so aggressively, the door shook.

"Vanessa, are you in there?"

Once again there was no answer. "Fuck this," he said then stood back and shoulder-charged the door. And again. As she watched, Britney withdrew her baton from her belt, having learnt the hard way never to leave it in the car no matter how uncomfortable it might be. Although any potential threat from Lyons was hampered by the small fact of him being comatose in hospital, they had no idea what was facing them inside. On Joe's third attempt splinters flew from the door jamb and they were in. Blood pounded in Britney's ears as she braced for a potential onslaught, but nothing faced them only an empty utility room.

After ensuring it was clear, they quickly moved through a door that led into the kitchen. Britney hit a light, at the same time scrunching her nose as she was assailed by a sickly stench. The room was a mess of unwashed pans, crockery and cutlery that had been so long discarded on the worktops they were mould-ridden. Otherwise, it too was empty.

"Vanessa," Joe called again. "Are you here?"

Drawn by the silence they moved further into the house, all the while keeping one eye on the stairs. Someone must have turned that light on up there, faint and all as it was. Britney hoped it was the girl, alive and well, but before investigating, they had to ensure the downstairs was clear. They tentatively stepped through another door.

When it came to tidiness the sitting room was in no better shape than the kitchen. Sheets of newspapers were strewn all over the floor while the couches and coffee table were buried beneath an assortment of files and loose paperwork. A swivel-head reading lamp sat on the table. Britney switched it on.

"These are all dossiers on the victims," she said as she searched through the files. "Here's one on Miss Cox. And this one's on Cullen." She picked one up from the pile and flicked through the pages. "This one is all about the doctor. It goes back years, Joe. Long before this investigation even started."

As he listened, Joe stared at the floor. "These old newspapers. Look, they're all from the Independent news." He glanced at Britney. "The gift-wrapping!"

Britney nodded then turned for the downstairs bathroom. Finding that clear, she made for the stairs. Joe stared at the papers a moment longer then followed her lead. With the weapon held in front of her Britney started to climb. One step at a time, her eyes raking all before her, ready to swing the baton at the first sign of movement. The stress of remaining alert proved so intense that her heart was a hammer in her chest by the time she reached the top. She was about to climb off the last step when she heard a soft, whimpering sound. She paused in mid-step as thoughts of balaclava man came back to haunt her. The sound had come from the room directly in front of her where a faint light drew a thin line beneath the door. She pricked her ears but heard nothing more. Silence. Inhaling deeply, she pushed on, noiselessly covering the three paces which brought her to the door then quickly stepping to one side and placing her back to the wall. Joe took up a similar position opposite. If danger awaited inside, they were well out of the firing line.

"Vanessa. My name is Sergeant Kent," Britney called. "I'm here with my colleague, Joe Murray. We're coming in."

She waited a moment then slowly turned the handle. The door squeaked as it swung inward. Britney followed through the gap, careful to keep her foot against the door to avoid a repeat of being rammed against the jamb. Halfway in, she stopped in her tracks. What assailed them first was the smell. Warm and pungent, it wafted toward the door to hit them full in the face, carrying traces of urine and faeces. Of sickness. Hospital smells thriving in the absence of bleach. The next assault was on the visual senses. Wispy hair and hollowed cheeks. Grey, waxy skin. Wide, staring eyes, registering nothing. The fixed irises told her the girl lying chained to the makeshift bed was dead. Britney slowly lowered the baton. There would be no need to defend herself this time.

Moving further into the room she saw discarded water bottles and food cartons on the floor. A wash basin and a soiled bedpan. Both plastic. Another step and she noticed the polythene screen and the bars on the window. The shackle that bound the girl's wrist. And her freedom.

"My God, Joe. This is a prison."

Joe nodded sombrely. "His killing roo…"

Suddenly the girl sprung from the bed with a terrifying screech. She was on Britney before she could react, her mouth wide open, displaying jagged teeth, bared as if searching for soft flesh into which to sink them. Britney swung the baton, but the girl was too close for it to have any effect. Luckily, Joe had seen the movement and reacted quickly. Before she could sink her canines in, he wrapped an arm around the girl's neck then grabbed a tress of the girl's wispy hair and hauled her backwards. She clawed and screamed as if fighting for her life, her savage strength belying her skeletal frame. Joe struggled to overpower her. He finally got the upper hand and with one mighty heave, he tore her away from Britney and tossed her backwards onto the bed. Together with Britney he leapt on her and pinned her down, calling to dopey Tim for back up.

"Get her strapped down," he instructed when Tim and his colleagues eventually arrived. "And call an ambulance. We need to clear the other rooms."

Britney judged there was every chance they'd find David Fagan imprisoned in one of them. Perhaps already dead. She was wrong. The rooms proved as empty as the girl's eyes.

Chapter 19

In the days that followed, the fallout from the 'Warehouse Shootout,' as it had been dubbed by the media, proved bitterly divisive within the Garda Síochána, while conversely served to unite public opinion. But not in a good way.

When initial reports leaked out regarding the critical shooting of the serial killer known as The Courier, it seemed the entire country drew one massive sigh of relief. However, when it was suggested, the perpetrator may have been a Garda and a detective at that, the sense of relief quickly turned to outrage and disbelief.

The public wondered how it could be possible that a Garda Detective could have committed such heinous crimes without his superiors being in any way suspicious of his wellbeing. Was it not the case that all Gardaí's mental health and stability were monitored? Were they not required to pass a regular psychological assessment? If so, how come this detective had gotten away with killing so many. Because he was one of them, many whispered. Others went even further by suggesting the killing hadn't begun with Cullen and that there were more bodies waiting to be uncovered. Bodies ranging through the various degrees of decomposition, from relatively intact corpses to fleshless, unrecognisable accumulations of bones. And the force was covering it all up. Like they covered up the trafficking and the brothels. The money laundering. The penalty points scandal. If this wasn't the case, they asked, why not name and shame?

To quell the rising tide of public resentment and to galvanise the force, Commissioner Wilson made a public announcement appointing a squad from Garda Internal Affairs to investigate the events leading up to the shooting and probe the level of corruption within the organisation. Every single Garda at Oldcastle Garda Station had been ordered to cooperate "to the very best of their abilities." Though never said in so many words, everyone understood the latter was just IA speak for, "Your entire squad is under investigation, guilty until proven innocent. And, if you're the one caught in a lie, you'll be writing parking tickets for the rest of your career. Or worse."

It didn't stop there. Anyone found to have even a tenuous connection, professionally or otherwise to either Superintendent Halley or Detective Flynn, came under the microscope. Even those invited to the Mayor's function, which Superintendent Halley had been due to attend the night of the shooting, had been questioned. These included local councillors, the President of the HAI, and the mayor himself. All were quick to distance themselves from any collusion with the corrupt pair. Britney didn't believe a word out of their mouths, especially Ade Fagan's. The fact that his son had been targeted and was still missing led her to believe he was far from innocent. As did the Commissioner's continued insistence that his disappearance be kept under wraps. 'But why?' was the question that played on Britney's mind. What was he trying to hide?

On her first morning back at the station, Britney had been met on entering with a slow handclap. This universal sign of appreciation initiated by Joe, was soon followed up by Ben and Triona, until it developed into a standing ovation by all present. Having been retrieved from the scene, the video of the shootout was secretly doing the rounds, leaving all viewers gobsmacked at the level of courage their colleague had displayed in the face of the most challenging of adversities. Britney saw the leak as just another sign that not only the triad of Halley, Flynn and Fiona stank, but every shiny button and creased epaulette of the force.

"Why not ask the public for help, Joe?" she asked in frustration as she manoeuvred through a glut of funeral traffic, the onerous task of finding the president's missing son having been discreetly handed to the pair. "I mean if The Courier is lying in a coma, what difference does it make? Except to hinder our ability to find the young man, of course. What is Fagan not telling us, Joe? What is he trying to bury?"

Joe shrugged in the seat next to her. "No one climbs to the top without having skeletons in the closet, Britney. I'm guessing that man has more than most. They do call him Hitler, you know."

"But at the price of his son?" Britney asked. "David Fagan could be anywhere, perhaps without food and water, or worse, bleeding to death, meaning the clock is ticking. With Lyons not telling us anytime soon, we need all our resources made available to find him."

"I'm still not sure Lyons took him," Joe argued. "I mean we only have Fagan's word. He said there was a note, but who saw it? I didn't."

"You mean you don't want to believe that Lyons took him, Joe. Just like you didn't want to believe the rest of it. But you saw that girl with your own eyes. She was death warmed up."

"And there was all the other stuff," Joe admitted, sounding as if feeling dispirited had become a chronic condition.

Days of investigation into Lyons had uncovered some unsavoury truths about his one-time colleague. According to doctors who examined her, the girl called Vanessa, who was now receiving treatment in a mental hospital, had been locked up for at least twelve months, if not more. During that time, she had been forcibly drugged – doctors had found vast quantities of a drug called Ketamine in her system and vials of the stuff were found in Lyons' house. The girl had uttered only a few words since her rescue, but enough to throw a spanner in the works. It turned out she was Lyons' niece. His brother's daughter. Which seemed to explain Lyons' cryptic confession of 'It was his child.' Further investigation substantiated this and found her parents had been killed in a car crash some years earlier, leaving Lyons and Molly as her legal guardians. That being the case, it seemed she had no connection to Halley and Flynn's trafficking enterprise, suggesting this was a personal thing for Lyons. Kicked off, Britney believed, by his wife's untimely death. The in-depth dossiers on his victims suggested as much. Detailed dossiers on their lives. Their careers. On their connections to the HAI. The level of detail he had compiled on the doctor in particular indicated that he had been stalking him for nearly two years. More or less since his wife died. Following up on this, they learnt that despite numerous checkups, Doctor Carmody had failed to diagnose his wife's cancer, leading them to believe they had found a motive for his murder at least. Negligence.

"It seems Lyons blamed him for her death." Britney explained as she sifted through the evidence. "I'm guessing that having known him from his hurling days he recommended Carmody but soon discovered Carmody wasn't quite the doctor he thought he was. Claimed he was too busy focusing on extracurricular activities like improving his golf swing rather than doing his damn job. He even registered a complaint with the medical board."

"Let me guess," Joe said, "it was brushed under the carpet?"

"Yes. I'd imagine that only served to infuriate Detective Lyons even more. I think it was after that he began to follow the doctor. Perhaps initially to gather evidence of misconduct," Britney shrugged. "But somewhere along the line, his intentions became more sinister until finally, he decided to exact revenge by killing him."

"But what about the rest?" Joe pointed out.

"Well, we believe he had an affair with Marie Cox. Perhaps in his grief, his guilt over having cheated on Molly intensified, driving him to resent the reporter. To blame her. If Halley is to be believed, she had seduction down to a tee. As for the rest, we're working on it. Lyons hinted the answer was in the newspapers, so I have Triona Maguire scouring internet archives looking for any connection there. Ben Youngs is following up on the individual victim's backgrounds to see what might have drawn Lyons to them. But it's clear he deemed them all corrupt in some way, perhaps through a connection to Halley and Flynn.

"Maybe he learnt about the brothels from Cox, and it appalled him," she suggested. "Went against all his principals."

"But then why keep that poor girl locked up?" Joe asked, sounding far from convinced. "And why keep her laced with enough Ketamine to fly her to the moon?"

Now as they turned onto the church road, they were faced with another problem. Where to park?

****

Be it down to morbid curiosity, genuine grief, or simply the cleansing of a collective conscience, the funeral of Jim Rourke was an extremely well-attended affair. The ceremony took place at twelve noon on the Saturday following his body's discovery. It was held in St Mary's Cathedral, the same church that served as the location for the prayer vigil beseeching Jim Rourke's safe return a little over a week earlier. The church was packed beyond capacity with mourners pouring out through the doors, into the carpark, and even onto the street more than forty yards away. Amongst the gathered mourners, the nature of the discovery of Jim Rourke's body was the main topic of conversation.

Suspended from the gates of a hurling field, the body had been found by a local builder who pulled in for a piss on his way home from the pub. At first, the builder's alcohol-fogged brain thought some prank-minded kids had hung a scarecrow from the entrance, but when he pulled over for a closer look, he could see how wrong he'd been. There was nothing fake about what he was looking at. It was a body. And not just any body. He recognised the face even in death. He had watched the young man hurling many times. Admired the young man's courage on the field, wondered about his attitude off it. Still, they would have won nothing without him. The builder was fairly certain of that. Now, however, he would win no more. Not in this life anyhow, the builder had observed as he blessed himself.

When the authorities arrived soon afterward, they found the body hanging by the neck with its feet dangling a foot or more above the ground. One end of a thick rope had been thrown over the top bar of the eight-foot gate and tied off securely. The other end formed a noose which, yanked by his own body weight, had jerked so tight around Jim Rourke's neck that it had almost buried itself into his flesh. The Gardaí's first instinct had been to judge it as suicide, but they soon realised by the specific posing of the body that suicide just wasn't possible. Jim Rourke's arms had been pulled out from his sides at right angles to his torso and tied to the bars of the gate with what looked like fishing gut. His legs were slightly bent at the knees and his feet tied side by side. His head was bowed to the right. 'Saint-like,' a Garda observed.

The image of Our Lord on the cross, except fully clothed where Jesus was stripped to a loincloth.

The question on the investigator's lips was why? Why had Lyons posed him like that? Like the others but different. More respectful. It was a question that bothered Britney as she entered the church grounds. As did the fact that he didn't appear to have been tortured like all the others. What made him so special in Lyons' eyes?

Despite the traffic they arrived early enough to procure a seat halfway up the church and therefore have a clear view of the family and chief mourners. As she shuffled into her seat Britney's phone vibrated with a message from Triona. Conscious of the solemn occasion she discreetly slipped it out of her pocket to check the text, keeping the phone low in her lap as she sat.

'I'm not sure if it matters now but I found what links the newspapers. We missed it before because it's not what you see. It's what you don't see. Call me and I'll explain.'

On reading it, her curiosity briefly tempted her to find the nearest exit, but the harrowing scene in front of her was far too unsettling for her to contemplate getting up and leaving. She had already disrespected the family enough. Not to mention the unnecessary burden she added to their woes.

If the disappearance of Jim Rourke and subsequent search had taken its toll on the family, then his murder, especially the manner in which it had been carried out, had all but destroyed them. His wife Stacey looked totally bewildered as she hugged her two children. Her overwrought eyes staring vacantly at the oak coffin, tears rolling freely down her cheeks. The children clung to their mother, their wide eyes frightened and uncertain as if knowing something big was up but not entirely comprehending the enormity of what was occurring.

It was his father Alan who seemed most affected of all. As with Stacey, his face was ashen with the notable exception of his excessively dark and puffy eyes, their stare also fixed on the coffin but in a resolute fashion, as if by staring at it hard enough, he could encourage his son to rise from within his oaken tomb and rejoin them in life. To Britney's eyes, he seemed to have become an old man overnight, a fact she regarded as further evidence of the devastating power of grief – his shattered appearance reminding her of the stark deterioration of Lyons, which seemed to rapidly accelerate in the short time she knew him. Vera sat next to her husband but slightly aloof, as if the ordeal had severed a bond that might never be restored.

Seeing the family like this, her heart very nearly broke for them. The pain they were suffering was clearly overwhelming. Understandably so. She couldn't help but wonder how much she had contributed to it with her unfounded accusations. Quite a lot, her guilty conscience forced her to admit. In mitigation of that guilt, she reminded herself that she had been a key player in unearthing and finally stopping the real culprit, thereby clearing Jim Rourke's name. Still, it was scant comfort to her now as she sat beholding their collective and overwhelming grief, knowing that once the service was over, she would have to face them. To sympathise, of course, but also to apologise. It was the reason she had taken time out of their search. Joe too.

When the priest finished the ceremony, Alan rose and approached the altar to say a few words on behalf of the family. Strained and emotional, he kept it brief, simply thanking wider family and friends for their support and anyone else that had helped them through this toughest of times. He gave a brief but moving homily for Jim, describing him as a loving son, husband, and father, a saint of a boy who had grown up to be a hard-working family man. "He didn't deserve what they did to him," he stated. Britney noted the use of the word 'they' and wondered if he was blaming his son's death on the Gardaí in general rather than Lyons, acting as a rogue member.

Finally, Alan Rourke asked that, once the dust had settled on this saddest of sagas and everyone's lives had returned to normality, please continue to support Stacey and her two children, Cathy and Zac.

"They will need your support then more than ever," he stated from behind the lectern. "A family without a father figure is a boat without a keel. Please look out for them," he begged tearfully. "They are the most innocent of victims in all of this."

Glancing around her as he finished, Britney noted there wasn't a dry eye in the house, including those of Joe who sat next to her. Directly in front of her, several women were openly crying, while to her left a father reached out a protective hand to pull his young son close. Perhaps it was the emotion of the occasion or perhaps it was the stuffiness caused by such a large crowd, but suddenly Britney felt sick to her stomach and actually had to get up and sidle past Joe to get out for fresh air. Once outside, she pushed her way through the mourners until she reached the street where she took a moment to settle herself, breathing slowly as she leaned against the church railing.

"You ok?" Joe asked having followed out behind her. Close up she looked worryingly pale.

"I'll be fine," she replied. "The crowd just got the better of me."

"It's emotional in there," Joe admitted. "The father spoke really well." He gave a rueful shake of his head. "If it was my son or daughter, I don't know how I would have handled it."

"You have children?" Britney asked in surprise. Family hadn't been part of his cover story.

"Yes. A boy and a girl. Teenagers. If something like that happened to one of them, I'd die. Or kill the bastard."

"Not if he killed himself first," Britney pointed out. Lyons was as close to dead as he could come without his heart actually stopping. Though the official line was shot in the course of duty, Britney believed Lyons' heroic act had a selfish undertone. He had been prepared to die. Welcomed it.

"True. Don't think I could get up there and be quite as dignified though. Not if it was my child."

Britney looked at him sharply as something familiar tugged at her memory. The phrase Lyons had used. *It was his child.* When he said it, she'd thought it strange but had dismissed it as the cryptic ramblings of a dying man. Now a nagging doubt punched its way into her subconscious.

"Did I say something wrong?" Joe asked, looking at her quizzically.

"Nah, its nothing," Britney replied, though in reality, it bothered her like a thorn. Try as she might, she couldn't put her finger on why, so she shoved it aside.

"What do you think he meant by, 'they'?" she asked then. "When he said he didn't deserve what they did to him. Do you think he was referring to us? The cops? Me, in particular?"

"For accusing him, you mean?"

"Yes. And not focusing on the real killer."

"Probably, but you can't blame him. It was his child, after all. And you accused him on live television."

There it was again, that little thorn. *It was his child.*

"Don't remind me," Britney winced at the memory. "I have nightmares about that still." She shook her head. "I was so sure it was all centred around Jim Rourke. So sure. Next time I'll just keep my mouth shut."

Joe smiled at the idea of that. "I don't think that's possible, Brit. Anyway, look on the bright side. You were right about Flynn, and you were right about Richie Lyons. As the song goes, two out of three ain't bad. So, don't be so hard on yourself. We all make mistakes."

Just then, the mourners started to spill out of the church and gather out on the street. Soon the coffin appeared. Brian Farrell was amongst the pallbearers, which included close friends and relatives. Following on closely were the grieving family. Stacey Rourke was hunched over and sobbing as she robotically placed one foot in front of the other, her children clinging to her coat, looking up at her every now and then as if to reassure themselves she was ok. That they were ok. Alan Rourke walked beside them, his expression a dark cloud, his jaw set and his eyes focused, the epitome of a man determined not to give way to his emotions. 'So stoic,' Britney thought as she watched him. Old school. Just like Lyons. That generation kept it all locked up inside. His head bowed, Timmy Dunne followed a few steps behind. On this occasion, and despite the attraction of a heavy media presence, Britney saw no sign of Ade Fagan. Clearly, he was lying low.

"They are all devastated, Brit," Joe observed. "I really don't think we should be here. At least wait until things have settled down before we approach them."

Britney nodded in agreement. Swayed by her own guilt she had judged it wrong. Now wasn't the time. It would only serve to upset them all the more. Better to wait a week or two and then call to see them in private. Perhaps things wouldn't be quite as raw then.

With the funeral cortege now reaching the waiting hearse, the pallbearers slowly lowered the coffin from their shoulders to ease it into the rear of the vehicle. Several cameramen pushed through the crowd angling for the front-page shot, their cameras held high above their heads. One of the bolder vultures had perched himself on the boundary wall, balancing himself against the church railing while snapping shot after shot of the coffin, the family, the pain.

"People just can't get enough of morbid, can they?" Britney observed. "Thank God we placed Gardaí at the funeral home or there would be images of Jim Rourke's dead body all over the Sunday papers. I can imagine the headline. 'The Courier's Latest Delivery' or similar tripe."

"I know," agreed Joe. "I was at the rosary last night and hundreds of people turned up. It took hours for them to filter through the parlour because every damn one of them had to get a look inside the coffin." He shrugged. "But then, deep down we're all voyeurs, aren't we? I'd probably be looking too only I already know what ligature marks look like."

"But they were covered with a scarf of some sort, surely?"

"Of course, but that doesn't stop people from imagining what's underneath. Might even make it better. Either way, our warped curiosity always compels us to look inside the damn box," he paused as Britney suddenly leaned back against the railing, grasping one of the iron bars as she tried to steady herself. *It's not what you see. It's what you don't see.* Turning deathly pale her eyes now turned to stare in the direction of the mourners as the hearse carried the coffin away from the church.

"Are you sure you're ok?" Joe asked, in a concerned tone.

Britney slowly nodded, then looked at him with what he could only describe as a dawning of horror in her eyes. "He didn't though," she said, almost to herself.

"He didn't what?"

"It was his child, don't you see? Lyons was trying to tell me."

"Tell you what, Britney?"

Scrambling through her own thoughts, she didn't seem to hear him.

"And that's why he didn't look inside the damn box." She hurried to root her phone out of her pocket and call Triona. After a brief exchange of words, she hung up and made a dash for the car. "We've got to get back to the station."

"Why?" Joe called as he pushed through disgruntled mourners to follow her. "And what do you mean about not looking inside a box?"

With the car abandoned in the only parking space they could find – a school gate over two hundred yards away, it was quite a dash. Despite not feeling the best, Britney reached it first. Joe was out of breath by the time he caught up.

"For God's sake why the sudden rush?"

"Because we can't arrest him without proof," she replied as he hopped into the passenger seat. "Not after the mess I've made."

"Arrest who?" Joe wheezed as he got behind the wheel.

"The real Courier. Don't you see? Richie Lyons was right all along. This was never about sex trafficking or corrupt Gardaí. It was about corruption in the HAI. But I was right too. It was about Jim Rourke. Only not in the way I first thought." She shook her head in dismay. "It was about the injury. The damn knee bandage! Christ, it was staring me in the face from the very beginning. He was staring us in the face. Taunting us all along. That was the reason for those newspapers. To highlight all he'd missed. Oh, it's so clever when you think about it. So sick, but so clever. And tying the body with that nylon string was so damn devious. Marie Cox's hair too. Don't you see? By pointing the finger at his colleague, he wasn't just trying to buy time but was pointing a finger at the grassroots of the organisation. The people like himself that stood back and did nothing."

"The HAI?" Joe asked breathlessly, while struggling to manoeuvre the car past groups of mourners.

"Exactly." Britney ran her hands over her face in frustration. "Alan Rourke told me about Timmy Dunne's son getting hurt. That's why his wife left him, he said, and I just took it as a throwaway comment. But how did he make it look like murder?" As she asked herself that, a further thought struck her. She picked up the phone once more and made another call. "Put me through to the coroner who carried out the autopsies, please. And quick. This is a matter of life and death." She glanced at Joe who, after the sudden dash, was sweating heavily in the heat of the car.

"What was it the Garda on duty at the scene said about Jim Rourke's body?"

"He was posed like a saint," Joe replied.

"Yes. A saint of a boy. But he also remarked that when he helped cut down the body it felt really cold, right? It was in the case notes."

Joe nodded. "Yes, I spoke to him myself. He said the body was so stiff and cold that it felt frozen." He changed gears then picked up speed. Having cleared the crowd, he was finding some freedom at last on the Oldcastle streets.

"But Triona checked the weather for that night. It was chilly, but far from freezing. So why would the body be that cold?"

Just then a male voice came on the line, drawing Britney's attention to the phone in her hand. She quickly outlined to whoever was listening exactly what Joe and herself had just discussed then explained what she needed.

"The coroner is checking his file," Britney informed Joe, then paused to listen closely as the coroner came back on the line and confirmed what he had found. Britney thanked him before passing the information onto Joe. "Jim Rourke suffered a kneecapping just like the rest of them. But, years ago. The coroner also found faded bite marks on his left side and evidence of multiple historical fractures in his nose."

"Fighting?"

Britney nodded. "His wife alluded to it. Said he used to get a lot of abuse over hurling." She returned her attention to the phone. "And could you confirm that the nylon string we found is the type used for fishing?" Again, she waited a few moments for an answer. "And I'm right in saying Ketamine is a sedative? Could be used to pacify a drug addict, perhaps?" Another nod. Finally, she asked the coroner if he could explain the low body temperature. On receiving her answer, she thanked him and hung up.

"Bingo," she declared, but without any sense of elation. "They found cell breakage. On both Jim Rourke and to a lesser extent on Doctor Carmody. It can happen when a body is frozen then thawed. It seems the blood cells rupture and leak what's called intracellular fluid." As she finished explaining, she cursed to herself. "The coroner had informed Flynn about his findings, but he never followed up on it."

"Never informed me either but why doesn't that surprise me?" Joe asked sarcastically. "So, what does it mean? And what's it got to do with The Courier? I mean, isn't Lyons The Courier?"

Britney shook her head as she stuffed her phone back in her pocket. "Lyons was only a demented father trying to save his adopted child from the addiction that was killing her," she stated. "I think Ade Fagan knew the truth all along. And that's why Wilson insisted on a vow of silence."

"Why?"

She met Joe's questioning look. "Because The Courier is still out there. And Ade Fagan is terrified."

Chapter 20

Hours had passed since the room had stopped moving, at least to the best of David Fagan's calculations. But, in reality, it could have been days. Between the drug, the darkness, and the waves of terror, he had completely lost track of time. Of direction. Of reality.

All he knew was he was lying face down in the dark and he was freezing cold. His hands were tied behind his back with some sort of flex or cable that cut deep into his wrists. The same cable ran down his back to secure his ankles then ran up to his neck where he felt it wrapped around his collar like a noose.

All the while he shivered uncontrollably; the terrible cold of the place having wormed itself so deep into his bones that his body already felt halfway to rigor mortis. He doubted he could move his limbs even if he wanted to and moving was the last thing that crossed his mind. Just lying there and waiting to die was fast becoming a welcome alternative. He had no idea where he had been taken, or even if the journey was at an end, but prayed he hadn't left the country. Because then his father might still find him and save him from this monster. And then it would be the monsters turn to shit himself. Literally. As David had.

It seemed like a lifetime ago when he had been sitting in his favourite restaurant with his girlfriend wondering if tonight was to be the night she would finally put out. God knows, he had pampered her enough. Put enough time into her to have the right to insert what he really wanted. He'd felt himself stir at the prospect when the waiter had ruined his thoughts with an urgent message from his father to meet him outside. It had been a hoax, of course, and here he was now, squelching in his own shite. But why?

That waiter had yet to reappear. David still tried to think of him as the waiter even though he suspected he was far from that. Not least because he found the man's face vaguely familiar. But thinking of him in any other way only served to make his blood run cold.

Which it did when the door suddenly opened with a loud metal thud and a broad beam of light shot into the room, illuminating the area where he lay. It was an erratic light, shifting back and forth as it came closer, and somewhere in David's foggy mind, it registered as that of a hand-held torch. He tried to focus on it, but his eyes had grown so accustomed to the dark that they stung from the glare. He was desperate to rub them, but his hands remained firmly tied behind his back. Blinking rapidly, he willed his vision to adjust.

"Who are you?" he called, unable to hide the fear in his voice as he strained to see through the gloom. He regretted the question almost immediately for the torch-bearer shone the light directly into his eyes, causing them to sting even more painfully than before. He fought against turning his face away.

"I'm your worst nightmare," came the taunting reply, "or should I say, your father's worst nightmare?"

'There it is,' David thought. 'This is about my father. Not me. Dear God, I did nothing wrong. Help me,' he silently pleaded.

The torch moved closer.

"You stink," the man asserted. "Just like I knew you would. Just like the rest of them did. But your stink is worse. Far worse. I guess the more corrupt the man, the stinkier his shit, eh? Perhaps it's because of all that rich food you devour."

Squinting, David's eyes stung as they struggled to discern so much as his tormentor's outline.

"I'm sure you're wondering why you are here."

"Yes," David replied weakly. Wherever here is.

"You're here to pay for your father's sins," the man replied. "Of which, I'm sure you are aware, there are many. But only one concerns me."

In the silence that followed, the man shone the torch across the room, drawing David's eyes towards a long rectangular box. On top of the box was placed a rather nasty looking electrical gadget next to a coil of electrical cable. The man slowly drew the beam across the lid of the box until it came to a set of industrial knives, their blades glinting in the torchlight. On these he allowed the light to linger before moving it another yard to the right where a tripod stood supporting a large video camera. For some reason, this frightened David even more than the other items.

"What's that for?" he whimpered.

"For posterity," the man replied coolly.

"Posterity?" David mouthed. A relatively benign word but delivered in a tone that made it anything but. "If it's money you want, I can pay you," he offered desperately. "Just tell me how much and I will have it arranged."

"I don't want your money. And I certainly don't want your father's money. It's only stolen money anyway. Siphoned from the ignorant. From naïve gobshites like me who all our lives have blindly believed in people like him. So, you can keep your ill-gotten gains. I have no interest in taking that from you. But what I have an interest in taking is your dignity. And in doing that, I intend to see you suffer. And for your father to see you suffer."

As he spoke, the man rummaged in his pocket then held a mobile phone out in front of the light. David immediately recognised it as his own gold-plated iPhone Pro.

"I know what you're thinking," the man said. "They'll track your phone. But I'll change the sim and that should confuse them for a while. Oh, I know they can still track it, but I'll have it turned off soon enough and then they'll be just like you. Fumbling around in the dark. So, while we're waiting for them to catch on, we're going to play a little game," the man informed him. "A little role reversal. We are going to contact your father and we are going to let him hear you scream."

The man dialled the number and in the silence the phone ringing sounded like a bell tolling in David's ears. A moment later he heard his father's voice.

"David?" Its tone remained authoritative still, but now contained an underlying hint of uncertainty. Of fear.

"No, not David," the man replied. "Although David is here. Right beside me. We have been making friends."

"David?" Ade Fagan called. "Are you ok?"

"Help me, Dad," David called in return. "He's going to kill me."

"Now, now," the man intervened, "let's not get ahead of ourselves. And let's try and be civil."

"You bastard," Ade replied. "You let my son go or I'll…"

"You'll what?" the man cut in. "Get your friends in the police after me?" he sniggered. "Not much of a threat considering how long they have been trying to catch me. They're so inept they've even destroyed the legacy of one of their own, thinking it was me. No, the best thing you can do is what I tell you to do. Otherwise, the heir to your little ill-gotten fortune dies. And I promise, it won't be pretty."

There was silence for a moment and David could tell his father was trying to think of some angle or other like he always did. Some rule to bend. Some buttons to press. Some escape clause. David sensed there were none. Not with this man.

"Ok," Ade Fagan replied somewhat meekly, as his frantic mind unwillingly came to the same conclusion. "What do you want from me?"

"By now you will have guessed why your son is here. You will also have guessed who I am?"

"Yes." It wasn't lost on the man that Fagan sounded defeated on the other end of the line.

"So, you remember then?"

"Yes."

"Oh, I don't mean our recent meeting. I mean from before."

"I remember."

"I don't believe you do. Not really. A man like you would have no reason to remember a nobody like me. Not after such a brief encounter. But you will remember. And you will remember my son. Forever."

"Tell me. Please. What can I do to stop this? To make it right."

"You can never make it right. But you just might save your son. Whatever will be left of him."

With that, the man calmly set the torch down. His voice took on the tone of a teacher divulging precious knowledge. That of an educator. An enlightener perhaps.

"You know a hurley stick swung in anger travels at approximately sixty miles an hour, imparting almost three tons of force on impact. Quite a lot of force, don't you think, when applied to the relatively fragile mass of flesh and bone that surrounds say...a kneecap?"

No sooner was the word said than David felt strong hands grip his leg and force it into a straight position.

"No," David pleaded, suddenly realising what was about to happen. "Please God no!"

"Please," Ade reiterated on hearing the terror in his son's voice. "I didn't mean your son harm. It was just the way things were done back then."

"Funny," the man replied, "that's exactly what Dunford said. Only he blamed it on following orders. Your orders."

David imagined the man shake his head in exasperation.

"Well, this is the way things are done now. And I'm just following orders. My orders."

David tensed as he felt one of the man's hands grip his upper leg tightly, pinning it to the floor. Then in the half-light offered by the torch, David saw some sort of cudgel shoot upwards and hang in the air for a moment before it came hurtling down at terrific speed, directed towards David's left kneecap. Almost instantly tremendous pain shot through him and somewhere in a distant place, he heard himself scream. A moment later, he passed out. As he did, he saw the image replay in his head and realised he'd just been struck by a hurley.

Ade Fagan heard the scream too. Clear and vibrant and so full of pain that it threatened to bring tears to his eyes. "Please," he begged, "not my son."

"Not your son, but mine, eh?" the man replied with a sneer. "Because yours is so special? Mine was a piece of dirt?" His sigh was followed by a long silence. "No response? Ok... If you want to see your son again you will carry on as normal. You will go to the game on Sunday, and you will accept all the adulation those brainwashed clowns watching will throw at you. You will be every bit the president they have come to know. Then you will make a choice. The ultimate choice. You or your son."

With that, he left the sanctuary of the room. Keeping close to the other vehicles he ventured out from his latest hiding place and into the square known as The March. He took a moment to look back at the castle's grounds. With golden leaves flitting on the breeze, he could imagine the perfect ending. The crowds, the colour, the high spirits fading into shocked disbelief. If truth were told, it wouldn't be the first hanging overlooking the great square. He was sure that, rightly or wrongly, plenty of other men had died there over the years. An ancient building like the castle didn't navigate its way through history as an innocent bystander. Power, greed, corruption would all have found a foothold within its walls leading to tyranny, treachery, and, undoubtedly, murder. Yes, the place had history. Tons of history. That's what made it perfect for his purpose. Better still, the Gardaí would see it that way too. At least the girl would. Eventually.

****

Not long after making his way home, Timmy Dunne was out the back of the house when the two Gardaí came looking for him. He immediately recognised the female Garda as the one who had called previously. The older man he had spotted with her at the funeral. When he saw them march around the corner of the house, he knew why they had come. In truth, he'd known it would be only a matter of time.

"Not at the meal, Timmy?" Britney asked as she slowly approached. She noted he was wearing the same long coat he had worn in the photograph she had spotted in Alan Rourke's house. Bound at the waist by a blue and white cord. "I thought everyone at the funeral was invited back to the hotel for dinner. And I thought with you being such a close friend of the family, you'd take pride of place."

Timmy shook his head. "Not my scene," he shrugged evasively. "Prefer to keep myself to myself."

"I understand," Britney replied with a slow nod. She glanced around, then looked in the direction of the hut where he had been working the last time she called. "No fish to be gutted today?" she observed.

"No."

"Had your fill of killing things, then?" she enquired, and understood when Timmy nodded in reply.

"I'll never want to see blood again."

Britney moved closer but kept her eyes on him all the while as she tried to get a sense of the mental state the man was in. She didn't think he would be any danger to her, but she had learnt the hard way that trust given too easily only invited a knife in the back. She halted a few feet away from him, making sure to keep herself between him and the exit from the haggard. The last thing she wanted now was for him to think they were going to arrest him on the spot. He might panic and make a run for it.

"Remember when I was here before?" Britney began evenly. Dunne nodded warily. "Well, I meant to ask you about something. Alan Rourke told me your son had an accident a while back and your wife left you because of it?"

"Did he now?" Dunne's expression turned as dark as the shadows lingering in the haggard.

"Do you mind telling me the nature of the accident?"

He looked away, clearly struggling with the memory the question evoked. "We were fishing, and the boat tipped," he finally declared. "Hit his head off the gunwale. Left him paralysed for life, not that it's any of your business."

"But it is, because that's why you hated Jim Rourke, wasn't it? He was with you then but survived unscathed while your son's life was ruined. Any dreams of a hurling career shattered. You hated Jim Rourke because you believed he flippantly threw away the kind of career your own son could only dream about. Probably had dreamt about every day before he got hurt. As you had."

Dunne shrugged indifferently but the cloud descending over his eyes gave him away.

"But when you realised the truth, you did your best to cover for your friend, didn't you?"

Again, he shrugged.

"How long have you known, Timmy?" she asked in her friendliest tone. In a way, this was the crunch question where Timmy was concerned. How much had he covered up?

Timmy stood staring dumbly at her for a moment as if he didn't understand what she was asking, then glanced warily at Joe and back again. He was clearly frightened, but stubbornly maintaining a brave face. To hide his guilty conscience?

"He's not worth protecting, Timmy," she pointed out, as gently as she could. "And we're not here to cause you any trouble. But he would have. If we hadn't discovered the truth, he planned on leaving the blame at your door because of how you openly criticised his son. So, please tell me. How long have you known?"

With that, Timmy's body language visibly changed. His shoulders slumped and his hard, defensive expression softened. "Since young Jim was found," he replied. "I wondered before then but after that, I knew for certain. That reporter had interviewed us, you see, last year when we reached the Club All-Ireland. That twigged with me. And, of course, he knew Cullen. But as I say, when I heard about the way Jim was tied up, I knew for sure."

"The fishing gut?" Britney asked.

"Yes. And the way the body was posed – like a saint, one of the papers said. Not cut up like the others," he gave a slow shake of his head. "I didn't say anything because I thought it was over. And…"

"And he's your friend," Britney finished. "That's why you didn't go to the hotel after the funeral, isn't it? You couldn't face him. Not after realising what he'd done."

Timmy nodded. "I still can't believe it," he proclaimed as the tears that had welled in his eyes started to leak onto his weathered cheeks.

Britney sighed. "Nor can I, Timmy," she replied in consolation. "Even though I know it to be true. What I don't know is why. Do you?"

Timmy looked at her as if she had just asked the most ridiculous question. "Because Jim wasn't murdered," he replied, his eyebrows raised. "He hanged himself. That's why he was missing all this time. And Alan blamed the HAI for it."

"And that's why Alan hanged his victims. To replicate his son's suicide. But why blame them? What exactly did the people he targeted do to his son?"

Timmy shook his head. "I'm not sure. Jim was always hard to handle. Could have been a great hurler but didn't have the discipline. Drinking and clowning around. And he only trained when he felt like it. Always claiming to be injured. No one in the club could talk to him. To be honest, I think Alan was always embarrassed by his carry on."

"But he did get a serious injury, didn't he?" Britney pointed out. "Kneecapped." Clearly this had a critical part to play. Timmy didn't seem to think so.

"I'm not sure it was quite that bad," he replied dismissively. "Anyway, that was years ago, and everyone knew it was only an excuse. Even Alan thought so. But when Jim went missing, Alan changed. He started bashing the HAI like Jim used to. Constantly harping on about their corruption, even while he was looking after the pitch. Saying it was full of self-serving pricks who lied through their teeth. I never heard him talk like that before. And I'd never heard him curse."

Britney nodded as she digested what they had been told. At last the picture was becoming clearer. "Thanks Timmy," Britney replied sincerely, genuinely grateful for his help so far. But right then, there was a more pressing question. "Now we need to know where he is. Can you tell us? Can you tell us where Alan Rourke is?"

"Isn't he at the dinner?" Timmy asked, with a frown.

Joe shook his head. "We checked. His wife said he left soon after the burial. Had been coming and going like that since Jim disappeared. And now another man is missing, so we need to find him and quick."

Timmy didn't look surprised. "Ade Fagan?" he asked. "Alan really hated him."

"No," Britney replied, deciding she was sick of all the secrecy. "His son."

Timmy gave a slow nod. "An eye for an eye." He sighed. "If he's not at the dinner I don't know where he is. Have you checked his house?"

"Yes. There's no one home. Is there anywhere else he would go? A warehouse or store? Somewhere he might have access to a large freezer?"

Once more Timmy looked at her as if she were stupid. "He doesn't need a warehouse," he explained as if it was the most obvious thing in the world. "He has his own freezer. It's in the back of his truck."

"Shit," cursed Britney, as she wondered how she could have been so stupid.

"That's how Rourke got Cullen into the dressing rooms." She turned to Joe as she put the sequence together in her head. "He killed him earlier, having already cut off his hand then using the truck, he transported the body to the hurling field and stored him in the changing room for later. Along with the sheet of bloodied newspaper and a lawnmower belt. Probably wrapped the stump in plastic so it wouldn't leak blood all over the place. Then drove home."

"Perhaps that's when he killed Marie Cox too," Joe suggested. "At home in the back of his truck. The timing would work."

"Very likely," Britney agreed. "Then claiming he was running late, he called Timmy here for a lift to ensure they arrived together. When they got to the field and cleaned the changing rooms, Rourke made sure he cleaned the one with Cullen's body in it. Then later when he made the excuse of going to the shed to get the belt for the lawn-mower, which he had no doubt earlier sabotaged, he simply had to transfer the body over via the internal hallway, hoist it up, remove the plastic from the stump, pocket it and stage the scene for Timmy to find. Using the back door, the building itself kept him hidden from view and when he arrived back with the replacement belt in hand, Timmy was none the wiser."

Timmy nodded. "That's the way I figure it. I think he broke the window in advance to divert suspicion then used me as his alibi. And that truck as his personal abattoir."

'And that's how he transported the bodies,' Britney added in her head. 'No one would have considered the presence of a delivery truck suspicious.' Britney scowled. She had seen that truck on visiting Rourke's house but thought no more of it. Never in her wildest dreams would she have thought he was using it to facilitate torture and murder. All done in the presence of a witness. His dead son.

She turned to face Joe. "The delivery truck he drives for a living," she exclaimed, "is a food delivery truck. It has a bloody freezer in it. Literally bloody. That's what we need to find."

Joe quickly pulled his phone out of his pocket and called the station.

Britney glanced at Timmy. "There's a name on the truck. The name of the company he works for. Quickly, what is it?"

"Quinn," Timmy replied. "He works for Quinn Foods."

With that, Britney headed for the car. The search for The Courier was no longer an investigation, it was a manhunt. And with darkness closing in, he had the advantage. For now. But tomorrow the sun would rise, and the hunt would begin in earnest.

****

He was on the home stretch, at last. The final night had passed without incident and now, with his preparations made, he could breathe more freely.

From where he stood in the VIP box, Alan Rourke watched Sunday morning's dawn break over the stand at Fenian Park. Observing the dark canvas of the night slowly give way to the blended shades of grey, purple, and orange was like watching the meticulous creation of a priceless work of art, performed by a master painter at the height of his powers. As further light seeped into the morning, the orange and purple hues turned to softer shades of pink and red, the grey bleaching to a dubious looking white. An oil painting of a morning to herald his day of reckoning. He smiled to himself. If Timmy or any of the rest of his peers could overhear his silent ramblings, they would think him in need of an exorcism.

All his life he had kept his thoughts to himself. Kept his imaginings in his head and did what was expected of him. Waived any venture into a descriptive vocabulary for the banal language of the everyday, the every man. In short, he'd kept his head down and did what he was told. Even when his instincts told him it was wrong. As a boy he had obeyed his father's wishes without question, did his chores, his schoolwork, his duty. As a young man, he had enrolled as an electrical apprentice with a local builder, a position arranged for him by his father. A man with a trade is a man with a passport for life, his father had told him. Alan had accepted the position without question. Even though he had loftier dreams in his head.

When the economy collapsed in 2008, he was out of work for two years. Still, he never drew the dole. Never asked for a handout. When the job as a delivery driver came along, he grabbed it with both hands and worked like he had all his life. Hard and without complaint. He put food on the table and paid his bills. He supported his family, his church, his local HAI club. All without question. And all the while keeping his thoughts to himself. He knew what people thought of him and that was why he had gotten this far undetected on his path for revenge. Who would have thought that such a simple, semi-educated but hard-working man, who all his life had toed the line, would suddenly buck and kill all those people?

But now as he watched the dawn break, he would appreciate his own thoughts. He would embrace them. Let them flourish. He was more than just a simple man. He was a 'yes man' no longer.

Soon the groundskeepers would come. And not long after that the officials would start gathering. Then the teams and the crowds and finally, the 'great man' himself. None of them would suspect he'd been there and gone. Or guess at the preparations he'd made.

God willing, they would be enough.

****

Stale body odour scarcely disguised by hurriedly applied perfumes and aftershaves merged with the smell of burnt coffee as the small team of investigators gathered in the incident room that Sunday morning. The evidence of baggy eyes and thin lips portrayed how each and every one of them had spent the night troubled by the mounting pressure. With all that had happened, Oldcastle Garda Station was the focus of national headlines and IA were like dragons breathing down their necks. They all knew there was only one way to rebuild the station's reputation. Find David Fagan. And find him alive.

"He simply puts on a uniform that loosely resembles that of a waiter," Britney observed, "then strolls into the restaurant unchallenged. A few minutes later strolls right back out again with David Fagan in tow, like the pied piper leading an enthralled child." She sounded every bit as frustrated as she felt. It was well into Sunday morning and despite a nationwide alert there was still no sign of the missing truck. No clue as to where Alan Rourke had taken David Fagan.

"It seems that way," agreed Garda Maguire, who had taken charge of collating any available video footage from David Fagan's abduction. Any earlier doubts Britney may have had concerning her loyalties had been dispelled by Triona's assertion that she had never pinpointed the warehouse. Fiona had simply used her as a pawn in the setup. For her part, Triona made it clear she took no sides in anything apart from that of the data. "The data never lied," she stated while looking reproachfully out over the rim of her spectacles.

"I don't see any gun or other means of coercion. He must have duped Fagan in some way to get him out into the carpark then doped him with something like chloroform and bundled him into a car like he did with the doctor."

"Did we get a view of the car?" Joe asked from where he stood behind Maguire. "A number plate?"

"Nope. The lens was broken on the only camera behind the restaurant. I'm guessing Rourke busted it when he smashed the outside lights."

"It wouldn't matter anyway," Britney said. "The car will prove to be untraceable like the one he used at the doctors' clinic. If we ever find it, that is."

"He's certainly a cool one," Joe observed. "Just waltzing in and abducting people in plain sight. Not even a disguise this time. He has nothing left to lose, I guess."

"That's what makes him so dangerous," Britney pointed out. "He's not afraid of being caught anymore, so he can focus completely on his mission. Ok," Britney said as she turned away from the computer. Even though he was her superior in rank, Joe didn't mind stepping back and letting Britney take the lead. In his mind, she had well-earned it over the last few weeks. "This is our suspect," she said as she held up a printout of Alan Rourke's face in front of the small team which had gathered in the incident room. "His name is Alan Rourke. He is sixty-seven years of age and is married to Vera. They had one son, an only child, and their son is what this is all about."

Ben Youngs at the back of the room caught her attention by shifting in his seat. "He killed him, right?" he said as he looked up at her. "Hanged him like he hanged the rest of them?"

Due to the recent upheaval and subsequent suspension while under investigation of any personnel linked to Flynn, Ben Youngs could almost call himself a senior Garda now, at least if measured by time served at the station.

"No. Not right," Britney replied.

"But I read the autopsy," Ben argued. "It said Jim Rourke died of cerebral hypoxia as a result of hanging. Which is how he was found."

"True. But Jim Rourke killed himself. He hanged himself from the gate of the local HAI field. His father, our suspect, happened to be the one who found him."

"But he couldn't have killed himself surely," Ben replied while glancing around at the others for support. "He was tied up in a way that made that impossible. And I thought it was the builder who found him?"

"On the face of it, suicide looked impossible and that's exactly what I initially thought," Joe explained patiently. "That's what we were meant to think. Murder had to be the cause of death. But the thing is, the builder found him the second time around when his father wanted him to be found. In fact, Jim Rourke had hanged himself weeks before that. It was actually his suicide that kicked off this killing spree."

"Exactly," Britney said. "We think Alan Rourke found his son's body one morning when he went to the hurling field to carry out his maintenance work. The reason Jim Rourke killed himself is not exactly clear yet, but we do believe that Alan Rourke held certain members of the HAI responsible. Anyway, we're guessing that soon after finding the body, Alan Rourke cut it down and placed it in the back of his truck, probably with the relatively innocent intention of taking his dead son's body home. Perhaps to in some way cover up the fact that he had committed suicide. From what I gather, Alan is a fairly religious man, so would have considered his son's suicide a mortal sin. Perhaps the worst sin." She shrugged. "Who knows the real reason but somewhere along the line, this new and far from innocent plan, formed in his mind."

"Isn't that a little farfetched?" Ben asked. "I mean to cover up a suicide by killing five innocent people."

"Not so innocent," corrected Joe, "at least not in Alan Rourke's eyes. He believed they were the cause of his son's woes which, in turn, led him to kill himself. And you have to understand what Britney just explained about Alan Rourke. He is a devout Catholic. The type who would say the rosary every night before going to bed. It's likely that being crushed with grief, he couldn't deal with the shame of his son's suicide as well."

"So, he decided to cover it up," Garda Maguire ruminated from her seat in front of the computer. "And take revenge on his son's tormenters at the same time. On that note, I found some vile stuff online. Abuse aimed at Jim Rourke going way back. I don't think the HAI is as perfect as people think it is." She continued to fill Britney in on what else she had found.

"But why not just bury the body?" Ben asked once she had finished, clearly determined to get at least one point on the board. Britney admired his resolve, even if it was misdirected. And though she was growing a little impatient with his questions, she had to admit the fact that he was cute swayed her a little. "I mean, he could still have killed the others."

"True," said Joe. "But you're looking at it with the unencumbered perspective of youth. I'm presuming you don't have any children?"

"No," Ben admitted.

Joe nodded. "You see if you did, you wouldn't have to ask that question. The body had to be found simply because it was the only way he could give his son's wife and children closure. His own wife too. The fact that their loved one was dead and gone was bad enough but imagine the added pain of not knowing where he was. Or what had happened to him. If he was alive or dead, run away or hurt somewhere. And not knowing indefinitely.

"And when you think about it," Joe continued, "if his family had discovered that Jim Rourke had killed himself, the torment would be every bit as bad. His wife would forever question herself as to why he did it and probably blame herself for not being attentive, supportive, or loving enough while his kids would grow up believing they were unloved by their father. That he didn't think they were good enough to live for."

"So, he decided to cover up his son's suicide as murder," Ben acquiesced finally with a slow nod of his head. "And he used the truck to store the body."

"Exactly," Britney stated as patiently as she could. "And to preserve his son's body. It gave him the time he needed to set his plan in motion and lay the blame for his son's death at the door of the HAI. He used it for the other murders too and relied on the freezer to distort the timeline of his kills. Now he's using it to keep David Fagan captive." 'At least that's what we hope,' she added in her head then paused and cast an anxious look at Garda Maguire. "Any trace on the phone?"

Triona Maguire shook her frizzy head. "Not yet. When we tracked it earlier, it was somewhere in the vicinity of the city, but it was switched off before we could pinpoint an exact location. Still, I believe if we find the phone, we find the truck."

"And we find David Fagan," Britney added. "What about the cars he used? His son's van?"

"Burnt out in the Brown mountains," Joe said. "When he found his son dead, he must have put him in the truck while he got rid of the van, somewhere nearby probably. Then came back for it later to get rid of it for good. As for the cars we've no idea where he got them but I'm thinking Timmy Dunne might have helped. But he's not admitting to anything."

"He won't, and I think we shouldn't push him. He's suffered enough." She glanced around at the rest of the team. "Ok, that's what we don't know. What we do know is that if we don't find David Fagan and find him soon, he will end up like all the others. I think it's clear The Courier has his sights set on the President of the HAI from the very beginning and he's using his son to get to him. Rourke's own son is dead, and if he blames the HAI President, he won't think twice about killing his son too."

"What's the President's stance on this? Is he still being a total asshole?" Joe asked.

"Yes. Totally uncooperative. Speaking only to the Commissioner and refusing to alter his weekend schedule. He'll be a sitting duck if he goes to Fenian Park today as planned."

On spotting the confused look in Triona's eyes, Joe turned to explain. "He's stepping down as HAI President, so they have a commemoration organised for him. Going to rename the grounds Fagan Stadium, seemingly. His ego refuses to cancel."

"Does he even give a damn about his son?" Ben asked incredulously.

"Only cares about his profile, as far as I can see," Joe responded. "And the power that goes with it."

"Makes me sick to the stomach, literally," Britney replied, noting the nausea was back. She glanced out the window to see the sun was rising toward midday. "Whatever the case, the commissioner has made it our job to protect him. And that means finding his son. And before this match kicks off. Anything at all on a possible location? It's not a bicycle he's using. He has to have hidden that truck somewhere."

"Nothing yet," Joe replied. "We've been through his finances and there's definitely no secondary mortgage. The bungalow is the only property registered in either Alan Rourke's or his wife Vera's name. Nothing for Jim Rourke either."

"What about a lease on a warehouse or other commercial space?" Britney asked Triona. "Maybe he had somewhere to hide the cars he used. And his son's van? Before they were discovered burnt out in the Brown mountains."

"Nope. The only standing order on any of their accounts is for electric while the biggest transaction we could find was for a holiday back in March. There are some weekly withdrawals, but they are only for insignificant amounts. Nothing that could possibly pay a mortgage or a lease. They live a meagre life."

"Was his wife any help?" Ben asked.

"Nope," Joe replied. "She was in a terrible state when we spoke to her after the funeral. Collapsed into a chair when we informed her about Alan. Told us she suspected something was wrong because he was gone all the time. Then when she both called and texted him early on the night her son was found, and he didn't answer, she couldn't help but wonder about it all. But was adamant she has no idea where he could be."

"Ok. If he has no secondary premises in his name, where could he be possibly holding David Fagan? Think, folks," she urged. "We're running out of time!"

"If he's not dead already?" Ben commented.

Britney shook her head. "I don't think so. This is about Ade Fagan, not his son. Whatever Rourke is planning, his intention is to cause Ade Fagan as much pain as possible."

"Torture his son, you mean! In that case, it has to be somewhere secure," Joe suggested. "Somewhere he won't be disturbed. But at the same time, he surely wants Ade Fagan to witness his work."

"And it's confirmed he's not holed up in Fenian Park?" Ben asked.

"Definitely not," Britney replied quickly. "We had a team of Gardaí sweep the stadium this morning and they came back with zilch. Apart from the groundskeepers preparing for the game, the stadium is empty. And before you ask, all the groundskeepers have been verified."

"Then what about a derelict house?" Ben offered, pursing his lips thoughtfully. "There's plenty of them in the city."

"It's a possibility," agreed Britney, recalling the properties which had been used off and on as brothels for the best part of two years with none of them the wiser. Apart from Halley, Flynn, and half the rest of the damn station, of course.

She glanced at Joe who had a dubious look on his face. "Too easy?"

Joe shook his head. "Not too easy," he replied quickly. "I just don't think it fits. He's been planning this for weeks so why hole up in a derelict house. Why not go straight to the grand finale? He has timed everything else to perfection. Controlled everything else. And just because a house is abandoned wouldn't guarantee privacy. Any neighbour who noticed unusual activity might easily report it, or the owner of the house could easily pay a random visit at any time. The presence of that truck alone would surely make it too risky."

"And?" Britney urged, sensing there was more.

"And I don't think an abandoned house would suit his needs. Or a warehouse either, for that matter. He's doing this to get attention, after all. To make a point. He needs a theatre, not some rundown hovel."

"Then he also needs a crowd," Ben pointed out. "What's a grand finale without spectators?"

Triona Maguire who had been fervently clicking keys paused to shove her glasses up on her nose. "I've just got a lock on David Fagan's phone," she said matter-of-factly. "It's somewhere in the vicinity of The March, accurate to within a hundred metres but I should be able to narrow that down significantly if the phone remains active."

"Shit," Britney suddenly exclaimed. "The Castle! I've seen Rourke deliver to the café there, so he'll know his way around. And with the match on, all the pubs nearby will be packed. The crowd will spill out onto the square right in front of it. All HAI supporters, making the perfect audience."

Joe nodded. It made sense. If David Fagan wasn't stashed at Fenian Park, then the castle was the next obvious choice. It was the city's most important building and main tourist attraction, drawing huge crowds to the city every year. There was a clear view from the castle onto the square called The March and vice versa, which meant any revellers would have front row seats for Alan Rourke's final act. And even if Ade Fagan weren't present to witness the act, phone cameras would ensure it would be all over the media. The internet. Gone viral in no time. There to torment the HAI President forever.

Even as Joe was running through it in his head, Britney had started out the door.

Before she got out of earshot Triona called after her. "I also meant to tell you. We got a call earlier from Commissioner Wilson. He's on the way down from Dublin as we speak to take over the operation."

"Great," Joe replied as he followed Britney out of the station. "That's all we need. A psycho on the loose and our strings being pulled by a damn pencil pusher."

Chapter 21

A cool breeze had picked up by the time they had reached the city-centre and with it, flurries of leaves carried across The March. Not many but enough to herald the beginning of the end. Broad and golden brown and being swept as they were from the trees to the rear of the castle, each one resembled a mini kite drifting down from the battlements. An uplifting sight on any other day, but today Britney could only find reason to groan. The leaves may have been sparse but there were people everywhere. Families, couples, strays, all merging into larger groups draped in tribal colours in the form of hats, flags and headbands. Some gathered outside the pubs, drinking, more wandering up the street towards the stadium, having already well-oiled their voice-boxes.

"Jesus!" Joe cursed as he waded into the buzzing crowd. "It's like the whole country is here. I knew the club final was a big draw, but do they all have to get pissed first?"

Glancing around Britney felt her heart sink. Not only was there a massive throng to work through but there were all sorts of vehicles parked along the streets, abandoned in gateways and down alleys. Even though the truck they were looking for was no small vehicle, it was going to take time to locate. And time was something they didn't have.

Worse still, if Rourke was to change his MO and stoop to using a bomb to make his point, they were facing carnage. With The March enclosed by high buildings on three of its four sides, Britney judged it would make a natural amplifier for any blast, first containing its force then directing it inward towards the area where the crowds gathered. Surveying the surrounding buildings, she judged that a bomb set off at the right time could kill dozens, if not hundreds.

She was tempted to call Wilson and ask for backup but quickly decided against it. This was personal for Rourke. A bomb would be too indiscriminate. Too detached. His MO suggested he preferred to look into the whites of the eyes of his victims. Needed to. Revenge wasn't complete unless he could taste their fear and watch the lifeforce drain out of them.

Just then her phone rang. Thinking it was Techie Triona calling with further info on David Fagan's cell phone, Britney quickly answered. To her dismay, it was a male who immediately announced himself as Commissioner Wilson. His was a gruff voice, one she'd only rarely heard and then mostly on television.

"Where the hell are you at, Garda Kent?" he barked, cutting straight to the chase.

"At the castle, sir. Triangulation of David Rourke's phone gave us this location. And with the crowds gathered outside the pubs, I think the area is primed for whatever he intends."

"But his target is in Fenian Park, Sergeant?"

"I know that, sir, but his son isn't. We did a thorough check. At the moment he's the priority."

"The President of the HAI is the priority," the Commissioner corrected. "I've placed a team of plainclothes inside the stadium in his close proximity. They are directly under my control. I don't want any interference. They alone deal with the President, meaning you're to stay well clear. Understand? We can't afford any further crossed wires on this!"

"Yes, sir."

"Now, Sergeant, apart from the phone signal, have you found any sign of David Fagan? In other words, can you give me any reason why I shouldn't drag you back here to patrol the outside of the stadium with all the other uniforms?"

'Apart from the fact that a young man's life hangs in the balance, sir, and we may be the only ones in a position to save him,' she was desperate to retort but somehow managed to bite her tongue.

"The castle itself. It's the showpiece of the city and with all the crowds around, it's perfect for a public execution. If you know your way around. And he does," she replied quickly. "That allied to the tracking on his phone, gives us good reason to believe he's stashed David Fagan somewhere close by. If he's not at the stadium, the castle and the area around it seem to be the most likely location for whatever he has in mind." She paused before stating what she considered the obvious. "Surely if we find his son, we're halfway to protecting Ade Fagan, sir?" The formal address sounded like it was dragged out of her. From what she'd heard so far, the Commissioner seemed only interested in saving face, and to her, that made him no better than the rest of them.

"Well then, you find him, Sergeant," the Commissioner barked. "And find him quick. First sign of that truck, you call me. Understand? Because if this blows up, it's on you."

The threat couldn't have been clearer, but Britney didn't care. The only objective that mattered right then was stopping Rourke from killing again.

"And one more thing, Sergeant Kent. This is a highly sensitive operation, meaning any intelligence uncovered relating to the HAI President is to be handed directly over my desk. And is for my eyes only. Is that clear?"

"Perfectly, sir." Again, she made little effort to hide the scorn in her tone. With that, she hung up the phone and catching up with her colleagues she filled them in.

"I guess we better find that truck then," Joe said.

"Yes. And I've been thinking about that. Rourke delivers to the café so there would have to be a parking space close by. Somewhere in the castle grounds." She took off running without waiting for an answer, pushing through the crowd without apology. Joe and Ben followed her lead until they stood together in front of the castle, staring up at the impressive walls of the massive structure. Britney had always considered the castle an astoundingly beautiful building but looking up at its grand façade now, the beauty of it failed to register. All she could see were the possibilities offered by the ramparts, the battlements, the towers themselves. All of them directly overlooking The

March and in their own way, offering the perfect stage for The Courier's objective. Rourke could stand on the ramparts and play out the final act of his twisted little play or he could climb the battlements and ransom David Fagan with the threat of a fifty-foot fall. The towers themselves were higher again, offering even greater opportunity. If it was a gallows Rourke was after, where better would serve his purpose? As these unsettling possibilities ran around in her head, Britney hurried into the castle' yard.

Seeing no immediate sign of the truck, Britney sprinted toward a massive doorway that she knew led into the castle proper.

On entering, Britney saw that the doorway led onto a great hall, with vaulted ceilings and double-height, stained-glass windows. The walls of the hall were at least three feet thick and were adorned with huge tapestries, ancient weapons, and suits of armour. It being a Sunday, the castle was buzzing with sightseers. They hung around in rucksack-clad groups or formed bored looking lines as they queued for the ticket kiosk. With so many distractions, it took Britney precious moments to locate a staff member who was free to assist. Eventually, she commandeered a young lady in a navy uniform who had just completed leading a tour and was in the process of expressing her gratitude to her group for their interest and attention during the previous hour.

"Has this man been here lately," Britney interjected while holding up the printout of Alan Rourke for her to see. Clearly not taking kindly to the interruption, the young woman shot her an irritated look but otherwise ignored her. Britney pulled out her Garda badge and shoved it in her face alongside the photo.

"Has this man been here?" she repeated in a tone that left no doubt but that she expected an answer. And quick.

"Every week," the girl replied, looking bemused. "He delivers food to the cafe."

"Was he here today?"

"This morning." She paused. "Which was strange, come to think of it. We don't take deliveries on a Sunday."

"Where does he park his truck?"

"Down the side. You should have seen it as you came in."

"We didn't. It's not there."

She frowned. "The only other place is the coachyard. But that's reserved for buses."

Britney caught Joe's anxious look. "I need you to take us there now."

The woman hesitated, glancing around the hall as if for support, clearly unsure how to proceed.

"NOW!" Britney's shout cut over the hum of the crowd, the crack of her voice splitting the air like a whip. A muffled silence fell in the hall as those present turned to see what the commotion was about.

The guide hesitated only a fraction longer then took off running. "This way," she called as she headed for a large double exit with Britney and the others hot on her heels. They exited the hall into a smaller chamber then out a backdoor and onto a narrow laneway. It led to a large, gravelled yard in which over a dozen tour buses were parked.

"Have these been here overnight?" Britney asked.

"Most of them. They buy weekend permits so even if they're not visiting the castle on any particular day, they still get to park here."

Britney nodded then took off running. Where better to hide a large vehicle than amongst even larger ones? And static ones at that. Taking the left side of the yard she passed off the buses one by one until she came to the very last parking space. There, nestled next to the high boundary wall and hidden by a large tour coach was the elusive truck.

"Over here," she called. Joe and Ben who had been focusing on other sections of the yard, quickly joined her. Together, they slowly circled the vehicle, all eyes peeled for movement. Joe pulled his gun and held it ready. They knew all too well Rourke was armed and dangerous. More than dangerous. And if he was trapped inside, only God knew what he would do.

On first inspection that didn't seem to be the case. The truck looked abandoned. A quick scan beneath the chassis found no one hiding underneath. Joe checked the rear door and found it locked. Perhaps from within. He couldn't tell.

Keeping her body tight to the truck, Britney sidled toward the driver door and found it open. She tentatively peered inside. Unless Rourke was hiding in the glove compartment the truck's cab was empty. She pulled herself up onto the step to get a better look and immediately cursed. There on the seat lay the remnants of a bloodied shirt – the one she recalled David Fagan wearing in the video footage taken from the restaurant. Next to it lay a dark weatherproof coat – again an item she recognised from video footage of the doctor's abduction. Checking its pockets, she found a phone. David Fagan's, she presumed. Crumpled on the seat as they were, the items looked inadvertently discarded but Britney knew otherwise. Everything The Courier did was intentional. It was left as a sign, she suspected. A taunt. Close, but not close enough. And, also, a sign of the confidence he had in his own invincibility. He no longer had a need for his disguise. Why would he? He had them chasing shadows from the start.

She took out her phone and dialled the commissioner's number. "We found it, sir. We found the truck so we're going to need a team of forensics."

"And Rourke?"

"No sign. Looks like he's abandoned it. But we haven't checked the…"

"But nothing Kent. You'd better find him. And find him quick. The president will soon be making his speech. And standing in front of that microphone, he'll be a sitting duck." With that he hung up.

Just then Britney heard faint noises coming from the freezer compartment of the truck. A human voice but muffled by the thick insulation that regulated the temperature. There it was again. It sounded like pained screams.

"He's inside," Britney shouted as she pocketed her phone and leapt down onto the gravel. "Ben, call backup. Then give us a hand to get that goddamn door open."

'Because as I was trying to explain to that pencil-pushing ignoramus, we have yet to check the back.'

****

Throngs of supporters had slowly filtered from the city centre pubs into the grounds of Fenian Stadium. It was almost full. Stands, terraces, reserved boxes, each awash with colour and heaving with anticipation. The media section was crammed; its usual assortment of local scribes and photographers slightly unsettled by the unprecedented influx of national broadcasters. On the face of it, they were all present to appreciate the biggest match of the local calendar year – The Club Final. But Ade knew different. The vultures weren't present for just the match. Or drawn by the rotting offal of a vicious killing spree, which included one of their own. No, in his mind, they had come in their droves to honour him. Despite the weight of his concerns, he felt extremely proud.

As the first notes of *A Soldier's Song* drifted up from pitch-side, the entire crowd climbed to their feet, turned to face the national flag, and, almost in unison, began to sing the words of the Irish national anthem with gusto. The players, who had taken up their positions on the field, stood shoulder to shoulder with their direct opponents, all facing the Tricolour which billowed in the gentle breeze to the left of the stadium. They too stood to attention. Their chests proudly pumped as they joined the crowd in patriotic song.

Having already taken his place in the VIP box, which separated him from the generality of the buzzing crowd around him, and in doing so, distinguished himself and the other District Board members from the ordinary man, Ade stood to attention with them. He was nothing if not a man of ceremony. Especially when he was to be the focus of attention. He knew every TV camera, photographer's lens and reporters pen would be focused on him at that moment. It was his day, after all. He was the guest of honour. A fitting tribute to his stellar career is how the local paper had put it. 'HAI Legend' suggested another. Perhaps the District Board should have taken some pointers from the articles, he thought to himself as he glanced around the drab VIP box. It contained little to suggest his accomplishments were being celebrated at all – a few rows of plastic seats segregated by a low wall from the rest of the stadium being the extent of it. Nothing like the corporate boxes he was used to in Gaelic Park, home to the national headquarters of the HAI.

They could have at least given him a more regal-looking chair, he thought. Or, as he had requested, made more of an effort to embellish the area for the occasion. Apart from the Oldcastle colours of black and white depicted on flags here and there, and some lengths of similarly coloured bunting that hung from the roof of the stand and ran downwards to be tied to the railing in front of where Ade would be later positioned by the microphone, little had been added to adorn the setting. Fagan was well aware the lack of effort reflected how the District Board members really felt about him. Sycophantic to his face, knives out behind his back. And when they learned Rourke was hunting him, they would be secretly jumping with joy because on this occasion they wouldn't even have to hold the knife. Once this was over, he promised, the smile would be on the other side of their faces.

Standing there alone, like a sitting duck, it seemed even the bunting was laughing at him – their lines of colour snapping in the breeze, fluttering and dancing as if overjoyed by the situation Ade found himself in. The snapping annoyed him so much that he had to resist an urge to reach out and rip the offending bunting from its tether and instead, force himself to exude outward calm, even though his heart was pounding all the while as he discreetly scanned the crowd.

Not knowing was the worst. Not knowing where his enemy was hiding. And not knowing whether David was safe. As yet, he had not received a call from the commissioner which likely meant Rourke was out there somewhere, mingling amongst the supporters. Hiding in plain sight. Watching him just as he watched the crowd. All Ade could do was await further instruction. Carry on as normal as the man ordered. For his son's sake, Ade would obey. But only be seen to because no one told Ade Fagan what to do. On his way to the stadium, he had forced himself to look at things through Rourke's eyes; a strategy he always employed when facing a dangerous adversary. While doing so, he'd had a moment of clarity and consequently, made an unscheduled visit to the equipment room before entering the stand. Now, looking out at the crowd he felt buoyed by his reading of the situation. He was sure he knew what Rourke's instruction would be. If you thought about it rationally, Rourke would want it to end no other way.

The rendition of the national anthem lasted approximately two minutes. As the last notes of patriotism faded into the matchday hum and the crowd resumed their seats, Ade remained standing as he awaited introduction. Shane Fitzpatrick briefly commandeered the microphone to provide a foreword, but his words barely registered with the president. He had spotted a man watching him. A large man, semi-disguised in a long overcoat and hat and for a moment he was certain that it was Rourke. However, as he peered closer, he saw that the man was too young to be his tormentor. When Ade caught his eye, the man nodded in return, as if to reassure him, prompting the president to conclude that he was one of the undercover Gardaí. His protection detail as the Garda Commissioner had put it. There would be at least another four Gardaí close by. All watching. All armed and ready for action. Ade felt somewhat reassured. But where was David? Where was his son and heir?

"It is my pleasure to introduce the outgoing President of the HAI," he heard Shane Fitzpatrick say as he concluded his intro, "Mr Ade Fagan!"

Hearing his name, Ade stepped close to the railing and waved to the crowd. As he did so, he could see his image transmitted on the giant scoreboard screen which was strategically placed in the east corner of the stadium to provide everyone in attendance with a decent view of proceedings. He was pleased to see that even stressed as he was, he looked every bit the president in his handmade suit. Despite this, the crowd's response was more muted than he would have hoped, but he had become used to that kind of reaction over the years. It never fazed him. It wasn't a popularity contest he was involved in. It was a power struggle.

"Thank you, Shane," he said as he leaned closer to the microphone with a perfunctory glance in the direction of the future District Director. "And thank you," he said to the crowd, "for such a warm welcome." His second chin wobbled as he cleared his throat, in a vain attempt to override his annoying nasal whine. "It has been my honour and privilege to act as your President over the last four years." He forced what he hoped would portray as a gracious smile, feeling more himself as he warmed to the task. Despite the stress, he was in familiar territory now. "In that time, I have endeavoured to strengthen the bonds of our community and to promote our games to a wider audience. In that, I think I have succeeded. But it wasn't easy. I travelled every corner of this country, as well as America, Europe, and twice to Asia, visiting Irish communities and HAI clubs. I met with dignitaries and state officials with a view to opening up new markets for our product, and with it, extra revenue for our young players. Revenue that will go towards better training facilities, better equipment, better…"

His flow was interrupted by the phone beeping in his pocket. He quickly pulled it out and glanced at it, hoping it would be the Commissioner getting in touch with good news, but a glance at the screen told him otherwise. It was

Rourke, now using an unknown number to deliver his new set of instructions. Or in this case, admonishments. Ade's heart sank as he scanned the text.

Asia? A future hurling stronghold, I'm sure. No guesses who paid for those little junkets. By the way, you cheated – again! You involved the police. Now, your son will pay.

Out of the corner of his eye, he noticed the giant scoreboard flicker as if the signal had been temporarily interrupted then a moment later, he saw the outline of a man appear on the screen. When the image cleared, he saw that it was Rourke.

"Shit," Ade cursed to himself, but loud enough for it to be picked up on the microphone. Several people close to him cast concerned glances in his direction, but he ignored them. He couldn't take his eyes off the screen. He knew every nook and cranny of the stadium from his days as District Director and was pretty certain that the room Rourke was standing in wasn't part of it. With the pallets piled in the background it looked like a section of a warehouse. He glanced downwards hoping to catch the eye of the undercover Garda he had spotted earlier but the man was staring at the screen with a concerned look on his face, having obviously reached the same conclusion as Ade had.

All their preparation, all their covertness, yet Alan Rourke wasn't even in the fucking stadium.

But unlike the Garda standing with his mouth open in front of him, Ade Fagan had foreseen that possibility. And he had prepared for it. What he hadn't foreseen was Rourke's use of the HAI's own technology to spread his poison – the very technology Ade had installed during his tenure as District Director. That was clever, he had to admit. Ironic even. It seemed he was to be hoist by his own petard.

However, despite Rourke's cunning, Ade was confident he could still come out of this with his reputation intact. Perhaps even enhanced. He would have to follow Rourke's instructions to the letter, of course. But if Ade was reading it right, those very instructions would lead him to the promised land.

After all, what better way to cement your place in history than to die, only to live a hero.

"My name is Alan Rourke," said the man staring coldly out from the giant screen introduced himself to the crowd and instantaneously all eyes turned to the eastern corner of the stadium.

"What the hell is going on?" one spectator asked another. In reply, he received a dumb shrug and a troubled frown.

Slowly a disquieted hum permeated the crowd as eyebrows furrowed and quizzical glances were cast about. Many of the people in the stadium recognised Alan Rourke as the mild-mannered man they'd bumped into at hurling matches over the years and also as the assiduous and loyal caretaker of the Ballyfeud hurling field. However, they'd also heard the stories that had been circulating over the last few hours. Rumours that had started with an incredulous whisper at the back of a church or in the local shop but had proliferated to become the talk of every house, pub, and pavement.

"Alan Rourke?" another whispered, as realisation slowly dawned. "Isn't that the man they're looking for?"

"The Courier," shouted another, fearfully pointing at the screen. "That's the Courier."

Then suddenly the entire crowd gasped as the man confirmed their fears by producing a large, serrated knife and holding it up in front of the camera. "Most of you will have come to know me as The Courier…"

On hearing that, the spectators closest to the screen shrunk away from it as if afraid he would somehow step out and start slaying all around him. As if to underline that possibility, the knife glinted coldly, possibly as a result of reflecting the light from the camera. Intentional or not, the gleam served to make the weapon appear all the more menacing.

"Those of you who really know me, know me as Jim Rourke's father. It is my aim to execute the man who just addressed you. Execute him for what I consider tantamount to treason."

Now, to a man, the crowd shifted uneasily. The murmur of noise increasing as they turned to stare at Ade Fagan.

"You see the man who addressed you is a charlatan. A con man. A thief. He dictates to you all under the pretence of leadership when all the while he usurps and twists all that is decent in the association. Since he has taken office, he has paid himself hundreds of thousands while his expenses run at double, if not treble that. Unvouched for the most part. Under the table. And that is only since he has taken up office as president. His record down through the years is no better. Secretly siphoning money that should have been directed to youth development and club structures. He has consistently withheld from the needy to line his own pockets. I can personally vouch for that. Once his tenure is over, he will no doubt create another official post for himself to step into or perhaps take on an advisory role," he added with derision. "Either way, he will continue to pay himself handsomely at the expense of those with no voice. But I intend to be their voice. I intend to be your voice. I say enough is enough. Ade Fagan, your era of hedonism is over."

As Alan Rourke's words resounded through the stadium, Ade noticed the inevitable stirring of movement in the crowd – reporters and cameramen jostling for position in front of the VIP area to get close enough to pick up his reaction. Cameras flashed and TV lenses aimed in his direction. Either side of him, the District Board members moved to distance themselves, leaving him to stand alone, thus silently inferring the corruption was his alone, not theirs. Shane Fitzpatrick stood further away than most.

Isolated now, Ade felt a trickle of sweat run down his back. 'Calm yourself,' he urged. 'It's not over until the last ball is struck. You have one more card to play, remember? The most…'

His edgy thoughts were cut short. As he watched, Alan Rourke shifted the camera until it was aimed toward a wooden, rectangular box sitting on the floor directly behind him.

"This, as you may have guessed, is to be your son's coffin but for now, I will call it my torture table," he said with a grand flourish of his arms. "And this is my muse. My torture toy." He focused the camera on the young man who was lying, spread-eagled on the box, his arms and legs strapped to either side, his bare torso bound to the wooden top. Despite extensive swelling around the eyes and caked blood disguising his mouth and jaw, Ade was in no doubt the face was that of his son, David.

"This, as you might realise, is David Fagan," Ade Rourke addressed the crowd. "A young man created entirely in his father's image. It is he who must pay for his father's sins. As my son paid for mine." With that, he paused as if to gather himself before continuing. "Most of you now see me as the killer of innocent victims. But believe me, none of them were innocent. Each one was corrupt. Each one of them a sinner. Rotten in their own way. But you, Ade Fagan, are the embodiment of all their sins. In you resides every evil that they displayed. Every greed, every corruption. That is why your son must die the slowest," he smiled a most wicked smile. "The purging of your level of sin takes time."

Alan Rourke then leaned down and took a firm hold of Fagan's right forearm.

"I have already maimed him," he continued. "Just as my son was maimed. By that most horrific of tortures – kneecapping, so now I shall turn my attention to that age-old sin of greed." He paused for effect, then raised the knife, allowing it to hover above the table before slowly lowering it, like a magician dramatically engaging in the final flourish of his act. Though the hand to be severed was disguised by his victim's torso, Rourke's intention was clear. David Fagan's body suddenly went rigid then his head began to jerk from side to side as realisation of what was about to happen dawned. The pleading looks in his eyes would have unsettled most people, but Alan wasn't swayed. Without flinching, he engaged the blade. And David Fagan began to scream.

"Greed," Alan stated, "is a deadly sin."

Bombarded by the young man's howls, the crowd recoiled in horror, revulsion written all over their faces. Yet they were captivated too as David Fagan's body writhed before them, his eyes bulging in his head, beads of sweat pumping out of his brow. Live mutilation may not have been what they came to see but down to the last man, they couldn't take their eyes off the screen. They were enthralled. This was reality TV at its best.

Ade Fagan's façade dropped. This was beyond his control. No strings could be pulled to sort this. No favours called in.

"Somebody stop him, for God's sake!" Ade bellowed into the microphone, a mixture of fear and frustration straining his voice. "He's a butcher. A psychopath. He's going to kill my son!"

No one moved. No one knew where to move to.

"At least someone cut the damn power…" His voice cracked as he glanced desperately at those nearest to him.

"We tried," came the feeble reply from his right, "but he's bypassed our system."

Fagan wondered if he detected a hint of grim satisfaction in Shane Fitzpatrick's tone.

As if to underline their powerlessness, further screams rang out across the stadium.

After a few moments, the agonised screaming stopped but Alan didn't give anyone a chance to take their eyes off the screen.

"My boy screamed too, if you recall," Rourke said as he turned to face the camera, the knife in his hand dripping with blood. "He writhed around on the ground and screamed. But you didn't pay him any heed. Just ignored his cries of pain. In other words, you too turned a deaf ear. One guess at what I am taking next?" He grinned the cruellest of grins.

Once again, the crowd witnessed Alan Rourke turn to face his subject and begin to slice with the serrated knife.

"I take this ear for Ade Fagan failing to heed the needs of his subjects. Because that is exactly what he thinks of you all. His subjects."

When Rourke turned back to the camera, he held up a grisly piece of flesh, so bloodied it was unidentifiable as the young man's ear. However, it was plain to see that the right side of David Fagan's face was now a mess of blood and gore. Many members of the crowd had blanched at what they were witnessing. Others felt their stomachs lurch. A young girl leaned over the railing of the VIP area as she began to retch.

The HAI President ripped his phone from his breast pocket and dialled the Garda Commissioner's number.

"Have you fucking found him yet?" he barked, before the Commissioner could answer, then on hearing the negative retort he cursed. "You'll pay for this. Every man and dog will know about the dummy security contracts I sign off for that shell company of yours. You hear me, Commissioner?" He hung up the phone without waiting for some feeble excuse. His boy was being butchered for all to see and those worthless Gardaí were running around with their thumbs up their collective asses.

"The next sin I wish to purge is that of unfairness. Inequality. Bias. Let's call it injustice. They say justice is blind, but injustice is not. It sees all too clearly, but with only one eye. The eye of self-interest." He leaned towards his victim, the tip on the knife pointing downward, aiming for his left eyeball. "People afflicted with this sin are the grey of this morning's dawn. You see the world in various shades of debauchery and corruption. Always looking for what you can gain. Never for what you can give. Your kind is the darkness of the world."

He stood then and looked down at the prone man. Spoke to him. "Now that part of your world will be dark. Dark as you are. Dark as your father." As the knife approached, Fagan made no effort to dodge it or to writhe on the table. He was clearly unconscious now, passed out due to the extreme trauma he'd already experienced. It made Alan's work easier but did little for the experience of the viewers. Little to build the tension. He needed Fagan awake and reacting. He needed him screaming. So, before he completed his task, he took out the small vial of smelling salts he'd used to good effect on previous victims and held it under the young man's nose, moving it back and forth to allow the acrid odour waft into his nostrils. After a few moments, Fagan came to with some feeble splutters and coughs.

"For you, blindness may be a path to a far clearer vision," he informed the semi-conscious man, who was conscious enough to register pain. "If you are willing to embrace the lesson, that is."

David Fagan groaned in reply.

Alan Rourke plunged the knife, and to his satisfaction, David Fagan screamed anew.

By now the intensity of the young man's suffering had driven the crowd to fever pitch. They screamed and shouted, comfort hugged and desperately clung to each other. Some were openly retching. More had turned away in disgust, while still others were baying for someone to stop the man on the screen. To stick that damn knife in Alan Rourke himself.

The players, with chests no longer full, seemed unsure of what they should do and obviously feeling exposed out on the field, ran across the pitch as one to be close to the crowd, finding security in the masses. Masses that seemed outwardly appalled at what they were witnessing. Sick to their collective stomachs. However, not one person left the stadium. A herd of voyeurs. Captivated and appalled. Seduced by their instinctive desire to witness another's suffering, to bear testament to their fall from grace. Outwardly dismayed but secretly, in the deepest recesses of their souls, baying for blood. Repulsed as much by the innate lust they recognised in themselves as by the butchery they were actually witnessing.

The most debased amongst them broke out their mobile phones to record this one in a trillion moment, holding the gadget high above their heads like the most devoted fans at a pop concert. All the while, the TV cameras kept rolling, cutting between the horror movie being transmitted through the scoreboard and Ade Fagan's reaction to his son's gruesome torture. Outside the stadium, the entire country had come to a halt as news filtered out about what was happening in Fenian Park. In their homes and at work, practically wherever they stood, people stared at phones, tablets, and TV monitors as they live-streamed The Courier in action. Patently aware of the attention he had gained, Alan Rourke seemed to revel in it all.

"Finally," he said dramatically from his position behind the camera. "It's time to take your son's heart. For it is in the heart where all the darkness dwells."

The President of the HAI looked past Rourke at his son. David gave no reaction on hearing the announcement. If, in fact, he had even heard it. He seemed beyond reaction. His life was a sea of pain now, Ade reasoned, and no external influence would register with him to any meaningful extent. Ade never felt so helpless in his life, so lacking in control. He had to hand it to Rourke. He had planned everything down to the last detail and now he had him where he wanted him. Almost.

"But with this, I give you a simple choice," Rourke offered. "A choice I would have gladly made. Your life for your son's. Let's see how corrupt your heart really is."

With that, the image on the screen seemed to jump. It went fuzzy for a moment then blacked out. Ade Fagan stared. Around him, the crowd gasped; its disbelieving eyes turned questioningly toward the president. Alan Rourke had given him the attention he craved. In spades.

****

As Alan Rourke broadcast his terror from the scoreboard the trio at the castle desperately struggled to force open the door. But failed. No matter how hard they pulled, the door refused to budge, even with the weight of three of them swinging out of the handle. Eventually the steel lever had enough, and in breaking free from the door, landed them on their collective arses.

Painfully aware of David Fagan's screams inside, they quickly rolled to their feet and went on a desperate search for some sort of tool to force the door. Rooting around in the cab, Ben discovered the truck's wheel brace which he hurried to extract from where it was secured under the seat. It was a hefty iron formed into a lug wrench at one end and tapered to a flat prybar at the other. Using the tapered end, he desperately tried to jemmy the rear door upward. But the lock was securely built into the door so despite his best efforts it held.

"Rourke," Britney called as she banged on the truck panelling. "It's over. You've nowhere to go. The best thing you can do is give yourself up."

No answer. Worse still, David Fagan had stopped screaming which suggested time was running out fast. In frustration Britney grabbed Joe's gun out of his hands. "Step back," she barked before firing four shots into the lock mechanism. The sound of the metal on metal echoed through the yard. A ricochet could have killed any one of them, or the bullet could have punched through and struck whoever was inside, but she got lucky. The bullets lodged and the lock popped. A gap appeared beneath the door, inviting Ben to insert the bar and prise once more. With a grunt the door slid upwards enough for himself and Joe to get their fingers underneath. One heave and it was open.

Holding the gun at the ready Britney peered into the truck, scanning left and right, bracing herself for any form of attack from within. None came. She moved closer but suddenly halted, her breath catching in her throat as what she was seeing registered; the bound and bloodied body of David Fagan trussed up like a pig on a market cart. The said cart looking disturbingly like a makeshift coffin. With the amount of blood caking his face, Fagan was almost unrecognisable. Familiar bile rose in Britney's stomach which she forced back down.

"We've got Fagan," she announced to her colleagues while silently praying he was still alive. She peered further into the gloom but all she saw were discarded pallets and a reel of electrical cable. Next, she noticed the tripod overlooking the coffin. And the camera sitting atop it, its red light still blinking. Directly below it, a strange electrical implement lay strewn on the floor. Struggling to comprehend what she was seeing her eyes followed the cable running from the truck's cab to power the camera. Amidst all the peculiarities there was no sign of Rourke.

It's not what you see. It's what you don't see.

"Shit," she cursed, wondering now if even his timely delivery to the Castle Café was staged to plant a seed. "He's played us." She pushed away from the truck and searched for the nearest exit. "And he's played, Fagan. Ben, wait here for an ambulance. Joe, we've got to get to the stadium."

Spotting a narrow gateway, she stuffed the gun into her belt and took off running. Joe followed. They exited out onto The March and sprinted for their car, Joe taking the wheel while Britney rooted out her phone. She needed to warn the commissioner. The Courier was in position to complete his final kill. Joe heard her swear in frustration when all she got was an engaged tone. A moment later Joe swore himself as he struggled to negotiate the match traffic. Cars lined the streets and were backed all the way up the March, from the traffic lights at the centre of the square to the castle. It seemed all exits were blocked, effectively hemming him in.

"The bastard planned on this," Britney exclaimed. "To delay us. We're never going to make it."

Just then Joe spotted an opening in the traffic heading away from the city centre. He hit the gas and the car lurched forward, its engine roaring as it picked up speed. The direction he chose led towards the ring road that circled the town – a less direct route to the stadium than through the town centre but not nearly as congested.

The further away from the castle he got, the more the road opened up and soon buildings were flying by in a blur. Despite her training, Britney felt terrified by the speed at which he drove, even if, belying his sedentary appearance, he managed the car like a rally driver, weaving in and out between other cars and overtaking in the tightest of spaces. Onward they sped, straight through roundabouts and traffic lights, over speed bumps like they were stunt ramps. Still, it seemed like the stadium was a million miles away. They would never get there in time. In fact, Ade Fagan could already be dead. As a hundred and one scenarios ran around her head, Britney desperately tried to steady herself in the passenger seat and redial. This time the call went through, and the Commissioner answered.

"What the hell is going on, Kent?" he shouted. Britney could barely hear him over the screech of the tyres as they desperately clung to the asphalt. "Ade Fagan is about to fucking die," he exclaimed, "and all we can do is sit back and watch."

"We found him," Britney shouted in reply. "We found his son."

In the background Britney heard a thunderous gasp as if a thousand voices had inhaled at once.

"Can you hear me, Commissioner? Are you still there?"

"It's happening, Kent. It's happening now. Where are you?"

"I'm on the way to the stadium, Commissioner. I'll be there in minutes."

Britney cursed then hung up the phone and stuffed it back into her pocket. Clinging to her safety belt she closed her eyes and silently urged Joe to go faster. Every damn second counted.

****

While staring up at the scoreboard, Ade Fagan's mind worked overtime. This was the moment he had anticipated. The flaw he had seen in Rourke's plan. The Choice. The life of his flesh and blood, his heir, over that of his own. A man in his position should never have to make such an unconscionable decision. He certainly should never have to bow down to the demands of a nobody like Rourke. He had never done so, and he didn't intend to start now. No matter what was at stake. He hated to think how he would have chosen otherwise but with the preparations he had put in place, it would now be an easy choice for Ade to make. But where had Rourke disappeared to? Was he still lurking behind the screen?

After long moments of dead air, the screen flickered back to life, grainy at first but soon the picture cleared. And, sure enough, there was Rourke staring out at his enthralled audience once more.

"If you look directly in front of you, Mr President." The words may have been respectful, but his tone was one of disdain. "There is a rope. It is disguised in one of the buntings. At the end of the rope, there is a noose. Please put it around your neck."

Ade Fagan stared at the screen for a moment longer before dragging his eyes away to search the mocking bunting for the concealed rope. An instant later, he spotted it. Directly in front of him. Just as Rourke had said. He hadn't noticed it earlier, but now that his attention had been drawn to it, he could clearly see that one of the lengths of bunting had been entwined with a thin rope, little more than a cord, and at the end of the bunting this cord was tied off in a circular fashion to form a noose. Very clever indeed. Hidden for all to see. He almost laughed at the simplicity of Rourke's little plot.

As Ade stooped down to untie the rope from where it was secured to the steel railing, Alan Rourke stared coldly out from the screen. "I want to see you hang. I want the world to see you hang. Just like I saw my son hang." Then he addressed the crowd. "If anyone moves to help him, David Fagan dies. It's the President's choice. Not yours. And no dramatics, President. Your son's life depends on it."

Ade raised the rope over his head and slowly slipped the noose down around his neck, settling it around his collar then tightening it with a sharp tug. He took his time. Tempting fate was not something to be rushed.

Satisfied the rope was secure, he gripped the stainless-steel rail that cordoned off the VIP area. Then with a grunt, he hauled his great bulk upwards until he was standing on the edge of the low dividing wall, neither a VIP nor a commoner now. Something in between? No, not between, but above. He nodded to himself. His name would live on forever.

The section of the crowd directly below him watched closely as he stepped onto the precipice. They started to shout and point animatedly in his direction. Soon the rest of the crowd turned until all eyes were once again focused on him, keen to witness this latest twist in the gruesome saga.

Just then a female Garda appeared out of nowhere, pushing through the crowd, desperately trying to make her way toward him. Ade recognised her from TV as the girl who had recklessly accused Jim Rourke of being The Courier.

And yet here The Courier was, butchering his son.

"You don't have to do this," she screamed up at him. "We've located David. He's safe. President Fagan, we've found your son."

Ade didn't let on to hear her above the hum of the crowd. She was damaged goods. Not someone to be associated with. The fact that she had been so wrong about The Courier, not once but numerous times meant she would be slaughtered in the media once all this was over. He didn't plan on being slaughtered with her. Balancing precariously on the railing with the rope hanging snugly round his neck, he looked down at the crowd. His audience.

To the man, they were looking back at him. Waiting with bated breath to see what choice he would make, but crucially, with no idea his son was safe. They only knew what they were seeing and would judge him on this moment. On his choice. Himself or his son. If he jumped, he would be seen as a hero, a miraculous martyr, something akin to a god and he would be able to spin this story whatever way he wanted. People needed heroes. Believed in them. Gods, they worshipped.

With this deific ascension foremost in his mind, he focused his eyes on some imaginary spot in front of him and blocked out everything else. Despite the precautions he had taken, he was terrified of what he had to do next. It was a long way down and if his plan failed, it was all over for him. All over for good.

"Can you hear me, Mr Fagan? Your son is safe," the Garda shouted once more, as she climbed the steps of the stand two and three at a time. "You don't have to do what he wants."

Ade Fagan barely glanced at Britney as she neared him. "But I do," he shouted in reply as he shifted his weight forward, preparing to dive. "I can't let that nobody win."

Then in the minds of the crowd watching below, he made his choice. For all to see, he bravely chose his son.

"Noooo!" Britney screamed as she stretched out a hand hoping to catch a leg or foot before he cleared the wall. But she couldn't reach him. As Ade Fagan stepped off the railing, he swung outward in a wide arc, the toe of his expensive leather shoe brushing the tips of her outstretched fingers as it flew past. Then he was gone, and she could only look on helplessly as the rope around his neck tautened and propelled by his own body weight, he swung further outward, his feet clearing the seats beneath him by mere inches.

With the steel roof support to which the rope was tethered overhanging the pitch by at least a dozen feet, onward he swung, gravity carrying him way out of Britney's reach. Out of everybody's reach. His hands clung to the rope as he desperately tried to take the pressure off his neck. To onlookers below, he appeared as a modern-day Tarzan – brash, bloated and overdressed, the stadium his jungle, the constricting rope his supporting vine. Once the rope reached the end of its natural sweep, Fagan slowed before swinging back in the direction of the stand, his momentum carrying him within tantalising distance of Britney's outstretched arm. But not quite close enough. She knew that had been her only chance. From now on, his return would halt further and further out of reach, the range of the swing becoming shorter and shorter with each pass, his weight a killing pendulum.

On witnessing him jump, the crowd screamed, almost in unison but now a stunned silence settled over the stadium. Every spectator present watched the HAI President swinging back and forth in the air above. Rooted to the spot, Britney looked on helplessly as little by little the energy petered out of the movement until Fagan's body settled into little more than a swaying motion.

All around the stadium, observers ran their hands over their heads in dismay or covered their faces with the onset of a common grief, while the more spiritual amongst them pleaded for help from God, Mary, or St Jude. Whether what they'd heard from Rourke was true or not, no one wanted to see the president die like this. To see anyone die like this.

Minutes passed. In the background, the homemade movie had ended abruptly, so Alan Rourke's voice no longer carried from the scoreboard to permeate the collective conscience. It didn't need to. All the strings were pulled and despite their best efforts to thwart him, Rourke had achieved his goal. The HAI President was dead.

In the strange silence that followed, Britney's phone rang. It was the Commissioner. "Fuck off," Britney cursed on seeing his number, but even as she did, she turned and flew back down the steps, the reverie suddenly breached. Finding strength, she never knew she had, she leapt half a dozen in a desperate bound. Was it her instinct telling it wasn't over, or just blind hope? Whichever was the case, she couldn't give up on him yet.

"Cut him down!" she screamed to no one in particular. "For God's sake, cut him down!"

Suddenly, with the spell broken, people began to rush from all sides to gather directly beneath the hanging man, their eyes straining upward as they reacted to Britney's cries. Players, officials, match day medics.

"Hurry!" one of the latter called out desperately. "He may still be alive."

Thinking about it rationally, a drop from that height would have broken his neck in an instant and severed his spinal cord. In the unlikely event of that failing, he would surely have been strangled due to the length of time he'd been hanging. In reality, there was little chance he could have survived the plunge. But there was something odd about the stillness with which his body hung that registered in Britney's mind. Something that spurred her on. Ade Fagan hadn't kicked out. Not in the animated way she imagined he should. From the moment he jumped, his arms had remained near motionless while he swung from the tether, his lower limbs static as they cut through the air. Now, they simply dangled, slightly bent at the knee, like those of a parachute jumper coming in to land.

Britney was on the verge of calling out again, but as she hurried onto the field, she saw that Joe had reacted every bit as quickly as she had, if not quicker. He had spotted where the end of the rope was tied off. It had been thrown over a roof beam and dropped to a lower stanchion where it was secured within reach. Joe was in the process of loosening the knot. As he did so, Ben joined him. Together, they untangled the rope, then bracing themselves against the sudden and immense weight, they slowly eased Ade Fagan's body towards the ground where many hands reached out to grab hold of the stricken man's limbs. To Britney, it looked like a case of too many cooks but as she pushed through the gathering, one of the medics stepped forward to take control.

Dressed in a green uniform and cap, the medic had an air of authority about him as he instructed all but those closest to push back. Though Britney hadn't yet got a look at his face she sensed a calm air of experience emanating from the man.

"Lay him on the ground," the medic instructed once those closest to him had safely gathered the president in their outstretched arms. "On his back. I need to loosen that rope. Quickly!" The voice struck a chord with Britney. Its tone resonating in her mind like a hammer striking a vaguely familiar bell. But what bell?

Once the men had done as he asked the grey-haired medic quickly pushed past them then set down the medical bag he was carrying and stooped to examine the now recumbent body.

"Is he alive?" Britney asked desperately.

"Too early to tell," replied the medic, "but it would be a miracle considering how long he's been hanging. And I don't believe in miracles." Standing directly behind him now Britney could see him frantically working to loosen the knot around Fagan's neck.

"Still, everybody should move back and give me room. That includes you, Garda."

Although she was desperate to help, Britney was well aware the medic was her superior in this scenario, so she did as she was ordered, taking up a position approximately two yards from the scene. A moment later Joe arrived to stand by her side.

"Any sign of Rourke?" Britney asked.

He shook his head.

"Looks like he's long gone. Good news is the kid is fine. It was all a camera trick. Recorded sometime earlier. Both the flesh and blood were fake, and the poor lads screaming was caused by electric shocks from a cattle prod. The screaming we heard coming from the truck was him calling for help before he passed out. He was a bit roughed up and his knee was badly busted but otherwise, he'll be ok."

"Well, that's something, at least," Britney replied just before she got a nudge in the back from a member of the jostling crowd which had gathered around the scene.

More and more supporters were pouring out onto the field and becoming increasingly animated in their desperation to see if the HAI President was alive or dead.

In the distance she spotted the grizzled head of Commissioner Wilson watching on. Almost detachedly, she noted the cool facade he reserved for his TV appearances now cracked by a look of thunder while his squinting eyes danced a jig of condemnation beneath the bureaucracy of his peaked cap.

'To hell with him,' Britney thought, an irreverent growl gathering in her throat. "Everyone, step back," she called. "Give the man room." Then to the medic, she said, "Any help you need, just shout."

"Will do, Garda," the medic replied over his shoulder.

A moment later, having managed to loosen the rope from around Ade Fagan's neck, he leaned closer to check for any sign of breathing. Judging by Ade Fagan's complexion Britney feared the worst. His round, chubby face had turned a deep shade of red, almost purple but the hope in her reasoned that excessively fat men often looked that way, especially when under stress. In the next instant, her heart leapt when she imagined she saw the president's large chest slowly rise and fall underneath his jacket, but her hopes were dashed again when she realised the movement was just the result of the medic checking for signs of life.

'Please,' she begged silently, and if she were honest, she would have to admit she was pleading as much for her own sake as his. She knew that she would be blamed if he died. She believed that was what the Commissioner was calling to tell her just now. The look she had spotted on his face said as much. He would need a scapegoat and she would be it, despite her recent successes. Or perhaps because of them. And they would be right to blame her. She had been too quick to jump to conclusions. Too slow to listen to others. Now, because of her pig-headedness, another death would be on her conscience. As she looked on with increasing dejection, she wondered if perhaps Flynn would get the last laugh after all and that his caustic warning would prove to be all too true.

Nights can seem very cold after a day in the sun.

As he worked, checking Fagan's pulse on both his wrist and neck the medic shook his head sadly. Britney's heart dropped. They'd lost him. The HAI President was dead.

Strangely, the medic then reached for his bag and as he did, he leaned forward and whispered something into Ade Fagan's ear. Britney didn't quite catch what he said over the noise of the crowd but presumed it was a prayer of some sort. Last rites perhaps. No, she decided, as she watched what was playing out in front of her. Not last rites, she corrected in amazement, but some sort of miracle intervention! Because suddenly Ade Fagan's eyes popped open drawing a cheer from the crowd. Just as suddenly, his body went stiff, the vivid colour draining from his face.

"What did you sa…" he spluttered. "Son of a bitch… It's you!"

The medic didn't seem surprised by Fagan's sudden exclamation but calmly dipped his left hand into his bag.

"Yes, Fagan, fate has caught up with you," he said, and now the familiarity of his voice was even more pronounced, that bell ringing louder. As he spoke, he cast a furtive glance in Britney's direction. Only then did she get her first proper look at his face. For a split second, she froze in disbelief as the man's features merged with the vague familiarity of the voice she had in her head. It was a delay that would prove costly because by the time her training kicked in, the medic had withdrawn a large, serrated knife from the bag and was now holding it with its point lodged into Ade Fagan's chest. If forced, the trajectory of the knife would drive the long blade directly into the prone man's heart.

"Freeze Alan!" Britney shouted as she grabbed Joe's gun from her belt where she'd carried it since leaving the castle. Steadying herself, she directed the barrel towards the centre of The Courier's back. "One more move, and it will be your last."

"You're too late, Sergeant Britney. The time for atonement has come. His. Mine."

The silence that followed was filled by a metallic click as Britney pulled the gun's slide back to chamber a round. On registering her intention those standing closest to her panicked and terrified screaming quickly overrode the earlier sounds of elation as the basic instinct of self-preservation kicked in. For a moment there was absolute mayhem as people fell over each other in their haste to put as much distance between themselves, the gun, and the psycho with the knife. Some people crashed into those next to them, knocking them to the ground while others fell of their own accord, losing their footing on the grass only to spring back up and make a dash for the relative safety of the stands. In a matter of moments, the once congregated group had scattered in all directions leaving Britney, Joe, The Courier, and his final victim the only people remaining on the field. So focused was she on Rourke, Britney hardly noticed the chaos that had developed around her. Her eyes were fixed on the hand that held the knife. If it so much as twitched, she was going to bury a round in Alan Rourke's back.

"You don't have to do this, Alan," Britney advised in the most reassuring voice she could muster. "He's not worth it."

"Oh, but I do, Sergeant Kent," Alan Rourke replied without the slightest hesitation. "You see, I must. My redemption dictates it. But I do agree with you on one thing. He's not worth it."

Britney would have shot him right then and there, but the knife looked razor-sharp and now Rourke had cleverly positioned himself over Ade Fagan's torso in such a way that she feared that even if she killed him instantly gravity would cause him to fall forward and plunge the knife deep into his victim's heart.

"I know what happened to your son," Britney said, deciding the best option was to try and talk him down. "I know all about the way they treated him when he got hurt."

"You know nothing," Alan replied in a weary voice. "Because you don't want to know. Just like the rest of them. The rest of us. We only hear what we want to hear."

"I know that he got badly hurt when he was a young man while hurling for Oldcastle, and they treated him like a piece of shit afterwards."

"Hurt? Is that what you call it?" growled Rourke in reply without casting the slightest glance over his shoulder, making it clear to Britney he wasn't going to be easily distracted from his appointed task. "He got kneecapped. His knee practically cut in half by a hurley. That's the way the surgeon put it."

"I heard. I heard he screamed in agony, and they didn't even offer him a splint for his leg. Forced you to take him home in the back of your car. Limerick to Oldcastle. A three-hour journey. It must have felt three times that with his knee the way it was."

"Yeah. And my boy didn't even open his mouth. Not then and not through all the pain afterward. They talk about integrity and honesty. About teamwork and loyalty, how so much could be achieved by working together, but my son was a piece of shit to them. When he got hurt, they just picked him up by all fours and threw him right back at me. The damage was so bad that it took five hours for a team of surgeons to put his knee back together. Afterwards, he didn't get so much as a phone call from the District Board. No physio, no rehab, no compensation. Nothing. He was a piece of shit to them. A nobody," he sighed and put his weight on the knife, drawing whimpers from Fagan that sounded just like those of his son. "And still, despite it all, he went back playing for them."

"Why?" asked Britney, part of her buying time, part of her genuinely interested to hear the intricacies of the hate that was driving this killing spree.

"Because the game was his life. He practiced every day. Every minute of every day if he could. The injury should have ended his career, but he was determined it didn't. Two years later, he was back playing. By the end of that year, he was on the Oldcastle senior team. Centre-back on the top team in the land."

"Jeez, he must have been better than good," Britney observed evenly. If she sounded genuine, it was because she really believed what she was saying and wasn't just telling him what he wanted to hear. However, she'd do that too if it would mollify him. Perhaps enough to get him to relax his grip on the knife and hopefully lower his guard. As she spoke, she edged to her right hoping to discreetly manoeuvre herself to an area in front of Rourke, thinking if she did get a chance to take a shot, the force of the impact would propel him backward rather than forwards onto the waiting knife. Joe moved in the opposite direction.

"Some say he was as good as they ever saw. For a while, it looked like he'd never been injured at all or that the injury might have somehow made him better. But it was his anger that was driving him on, not love for the game like it used to be. That's why it couldn't last. He was playing through pain just to prove a point. After a few months, the pain won out and the inevitable happened."

"He got injured again?" Britney guessed. She had managed to work her way around and was now able to see the side of his face. She wasn't sure if she should be surprised or not by the fact that Alan Rourke, The Courier, the cold-blooded killer of men, was crying.

"Yes," Alan Rourke replied. "Busted up his ankle really bad. Then ruptured discs in his back. One injury after another. It was his body's way of telling him to stop. But even though he was playing for the top team now, it only gave them a chance to treat him like shit again while his teammates were treated like royalty. They got physio if they needed it. Got compensation while they were injured. Hell, they even got fancy gear to wear. But my boy was a nobody. The son of a nobody – a simple caretaker, their grasscutter. And the dreams of a grasscutter's son mean nothing. But what's a young man without dreams? And all because this prick said the District Board couldn't afford it."

He shook his head at the idea of it. Leaned further on the knife.

"When he tried to stand up for himself, to demand his rights, they told him to fuck off. To shut up. To stop complaining. 'No one is above the District Board,' they told him. He thought that anyone with basic human decency was above those bastards. He said if he was black or gay, or one of those fluid-gender types he'd have an entire army up in arms over it. But he wasn't fashionable. Not even close. After that, he refused to play for them anymore. And that's when it got a whole lot worse."

"Worse," Britney asked. "In what way?"

"They accused him of being a disgrace," Rourke replied bitterly. "A waste of talent. Made him out to be a lazy good for nothing. A whinger, too full of himself to train. All he wanted from the beginning was to be treated fairly. But he wasn't. When he stood up for himself, they twisted it and labelled him as 'hard to manage.' A prima donna, they called him. A troublemaker. And worse, a prick, a wanker, a dickhead. When you get branded like that, it sticks with you for life. Follows you around like a bad smell."

He took a deep breath and released it slowly as if to stop himself from exploding.

"You see, no one stands up to the District Board. You're meant to just take whatever shit they throw at you and shut up. No matter how people like Ade Fagan treat you. But Jim did more than just stand up to them, he stuck his two fingers up at their corruption. At this prick here especially. You see, with Jim being so good, they still wanted him to play for them, but he refused. Went to America instead. Would have gone to Afghanistan to get away from those bastards if he thought it would be better when he came back. He was wrong. It was worse. So, he only played when he felt like it, and point-blank refused to pay their membership fees. Why should he? They treated him like dirt. That refusal really stuck in their craw. To people like Ade Fagan, money is all that matters. Money and reputation."

Britney found herself torn. Between her responsibilities at that moment and the forlorn man in front of her. Despite what he'd done, her heart went out to Rourke. He had clearly been destroyed by his son's suicide. As Richie Lyons had been by the ruination of his niece. But where

Lyons took his fight to the drug culture, Rourke took his to the HAI. He considered the man on the ground as the root cause of his son's troubles. The genesis of the shitstorm that Jim Rourke endured. It was becoming clear to Britney that Fagan thought himself above basic human decency, above the constraints of the common good that bound most people. Thought himself superior to everyone else. Harder. Smarter. And obviously thought that to the very last.

From her new vantage point, she could now see the rope that had saved Fagan's life. Hidden beneath his jacket it was wrapped tightly around his torso to run under his arms and connect to a metal clip that protruded above the collar of Fagan's jacket. The clip was fastened to both the rope and the knot of the noose, therefore effectively taking his weight when he jumped.

'Clever,' Britney thought, realising now why Fagan had so freely taken the plunge. His plan was to play dead until he was carried to an ambulance. If Rourke presumed him dead, he would have no further reason to hurt his son and would surely let him go. Later, once The Courier was apprehended, Ade Fagan could suddenly appear like Lazarus out of the tomb. A martyr and a heroic father rolled into one.

Yes, very clever indeed. But not clever enough. Rourke had obviously foreseen that Fagan couldn't help but try and con the system, even if it meant jeopardising his own son. He knew Fagan's conceit dictated it, Britney supposed. A leopard doesn't change its spots, she reminded herself, thinking of Flynn.

"And once he was labelled a prima donna, everyone else jumped on the bandwagon, I presume?" Britney knew how it worked. People the world over are all the same. Their first and foremost instinct is to fit in. All other considerations are secondary.

"Yes. Players, supporters, his own club. They took it on themselves to put him back in his place. They taunted him, ridiculed him, assaulted him. Walked up to him and spat on him in public. Imagine standing there in front of everyone with somebody else's spittle running down his face while they all laughed. One of those animals even bit him, for God's sake. Caught him in a rugby tackle and pinned him to the ground then sank his teeth into his side. Bragged about it afterwards. But the worst was when they targeted Stacey, Jim said in his letter. Caught her by the hair and forcibly kissed her in front of him. All to humiliate him. To drag him down. Whatever about the rest of it, he couldn't handle having his troubles visited on the ones he loved."

"That's why he started drinking?" asked Britney. "To soften the blows."

"He'd always drank. He wasn't perfect. He could be shy and socially awkward, and like a lot of young men, he tried to cover it up with drink. But yes, that's when his drinking got out of control. Why wouldn't it? He'd done nothing wrong. Nothing only to try and stand up for himself. Yet he received constant derision. Personal attacks. The kind that can really hurt. To his face and behind his back. Even on that damn Facebook. Over time, the abuse really started to weigh on him. But drinking only made it worse. He started getting into arguments, fights. Fights he was never going to win. It was always him against them. Groups of them. The great HAI."

"That's how cowards work," acknowledged Britney. "They gain courage in numbers. Egg each other on. But run away if they're on their own." She inched a few steps further to her right.

"You're damn right there," Alan agreed. "He said it got so tough that sometimes when he was alone in the van, he'd scream to himself that he wasn't going to let them beat him. But they kept at him until they did." Now Alan Rourke took a deeply anguished sigh. "Just when he thought he was getting past all that, some bastards broke into the site he was working on and sabotaged his work. Did thousands of euros of damage. The builders said that seeing as he was the target, he had to pay for it. They also rescinded his contract. Those greedy bastards told him he had to finish up at the end of the month."

That must have been when he started hiring out his van, Britney decided. To pay what they deemed he owed for the vandalism. He would have had no idea what it was being used for. Clearly Alan had no idea what his son had gotten involved in either.

"I mean, he couldn't even run his business without it being targeted. It was never ending. He went to local members of the HAI and pleaded with them to put a stop to it. Even went as far as apologising to the bastards for any trouble he had caused. Imagine…trouble he had caused."

'But he wasn't the target,' Britney wanted to say. 'It had nothing to do with Jim.' She sighed as she realised that Halley owning the site wasn't just a coincidence in all this. The vandalism was a revenge attack on his nephew. Flynn's thuggery was what kicked it all off. Jim Rourke would still be alive only for Halley and Flynn. As would all the others. The Courier would never have existed. Sensing this might only agitate him even more, she kept her mouth shut.

"But they made a joke of it," Rourke continued. "My so-called friend Timmy Dunne even accused him of just looking for sympathy as usual. Jim was so desperate to be left alone that he approached this pig," he spat the word and pushed further down on the knife, digging it into flesh and drawing another terrified whimper from Fagan. Blood now began to seep through the president's shirt.

"But our great president's attitude hadn't changed one bit either. None of theirs had. They just scoffed like before. Told him that's what happens to troublemakers. His club told him the same. My club. The great Ballyfeud. They literally told him to fuck off, exactly as they had done when he got hurt in the first place."

"That must have really cut," Britney said, genuinely appalled by this side of the HAI. An organisation she'd always thought above reproach.

"It was the last straw, what broke him in the end," explained Alan. "Not just the way the HAI treated him when he got hurt, and all the verbal abuse he endured over the years, but that he wasn't left alone to support his family the way he wanted to. The way he thought a man should. He was going to lose his house, his business. Everything he had fought for. Fought for more than any man should have to fight considering the constant pain he was in with that knee of his. Other joints too, over time. Hips, ankles, back – all aggravated because he was compensating for that busted knee. It was the next morning, after hearing that belittling reaction from his club that I found him hanging from the gates of the hurling field. I guess it was his final protest," Rourke said. "Against the club. And against me." He paused and glanced out over his shoulder at Britney. He was clearly haunted by the memory of what he'd seen.

"He was a good boy," he continued, "trying his best for his wife and kids. But everyone had turned against him because he tried to stand up to this tyrant."

Britney had manoeuvred herself into a position that offered her a favourable shot. She aimed the gun at Alan Rourke's right shoulder in the hope that she could disable him, rather than kill him, perhaps force him to let go of the knife. Out of the corner of her eye, she could see Joe, silently urging her to squeeze the trigger, but she hesitated. When interrogated about it later, she couldn't explain exactly why she had delayed. Not in a way that any of them would understand. But at that moment, standing there with the gun pointed at The Courier her finger froze.

The injustice of it all played on her mind. The image she had pieced together over the last days of Alan Rourke was of a decent and hardworking man who had gone rogue. Now, she knew exactly what was driving him. In his own twisted way, he was making a stand against corruption. An insidious corruption that had targeted and ostracized his innocent son, leaving him with nowhere to turn, and in the end, forcing him to take his own life. A corruption driven by the likes of Ade Fagan and his associates and readily embraced by a mindless and conformist public. The same HAI mob she'd seen streaming out of the city centre pubs some minutes earlier.

In many ways, Alan Rourke was the righteous one, the hero, while Ade Fagan was the coward. The callous and indifferent destroyer of a young man's dream. Of his soul. He was a usurper. A bully. A killer in his own right. Only his type of killing took years to take effect.

"But the worst thing of all was I believed in those people," Alan Rourke confessed as Britney wrestled with the thoughts in her head. Tried to fight against her convictions so as to free her mind to take the shot.

"I took their side against my own son. Even when they refused him the ambulance, I defended them. Told him what I'd been told since its foundation; that the HAI was an amateur association and as such, couldn't afford to spend money on players. Even ones injured as badly as he was. I told him the same when they cut him loose, discarding him like an unwanted animal, with no support to rebuild his knee. His career. I explained that the HAI hadn't the funds. That the only way they survived was through the efforts of volunteers like me. We often argued over it. Bitterly sometimes. But all the while, this guy here and his cronies were getting fatter and fatter. Literally. And I continued to volunteer for them. That must have felt like I was twisting a knife in our Jim's back."

"It's hard to question people in authority," Britney acknowledged by way of consolation. "They're masters at indoctrination, of creating automatons with their propaganda. Feeding on our inherent fear of social isolation, they condition us to presume they know best and to trust their every action. Their every word. They have us thinking it automatically. That they'll do the right thing by us. But they don't, do they? They look after themselves, number one. Our welfare comes in as a poor second."

"I'm sorry," Ade Fagan whimpered then, glancing beseechingly from Rourke to Britney and back again. "I'm sorry for any hurt I caused your son."

Alan Rourke shook his head, the disgust evident on his face. His tears were flowing freely now, falling from his cheeks to land on Ade Fagan's shirt, staining the white material with little water blossoms of grief.

"You're not sorry," he replied. "People like you are never sorry. They take and never give back. Using words that are every bit as conniving as their actions."

"No. I mean it, Alan. I am sorry. And you're right in everything you said. I treated your son despicably. But if you give me a chance, I'll show you I'm sorry. I'll prove it to you."

Tears ran from Ade Fagan's eyes too, sidling down the side of his face as if determined to get out while the going was good. Cowardly entities spawned in the image of their creator.

"Too late," Rourke stated. "I believed in you before. In all of you. I don't believe in you now." His head dropped despairingly, and Britney noticed the grip he had on the knife relax ever so slightly. Hope blossomed like the falling tears. Maybe he was about to give up. Maybe she wouldn't have to shoot him after all.

"In fact, I don't even believe in myself," he continued in that same desolate tone as she inched a little closer. "Because I'm just as bad. I said nothing. Not then. Not when I should have. I should have stood up for my son. I should have made sure they treated him properly. But I believed in them. Believed all their bullshit." Suddenly he raised the knife high above his head.

His movements so quick, he caught Britney by surprise.

"Well, I don't believe anymore," he growled furiously. Then mustering his anger into terrific force, he brought the knife down at lightning speed. A fraction of a second later Britney fired and saw the bullet tear into Alan Rourke's shoulder, but it wasn't enough to halt his momentum. She fired again, and this time Rourke took the bullet in the chest, the impact forcing him to fall sideways and collapse to the ground. Britney darted forward, the gun pointed at her target's head.

"Don't move," she warned but even as she said it, she knew the words were wasted. The bullet had ripped into Rourke, just above the heart, and already his shirt was soaked with blood. His breathing was quick and laboured and his eyes stared upwards as if searching the heavens for the gate he would once have been destined to walk through. But not now. Even the lord couldn't forgive what he'd done.

As she stood over him, he slipped a bloodied hand inside his jacket.

"Don't," Britney's pleaded, her hand stiffening on the gun. She breathed out in relief when all he withdrew were folded sheets of paper. His fingers trembled as he slowly unfolded them.

"My atonement," he said as Britney knelt next to him. Then using the tip of his finger, he scrawled a bloody line across an already bloodied page. And then another. Two lines for two names. Britney could see the last was the name of the person the letter was addressed to. His own.

"I'm not sorry for what I've done," he said as she leaned close. "They all deserved to die. There has to be some give for everything you take." He grasped her hand with both of his and shoved the folded paper into her palm. His final offering.

"My son left this letter for me to find. Now I give it to you. Perhaps after you read it you won't think me so evil."

"Sssh," Britney urged, feeling her own eyes well. She took the letter then grasped his hand and held it tightly so that, when he drew his last breath, he would at least feel the touch of another human being. She sensed that his horrific crimes apart, he had been a decent man. A good man. A man twisted by the loss of his only son. Evil invades even the most virtuous of souls she reflected as she looked down at his ashen face.

"But the evil was not yours to begin with," she said out loud.

"No," Rourke whispered, "nor my son's. But now, because of what they drove him to, he is destined to burn in the fires of hell." He coughed and swallowed as blood began to fill his throat. A dark trickle escaped his lips and ran down his chin. Still, he managed to force a smile. "He will not burn alone, Sergeant Britney. I will be there to burn with him. To hold his hand." His eyes flicked to where Ade Fagan lay. "And to fan the coals for others."

Glancing over her shoulder, Britney saw that Joe was kneeling next to Ade Fagan. For a moment he held her hopeful gaze, then he gave a brief shake of his head. Ade Fagan was dead, the long knife buried to the hilt in his heart. She had left it too late. Too late by a long haul. Joe knew it. She knew it too. The shot was there to be taken but she had refused it. Why? She couldn't be sure. Perhaps to give Rourke a chance to cleanse his soul before he met his maker. A final confession of sorts. Or perhaps deep down she felt he deserved to get his revenge. Evil begets evil.

Whatever the case, questions would be asked, she knew. Allegations made. At best, she would be reprimanded, at worst she would be discharged. But she didn't care. Nothing they could do would change the fact that she was about to have two more deaths on her conscience, one of which would weigh far more than the other. And not just because she had fired the killing shot.

She turned back to Alan Rourke whose weathered face was now a deathly shade of pale.

"I hated you for a while," he said. "For what you said about Jim. And wanted revenge. But now I see you for what you are." He forced a smile. "You're just like me." That said, he took a shallow breath, and suddenly his eyes became crystal clear. "Tell Vera, I'm sorry," he pleaded, his voice weakening. "And Stacey and the kids. Tell them I love them." Then his grip tightened on her arm and his pain-wracked eyes bore into hers as he drew her close. "Take care of your child," he urged. "Even when the world conspires to distract you. To con you. Protect her. Nothing else really matters."

"I will," Britney promised, a little taken aback by the random comment. "And you take care of yours."

Alan Rourke didn't hear her. His eyes were closed, his head lolled to one side. The man who had terrorised Oldcastle for weeks, had now completed his killing spree and would kill no more. Neither would she, swore Britney to herself.

Chapter 22

Weeks had passed and all the incident reports had been written. Filed and scrutinised, with directions sent down from Commissioner Wilson for them to be revised and written again. But Britney had stuck to her story. Her hesitation had caused the death of the HAI President. She was certain of that. And she wasn't going to lie about it. Or try and paint it a different colour than it was, even if the hierarchy were demanding the narrative be altered. It wouldn't reflect well on the force, Wilson warned. Or on her career.

'And lying would,' she thought with dismay.

"It may not," she replied, "but it's what happened." Despite mounting pressure, she stuck to her guns, and finally, the report had been accepted. It was then that she handed in her resignation. They would have no choice but to accept that too.

"You don't have to leave," Joe said after she had aired her intentions of calling it a day. "I'll back you all the way. You know that. Soon it will all blow over and someone else will be in their crosshairs."

They were sitting in the canteen of Dublin's Beaumont Hospital, sipping beverages that were not quite on a par with the Castle Cafe. But then, they weren't there for the coffee. In fact, Britney wasn't drinking coffee but sipping herbal tea. Ben nursed a latte while Joe had a black tea with milk – a choice which reminded her of the far too young and innocent Danny Owens. A sadness crept over her which she embraced for a moment before battling to push away. It wouldn't be so easily dismissed.

"I know," she replied, "but I want to. I've seen enough of death to last me a lifetime. And I'm tired of all the corruption. Inside the Gardaí. Outside it. It's all making me sick."

They could see by her unusually pale complexion and generally jaded appearance that she wasn't exaggerating. The stress of recent events had clearly taken a toll on her.

'Who could blame her after all she had been through?' Ben thought.

"Why not take an extended holiday?" he suggested. "Portugal is nice this time of year."

"I need more than a holiday," Britney replied. "I need a life change." Getting one too, she thought to herself, whether I like it or not. "None of this makes sense to me anymore."

"You have empathy for Rourke," Joe said as he sat back in his chair. "Part of you even admires him for what he did – standing up to corruption. That's why you're really thinking of quitting the job. You can't reconcile one with the other?"

Britney shook her head. "I told you why I'm quitting."

"Nor can you reconcile that admiration with the fact that you had to shoot him."

"Not true," she replied adamantly. "What he did was wrong. Terribly wrong. And, yes, he deserved to die. But you're right too. I don't like killing anyone. Not even a serial killer. Do you?"

"No. But in this line of work, it happens," Joe replied. "You knew that when you signed up."

"Yeah, I knew it was a possibility. But a possibility is a far cry from reality. To have the man you shoot die in your arms is far too real for me. And then there's Danny and the way he died. It's just too appalling to think about."

"Sounds to me like you're implying Rourke was in some way innocent," Ben remarked, "cause I'm with Joe. He was an evil, cold-blooded killer."

"I know. But he was human too. Ever since I read the letter he gave me, I've been questioning what I would have done if I was in his shoes. I mean, the way they treated his son was horrific. Chronic." She glanced from one man to the other. "I'm not saying that I agree with what Rourke did, but if it was my child, I think I'd be tempted to kill someone too."

"But five people?" Joe asked.

Britney shrugged. "They destroyed his son. All of them in their own way. That's how Rourke saw it."

Joe took a long draw of his tea, his face grimacing. Britney couldn't tell whether it was due to the poor quality of the canteen beverage or the thoughts he was wrestling with. From start to finish, the whole thing had been more than just a trying experience. It had very nearly been the end of them. Now that they were physically safe, it had become a real test of conscience.

"Ok, I can see why he hated Ade Fagan," Joe admitted. "He was corrupt to the core, like the majority of the people who make it to the top of these organisations. But what did Cullen and the others do to deserve to die the way they did?"

"They were all part of the corruption. All there on the day that Jim Rourke got hurt, and every single one of them stood by and did nothing. Or worse. Like Donie Cullen, for instance. After the incident, he ran a fund-raiser in Jim Rourke's name. It was backed by the HAI, but not by Jim Rourke. I think, knowing the man's track record, he suspected Cullen was arranging it with the intention of appearing as a kind benefactor to a young man who was badly hurt but in reality, was arranging it so he could reap the profits. Even if that wasn't the case, he didn't want their charity. He just wanted to be treated like every other player. He made that clear to Cullen but still, Cullen went ahead. Made a big fanfare out of the whole thing with a private hall and a band. Sold raffle tickets all over the district. Must have sold hundreds of them, if not thousands. Afterward he gave Jim Rourke a couple of hundred euros to pacify him even though revenue was estimated at more than ten times that. No one knows what happened to the rest. Jim Rourke felt used. A pawn in Cullen's greed. So, Alan Rourke cut off that greedy hand."

"And the doctor?"

"As team doctor he should have ensured Jim Rourke got proper medical treatment. But he didn't issue so much as a splint for Jim Rourke's leg when he got hurt. And then he backed Fagan when Fagan point-blank refused access to the ambulance that was on site, forcing Jim Rourke to go home in the back of his father's car. Just imagine the unnecessary pain that caused the boy. Three hours with nothing to stabilise his leg and his knee swollen up like a football. The soft-tissue damage alone must have been horrendous. Any doctor worth his salt would have objected to that kind of cruel and indifferent treatment but just like the rest of Fagan's cronies, he was so desperate to toe the line that he didn't object. Remaining the Oldcastle team doctor was far more important than any Hippocratic Oath he had taken."

"And then later when Alan Rourke finally got his son back to hospital in Oldcastle, the doctor turned up acting all concerned and professional in front of the hospital staff. He dismissed Alan. Sent him home, arrogantly stating he would take it from there. And having grown up in an Ireland where directives from men in authority were accepted without question, Alan left. Five minutes later, after he had covered his ass with his peers, the doctor was gone too, and the lad was left lying on a trolley by the door, for hours. Shivering from shock and cold. Hungry because no one had given him so much as a bite to eat, even though Fagan and the rest sat down to a post-match four course meal. And worse, urinating on himself because no one thought to ask if he needed to use the toilet. Imagine the indignity of it. One minute he's hurling for Oldcastle, and the next he's lying there helpless, with his own urine running down his leg.

"Alan Rourke deemed the doctor as heartless, so felt justified to take his heart."

"And with Peter Dunford being Fagan's right-hand man, The Courier took Dunford's eyes because he just looked on and did nothing?" Joe asked.

"Yes. As district secretary, Dunford was Fagan's right-hand man. He was the one that filed the incident report, registering the injury as ligament damage, not a knee-capping. There's a big difference, especially in the level of treatment the injury required. I mean, this was far from keyhole surgery. They had to cut his knee open from one side to the other. More than ten inches across. Then insert pins and stitch the soft tissue. Staple the whole thing back together. All in all, it amounted to the kind of expensive treatment they didn't want to pay for."

"When Jim challenged them over it all, Dunford backed Fagan all the way. Presented a united front for all the others to fall in behind. At the District Board dinner dance that year, Jim Rourke confronted Fagan. Asked why he wasn't getting assistance for his injury like everyone else. Fagan belittled him. Laughed in his face. Dunford sided with Fagan. Made a joke of it all, is how Jim put it in the letter. When Jim pushed the point, Ade Fagan gave him a cheque for a paltry two hundred quid just to shut him up. Imagine. Two hundred quid for a kneecapping. An injury that would last a lifetime. Jim never told his father about any of this, until he wrote it all down in the letter. He didn't want to bother his parents with it. Thought he could handle it himself."

"Obviously, he couldn't," Joe observed sadly. "But I don't blame him. He was little more than a boy then. An innocent standing up to grown men."

"An innocent," agreed Britney. "Exactly like Alan tried to convey when he staged his murder in the hurling field." She shook her head and looked from one to the other. Her brown eyes were as sad as Ben had ever seen them. "Imagine his level of disconnection to go to that extreme of subterfuge with your own son."

"That's what I mean," intervened Joe. He had to admit he had a certain sympathy for Rourke but no matter how his son was treated, it could not justify the terrible things he had done. "You shouldn't be quitting over a guy that could do something like this."

Britney scowled in frustration but didn't reply. She couldn't. Not honestly. She still had to get her head around the truth herself. Ben could sense there was more to why she was stepping down, but he didn't push it. She'd tell them everything when she was good and ready. If not... well then, it was probably none of their business anyway.

"Ok," he piped up to nip the developing silence in the bud before it became awkward. "So, that explains Rourke's hatred for Fagan, Dunford, the doctor, and Cullen. But what about the reporter, Marie Cox? Where does she fit in?" Having only been an observer for much of the case, Ben was struggling to put names and faces in order in his head.

"With it being an underage game, Marie Cox was the only reporter present at the match the day Jim Rourke got hurt but never once mentioned the incident. Imagine, a young player received a career-ending injury in front of thousands of people, the game was brought to a halt for a long period, yet it didn't warrant a single word. She was also the reporter he approached after he got injured the second time but again, she considered it irrelevant. A non-story. Then years later when Jim Rourke was reaching the end of his tether, he went to her once more with the story about the corruption he believed inherent in the HAI, the cruelty, the bullying, the ongoing hostility, but she didn't give him the time of day then either. Instead, she accused him of being a whinge and told him to go off and waste somebody else's time. We've found out since that Marie Cox and Ade Fagan were known to exchange 'favours.'" Britney used her fingers as inverted commas. "I think Alan Rourke might have spotted them together and suspected Fagan had ordered her to kill the story."

This was new to Joe. He pursed his lips thoughtfully. "Is that why he used the newspapers? To highlight this omission."

"And to highlight what his son missed out on," Britney agreed. "All the papers he used were from match reports that Marie Cox had compiled as part of her job. When Triona checked she found they all contained names of players who had hurled with Jim Rourke on the day he was injured. Players who went on to have stellar careers as a group, winning numerous titles, medals. All considered heroes, lauded in the community while his son was ostracised – not once mentioned in these reports."

Ben nodded in understanding. "And he was also telling us that Cox turned her nose up at his son's story. She refused to listen, especially when he was at his wit's end. So, when Jim Rourke hangs himself, Alan gets his revenge by cutting off her ears. "Poetic justice, some would say."

"He killed her as well," Joe reminded him starkly. "Traces of DNA confirm it was done in the back of his truck. Like some might slaughter an animal."

Ben shrugged sombrely. "An eye for an eye, I suppose." Then corrected himself with a humourless smile. "Or will it be an ear for an ear from now on?" He paused as he deliberated. "What I don't get is how Rourke thought he could disguise his son's suicide forever. Surely, he knew that once he killed Ade Fagan so publicly, everyone would learn the truth?"

"I don't think that was his plan originally," Britney explained. "I think he was going to force Ade Fagan to admit the level of his corruption by publicly torturing Fagan's son. But he intended to do it in such a way that he could avoid revealing his own identity."

"But how was he going to get Fagan to admit ill-treating Jim Rourke without drawing the attention to himself?" Joe objected. "Surely if Jim Rourke became the focus of Fagan's confession that would have been a clear indication Alan Rourke was behind it all?"

"Not if he got Fagan to admit his corruption on a grand scale. Which in fact, it was. And, also, to admit to his ill-treatment of players in general. He could then get him to admit to the cruel way in which he treated his son but as part of the wider context of abusing his power within the HAI. That way people would not necessarily suspect Rourke. It would be conceivable that a HAI member was defending the integrity of the organisation he loved. Someone who knew Jim Rourke perhaps."

"Like Timmy Dunne," Ben added with a nod.

Joe leaned back in his chair. He had to admit that he was feeling torn now that all the facts were clearer. He had often felt like killing someone when his children were bullied or treated badly. If one of them had committed suicide over it, who knows what he would have done. He shrugged to himself. It's a thin line between angry and crazy. Especially so, for a tortured parent.

"I still think it's hard to credit that The Courier came into existence because of what Alan Rourke saw as some sort of organisational conspiracy that forced his son to commit suicide," Joe stated. "I mean there are such variables when suicide is involved."

"You're forgetting the letter his son left for him to find," Britney reminded him. "Jim Rourke had outlined everything he experienced in that. And it wasn't so much a conspiracy as widespread corruption. His son was irrelevant to these people and that's the way they treated him. Worse still, they all prospered while the young man's career lay in tatters. Fagan went all the way to becoming President, Cullen became Director of his club and Cox was on her way to becoming Sports Editor of one of the biggest papers in the country. Dunford became wealthy beyond what a modest man like Alan Rourke could possibly comprehend. From their lofty positions, they completely disparaged Jim Rourke and any claims he made. Portrayed him as the problem."

"And this constant struggle eventually overwhelmed him, and he killed himself," Joe said. "Which, I think, explains the rope marks on the victim's necks. Rourke tied them up in such a way that their own struggles killed them too. Ultimate payback."

"Yes. And ultimate self-delusion. Because at the time, even Alan Rourke himself accepted his son's treatment. And worse, told Jim to do the same. But I can't blame him. The social frameworks in which we trap ourselves mean we are driven to fit in above all else. Consequently, we are afraid to think for ourselves. To stand up for anything. We're all the same. Allowing ourselves to be led around by the nose. You see it on social media all the time. On TV. Reality programmes have become hugely popular because as viewers, we don't have to tax our brains. I watch them myself to unwind sometimes. Love Island, Goggle Box, The Apprentice – they're hugely influential. I'm named after a pop singer for God's sake! And of course, the same blind thinking is why one of the most corrupt men in the world got elected to the highest office possible. And it's the reason why, no one objected when Ade Fagan was promoted up the ladder, from District Director to HAI President, despite his obvious failings – his monetary corruption, his blatant disregard for players' welfare, his draconian attitude – failings for which any conscientiously run organisation would have kicked him out. Yet even Alan Rourke himself accepted it. And worse, told his son to do the same." Britney paused to sip her herbal tea then pursed her lips as she returned the mug to the table. "To be honest, I think it was his own weakness that Alan Rourke hated the most. That's what he was really trying to kill."

Joe nodded to acknowledge he understood the reasoning, if not yet totally prepared to accept it. To stand in silence may be complicity, but surely carnage wasn't the answer. As his heart wrestled with his head, a doctor in light green scrubs entered the canteen and approached them.

"He's awake now if you want to see him," the doctor informed them, "but only for a few minutes."

"Lead the way, Doctor," Joe replied with a mixture of relief and trepidation evident in his voice. The recovery of his friend and colleague had been classed as something close to a miracle. Having initially written off any chance of a recovery, the doctors now reckoned he was over the worst. Despite his personal descent into darkness, he must have found something worth living for, Britney mused as she followed. Ben, having no connection to Detective Lyons didn't want to crowd the room, so he remained at the table to await their return.

****

There were no prizes for guessing to which room the doctor was leading them. It had to be the only door on the male surgical ward with a Garda stationed outside. Even though Detective Lyons was proved innocent of all charges regarding The Courier case, there were still question marks over the illegal detaining of his niece. By visiting the recovering detective, Britney hoped to get some further clarity on that, amongst other loose ends that bothered both herself and Joe.

As they followed the doctor into the private room, Richie Lyons was sitting up in bed. His head was heavily bandaged, and he was wired up to all sorts of medical equipment but still, he looked well for a man who had been shot in the head. Pale, thin, haunted. But alive.

"Luckily, the bullet entered at an upward trajectory and therefore missed the more vital areas of the brain," the doctor had informed them on their arrival. "Otherwise, he didn't stand a chance. And whoever staunched the blood deserves a medal for their quick thinking. It was critical."

Joe glanced at Britney as if to say you saved his life.

"With appropriate rehab, I believe he has every chance of recovering fully. In a physical sense, at least," the doctor added ruefully, "considering the stories I've been hearing."

Britney understood what he meant. Physical recovery was one thing. Emotional healing was another story altogether. After one last check on his patient, the doctor left them alone. A momentary silence followed which Britney broke before it dragged by pulling up two chairs, one either side of the bed. With the room to themselves, they dabbled in small talk at first, but then Joe steered the conversation around to the case. He was determined to get the facts straight, with the added hope of making sense of his friend's actions. Perhaps make peace with them.

"So, you were right, Richie. The HAI proved every bit as corrupt as the rest of them."

Richie forced a tired smile. He glanced at Britney. "I tried to tell you."

His speech was weak and intermittent. They had to be patient with every sentence. Every word.

"Animal Farm eat your heart out." He paused to take a slow, rattling breath, and a deep sadness crossed his face. "How is Vanessa?"

"She's doing ok, Richie," Joe replied. "A long road ahead."

"I know. I tried to help her. To save her. But I couldn't. The drugs… After Molly died, she…she got lost. So, I kept her in that room to protect her from herself."

'But chain her up,' Britney thought in dismay while at the same time wondering what else he could have done. Seemingly, Vanessa had been in and out of rehab for eighteen months or more. Then, about a year ago, she went missing from the centre. Just took off and the staff hadn't a clue where she'd gone. Ended up missing for months until Richie eventually found her shacked up somewhere in the north inner city with a drug-dealing scumbag who belonged to the notorious gang calling themselves The Redheaded Serpents. Richie later arrested the scumbag for theft. Gave him quite a thumping as well, from what Britney heard. She couldn't blame him for that. That was also the reason he had transferred to the Drug Squad – in the hope that he could develop contacts and get intel on the inner-city dens for his own personal war against the Serpent gang. Turned out one of those contacts was the man Danny had seen him pay off. The man Danny had referred to as Snake.

"After the car crash, we adopted her… She became our daughter. We never had children… But then Molly died, and I just couldn't cope…" he sighed. "Before I knew it, I'd lost Vanessa too. And no matter what I did I couldn't save her."

Britney nodded to herself as she struggled to contain the emotions rising in her chest. The killer had been driven by the pain of losing his child. That's what Detective Lyons had suddenly understood when news filtered through about the manner in which Jim Rourke's body had been discovered. He had tried to tell her as much when he said, 'It was his child,' meaning Alan Rourke was killing because it was his child who had been taken. Who would pose a body with the reverence Jim Rourke's had been shown, only someone who dearly loved him? The way Lyons himself loved Vanessa. Like a father.

"But you suspected earlier?" Joe encouraged.

"Yes," Richie took another slow breath which seemed to give him strength. His speech steadied. "Initially, I thought it was all centred around Marie Cox's illegal activities but there were just too many links to the HAI. The hurling field, the reports in the papers, the other victims. I knew from my own experience that the HAI was as corrupt as they come. Therefore, I was more than willing to believe that the killer could be someone heavily involved with that organisation. Someone with an axe to grind. Especially with the Ballyfeud club, seeing as that was where the first body was discovered. Then once Jim Rourke's body was found as it was…" He shrugged and looked at

Joe. "If you weren't so distracted with Flynn, you would have seen it too."

"Perhaps," Joe replied with a wry smile, "but then, I was never as bright as you." The smile faded as he pondered the next question. "But you did consider killing the doctor?"

Lyons nodded. "Thought of it every day. I followed him for almost two years but could never quite work up the courage. Kept track of it all in a file."

"We found it. And what you'd gathered on the rest of them during the course of the investigation. A substantial file on Miss Cox. You had an affair with her, didn't you?"

Richie sighed heavily then nodded. "It's something I'm not proud of. We met through Molly's work, and it lasted only a couple of months. But despite what some people thought, that's the only connection I had to her. When I learned about her illegal enterprise, I cut my ties with her completely." He sighed. "But the damage was already done." He glanced sheepishly at Britney now as if to say I don't blame you for doubting me all along.

"Alan Rourke knew about it too. Seen us coming out of a hotel in Oldcastle once. I think he knew Miss Cox would come to me with that hand. I think he counted on it in a way."

"Because he knew you from your playing days," Britney suggested. "And knew you saw the HAI for what it was. If he didn't succeed, he counted on you carrying on the investigation and shedding a light on Ade Fagan's corruption."

"Yes." Now he addressed Joe. "There's something else you should know." As he spoke, he dropped his eyes to stare at the white hospital sheets. There was nothing there to see only memories, starched and sanitised, but painful still. When he looked up at his colleague his eyes were heavy with guilt. "Marie Cox wasn't the only person I cheated on Molly with. You see, Vanessa wasn't just my niece. She was my daughter."

'So, that's why he was so protective of her,' Britney thought to herself. She was his child. Not just adoptive but biologically. Britney glanced at Joe. He looked completely taken aback by this revelation.

"Still, didn't give you the right to keep her locked up like you did, Richie," Joe accused. "Or drug her."

"I was sedating her," Richie countered, "to protect her from herself. And I'd do it all again. Because once those damn drugs got a grip on her, I had no choice. She was wasting away before my eyes." He sighed once more. "I know what you're thinking, Joe but you're wrong. I did love Molly, but I made mistakes. Those mistakes have been eating me up ever since. They'll haunt me 'til the day I die. Just like failing Vanessa will." With that, he closed his eyes. "I hope you'll forgive me someday, Joe," he said. "I've a feeling I'll need a friend."

Joe nodded. 'I'll forgive you,' he thought, 'but when the time comes for you to face her, will Molly?'

"And I must ask your forgiveness too, Sergeant," Lyons continued weakly, "for letting you down. For letting you all down." His haggard face took on a contrite expression. "You were right to call me out in front of all those people. I am a useless drunk. A liability."

Britney gave a non-committal shrug as she recalled the confrontation. His drinking had clearly cost him so much. As had his secrets. But they combined to cost Danny an awful lot more. It would take her a long time to come to terms with that. She might have said so if the doctor hadn't returned and called time on their visit.

"He needs his rest," he said, by way of explanation.

"One last thing," Joe asked. "Why didn't you just shoot Halley in the warehouse?"

"I…" Lyons hesitantly glanced at the doctor, and back again. "I just couldn't get a clean shot." He closed his eyes and lay his head back on his pillow.

Britney wondered if she saw a tear seep onto his craggy cheek. She glanced at Joe who met her eyes with a knowing look. Saving a life hadn't been the only reason for his heroic dive. He had planned on losing one.

As they returned to the cafeteria, Joe shook his head. Disillusionment clearly visible on his face. "You think you know someone," he said as they sat back at the table. They ordered fresh drinks then filled Ben in on everything that had been said.

"So, Detective Lyons tried to point you to Rourke after he got shot?" Ben asked, clearly feeling a little confused. "That's what helped you figure it out?"

"Yes, and no," Britney replied. "I thought what Detective Lyons said was terribly odd, even for someone delirious. But Rourke helped us too. Unwittingly, of course. By delivering the heart. You see, that was a mistake on

Rourke's part. Bringing the box to the station unopened like that. If I got something so strange delivered to my house, I would have been far too curious not to open it there and then – no matter what was being said in the media. Especially if I had already received gifts in sympathy, as they had. It could have been more buns for all I knew, meaning I would have at least had a peek inside. Unless I already knew what was in it. If that was the case, it follows that I must have delivered it myself."

"The wrapping on the box had been completely untouched?" prompted Ben.

"Not completely. Some of the newspaper was torn but not enough to have seen inside the box."

"So, he planted the box hoping it would make his son appear innocent?" Ben asked. This point rather confused him. "Why terrify his daughter-in-law and grandkids like that? I mean surely there were other ways."

Britney shook her head. "Don't you see, he had to plant the box at Stacey's to convince everyone that Jim was to be another victim. That way when his body was found, no one would suspect suicide. That was what he was trying to avoid from the beginning. Apart from the perceived stain on his son's soul, he didn't want those bastards in the HAI to think they'd won."

"Or for people to think he'd played a part in his own son's suicide, more like. I think it was cowardly and callous. Especially on the poor girl."

"Maybe," Britney said with an inclination of her head. "But I don't think the girl was meant to find the box. I think he secretly deposited it at the door on the way in, with the plan of making a show of noticing it on the way out. Stacey would then later be able to vouch for him finding it."

"But overall, I mean. To put his family through that?"

Now Britney sighed. "His mind was gone, so far gone that he couldn't see the pain he was causing. Or maybe he did, and that's why he was prepared to die in the end. Who knows? But I should have seen it. All the clues were there but I was too pig-headed to pick up on them. Too ready to judge everyone, including Detective Lyons. Perhaps if I hadn't been, we would have stopped this earlier."

"Is that the real reason you're resigning? You can't reconcile with your own failings," said Joe.

"That might be more like it," she admitted. "I discovered a lot of them over the last while."

"Didn't we all. Because we all have failings, Britney. We all make mistakes. Make the wrong choices. We can't keep beating ourselves up over them," he shrugged. "I don't."

"But you're not the reason so many people are dead," Britney argued.

"Neither are you, Britney. Alan Rourke is. Ade Fagan is. Flynn is. But you are definitely not. You are the best Garda I have ever worked with. I mean that. And you'd make an even better detective." Fearing her mind was already made up, he gave a resigned sigh. "All I'm saying is, think things through. I know you've gone through a lot, and it's raw to the bone right now, but that will change with time." He reached across the table and grasped her hand reassuringly. "I'd hate to see you make a rash decision." A wry smile tugged at his lips. "And that wouldn't be like you, Brit." That said, he leaned back and finished his tea. "I've got to go. The young lad has football practice."

"Oh, so your kids are living with you?" Britney glanced at him with surprise. "I suppose your wife didn't leave you either?"

Joe shrugged. "Nope, all a cover story. Didn't want my family to be an easy target if things went belly up. Truth is my wife loves me."

"Can't see why," Britney ribbed with a smile.

"Clearly my six-pack," he joked as he patted his spare tyre. "Built for comfort, not speed, as you know. And my wife likes her little comforts. Or not so little, before you say it."

"Would I?" Britney asked with an innocent expression.

"Uncle Buck?" Joe replied, with a knowing smirk. With that he pushed himself up from the table and took a few steps toward the door before stopping and turning back. "Whatever decision you make, we'll keep in touch. Right? Maybe meet up in Oldcastle for something a little stronger."

Britney nodded enthusiastically. "Proper coffee next time."

"I was thinking more along the lines of a cold beer or a good malt. Something to take the edge off. What's with that cat's pee anyway?" He scrunched his face in distaste, then smiling warmly he nodded to Ben in appreciation. "Nice working with you, Ben."

"You too, Detective," Ben nodded.

Goodbyes complete, Joe turned and headed for the door.

With Joe gone, both Ben and Britney remained silent for a while. Britney stared out a window at the street outside, her eyes drifting up and down the thoroughfare as if trying to figure out where to go from there. Ben fiddled with his coffee, torn in a different way.

"He's right, you know," Ben said eventually. "You are a great Garda."

Britney turned back from the window, an appreciative look in her brown eyes. "Was. I didn't tell Joe this, but I've already handed in my resignation. There's no turning back, I'm afraid."

"It's a shame," he said sincerely, "you will be a huge loss to the force."

"To hell with the force," Britney replied. "The 'force' is just another corrupt organisation powered by those who are out to promote their own selfish interests. Just like the HAI, the FAI, the GAA and worst of all the goddamn Church. Nothing in this country is sacrosanct."

"I agree with you," Ben nodded, "but isn't that because the building blocks of all these organisations are inherently corrupt? Humans, I mean. Us."

"Some of us more than others, I'd like to think. And just because corruption exists, doesn't give us the right to stand back and do nothing when someone in a weaker position than us is targeted. Surely as human beings we have an obligation to defend the innocent. Even the most savage of animals are known to display that instinct."

Ben nodded in understanding. "Ok, I get why you're resigning. You don't want to be tainted by all this anymore…"

"That's one of the reasons," Britney agreed but said no more. She finished her herbal tea and as she felt the watery liquid filter down her throat, she shoved the mug away with a look of distaste. She was desperate for a good strong coffee, but she'd had a mug earlier that morning, which meant she was already over her allowance. It was only day one but already she feared this new regime would kill her.

"So, what are you going to do now?" Ben asked, turning her mind from the path it would otherwise inevitably have gone down.

How was she going to cope?

"I don't know," she shrugged. "Maybe go freelance."

Ben looked surprised at first then smiled. "Britney Kent, Detective for hire. It has a nice ring to it."

Britney laughed. "Sounds like a B-movie. Or one of those reality TV series. Maybe I'll just take up baking instead. Or gardening."

"I can't see you in an apron, Britney. Or a pair of wellies for that matter but…" he hesitated, then before his nerves could scupper him, he forged ahead. "But I do see you as a beautiful woman. So…" he paused and glanced around the canteen nervously. The setting was far from perfect but then he might never get another chance. Soon they would be going their separate ways. He took a quick sip of his latte, wishing in his own head that it was the malt Joe had earlier mentioned. "Well, now that we will no longer be colleagues, I was wondering if maybe you'd like to go out sometime?"

Britney attempted a polite smile, but even the slight gap in her teeth appeared sad.

At least that's how it looked in Ben's amber-flecked eyes. "I'm sorry! I shouldn't have…" he mumbled awkwardly before she had a chance to reply.

"I'd love to Ben," Britney interjected quickly, hoping to offer relief to his obvious discomfort. She genuinely liked Ben and if circumstances were different, she wouldn't think twice about saying yes. He was certainly attractive – good-looking with a dry sense of humour that she liked, and he had proven himself to be a decent and honest man. The kind she could rely on. A rare breed in her recent experience.

"But?" Ben urged.

"It's not you," she apologised but even to her own ears, it sounded weak. Dismissive. The universal copout.

"What is it then?" he asked. "My age? You're into older men?" He forced a weak smile, but his eyes admitted defeat.

"No, Ben," Britney replied with a quick shake of her head. "It's nothing like that. Actually, it's the second reason I'm quitting." She sighed. "And the most pressing one." She hadn't planned on doing it like this, but she knew she was going to have to tell someone eventually. And Ben deserved a straight answer. Anyway, she wasn't going to get away with drinking herbal tea for the next nine months without someone putting two and two together.

Ben noticed her glance down at her empty cup then once again registered how pale she looked. He might have turned a little pale himself as he suddenly understood. "You mean?" he asked hesitantly.

"Yes, Ben," Britney nodded solemnly, doing her best to hold back the tears. She suddenly felt terribly afraid. Every bit as afraid as she had been in the warehouse. "I'm pregnant," she said. After a pause she added, "And this child will need me more than any force."

Ben didn't know what to say. He only knew Britney a short while but from the very start, he had felt drawn to her undoubted strength. All she had been through over the last few weeks would have broken most people. Now, she seemed ready to fall apart in front of him.

"Is there a father?" he asked before quickly realising how stupid that sounded. "Of course, there's a father. What I meant was, is he on the scene?"

She shook her head. "No. He's not on the scene. He never will be. Because…"

"Because?" Ben urged gently, wondering how any man could run out on such a beautiful and courageous woman.

"Because I killed him," Britney said simply.

Now, Ben was truly gobsmacked. He'd seen the video doing rounds at the station, and heard the rumours that went with it, but had dismissed them as exactly that – loose tongues exaggerating an already extraordinary event, but now it was clear the stories about her having an affair with a witness were true. Despite his best efforts, his shock must have been written all over his face.

"Great way to start a family, eh?" Britney said with a thin smile of resignation. "An unborn child already tainted by the sins of its father."

"But it doesn't have to be that way, Britney. You of all people must believe that."

"Must I?" Her voice quivered.

A moment later, the floodgates opened. She cried for herself and her unborn child. She cried for Jim Rourke. She cried for Lyons and Vanessa. Most of all, she cried for Stacey and the kids.

It was time to pay them a visit.

And perhaps make peace with Lily. Her mother.

THE END

About the Author

Jack Talbot was born and raised in Kilkenny. He lived for a short while in Australia, America and Europe before returning home to his native country. A carpenter by trade he has worked in clothes shops, bars and as a fitness instructor. This is his first novel.

If you would like to connect with me, you can do so at my website http://www.jacktalbot.ie.

Please Review

Dear Reader,

If you enjoyed this book, would you kindly post a short review on whatever bookstore where you purchased the book or on Goodreads? Your feedback will make all the difference to getting the word out about this book.

To leave a review, go to Amazon and type in the book title. When you have found it and go to the book page, please scroll to the bottom of the page to where it says 'Write a Review' and then submit your review.

Thank you in advance.

Printed in Great Britain
by Amazon